Published by Autumn Day Publishing

Copyright 2015
Cover by Toby Gray
Other works by L.S. Gagnon,
Witch: A New Beginning
Witch: The Spell Within
Witch: The Secret of the Leaves
Original release, 2015
ISBN 978-0-9962305-7-5
All characters in this book are fiction
and figments of the author's imagination.

WITCH: THE FINAL CHAPTER
Book Four
by L. S. Gagnon
Facebook/TheWitchSeries

Table of Contents

Special Thanks

I want to dedicate this book to my husband, Steven Gagnon. You are my rock, my soul, my friend, my love. Thank you for putting up with my strange writing hours and never complaining. You believed in me when no one else would. You cheered me on, gave me positive input, and most of all, you were there in my darkest moments. I'll never forget the day we were in that bookstore. I couldn't find a book I liked, and you said the words that would change my life: "So why don't you write your own book?" You never intended those words as a joke. You knew I could do it. You believed in me more than I believed in myself. I just want to say how much I love you. Thank you for being the hero in my dreams. You saved my life in more ways than one.

I also want to dedicate this book to my sisters, Angie, Lupita, Vicky, and Yvonne. I think of you every minute of every day. Words cannot say how much I miss and love you. I am a better person because I had such wonderful women in my life.

Next, I want to thank my assistant, Melanie Halliwell. You work for pennies and never complain. You run around for me and save the day. I can never repay you for all that you've done. You and your family have become a very important part of my life. I know our journey has just begun. I love you.

Next, I want to say thank you to Lori Bruno. Thank you for giving me the opportunity to come to your store, Magika, and sign books. Doing a signing in

Salem had always been a dream of mine. Thank you for making that dream come true. You are a true witch and friend.

A special thanks to Moses. (You know who you are.) You freed me from the darkness and brought the sun back into my life. There will always be a special place in my heart for you.

I also want to thank William Greenleaf. You are the best editor an author can have. I can't imagine having to edit a book that someone with dyslexia wrote. You wave your wand and put everything in order. Thank you.

Toby Gray, you're an amazing illustrator. You took the images right out of my head and brought them to life. I can never thank you enough for that.

Justin Santos, my second love, my best friend. Thank you for the hours of help when I was going crazy formatting my books. I couldn't have done it without you. Much love, my friend. You will never know how much you mean to me.

And finally, to all the people who inspired some of the characters in my books. Thank you for being funny, handsome, grumpy, good-hearted, wise, and beautiful. You made it easy to write these characters and bring them to life. You each gave me inspiration to make the readers laugh, cry, and be amazed. Thank you, Cory Urban, Sam Bentley, Kris Fisher, Javier Moniz, Joshua McCallister, Janice Gagnon, Michelle Kazen, Sharron Bell, Donna Valente, Kym Andreozzi, Melanie Halliwell, Steven Romero, Ryan Peace, Pete Paredes, Courtney Almeida, the Santos Brothers, Kimberly Roderick, Jennifer Silvia, Jason Corser, Morgan Scott Fielding, Martin Soto, Toby Gray,

Connie Ouellette, Meaghan Parker, Jennifer Silvia, Lori Bruno, Amanda Scanlon, and April Tripp.

And to all the fans of my books, thank you! Without you, there is no Witch Series.

In memory of Collette Gagnon, Ana Delia Palafox, and Bill Williams. You will be forever missed. We love you.

To Zach Halliwell, I say this: Dark clouds can fill our lives sometimes and bring us down. But know that you are not alone. We all have bad days, but don't let them overshadow the good ones. There is always a light at the end of the tunnel. What may seem impossible right now can turn into what makes you stronger. You are a bright light. I see you. I love you, kid.

A Note to My Mother, Ana Delia

When you left us, I sank into darkness and lost myself. I let the pain of losing you take over who I was. I never truly felt pain until I lost you. But one day, I heard your voice in my head. "Despierta," you whispered. You filled my head with memories of how hard you fought to give us a better life. All you ever wanted was for us to be happy. It was then I realized I wasn't honoring your memory. I decided that very day that I would live the life you intended for me. Now I reach for every star, follow every dream. I try to give more than I take. I work hard and try to be a good wife. I am the woman I am today because you loved me. I hope I've made you proud, Mom. Con todo mi Corazon, te quiero.

Prologue

I felt evil rising up from inside me and tasted its bitterness in my mouth. A battle between good and evil was underway in my head, and good was losing the battle. Tears streamed down my face as I tried to remind myself who I was. I couldn't find the strength to wave my hand and save myself. The darkness was too strong. It was time to pay for what I'd done.

My eyes grew wide as I found myself opening the crystal. What was I doing? I tried to put one hand over my mouth as I began to chant the spell needed to give Simon my powers.

"Don't fight it," Simon said, moving my hand away.

I cried as the crystal began to glow. Streams of energy flowed from my body and into the crystal. A crackling laugh escaped my lips. The darkness had won. My life was doomed. I had just killed any hope of saving my friends.

Chapter 1
The Signal

I should have been enjoying this beautiful evening as I sat on my windowsill and admired Salem, all covered in snow. Christmas lights were everywhere. Many homes were all decked out for the holidays. The town looked more breathtaking than ever. This was usually a happy time of year for me. I loved watching humans and their holiday rituals. I would walk the streets and inhale the odor of cookies baking in nearby homes. There was something about December that made my heart come alive. Even with all this evil living inside me, I somehow managed to smile sometimes.

Today was not one of those days. Instead, I felt out of breath as I paced back and forth in my apartment. I was getting tired of waiting for the signal. Time was running out. My good mood had faded. I was quickly changing into that evil witch again. Only James, my husband, knew how to keep her away.

Being near him seemed to be the only thing that would calm the rage inside me. But, where was he? He hadn't sent the signal to meet him yet.

We met in one of my memories as often as we could. It was the simple plan we had thought of to keep me calm. If things got too bad for me, I would just send the signal for James to meet me. But today, James was late. I hadn't seen him in two days. Every time we were apart, I would feel the darkness wash over me. The evil witch inside me would rejoice and darken my mood fast. I was trying everything I could to stay happy, but when James wasn't near me, it was almost impossible.

Delia, my best friend, couldn't understand my need to stay so cheerful. It bothered me when she said I had brought this on myself, even though it was true. She never missed a single opportunity to remind me of how I had made things worse. She made it sound so easy to stay happy.

"Just don't think about it," she often said.

That was easy for her to say. She spent every moment with Fish. They had married over a month ago and were now living on the second floor of my building.

Cory and the boys, my childhood friends, had removed all the workout equipment and fixed the place up for the happy couple. Delia wanted them to live in her house, but Fish wouldn't have it. He kept the house boarded up and begged Delia to stay away from there. I sometimes heard him yelling at her not to leave the house. Delia was becoming annoyed with his constant worry over her.

"We'll be safe here with Thea," he would tell her. He had no idea how wrong he was.

I was having trouble keeping the evil witch inside me from showing her face. A demon now lived inside me. I had made the worst mistake of my life: I'd made a forbidden blood promise to marry Simon, the man who had been hunting me for hundreds of years. I had traveled into the depths of hell and sealed that promise with my blood. That promise had changed me, both physically and mentally. My eyes were as dark as the night—and my heart, cold as ice.

Now evil thoughts constantly went through my head. Sometimes those thoughts made me smile. I thought of killing my friends, killing everyone. Voices filled my head and told me to hurt the ones I loved. Sometimes I had to leave the house when the temptation became too great. I would imagine their bodies covered in blood while my face lit up with happiness. Being around James was the only thing that made me feel like myself again.

There was only one problem: I wasn't always with James.

I was trying to find a way to break the blood promise I had made to Simon, but if my plan was going to work, I had to stay away from James. I couldn't let Simon see me with him, since it would reveal my secret to staying strong.

We had all moved out of the mansion the same day James and I had gone into Magia, the magical land my father came from. Everyone wanted to know why we had gone there, but I knew it was too dangerous to tell them. There was something James and I needed to do back in Magia. It was our last saving grace to fix what I had done.

James and I told no one of our plan. Only my wizard father, the king of Magia, knew the reason we had left. James and Martin, a wizard from Magia, had become fast friends. Martin approved of my choice to bring James there. He called James a man of honor, something I already knew. But Martin had been very disappointed in me when I told him I'd made the blood promise. He couldn't understand why I had resorted to that.

"You're a wizard, Thea," he'd said. "Wizards are not weak."

I was honestly getting tired of hearing that. I knew I had made a mistake but throwing it in my face wasn't helping. Although I could see things were bad, I wasn't stupid. I knew there was no turning back after making a blood promise. You either kept your word, or the darkness would take you.

In my desperation to get revenge, I had gone to Simon for help. I had called the demons from hell and given Simon a vial of my blood to seal the promise. The thought of my unborn son being dead had driven me mad. I saw Simon as my only way out. He had the leaves, and he had a way to kill Wendell, the wizard I held responsible for making me lose my son.

The leaves Simon had been able to take away wizards' powers. I planned on using those leaves to bring Wendell to his knees before I killed him. But, naturally, Simon wanted something in return for his help. He wanted to be king, and I handed him the way. I had given Simon everything he ever wanted. I even told him about my unborn son. He was surprised that was the secret I had been hiding this whole time.

~ 5 ~

But there was something Simon didn't know: I had never lost my son. Wendell had not killed him when he was torturing me.

Now I was doing everything I could to keep this from Simon. I put spells on myself, so I wouldn't show my pregnancy. I knew if Simon found out, he would find a way to kill him. There was no way Simon was going to let anyone take away his chance to be king. Simon hated the fact that he was half human. He thought Magia would give him the powers he wasn't born with. Now he had a way, and I had given him the ticket.

But I had a plan, a way out of this. And it started with me coming back home to my apartment.

Simon had to think I wanted no part of James. He had to believe that there was no longer any room in my life for love. Simon knew how the blood promise worked. He himself had made a blood promise to Wendell one day, and that promise was to kill me. Simon didn't know I knew about that. He also didn't know I knew where the leaves were. I had used my magic to hide them from him. Now Simon was furious, and he and his men were tearing Salem's woods apart to find them. Simon spent most of his days searching the area where he thought they might be. This had delayed his plan to go into Magia right away. Without those leaves, he knew he was no match for the wizards.

I had told Martin and the others what Simon was planning, but Martin didn't seem worried about it.

"We have dragons, Thea," he said to me one day. "Simon's leaves can't hurt them."

But Simon had an army of warlocks waiting to help him kill the wizards, and they were as hungry for power as Simon was. Going into Magia was all Simon and his men could think of. Simon had filled their heads with hopes of becoming wizards if they helped him, and the warlocks had believed the lie.

I knew Simon was only using them, and that he planned on killing them once we were in Magia. There was just one thing I didn't understand: if Simon killed everyone, who would he rule in Magia? He would have no kingdom if everyone was dead. I couldn't make sense of that. I knew Simon had something up his sleeve; I just couldn't figure out what that was. Right now, Simon was more worried about finding the leaves.

But as he searched for the leaves, I was busy looking for answers. I'd heard about a witch who had survived a blood promise. The promise was broken, and the darkness never took her. I had to find out why and how she did it. I was trying to gather information about her, but all anyone seemed to know was that she spent a lot of time near Salem Willows, a park here in Salem. I'd gone looking twice already, but to no avail. No one knew what her promise had been, only that she had broken it. They say she went mad after that.

"She hardly shows her face anymore," Sharron had said.

When she did show her face, you got the sense that you were looking at Satan himself. Her dark eyes scared anyone who looked into them.

I was starting to get the same looks. The glossy look in my eyes made others shiver when I looked their way. I hated the effect I was having on people. I felt like a monster that was scaring the town of Salem half to death. Even my friends backed away when they noticed my mood darkening. I was trying everything I could to fight it, but the darkness was starting to win the battle. I was back to hating who I was, back to hiding behind my loose clothes.

Right now, I couldn't think of that. I needed James. Where was he? We had agreed to meet in two days, no matter what. I kept pacing back and forth, waiting to hear the thunder. It was the signal James would send to let me know he was waiting. I was getting desperate. I could feel the evil thoughts taking over who I was. I wanted to hurt something; I wanted to cause pain. The thought of tasting blood sounded sweeter than ever, and I was having trouble shaking those thoughts from my head. I closed my eyes and whispered, "Please hurry, James."

The evil witch inside me was rising to the surface. It was getting hard to control my temper. Impulsively, I knocked over a box of Christmas ornaments Fish had given me, then spun around and kicked the tree Cory had cut down, sending it flying across the living room.

"Control yourself, witch!" I yelled at myself. I ran to the mirror and saw that my eyes were darker than ever. "Stop it!" I protested as I felt my heart turning black.

I couldn't imagine where James could be. He knew how important it was that I see him. He was my secret weapon to chase away the evil witch inside me. When I was near him, his love made her drift away. I felt normal again. The pain and anger disappeared. His scent flowed through me and made me think straight.

Nothing else helped; nothing else even came close.

I began pacing the room again. I froze when someone knocked at the door.

"Creepella, are you in there?"

It was Fish. I couldn't see him right now. My mood was too dark. I knew I would be nothing but rude to him.

I gave up on waiting and pulled out Delia's box. My hands shook as I forced myself to open it. Soap-like bubbles floated out of the box and hovered over my head. I quickly searched for the memory I wanted.

As Fish opened the door, I reached for the memory, and I was gone.

I was at my favorite lake. Here, the forest was green and beautiful. There was no snow, no chilling wind. It was the perfect day, saved in a little box. The memory was of one of the happiest days of my life. James was courting me, and he often met me here in secret so we could be together. I had spent hours with him here, swimming in the lake until the sun went down.

I looked around, but James was nowhere in sight. This wasn't good. What possible reason could he have for not coming here today? My blood was still boiling. I was having a hard time keeping the evil thoughts from winning.

I was beginning to hyperventilate when I heard the breaking of twigs behind me. Finally, I saw James running out from the trees.

"I'm here!" he yelled.

I wanted to wave my hand at him, but that smile on his face stopped me. He was more handsome than ever. I still could hardly believe this tall, beautiful man was mine. He had the face of an angel, a face too beautiful to be real. His eyes were a liquid brown but had turned blue when he fell in love with me. It was a sign of love that only I could see. Every time he looked into my eyes, I was reminded of how much he truly loved me.

As he made his way to me, I touched my hair, knowing he would notice how straight and dark it was. My hair was normally a tangled, knotted mess—a sign of true love among witches—and I tamed it by keeping it in a ponytail. But when the evil witch rose to the surface, all signs of my love for James disappeared. My hair turned black and straight, just like it was now.

James finally reached me and took my face in his hands. I felt an eruption of anger explode within me when he touched me. I tried very hard not to show how angry I was. When he attempted to kiss me, I couldn't help but turn away.

He gently turned my head and made me look at him. His blue eyes pierced through me. "Are you not going to say hello?" he asked in a soothing voice.

I scowled. "Where have you been? Why didn't you send the signal?"

He smiled that golden smile. "I sent it just before I got here, my love."

I fought the impulse to push him away. Instead, I shook my head. "You can't ever be late. You promised you would always be here."

A look of concern washed over his face. "I'm sorry. It won't happen again, I promise." He kept looking into my eyes. "Having a bad day?"

I tried to let his voice calm me, but the evil witch wanted no part of him. She hated when I was near him. So many times, I had to stop myself from hurting him. "I'm furious with you," I said, pushing him away.

He seemed surprised at first, but then grabbed my arm and pulled me toward him. "I guess we'll have to stay here until I'm forgiven, won't we?"

When our lips met, it felt like ice water being splashed on my face. His kiss was sweet; his touch, tender. I slowly wrapped my arms around his neck and gave into him. His scent traveled through me and calmed my soul. The evil inside me quickly drifted away. I could hear the birds again, feel the sun shining down on us. It was like I was being dragged out of hell.

"I missed you," James said between kisses.

"More—kiss me more," I said, pulling him closer.

We sat under our tree, his arms tightly around me. The evil witch was gone. Love had won the battle over evil for now. My mind was clear. I was the old Thea again. I closed my eyes and let James's scent fill my head.

He asked his usual question: "What are you thinking of?"

I smiled. Didn't he know I was always thinking of him?

He gazed down at me. "It must be something good, to make you smile like that."

"I was thinking of you."

"But I'm right here."

I looked up at him. "Does that mean I can't think of you?"

He smiled. "I'm sorry I was late today."

I leaned my head on his chest again. I didn't want him to know how hard it had been to stay calm, how it had felt like I was fighting off an evil demon. I knew James would get nervous if he suspected I was having so much trouble staying away from him. He was already nervous about my plan. Although he agreed with it, he didn't like the fact that I was risking so much. But I knew it was the only way. Simon could never know I had found a way to keep the evil thoughts at bay. I had to push myself to the limit in order to convince him I had become as greedy and evil as he was.

"Are you angry with me?" James asked, tearing me away from my thoughts.

I looked up at him and smiled. My dark eyes didn't seem to bother him like they did everyone else. James never cringed like Delia and the boys would. He only looked at me with tender eyes. "Of course not," I answered. "I'm sorry if I was rude."

"Was two days too long?" he asked.

I glanced away. I didn't want to answer that. He had stayed away from me for two days to see how I would do. We'd started off by being apart for hours at first, and then a day. This was the first time we had tried two days. I knew I hadn't handled it well, but I didn't want him to know that. I had to keep pushing myself. I couldn't always rely on James to keep me calm. Everyone was expecting more out of me. They made it sound so easy to fight the evil thoughts that filled my head. My father had told me many times to find myself, but I never understood what he meant by that.

"You're a wizard, Thea," he would say. "Find the wizard part of you. It will keep you strong." Why didn't he just tell me how?

When I didn't answer, James made me look at him. "Too long?" he asked.

I shook my head. "I say we go for three days next."

His eyes narrowed. I knew he didn't believe me. "I don't know about that, Thea."

"I'll be fine," I lied. "As long as you're here waiting, I can do it."

He thought about it for a moment. "Okay," he said, wrapping his arms around me again. "I'll wait three days before I come here again. But promise me one thing."

"What is it?"

"That you send the signal if you find yourself needing me."

"I promise," I replied, but I knew I was lying.

I had always promised myself one thing: if I felt myself losing control, I would not stay here and hurt him. There were so many things I couldn't take back, so many things I didn't see. I was ashamed of all the mistakes I had made, ashamed at how many people I had already hurt. I had to find my own way out of this. It was time to grow up and act like the witch I really was. Problem was, I didn't know how to do that.

I noticed James kept checking his watch, something he never did. "Feeling normal again?" he kept asking.

That was strange. Why did he keep asking me that? *Maybe he just wants to know how quickly I feel like myself again.* I decided to change the subject.

"Fish made me laugh yesterday," I said.

"What did he do now?"

"Delia keeps putting a spell on her hair to make it neat again. Fish insists she leave it alone."

"And what's funny about that? She should leave it alone, like you do." He glanced at my hair when he said that.

"Well, when she was sleeping, Fish cast a spell on her to make it messy again. He must have chanted the spell wrong, because when Delia woke up, her hair was blue."

We both burst out in laughter.

Chapter 2
A Better Goodbye

James ran his fingers through my hair. It was finally messy and knotted again, which meant our time together was coming to an end. I got an uneasy feeling that he was in a hurry today. He was worried about something, but I couldn't figure out what.

"Can I ask you something?" he said. "But I don't want you to get mad."

Why would I get mad? "What is it?"

There was a pause before he asked, "Have you seen Helena?"

I closed my eyes as my fingers sank into his skin. Just hearing her name made me want to tear that woman apart. I knew James had to preserve his relationship with her; it was vital to keep Simon thinking he had torn us apart. Helena thought she had tricked James into believing they had bonded on the night of Delia's wedding. He had been very drunk that night, and Helena took full advantage of it. She had no idea that James and I knew the truth, or that we had bonded ourselves again.

Helena believed her marriage to James was still on. She was running around making plans for the wedding and had even bought her dress already. Almost the whole town was invited—the whole town but me, of course. James was running out of excuses to delay the wedding. He'd lied and told Helena that he was waiting on a gift he had ordered. This only made her think that James wanted the wedding to be perfect.

"Thea, you're going to rip my arm away," James complained.

I hadn't realized I was squeezing it so hard. I quickly let go and looked up at him.

"I asked you not to get mad," he reminded me.

"I'm not mad," I lied.

"So, have you seen her?" he asked again.

"What reason would I have to see *her*?" I snapped at him.

"She was supposed to come over tonight, but she never made it. I'm a little worried."

"Then why don't you run and go look for her?" I said, trying to get to my feet.

James took hold of my arm with force. "Hey, this was your idea, remember? I never wanted to keep seeing her. It was your idea to give her hope, not mine. I don't like playing those games with anyone."

I immediately knew my reaction had been a mistake. "Just a few more days, please," I said as I leaned back again. "If you stop seeing her, she'll tell Simon, and he'll get suspicious."

He looked frustrated as he let go of my arm and relaxed against the tree. "Why did I let you talk me into this?" he said, shaking his head. "I'll never forgive myself if she gets hurt."

"Why would she get hurt?"

He looked at me with disapproving eyes. "That girl has no idea what she's gotten herself into by helping Simon. He'll dispose of her when he's done using her."

"That's her problem," I snapped. "No one told her to help him."

He gave me a horrible look. "I'm not going to have her death hanging over my head, Thea."

"Why would it hang over your head? You didn't force her to help Simon."

He ignored the question as he sat up again. "I don't know why you don't just let me drag Simon into Magia so the dragons can kill him. Why does it have to be you?"

I hung my head. "Because now he's protected by the promise I made."

He looked away. "All these rules—I can't keep up with them. First a spell that can't be broken, and now a promise that must be fulfilled. It's driving me mad, Thea. I want this to end already."

"The spell doesn't affect me anymore," I reminded him.

"And the promise?" he said, turning back to me. "It wasn't enough that a spell was making you hate me—you had to make a blood promise on top of it? Don't you think we had enough problems?" He shook his head.

This was the first time James had shown resentment toward me. I could put up with it from Delia, but not from him. I knew I had made things worse, but there was nothing I could do to change it. Couldn't he see I was trying everything I could think of to fix what I had done?

"Do you want me to leave?" I asked.

He looked at me. After a moment, he wrapped his arms around me and leaned back. "Don't be silly, Thea. I'm just frustrated. I don't like the way you get when you're away from me. I could clearly see you were having a bad day today. You didn't fool me for one moment."

I bit my lip. I was hoping he hadn't noticed.

"We're stronger together," he continued. "You shouldn't have left the mansion, and I shouldn't have continued my relationship with Helena. So, what if Simon knows I keep you strong? What can he do about it?"

I closed my eyes when he said that. I knew exactly what Simon would do if he found out. Simon still thought he would die if he killed James, but that didn't mean he wouldn't send warlocks after him. I knew it was safer if Simon thought I wanted no part of James. I even wanted him to think I hated James. I was willing to do anything to keep James safe.

He began running his fingers through my hair again. We watched the Thea and James that lived in this memory swimming in the lake. I was surprised when he said, "Do I help you find yourself, Thea?"

I bit my lip again. He'd been talking to my father. That made me angry. Now James thought it was his fault I couldn't find the wizard part of me. "I didn't know I was lost," I answered.

"Your father seems to think so."

There was a pause.

"You know I love you, don't you?" he asked.

I didn't like where this was going. "Of course, I do."

He looked down at me. "And, do you know I wouldn't change a thing about you?"

"Yes, I know that."

"Do you doubt *why* I love you?"

Yes! I screamed in my head. "Never," I lied. It was the one thing I had never understood. Why had he fallen in love with me? He could have any woman he wanted. Why me? I was so plain, so not what he deserved. I tried to look away, but James forced me to meet his eyes.

"You made me better than I was, Thea—made me more than I am. That's why I love you."

I didn't want to talk about this anymore. Whatever was wrong with me, it wasn't his fault. I was the weak one, not him. I didn't know why I was being so self-loathing these days, but I could tell it was only getting worse. It seemed the only time I was happy with myself was when the evil witch came to the surface. It was only then that I felt confident and beautiful, but there was no way I could admit that to James.

"How is my father?" I asked, hoping to change the subject.

"Oh, I almost forgot . . ."

"What is it?"

He stood and helped me to my feet. "We have to find a way to sneak you into the house, so you can

~ 19 ~

see him. He's been very worried about you. Steven has been asking about you, too. He misses you. I told him you would be over to see him soon."

"But my eyes—I'll scare him."

James laughed. "They're not that bad, Thea. Besides, I can't keep lying to him about where you are. Steven deserves better than that. And I hope you intend to restore his memories soon."

"I will, when this is over," I assured him.

"So, when will you go see him, then?"

"What if Simon sees me there? He'll know we're up to something."

"I have a plan," James said, pulling me into his arms. "And if it works, you can see your father and Steven whenever you want."

"How are you going to do that?"

The most beautiful smile spread across his face. I was glad to see that his angry mood had passed. His blue eyes sparkled. "Do you trust me?"

"You know I do."

"Then I will find a way."

I was going to ask him what he was planning when I noticed something odd. I was so worried about calming down that I hadn't noticed it before. A tattoo of a dragon covered his arm. I had never known James to have tattoos before. The ink looked very fresh. *Did he get that today?*

I stepped back and pointed at the tattoo. "When did you get that?"

He looked down at it. "Oh, this? I'd always wanted to get one—just never had a chance."

"I never knew you liked those things."

He gave me a nervous look. "I told you—I've

~ 20 ~

always wanted to get one."

I kept staring at the tattoo. The dragon was beautiful. Its red eyes reminded me of Attor, the dragon from Magia. It was almost the perfect image of him.

"So, three days then?" James asked when I wouldn't look away from his tattoo.

I raised my eyes. "What?"

"You said we should try waiting three days this time."

"Oh, yes. I'll see you in three days."

"Do I get a kiss goodbye?"

I was gazing at his arm again and couldn't look away. There was something about the tattoo I couldn't put my finger on. I could smell the fresh ink. That was odd. I had never known of a tattoo that gave off an odor. Why did his?

"Thea, I have to leave now."

I looked up at him again. "We still have no secrets, right?"

He became annoyed. "I thought you said you trusted me."

"I do."

"It doesn't feel that way."

As much as I wanted to question him, I decided not to. I had caused him enough pain in the past. I wanted to show him that I believed in him now more than ever. I forced a smile. "I'll see you in three days."

"I'll be here waiting." He gave me a short kiss goodbye and disappeared into the trees.

I couldn't help but feel confused. Normally, James would have asked that I not forget I loved him. He would have kissed me several times before he left.

Today, it seemed as if he couldn't wait to get out of here.

I couldn't drive myself crazy thinking about this. I pulled out Delia's box and opened it.

"Thea, wait," I heard James call out.

"Is something wrong?" I asked as he made his way back to me.

He slid his arm around my waist and pulled me toward him. "I forgot to tell you that I love you," he said with a big smile.

I dropped the box when he pulled me to his lips. I knew he would be seeing Helena today, so I pressed myself against him and persuaded him to stay. When I ran my tongue over his lips, he began to rip my clothes away. This was a much better goodbye. Those three days would be easy now. All I had to do was think of this moment.

I was still on cloud nine when I pulled myself out of the memory. My heart was filled with joy. I smiled as I breathed in James's scent, which had permeated my clothes. I dropped on the sofa and closed my eyes, imagining his arms holding me tight. I wanted to go back into the memory, to stay in his arms and never leave. How I loved the feeling of safety I felt when he held me. I didn't think of anything, not even the nightmare I was living.

"Um, should I come back?" I heard Fish say from the kitchen.

I opened my eyes, feeling embarrassed. "Fish . . . I didn't know you were still here," I said, trying to fix my hair. I knew I must have looked a mess. My blouse was still half unbuttoned, and my skirt was covered with grass. I straightened myself as Fish closed the refrigerator door. He had a sandwich in one hand and a can of soda in the other. With his boyish face and dirty-blond hair, he could easily have been mistaken for a fifteen-year-old. He was very handsome and always funny.

"Delia is pissed again," he said, "so I thought I would come up here."

I tried to hide my embarrassment from him. "Why is she mad *now*?" I asked, hoping he wouldn't notice I was blushing.

He took another bite of his sandwich. "You have grass in your hair," he said with a mouthful of food. "And your skirt is inside out, too." He took a sip of soda.

I glanced down at myself. He was right.

"Wow, I wonder what James looks like," he teased.

I couldn't even look at him.

"Don't be embarrassed, Creepella. Delia leaves the house with mismatched shoes all the time. She can't help it. Just look at who she's married to."

I chuckled. "So why is she mad?" I asked as I headed to the bathroom to fix my skirt. I was delighted at what a good mood I was in. "She's been mad a lot lately. What did you do this time?"

When I came out of the bathroom, I found Fish sitting on my bed, his smile replaced by a gloomy look. He stared at the half-eaten sandwich still in his hand. "I think Delia wants a divorce," he blurted out.

"What?" I asked, shocked. "Why on earth would you think that?"

"I think she regrets marrying me, Thea."

I couldn't imagine why he felt like that. I knew Delia loved him more than life itself. Maybe she wasn't the most affectionate woman I knew, but I did know she loved him. "Fish, she loves you," I said, placing my hand on his knee. "You know that."

He shook his head. "I never said she didn't love me. I said she regrets marrying me."

"But what makes you think that?"

He tossed the sandwich on my nightstand. "You ever regret marrying James?"

I was taken aback by his question. "No, of course not."

He looked down again. "I would do anything for her, Thea—even give her up, if that's what she wanted. All I've ever wanted was for her to be happy, and I think she's unhappy being with me."

I couldn't get over how heartbroken he looked. His boyish face had lost its golden smile. I knew Delia had been in a foul mood lately, but I hadn't realized it was this bad. Fish really thought Delia didn't want to be with him anymore. Question was, why?

I kneeled in front of him. "Fish, why are you talking like this? This isn't like you. I'm sure you're making too much out of it. Delia adores you."

"She used to. Not anymore. She's always angry with me, yelling and screaming. I can't do anything right in her eyes. The only time she's happy is when I'm not around. She used to think my jokes were funny, but now she thinks they're stupid."

I couldn't believe what I was hearing. What was going on with her? Couldn't she see what she was doing to him? "You want me to speak with her?"

He shook his head. "She'll only get upset with me."

"What can I do, Fish?"

He looked at his hands. "I was kinda hoping you could tell me what I'm doing wrong."

I had no answer. How could he possibly think he was doing something wrong? Fish did everything for Delia. She'd told me herself how Fish greeted her with breakfast in bed every morning. "I know I wore you out last night," Fish would say, placing her breakfast on her lap.

Delia loved that about him. She admired how Fish took pride in being her husband. "He treats me like a queen," she'd said one day.

I couldn't understand what was going on. Fish was clearly hurting. He was on the verge of tears. I tried to reach for his hand, but he quickly stood.

"Forget about it, Thea," he said. Trying to hide his anguish, he put his hands in his front pockets and forced a smile. "Hey, look at your eyes. They're not so bad right now. You actually look like yourself."

"Fish, talk to me."

He ignored what I said. "Need help getting up?" he said, offering me his hand. He helped me up, and I wrapped my arms around him.

"I'm sure there's a perfectly good explanation for this, sweetie," I reassured him.

"Yeah, sure there is," he said as he pulled away. "I'm just being stupid."

"Thea, is Fish—" Delia froze as she walked into my room. I noted the angry look on her face. Her long, dark hair made her look even angrier.

"Looking for me?" Fish asked.

"Why didn't you tell me you were up here?" she snapped at him.

Fish tried to joke with her. "Hey, Delia, I'm up here with Creepella."

Delia rolled her eyes and turned on her heels. "Idiot," she said under her breath.

Fish sighed as Delia slammed the door behind her. "Yeah, I'm sure she's perfectly happy with me."

I couldn't understand it. What the hell was wrong with her? "Let me talk to her, Fish. Maybe I can find out what's going on."

"Don't bother. I can see what's going on."

He threw the soda away and walked out of the apartment.

I felt so bad for him. I wasn't used to seeing him like this. *Maybe I should speak with Delia.*

Against his wishes, I decided to go down and talk to her. I knew it was a good time, too. My mood wasn't dark; in fact, I was in a very good mood right now. I could take Delia's jabs and indirect comments about how I had made things worse with no problem. And with that thought, I ran down the stairs.

Chapter 3
The Witch Christmas Tree

I heard Delia yelling at Fish as I descended the stairs. I stopped at their door, debating whether to knock or not.

"I don't want you upstairs with that witch," I heard her say.

Maybe this wasn't a good idea after all. I couldn't let anything darken my mood. Delia and I would probably end up arguing. I decided to go for a walk and get some fresh air instead. I could check Salem Willows. I remembered Sharron telling me that she'd seen the black witch there. Maybe tonight would be the night I found her.

I hurried back up the stairs and into my apartment. I grabbed my coat, put the wand in my pocket, and headed out into the night. I was surprised to see Kym, Jason's mother, walking into the yard as I left the building. What was she doing here? Kym had long, curly dark hair and blazing dark eyes. She was a very moody witch and usually had a trail of cats following behind her. I wondered if she was still casting her cat spells on the warlocks. I noticed she still carried the branch I had once cast a spell on to make her fly. Had she been using it?

She didn't look happy as she approached me. "What do you have my son doing now?" she hissed.

I had no idea what she was talking about. I hadn't seen her son, Jason, in weeks. "Hello to you, too," I answered.

She stomped her way closer to me. I admired how this witch never showed any fear of me. She didn't know it, but she was one of my favorite witches. "Don't play stupid with me," she growled. "What are the tattoos for?"

I froze. "What tattoos?"

She pulled out her phone and held it up. "I took this picture while Jason was sleeping. Why is my son getting covered in tattoos, witch?"

I was speechless as I looked at the picture. Jason lay on his stomach, exposing a large tattoo on his back. It was a beautiful lion standing over a massive rhino, clearly proud of the prey it had taken down. "When did he get that?" I asked.

"Don't pretend with me," Kym said, lowering her phone. "Why are you having him get these?"

"These? He has more than one?"

Kym's eyes narrowed as she studied my eyes. It took her a moment to realize I really didn't know about the tattoos. "If you're not making him get these, then who is?"

I couldn't help but wonder if James was behind this. He was also getting tattoos. What were they up to? "I don't know," I said.

She put the phone away. "Well, I'm getting to the bottom of this."

"You're not flying around Salem on that thing, are you?"

"What if I am?" she said as she placed the branch between her legs. "Are you going to stop me?"

She flew off before I could say another word. How I loved her tenacity. It was the reason I respected her so much. I thought about following her, but the truth was, I didn't want to lose my good mood. I wasn't going to see James for three days, so I had to stay as happy as possible. I didn't even want to think about the tattoos; that would only make me sick with worry. What harm could getting tattoos do, anyway?

I decided to go for my walk. I needed to clear my head. I buttoned my coat and headed down the street.

Salem looked even more beautiful at night. Almost every home was decorated for the holidays. I soon forgot all about Kym and the tattoos as I walked the streets, admiring the lights. I peeked through windows to see families decorating their trees and smiled at the sight of kids shaking their gifts, trying to guess what was inside. These were the moments I had dreamed of sharing with my son. Many times, I'd imagined him running to open his gifts while James sat on a couch in his pajamas, a smile stretching from ear to ear as he watched his son under the tree.

It was the human life I craved. I wanted to live a normal life, one without magic or spells. But who was

I kidding? Witches never had it that easy. Our world was filled with the fear of being found out and exposed. As far as humans knew, witches only existed during Halloween and in books. Magic was something only magicians did. The human world would have been turned upside down if they knew witches were real. I had to accept that my fantasy of having a normal life would never come true.

As I walked the streets on my way to Salem Willows, a house caught my attention. It wasn't lit up with the typical Christmas lights everyone else had. Instead, this house had orange and purple lights all over it. I crossed the street and peeked in the front window. Inside, a beautiful black tree was decorated with orange and green witch hats, purple silk ribbon, and tiny orange stockings. A black cat served as the tree top. It was the best tree on the block, I thought.

"What is making my angel smile?" I heard a voice say.

I spun around, and my smile instantly disappeared. I'd been so busy enjoying my good mood that I hadn't heard Simon walk up behind me. He wore a long black coat and a scarf wrapped around his neck. I couldn't get over how much he looked like James. He was just as handsome, just as appealing. What was he doing here? I expected him to be out looking for the leaves. What must he be thinking, seeing me smiling and in a good mood? This wasn't good.

I slowly moved away from the window. Simon's dark eyes looked past me and into the house. He seemed confused by what I was looking at. His brows arched when he saw the tree.

"Silly humans," he said, turning back to me. "They make such a fuss this time of year. Don't you agree?"

He tilted his head when I looked into his eyes. At first, I wasn't sure what he was looking at, but then I remembered what Fish had said: *Hey, look at your eyes. They're not so bad right now. You actually look like yourself.* I quickly looked away from Simon. My eyes should have been as dark as his right now. I knew Simon would grow suspicious and wonder why I was in such a good mood. I kept my eyes to the ground as he moved closer to me.

"What is my little dove doing out so late?" he asked. He looked through the window again. "It couldn't be to look at trees, could it?"

"I was just getting some air," I said, trying to avoid his eyes. I could feel his eyes on me.

After what seemed like forever, he offered me his arm. "Come, I'll join you."

I reluctantly wrapped my arm around his. I heard weapons being drawn the moment I touched him.

Simon laughed. "Please, gentlemen, this is my fiancée. She's not going to hurt the man she's promised to wed." He patted my arm. "Are you, my sweet?"

I tried to find his warlocks. I knew they were near. "No, of course not," I answered.

"See?" Simon said into the night. "All is well."

My eyes searched the darkness for them as Simon led me back to the sidewalk. As we made our way down the street, I finally spotted them. Two huge warlocks, massive in size, were following us in the shadows. They seemed to be getting bigger and bigger every time I saw them. Had they been taking steroids? They stayed several yards behind us as Simon led me away.

I got a little nervous when Simon began walking toward Salem Willows. Did he know I had been headed there? I kept wondering what he was doing out here tonight. I looked at his shoes but found no evidence of him being out in the woods. Simon usually wore hiking boots when he was searching for the leaves, but tonight he was very well dressed. It was like he had been out to dinner or something. His dark hair was well combed. He even had on cologne. I wasn't used to seeing Simon like this. Who was he trying to impress? I hated myself for even noticing how handsome he looked.

We walked a few blocks without saying a word. Simon kept glancing at me and shaking his head. I was going crazy wondering what he was thinking.

"You haven't come to see me lately," he finally said.

I looked away. "You haven't been around," I answered.

He gave me a sideways glance. "I was around tonight. I was on my way to invite my sweetheart to dinner—and perhaps ask her why she's been avoiding me." Again, a sideways glance.

"I haven't been avoiding you," I lied.

We continued walking as the warlocks followed. I was surprised to hear that Simon had planned on having dinner with me tonight. I couldn't imagine what my friends would have done if Simon had walked into my building tonight. That could have turned into a big mess.

"I was starting to think you had found a way to break the promise," he said. "Word has it that you've been searching for a witch who broke it long ago."

What? Who told him?

He stopped and faced me. "Imagine my dismay when I looked into your eyes tonight. They're so pretty and *brown*."

I swallowed thickly. *I should have known he would notice them.* There was no doubt in my head that Helena was behind this. She ran to Simon about everything.

"I don't know what you're talking about," I answered.

"Is that so?" He studied my eyes and slowly moved closer. "Do you know what angers me the most?" he said, stroking my face. "I hate when people hide things from me. You wouldn't be hiding something from me now, would you?"

Before I could answer, he struck me hard across the face. A wave of rage exploded inside me. When he struck me again, dark thoughts flooded my mind. I felt myself changing in an instant. Evil quickly rose to the surface.

My blood was boiling as I looked at Simon again. "I wouldn't do that again if I were you, Simon."

His warlocks quickly drew their weapons.

Simon put his hand up to stop them. He looked into my eyes again and smiled. "There is my bride," he said, lowering his arm. "You were starting to worry me, my angel. I had actually convinced myself you had broken the promise."

I felt an ugly hatred traveling through me and knew my eyes were dark again. All the evil thoughts that consumed me returned within seconds. I wanted blood; I wanted power.

"It's no use trying to fight it," he said. "You belong to the darkness now." He reached out and grabbed my chin with force. "And you also belong to *me*," he said and crushed his lips to mine.

I wanted to push him away. I felt repulsed as his tongue explored my mouth. I fought the urge to wave my hand at him. I had to stay calm; I couldn't ruin things now.

He grabbed a handful of my hair and pulled my head back. "I want you to know something," he said, kissing my neck. "If you're up to something, I *will* find out." He pulled my hair again and made me look at him. "No one forced you to make that promise. You came to me, remember?"

"I haven't forgotten," I hissed.

He smiled. "That's good to hear, my pet. You never know what tricks I may have up my sleeve. Remember, I am not a stupid man."

I pushed away and glared at him. I was finding it almost impossible to stay calm. I wanted nothing more than to hurt him.

Simon seemed pleased as his smile grew wider and wider. "Your eyes look beautiful, my dear. I like them black. It suits you. Why would you ever want to change them?" He moved closer. "The question is, what is making them turn brown again? I wonder where you've been this evening."

"What do you want, Simon?"

He laughed. "Come now, my little dove. Is this any way to treat your fiancé?"

How I hated all the stupid names he called me. "My little dove" was my least favorite. I was trying to fight the urge to hurt him when he reached out, took a strand of my hair, and held it to his nose.

"You know, I rather like it when your hair is so straight and dark like this. It only makes me wonder what you'll look like after."

"After what?" I asked.

I had never before seen a look of tenderness in Simon's eyes. As he brushed his fingers across my face, he seemed lost in some deluded moment he thought we were having. But as fast as it started, it ended in an instant when he suddenly pushed me away and began to laugh.

"You will not bewitch me, my sweet."

A cell phone rang, interrupting our conversation. Simon never looked away from me as one of the warlocks handed him the phone. "This better be good," Simon said into the phone. A pause. "I was busy. What is it?" Another pause. His face suddenly lit up. "That is good news," he said with a wicked smile. "I'll be right there." He handed the phone back to the warlock. "I'm sorry to ruin our little reunion," he said to me, "but I must leave now. I have a few questions to ask someone." He gave me the most evil smile. "Happy hunting, my little dove." He motioned to his goons, and they were off.

The moment Simon disappeared into the night, I began running home. I forgot all about finding the black witch and hurried back to make sure my friends were okay. That phone call Simon received made me nervous. Had he captured one of my friends? Who would he interrogate to get answers to his questions?

I ran faster. I tried to calm the rage I felt inside. My mood was dark, and I was already starting to hear the voices in my head. It didn't take me long to get back to my apartment. I knocked on Cory's door.

Javier was combing his mohawk when he answered the door. "Hey, Thea. What's up?"

"Is everyone home?" I asked.

"Yes, why?"

Without answering, I ran up the stairs and knocked on Delia's door. When she opened the door, she had an angry look on her face. I knew this could get ugly.

"Is Fish with you?" I demanded, my hands clenched into fists.

"Where else would he be?" she snapped.

Very ugly.

"Is he home or not?" I yelled.

Her face turned red. "Don't yell at me, witch. Who do you think you are?"

Fish came to the door. "What's going on?" he asked. When he looked into my eyes, he quickly pushed Delia behind him. He seemed to be the only one who used caution when looking into my eyes. He could tell when I was in a good mood, and he was always careful when the darkness washed over me. "Did you need something, Thea?" he asked nervously.

"She needs a new brain," Delia said from behind him.

"Delia, stop," Fish said, keeping his eyes on mine.

My eyes darted to Delia. I couldn't take the judgmental glare she was giving me. I wanted to rip her apart.

"It's kind of late, Thea," Fish said. "Why don't you go get some rest?"

"What do you want, anyway?" Delia asked, her voice like poison in my veins.

I knew I had to get out of there. I ran up to my apartment and slammed the door behind me. I slapped my hands over my head and fell to my knees.

I couldn't shake the dark thoughts that were going through my head. Simon had ruined all the progress I'd made with James today. I had been in such a good mood after being with him, but now I was living in hell. I wanted to run back down and hurt Delia. How dare she speak to me that way? I wanted to cut out her tongue and make her eat it.

"No!" I yelled, shaking my head. I heard laughter in my head, and a voice telling me to do it. "Go away!"

"Thea, open the door!" James shouted. His voice felt like a distant memory. I could hardly hear it, hardly make out it was him.

Then the voices in my head stopped. There was silence.

"Thea, open the door!" James repeated.

I slowly turned to look at the door.

Kill him, a soft voice said.

I smiled and got to my feet just as James burst through the door. He looked into my eyes, gasped, and pulled me into his arms. "I've got you, my love," he said, squeezing me.

~ 37 ~

I let out a grunt as I tried to pull away from him. "I hate you!" I yelled. The room spun as he held me tighter. For a moment, I thought I was falling, but then I realized he was pulling us into our memory.

"Whatever you do, just don't let go of me," he whispered into my ear.

I closed my eyes and tried to let his voice calm me. I tried to ignore the voices in my head.

"Send her away," he whispered.

I drew breath as his voice traveled through me. It was like hearing an angel singing into my ear. I took another deep breath as I heard the birds chirping around us. We were there, back in our memory. The voices faded. His scent filled my head. I didn't want to pull away. I held him tighter and inhaled his sweet scent.

"Better now?" James asked as he kissed my head.

I nodded and buried my face in his chest.

"What brought this on?" he asked.

I didn't want to tell him about my little encounter with Simon. "I don't know," I lied.

He leaned back. "You don't know what made you angry?"

I finally looked at him. "No."

He sighed and pulled me to him. "That doesn't make sense, Thea. How can you get angry out of nowhere?"

I didn't answer. I kept thinking of the voices I'd heard in my head. They were so clear, so loud. I'd heard them before, but now they were getting louder, more demanding.

"Are you okay now?" James asked.

I wanted to say yes, but the truth was, I didn't know. How could I tell him that being around him didn't seem to be enough anymore? It was making me very uneasy.

"Thea?" James said, leaning back again.

I looked into his sparkling blue eyes. It suddenly occurred to me how fast he had gotten up to my apartment. "How did you get there so fast?" I asked.

"I was talking with Cory when you knocked on the door. You didn't give Javier a chance to tell you that I was there."

"What were you doing there?"

I wasn't sure why I cared so much.

"It doesn't matter. Are you okay now?"

"No. I asked you a question."

James pulled away. "You can at least try to stay in a good mood."

I crossed my arms in defiance. "Maybe if you didn't keep secrets from me, I would."

"What makes you think I'm keeping secrets?"

"Then tell me why you're getting tattoos," I demanded. "Tell me why Jason is getting them." I could see he didn't like my questions.

"You really piss me off sometimes, Thea," he said, shaking his head. "You talk about trust and then show me the complete opposite."

Did he think I was that stupid? "This isn't about trust," I said. "It's about you keeping things from me. You said you wouldn't do that anymore."

"And you said you wouldn't ask questions!" he shouted.

"Well, I lied!" I shot back. I reached into my pocket and pulled out Delia's box.

"Don't you dare leave, Thea."

"Go to hell." I opened the box and was gone before he could reach for me.

Chapter 4
A Moment in the Sun

I threw the box across the room the moment I was back in my apartment. I looked around, expecting James to be pulling himself out of our memory. That didn't happen. I was all alone. He wasn't coming after me.

Maybe that was a good thing. My mood didn't seem to be getting any better.

"I need some air," I muttered and headed out the door.

I was walking downstairs when I heard Delia still yelling at Fish.

"I don't want you up there with her," she said. "She's nothing but a coward and a foolish witch. We have to face our own problems and not run away from them like she does. I can't take her childish temper anymore. How many mistakes does she have to make before you see she's not the same Thea we knew? That stupid promise she made is changing her. I don't know her anymore."

"Delia, she's our friend," Fish answered.

"She's a coward," Delia shot back.

Her words cut through me. I froze halfway down the stairs.

"She's gotten us into enough trouble," Delia continued. "We can't trust her anymore. Can't you see she's impulsive and crazy? Is that the way you want to live?"

I sat on one of the steps and listened to them talking about me. They had lost all faith in me. Delia was right—I did run away from my troubles. I was even doing it right now. Even James had probably had enough of my temper. I had done nothing to help the situation. The word, 'impulsive' kept going through my head.

I looked up the stairs and got to my feet. I had to go speak with my husband. I wasn't sure if he would still be willing to listen. I wouldn't blame him if he sent me away.

I walked back into my apartment and picked up the box. All I could hear were Delia's words as I went back into the memory.

James was sitting at the edge of the lake. He didn't even look my way when he heard me coming. "Are you done throwing your little tantrum?" he asked as he gazed out at the lake. He looked over his shoulder. "Or maybe you want to storm off again? Maybe tell me where to go?"

I didn't answer.

He shook his head and stared at the lake again. "Go ahead and run, Thea. But I'm done chasing after you. If you don't trust me by now, you never will."

I moved closer. "I trust you more than you'll ever know."

He didn't look at me. "You have a funny way of showing it."

"I'm sorry, James."

"Yeah, I'm getting really tired of hearing that."

"Could you at least look at me, please?"

"Maybe you should leave now." He threw a rock into the lake.

I walked around and stood in front of him. "You listen to me, James Ethan Wade. I can take this from anyone, but not you. I'm a fool, I know that. I never said I was perfect. I'm trying to be that witch you once knew, but I can't if you lose faith in me, too. I want nothing more than to be the witch you fell in love with."

He looked surprised. He got to his feet. "Well, this is a glimpse of her. For starters, you're not crying."

There was a pause before we both started laughing.

Within moments, I was in his arms. I closed my eyes and leaned my head on his chest. "I'm so stupid sometimes," I said.

"I know," he answered.

We both laughed again.

I was about to tell him how sorry I was when he took two steps back and held up a red stone.

"What is that?" I asked.

He smiled. "I'll be right back." He wrapped his fingers around it and vanished.

So that was how he was getting here. My father must have given him that stone. They were the same stones that were all over Delia's box.

I walked to our tree and waited for him to return. After fifteen minutes, I began to wonder if he had forgotten about me. Why had he left in the first place?

I was sitting under our tree when I heard the breaking of twigs behind me.

"Sorry I took so long," James said as he walked out of the trees.

I stood up. "Where did you go?"

He seemed worried about something. I didn't like the look on his face as he approached me.

"Is everything okay?" I asked.

He nodded. "I had to run back to the house."

"To your house?" I asked, confused.

He stood next to me and grabbed my hand. "No questions. Just look over there." He pointed to the trees.

At first, I saw nothing. And then my jaw dropped. I couldn't believe my eyes. My father was walking out of the forest.

"I told you I would find a way," James said.

I let go of James's hand. "Father!" I said, running to him. I had never felt more uplifted in my life. I quickly forgot about my worries and threw myself into his waiting arms. "Father!" I cried.

I felt a surge of energy going through me as he gathered me in his warm embrace. I drew breath and squeezed him tighter. I felt his love traveling through every fiber of my body. I felt calmer than I had in weeks. My heart connected to him at once. I closed my eyes as he put his hand on the back of my head and kissed my forehead. My heart rejoiced. "Oh, Father, how I've missed you."

"And I you, Thea."

I looked up into his sparkling green eyes. I loved how my father exuded confidence. He had salt and pepper hair— "strands of wisdom," as he called them. He was my rock, my strength. He had a way of making all my troubles go away.

"How is this possible?" I asked. "How are you here right now? I thought you couldn't go outside."

"I still can't," he answered. "But we're really not outside, are we?" He nodded at James. "A point James brought to my attention."

I turned to thank James, but he was gone. "Where did he go?" I asked.

When my father didn't answer, I looked up at him again. I followed his eyes; he was looking at his hand. With his arm stretched out, as if reaching for the sun, he moved his fingers through the sunlight and smiled. I almost got the sense that he was trying to capture the rays in his hand. He closed his eyes and turned his face up to the sky with a sigh.

Then I remembered that my father hadn't been outside for years. I took two steps back and let him have his moment in the sun.

As I watched him take deep breaths of fresh air, I realized something else. James was able to bring him here, so why couldn't I take him to Magia the same way? My heart began racing with excitement. I pulled the ring from my pocket, wrapped my arms around him, and put it on. I waited for the wind I usually felt while being carried to my father's magical world and searched the air around us for the speckles of light to carry us away.

My father chuckled. "Do you think I haven't thought of that?" he said, still gazing up at the sun.

I pulled away, feeling confused. I looked down at the ring. "I don't understand."

"You're in a memory, Thea. The ring can't find you here." He opened his eyes and looked at me. "And I am too weak for the ring to take me there. It will never work on me as long as it can't sense me."

"Why isn't it sensing me?" I asked, looking at it again.

"I told you, it can't find you here. This is one of your memories, a distant place that doesn't exist. The ring needs to sense what world you're in, and it doesn't understand where you are." He closed his eyes and took another deep breath. "It still feels real, nonetheless."

As he soaked up the rays from the sun, I couldn't help wondering why James had left. I had this gut feeling he was still worried about Helena. He'd seemed so restless earlier. She was probably with Simon. Why couldn't he see that?

"Walk with me, Thea," my father said, taking my hand.

I hadn't realized he was staring at me. He intertwined my arm with his, and we began to walk. I kept looking over my shoulder, expecting James to come walking out from the trees.

"James would be worried no matter who it was," my father said. "He feels sorry for that girl."

"So, he *did* go looking for her?"

"He just wants to make sure she's okay. Let him ease his conscience."

He stopped and took in the lake as if it were his first time seeing water. He smiled like I'd never seen him smile before. He walked slowly, appreciating every step he took on the grass. He stopped a few times to touch some leaves, then some flowers.

"Does this place remind you of your home?" I asked.

He cut a flower and placed it in my hair. "No. It reminds me of your mother," he said, touching my cheek. "She loved these woods as much as you do."

I couldn't help but ask the question he never wanted to answer. "Father, why can't you go outside?"

He smiled. "One day you will figure it out. The answer will come to you when you're ready. You don't realize I've already answered the question."

"You have?" I asked, surprised.

He chuckled. "Pay attention, Thea."

We began walking again. My father reached for my arm again and wrapped it around his. It was strange how I felt so calm from his touch. I had missed my father so much. I decided to think of nothing else and enjoy this moment with him.

"I still can't believe you're here," I said.

"That makes two of us," he answered.

"I also can't believe I never thought of this myself. I feel rather foolish right now. Seems logical when you think of it."

He smiled and squeezed my arm. "How are your friends? I haven't seen them lately."

"I'm worried, Father. Delia and Fish are not doing so well."

"Oh?"

I told him about Delia's foul mood. "Fish is heartbroken," I said. "I don't know how to help him. I have no idea what's wrong with Delia, or why she's treating Fish like that."

"I went through that with your mother," he said. "It will go away in a few weeks."

I looked at him, confused. "What will go away in a few weeks?"

He smiled. "You really don't know?"

"No."

"Witches have foul moods when they're with child, Thea. The first two weeks are the worst."

"Delia is pregnant?"

"I would say most definitely."

I smiled, knowing Fish would be over the moon about the news. Maybe I would suggest that he stay away from Delia, only until he found out.

"And how are you doing?" my father asked.

My smile faded. I looked away and didn't answer. I felt ashamed to tell him anything.

"I see." He stopped and turned to me. "And being around James isn't helping?"

I looked down. "Sometimes it does."

"What made you angry today?" he asked.

"I ran into Simon," I confessed.

He put his fingers on my chin and made me look at him. "How do you feel now?"

How could I tell him the voices in my head were getting louder? They made me desire power. It was all I could think of sometimes. I thought of ways of killing Simon and keeping it all for myself. Sometimes the thought of controlling this world and Magia made me feel alive. It was the sweet taste of power I couldn't get out of my mouth.

"I see," my father said again.

I looked away from him. I looked at the trees, the lake, at everything but him. I didn't know what to say. He expected so much out of me, but here I was, disappointing him once again.

"I don't expect anything from you," he said.

"I wish you wouldn't read my mind right now," I said, looking back down.

"Thea, the only thing I've ever wanted was for you to be happy."

I didn't answer, but I could feel his eyes on me. I was relieved when he began walking again.

"Tell me something," he said. "Do you think yourself capable of killing three warlocks?"

I laughed. "Of course, I do."

"And how do you know that?"

"I could kill an army of them if I wanted to."

"Yes, but how do you know that?"

"I don't know. I just know I can."

He stopped and faced me. "That right there," he said, pointing his finger at me. "That is the wizard part of you talking. Your bravery has never faded, but your confidence has been lost here in the human world. That is the part of yourself you must find, Thea. One day, you will need it to chase away the darkness. You will be tested like none of us ever have."

We began walking again.

"Do you think Simon is a confident man?" he asked.

That was an odd question. "I think he's a coward."

"A coward would not risk as much as he has, Thea. Think about that."

"Do you think he's confident?"

He looked straight ahead. "Yes, I do. But I also know he has a weakness."

"A weakness?"

He sighed. "Have you ever asked yourself why Simon hates humans so much?"

"Isn't it because his father left him?"

"Would that make you hate as much as he does?"

"No, I suppose not."

We continued to walk along the shoreline of the lake. My father's question was stuck in my head: Why did Simon hate humans so much? He always referred to them as disgusting animals. The fact that Simon himself was half human was the one thing he hated most about himself. It was his greatest reason for wanting to become a wizard. My father always said that Simon was fascinated with him because of that. Simon had even called my father his best friend.

"Father, may I ask you something?"

"Of course."

"Why did Simon betray you? Why did he turn on you so easily, if he loved you?"

My father didn't answer. I could see that the question caused him pain. He stopped, let go of my arm, and looked out into the lake. After a few moments, he said, "Did you know I had a vision of how I would meet your mother? I saw the exact spot where I would fall in love with her one day."

"You had a vision about that?"

He nodded. "I was stunned when I realized I would be meeting her in the human world, and even more stunned to learn she would be a witch." My father's eyes lit up whenever he spoke of my mother. "The vision never showed me when I would meet her. I only knew that I would love her like no other. It was then I began to come into the human world. The wizards couldn't understand my need to leave Magia so often." A smile broke across his face. "It took hundreds of years before that creature finally walked into my life. It was like seeing an angel walk right out of the heavens. I loved her at once. I knew at that moment my life would never be the same." He put his arms behind his back as he continued. "By this time, Simon had already been with me for years. He was a tortured soul when I found him, a scared, lost little boy. I never interfered with things in the human world, but Simon was suffering, so I took him under my wing. I became like a father to him and gave him all the love I could. He grew into a man by my side. I tried to make him forget the things his human father had done to him. He was with me the day I met your mother. She never liked him." He shook his head and looked out into the lake again. "When I told the wizards in Magia that I would be bringing home a queen soon, Wendell did not take the news well. Bringing home a queen meant having an heir to the throne, thus pushing back Wendell's chances of becoming king. He said he would never bow down to a mere witch, but I didn't see my true problems." He shook his head again.

"What do you mean?" I asked.

He looked at me. "You asked how Simon could betray me so easily. I'm afraid I gave him the motive for that."

"I don't understand."

"Don't you see, Thea? Love made Simon turn on me."

I was bewildered. "Simon doesn't know the meaning of love."

"Ahh, but he does. He has felt the true power of love, and I took it all away from him."

I gasped as I realized what he was talking about. "My mother."

"Yes. She was the only woman he ever loved—I would say more than life itself."

I looked into his emerald eyes. "You didn't know he was in love with her, did you?"

"No. But I figured it out the day I told him I was going to marry her. I could see that I shattered his dreams that very day." He shook his head. "I was a fool to never notice how he looked at her, how he made excuses to be near her. I thought he was merely trying to be helpful. Your mother found him annoying because of that. So many times, he was already there when I visited her. All I had to do was look into her eyes to know she didn't want him there. She didn't like the way he talked down to humans."

"If he loved her, why did he kill her?"

He took a deep breath and closed his eyes. "My Emma never knew of his love for her. She never realized Simon felt she betrayed him for choosing me and not him." He opened his eyes and looked down at me. "I know this may sound strange, but killing your mother was the hardest thing Simon has ever done. It took me years to realize that was the reason he had gone into hiding after killing her. The pain of what he did to her was too great for him. But it was a force stronger than him that made him do it." He gently touched my face. "You look just like her, Thea. You have her smile, her eyes. Everything about you reminds Simon of her. It's the reason he hasn't killed you, the reason he didn't follow Wendell's orders. Not even a blood promise could make him take your life. It would be like killing your mother all over again."

"But he tried to kill me many times," I pointed out.

"No. He's been punishing you for reminding him of her. I strongly believe that."

I thought of all the times Simon had kissed me and then pulled away. It began to make sense why he wanted me to hate James so much, why he'd asked my father for my hand in marriage. I reminded him of my mother. "He loves me," I said.

"He only loves what you remind him of."

I looked at him. "Did Wendell know Simon loved her?"

"I have no doubt. Wendell knew the blood promise would make Simon kill what he loved most in the world, and he needed her heart to get rid of me."

I swallowed thickly when he said that. I thought of the voices in my head and all the times I had to stop myself from hurting James.

"That's why I keep telling you to find yourself," my father said. "You will have to fight the same force Simon gave in to."

"What do you mean?" I asked, confused.

"Don't you see, Thea? The blood promise prays on the weak-minded. It grows stronger by feeding on your thoughts and desires. If there is a weakness inside you, it will find it."

"Am I Simon's weakness?"

He took my arm again and began walking. "You will have to figure that out on your own. But I will tell you this: the blood promise makes that weakness stronger. Simon grows greedier and more evil because those are qualities that were already in his heart." He stopped and faced me. "And you—you've grown up in the human world. You've never known the true power that lives inside of you. But one day, it will hit you like a rock, waking you up from these habits you've learned in the human world. Insecurity is a human trait, not a wizard one. We bow our heads to no one. One day, you will understand that."

I lowered my head, but my father made me look at him.

"Find the black witch, Thea. She will show you more than you hoped for. Sometimes it takes looking at ourselves to see what we are doing wrong. That woman will open your eyes to the truth."

"Will she tell me how to break the promise?" I asked.

He looked thoughtful for a moment. "It's not what she's going to tell you, but what she's going to show you. There is no breaking that spell, but a wizard can control it. I realize I am taking a dangerous chance by sending you to her, but it's a chance I must take. You will have to separate her lies from the truth."

I heard someone walking out from the trees and spun around. It was James, appearing more worried than before. He looked at my father and shook his head.

"I'm afraid we must go now," my father said.

"He didn't find her, did he?" I asked.

"My guess would be no."

James was looking down at his watch. I knew he wanted to go search for Helena.

"Will you meet me here again?" my father asked.

I threw my arms around him. "Of course, Father."

"Find her, Thea," he whispered in my ear. "Pay attention to only what she shows you."

"I will, Father, I will." I glanced at James again. "Three days, then?" I asked.

He only nodded and turned his eyes back to his watch.

I looked at my father again, pulled out Delia's box, and was gone.

Chapter 5
Stupid Witch

I noticed a small Christmas tree on my coffee table when I got back. It was decorated with twinkling lights and red bows. I moved closer and noted that the ornaments I had thrown on the floor were back on it. I reached out to touch it.

"You're not going to kill this one, too, are you?" Fish said.

I hadn't seen him lying on my couch. "Fish, what are you doing here?" I knew Delia would be furious if she knew he was with me. "You really shouldn't be here, sweetie."

He stretched his arms and sat up. "Why? You're not all creepy right now, are you?"

I smiled. "No, I'm not all creepy right now."

"Good. I couldn't take two angry witches tonight."

"What happened?"

"Delia threw me out."

I sat next to him. "Not getting any better, huh?"

"She hates me, Thea. She doesn't even want me sleeping next to her anymore."

"Why did she throw you out?"

"Oh, I don't know, because I was breathing?" He leaned forward and put his hands on his head. "I don't know what I'm going to do. I can't live without her. I'm no good without her in my life."

It was time to tell him the truth. I didn't want to take this moment away from Delia, but I couldn't stand seeing him like this anymore. I laid my hand on his back. "You know what you can do, Fish? You can start thinking of names."

"Names for what?" he asked with his head still bowed. Then, as it sank in, he lifted his head. His jaw dropped, and he looked at me.

I smiled and nodded.

His face lit up as he jumped to his feet. "I'm going to be a father?" he said in disbelief. "I'm going to be a father!" He pulled me up, and I threw my arms around him as he spun me around. "She doesn't hate me, Thea. She doesn't hate me!"

I laughed as he put me down. "You can't tell her I told you," I said.

"Does she know?"

"I don't think so."

He looked at the door again. "This explains everything. Why didn't I put it together?"

"Because you were too busy being heartbroken."

He picked me up and spun me around again. "I'm the happiest man alive."

His joy lit up the room more than the twinkling lights did. He was beaming with happiness. "This is the second proudest moment of my life," he said as he set me down.

"What's the first?" I asked.

He smiled. "When I married Delia."

"Oh, Fish, you're going to make a wonderful father."

"I'll die trying, Thea."

Fish gave me a kiss on the cheek and returned home. I had a feeling that no matter what Delia said, Fish was going to smile the whole time.

I went to bed thinking of them both. Delia was going to make a wonderful mother. Fish would be the cool dad any kid would love to have. I could see the happy life ahead of them.

~~~

I awoke in the morning feeling refreshed. I stretched and readied myself for another day. I had plans to search most of the day for the black witch. What my father had said about her was stuck in my head. What could she possibly have to show me? I hardly knew anything about her. In fact, no one seemed to know much about her past. I had seen her a few times over the years, but never gave her much thought. Maybe I would spend the day in Salem Willows looking for her. I had to run into her sooner or later.

I put the wand in my pocket and reached for my coat. I was hoping I wouldn't see the boys on my way out. I had no time to answer their constant questions. I knew James had asked them to keep an eye on me, but sometimes their questions did nothing but aggravate me. I threw my coat over my shoulder and tried sneaking down the stairs in the hallway without being heard, but luck was not on my side.

Cory popped his head out of his apartment when I reached the bottom of the stairs. "Where you going?" he asked.

Cory was my dearest friend in the world. We had been through so much together. He had once loved me. He had even passed himself off as my husband when I couldn't remember who James was. Now our relationship was back to normal.

Cory wasn't hiding the fact that he was dating human girls. They came to look for him often. He had his pick of them, but he never seemed to date the same one for long.

I tried to smile as I walked past him. I didn't want him to know where I was going. I thought of telling him a quick lie, but the smell of ink made me freeze. I turned toward him and realized the scent was coming from him. I moved closer, and the scent grew stronger.

"Did you get a tattoo?" I asked.

His face went pale. His smile turned into a look of panic. "W-what are you talking about?"

My eyes narrowed as I looked at his arms, which were hidden by long sleeves. I noticed a stain on his shirt and realized it was fresh ink, so I reached out and touched it. The strange ink spread across my fingers.

I looked at Cory again. "What is this?" I demanded, showing him my fingers.

He swallowed nervously. "I was painting."

~ 59 ~

Why was he lying to me? Better yet, why would he feel the need to keep this from me?

The front door to the building swung open before I could question him. I wiped my hand on my blouse as Pam walked in with tears in her eyes. Pam was Helena's cousin and a childhood friend of mine. I hadn't seen her in weeks. I noticed her shaky hands.

"Still nothing?" Cory asked her.

"What's going on?" I asked.

Tears ran down Pam's cheeks. "It's Helena. She's missing."

Just hearing her name made my temper rise. So, they still hadn't found that witch. "Why would I care about that?" I hissed.

She looked down at her hands. "I know you couldn't care less what happens to her, but she's been missing since yesterday. She hasn't called or even been home. James has been out looking for her all night. She was supposed to see him yesterday, but she never showed."

I made a fist. *He's been looking for her all night?* I thought of the phone call Simon had received last night. Maybe it was Helena whom he intended to ask questions.

Pam wiped her tears. "James can't find her. That's why I came looking for you."

How dare this witch come to me for help? Why would I care if Helena was missing? "And what do you want from me?" I demanded.

"Please, Thea," she said, stepping closer. "You have to help me."

"I'll get my coat," Cory said.

"No!" I shouted at him. "We're not going out to look for that witch."

Cory spun around and glared at me. "I've got news for you, Thea. I've already been out looking for her with James."

"Is that why James was here last night?" I snapped.

He stepped up to me. "You listen here, witch. This poor woman has been begging us for help since yesterday. This isn't about you. It's about finding someone who's in trouble."

Pam broke into a sob. "Please help me, Thea."

I wanted to slap them both. I hated Helena.

How could they think I would want to help her? If Helena was dead, it would only speed up what I already planned on doing. It was bad enough she had lied about bonding with James; she had also told Simon about my father. Although Helena thought my father was only James's butler, she had told Simon about him nonetheless.

Simon had quickly sent for him, but Porteus, a guard from Magia, had changed what he looked like and gone in his place. I still didn't know how Porteus had gotten away with that. How could Simon not think he was my father if Porteus had made himself look just like him? Simon and my father had been friends, so it never made sense how Porteus had pulled it off.

The more Pam cried, the more I felt like hurting her.

"All right!" I shouted. "I'll go look for her, but you're staying here," I said to Cory.

"Thank you," Pam cried.

"Shut up, witch," I replied. "I'm not going to

look for long." I walked past her and out the door. I stormed out of the building, not really intending to look for Helena. I would tell them a quick lie later and say I never found her. I didn't care where Helena was, or why she was missing. If she was hurt, she had it coming. I could only wish someone had done me the favor of killing her. After all she had put me through, I could only hope she was dead and gone.

I made my way down the street, debating whether I should even look for that witch. I decided I would check the house I knew Simon used sometimes. It was a few houses down the street. The old man I had once thought owned the house had turned out to be Simon—his way of keeping a watchful eye on me, no doubt.

I was approaching the house when I saw James's car pull up to the curb. He stepped out, holding his whip.

What was he doing? I broke into a run. "James, stop!"

I pulled him back when he headed toward the house. "What the hell are you doing?" I asked, blocking his way.

"Helena has been missing all night," he said. "I have to help her. Netiri called and said Simon might have her here."

He tried to go around me, but I pushed him back.

"You're not going in there."

"I have to!"

I took a step back. "Why is she so important to you?"

"Don't turn this into something else, Thea. I'm only trying to help. I know Simon has her."

"What do you care? Let Simon have his way with her."

He gave me a disapproving look. "What kind of man do you think I am? I'm helping her, so get the hell out of my way."

When he tried to get past me, I got in his way. "Okay, I'll help. Let me go in there and look for her. Just promise me you'll stay out of this."

"I'm not promising you anything. I'm going in there with you."

"And let Simon see you with me? He's probably looking out the window right now, wondering why I'm talking to you. This will ruin everything, James."

He thought about it for a moment. Finally, he said, "If you don't come out of there with Helena in ten minutes, I'm coming in after you."

His concern for Helena was cutting through my heart. I nodded and turned on my heels. I heard his car door close as I knocked on the front door of the house, then watched him drive away. When no one answered my knock, I waved my hand at the door, walked inside, and slammed it behind me.

"This witch better be dead," I said, looking around. There was no one here. I couldn't smell Simon anywhere. This was a good thing. That meant Simon hadn't seen my little encounter with James just now.

I searched the house, but Helena was nowhere in sight. I thought of places where she could be. Maybe I would check Simon's house out in the woods. It was very possible Helena was there with him, plotting and planning their next move. I turned to leave but stopped midstep when I heard a faint scream. Was my mind playing tricks on me? I turned in place slowly, checking every inch of the room. A small spot on the floor caught my attention. There was sand on it. I knew what that meant: Simon was inside the walls. He had done this before. I had never known where his secret passages led to, but I was about to find out.

I looked at the wall near the spot of sand. I waved my hand, and the wall began to crack. Muddy sand fell to the floor as the wall revealed a secret passage. I stepped into the wall and looked around. The smell of mold and mildew burned my nose. I watched the sand pack itself along the wall again as the opening to the passage closed behind me.

The passage was dark and damp. I could easily stand with no problem. It was like a big tunnel built into the walls of the house.

I walked farther in and saw that other tunnels were connected to this one. I wondered where they all led to. I wasn't sure which way to go. Then I heard a woman's cries coming from deep in the tunnel. I froze when I heard Simon laughing. He was here. Why hadn't his scent hit me yet? Then I realized his scent hadn't hit me last night, either. He'd been standing very close to me. In fact, he'd even kissed me. Why couldn't I smell him anymore?

I followed the voices. Echoes of pain filled the air around me. He was hurting her, and this pleased me. I walked faster. I didn't want to miss a single lashing he gave her. If she was dead when I got there, I would reward Simon for his service. Nothing would make me happier than to know that witch was dead.

I found myself walking deeper underground as the sound of dripping water surrounded me. It was like another world down here. More and more tunnels connected to the one I was walking through. I began to see sleeping bags scattered about. *So this is where the warlocks sleep at night.* I could never make sense of where Simon was hiding them. I wondered where they were now.

"I beg you," Helena cried. "Please stop."

When I got to the end of the tunnel, I peeked around the edge of the wall. It was a big room. I had seen it before, when I had followed the fake James here. I had to hand it to Simon—these tunnels were a very good idea. I would have never thought of looking for him down here.

It was bothering me that I hadn't picked up his scent. I could always smell Simon a mile away. It was the smell of rotting flesh I had marked him with so many years ago.

"I'll stop when you answer my question," I heard him say. His voice sounded almost playful. He was clearly in a good mood.

I looked around the room. I spotted Helena hanging upside down from a beam on the ceiling, her hands tied behind her back. She was badly beaten. I wondered what she had done to upset Simon so much. I knew she was helping him, so what had changed? I stayed very quiet as Simon walked around her.

"Hit this witch again," he said to his men.

The smile on Simon's face was truly that of a monster. Every time Helena screamed, he ran his fingers through his dark hair, and his smile grew, along with his good mood. He was clearly taking pleasure in hurting this witch. I couldn't help but smile myself. I was also getting pleasure from it. I wanted to run and join him in the fun. My fingers clawed into the wall as I watched him work his magic.

He stroked Helena's face as he put his lips up to her ear. "What did you do with the leaves?" he asked her.

I gasped. He thought she had them. *Of course, he would think that. No one knows I had been there that day.* I was the one who had hidden the leaves from Simon. I wondered if he also suspected Netiri and Toby, the two warlocks who were helping me, but Simon didn't know that.

"It wasn't me!" Helena cried. She was shaking, clearly terrified out of her mind.

Simon took a step back and punched her across the face. Helena's cries did nothing to soften his heart. He began pacing the room. "I can promise you this, witch. You will not leave this room alive if you don't tell me what you did with the leaves."

"I didn't do anything," Helena said in a shaky voice. "I never went there without you. I don't even remember how to get there."

Simon sighed. "Very well. I see I will have to force the truth out of you."

"No, please! I'm telling the truth."

"Bring me the needles!" Simon shouted.

Helena's face turned white as snow. She let out a scream. The sight of her fear was like a blast of pleasure going through my body. I wanted nothing more than to see Simon hurt her.

I didn't like this side of me. I never liked to see anyone in pain. The darkness was making me as cold as Simon. I was actually looking forward to watching this. What was wrong with me? Why wasn't I helping this stupid witch?

I glanced around the room as Simon waited for the needles. I was surprised to see only three other warlocks in the room with him. I couldn't get over how big they were. They didn't seem interested in what Simon was doing. They almost seemed bored as they looked through the morning paper.

I looked back at Helena. Her silky blond hair was a mess, her perfect face covered in blood. She was about to die. Meanwhile, I was still battling with myself over whether to save her or not. I knew the pain she was about to go through. I had to be honest—I didn't wish that pain on my worst enemy. But this witch had it coming. How could I feel sorry for her now?

When a blond warlock handed Simon the needles, I decided to let Helena get a taste of what I had gone through. I waited in anticipation as Simon ordered the man to cut her down. When he cut the rope, she dropped to the ground with a *thud*. The warlock removed Helena's shoes and socks as she screamed. Simon placed a chair in front of her and took a seat. He grabbed her foot and rested it on his lap. I knew he was about to give a little speech. This was all too familiar to me.

"Let me explain something to you," he began. "I put a spell on the water that fills that hole. Only a woman can get near those leaves without my spell killing her. So, you see, only you could have taken those leaves. You were the only woman who knew where they were. So, I will ask one last time: Where are the leaves?"

There was terror in Helena's eyes. "I . . . I didn't take them, I swear."

Simon looked down at her foot. Helena tried pulling it away, but Simon gripped it and smiled. "This may hurt a little," he said with an evil smile.

Helena gasped as Simon inserted the needle. A puddle of urine quickly spread around her.

He laughed as her screams echoed through the room. "That hurts, doesn't it?"

"P-please no!" Helena screamed.

"Do you have something to tell me?" Simon asked.

When Helena only cried, Simon got up and threw the chair across the room. The warlock handed him another needle.

"I don't need that, you fool," Simon said, slapping it away. He looked down at Helena. "She doesn't have the leaves. This witch is not strong enough to keep secrets from me."

"What now, my lord?" the warlock asked.

Simon began pacing. "Perhaps we should start asking all the witches our questions."

"What about Netiri and Toby, my Lord? You said they knew where the leaves were."

"No. It has to be a woman." Then Simon froze. I could almost see a light going on in his head. A wicked smile spread across his face. "I think I know who to ask," he said. "Yes, I'm past do for a visit."

"What about this witch, my Lord?"

Simon looked down at Helena. "Leave her. I have no use for her now."

They all disappeared into one of the tunnels. I wondered who he was going to question next. I had to follow him. There was no telling who he might go after.

Helena became delirious when she saw me enter the room. "Help me!" she cried. "Please help me."

I ignored her and peeked into the tunnel Simon had disappeared into.

"Please, Thea, don't leave me here," Helena begged. "You have to help me."

I wanted to slap this stupid witch. She actually expected me to help her out of here.

When her cries began to annoy me, I decided to untie her. She could find her own way out. I removed the ropes from her hands and feet, and she dragged herself into my arms and clung on to me.

"Don't leave me here, please," she cried.

I wanted to push her away, but I realized she was paralyzed with fear. I closed my eyes, fighting the urge to help her. I finally gave in and decided to get her out of there.

As I got to my feet, Helena wrapped her arms around my ankles. "Take me with you, please!"

"Shut up, witch. I'm not leaving you."

She broke into a loud sob when she realized I was going to help her.

I quickly leaned down again and put my hand over her mouth. "Shut up. He might hear you."

She nodded, and I pulled my hand away.

I looked down at her feet. She still had the needle thrust into her foot. I gently took hold of it. "This is going to hurt," I said, and pulled it out. I put

~ 69 ~

my hand over her mouth again when she gasped from the pain. "Helena, shut up."

Her cries became silent. She began shaking and staring into space. I pulled out my father's wand and watched as it turned into my stick. I threw Helena over it, took my place behind her, and flew through the tunnel. I checked for Simon before flying into the house. Helena clung to me as we finally made it outside. She held on to my arm like her life depended on it. I was actually starting to feel sorry for her. She was shaking so hard, I thought she was going to pass out.

"It wasn't me," she kept repeating.

I looked all around for human eyes. When I saw that the coast was clear, I began to fly to my apartment. I looked down at Helena when I felt her squeeze my hand. She stared into my eyes and didn't say a word. Tears ran down her face as she squeezed my hand again. Somehow, I knew she was saying "thank you." I nodded, and she lay her face on my chest.

This was different; Helena was my enemy. We hated each other. I knew she wanted nothing more than to take James away from me. I had always been jealous of her beauty, of her perfect hair and figure. She was everything I had always wanted to be: thin, beautiful, tall. But I had what she wanted the most: James, the only man she had ever loved. She had spent hundreds of years thinking of ways to get him back. I was starting to understand her bitterness.

Chapter 6
The Fat One Looks Hideous

I burst through the door to my building, still riding my stick. James and the others ran out into the hallway when they heard me and stared, shocked to see Helena shaking in my arms. Pam screamed when she saw Helena covered in blood. James pulled her off the stick and into his arms. She looked lost as he walked into Cory's apartment with her. Delia gave me a nasty look and followed them in. What was her problem?

James was placing Helena on the couch when I walked in. "What did he do to her?" he asked.

Everyone looked at me.

"He was torturing her," I said flatly. "He thought she had something that belonged to him."

Pam gasped. "What did she get herself into?" she cried.

James looked down at Helena. "Helena, you're safe now. No one is going to hurt you."

I glanced around the apartment. Something seemed odd. I got the sense that things had been hectic moments ago. James's whip lay on the floor, as if he had dropped it right before I got here. The others all had their coats on, as if they were getting ready to leave. Before I could put it all together, Delia walked out with a blanket and threw it over Helena, saying she would make her some tea.

"I'll go get Donna," Cory said. "She doesn't look very well." He left without even giving me a glance. He seemed aggravated with me.

When Joshua and Javier followed him without saying a word, I knew they were all angry.

What had I done? Had something happened while I was gone? I could feel James's glare as he began chanting healing spells at Helena's feet. Were they actually blaming me for what Simon had done to her? No one had forced her to join him. How could they hold me responsible for the choices she had made?

I looked at Helena. I could still see the terror in her eyes. She said nothing as James brushed the hair away from her face.

"Helena, please say something," he said in a soft voice. "Look, Pam is here." He motioned for Pam to get closer.

She grabbed Helena's hand. "I'm here, cousin. You're safe now."

Helena didn't answer. There was a faraway look in her eyes that told me she was still living through what Simon had done to her. James kept trying to snap her out of it, but Helena wasn't responding.

I wasn't sure how to feel about his worry over her. He hadn't asked me once if I was okay. It was like I wasn't even there.

"Helena," James called out to her, "it's over, sweetie." His soothing voice sounded so tender.

I felt invisible as everyone made a fuss over the witch I hated so much. Even Fish sat next to her, holding her hand and trying to make her smile. I felt betrayed. Didn't they remember all the things she had done? Why were they treating her like a victim?

Delia came back with a cup of tea. "Sit her up. Maybe she'll drink this."

James picked Helena up and sat with her on his lap. He tried getting her to sip the tea, but Helena only stared into space.

"She's in shock," he said. "I knew we never should have used this girl like that. We should have warned her that Simon was going to turn on her sooner or later."

"Please don't blame her," Pam cried. "She did it out of love for you."

"Don't say that to me!" James yelled. "I feel bad enough as it is."

"I'm sorry," Pam said, bowing her head, "but you know you're the reason why she's done all these things."

Delia got in Pam's face. "You're not helping things, witch. This wouldn't have happened if Helena wasn't trying to help Simon, and you know that."

Finally, someone was making sense. James made eye contact with me. I couldn't get over the cold look in his eyes. I knew he felt guilty. He had asked me so many times to leave Helena out of it. When he realized how far she would go to be with him, he had wanted to cut all ties with her. "I want her to move on," he'd said to me one day. Now he was angry, and I knew he was blaming me because Helena was hurt.

He looked away from me and started talking to Helena again. Her eyes were empty. She only stared into space and said nothing.

Delia walked up to me and grabbed my arm. "I need to speak with you," she said and dragged me outside.

My stick fell from my hand and rattled on the floor as it turned into the wand again. I had no time to reach for it.

As soon as we were outside, Delia let go of my arm. "You're never going to change, are you, Thea?"

"What the hell are you talking about?"

"What do you think was going on right before you showed up with Helena?"

"How should I know?"

"Did you know James went right back into Simon's house when you walked inside?"

"What?"

"Did you really expect him to just leave?"

I didn't answer.

"He knew you wouldn't let him help you, so he pretended to leave. He looked all over that house for you. He came here when he couldn't find you. He and the boys were about to leave right before you showed up with Helena."

"What were they going to do?"

"What do you think, witch? Are you that stupid? Did that blood promise kill your brain?" She shook her head. "You really think these guys are going to listen to you and stay put? Don't you see you put them in more danger when they go off looking for you? Why can't you see what you're doing wrong? Cory is pissed with you for telling him to stay."

"I didn't need their help," I said. "You think I want them getting hurt?"

"You're the whole reason they get themselves hurt in the first place," she shot back.

I didn't know what to say. I knew she was right.

"Look, Thea," she continued, "I've been very angry with you for a long time. You've done things I don't understand, made choices that affected all of us. The blood promise you made to Simon took the cake. But now it's time to snap out of it. You need to be the witch you once were. I am not going to let my husband get hurt again because of you."

I glared at her. "What the devil do you think I'm trying to do, witch?"

She shook her head again. "You've done nothing but try to fix the mistakes you've made. You give Simon more to work with every time you see him. He can read you like a book, Thea. You could have killed him long ago. I think you like playing games with him."

"How dare you say that to me," I said, stepping up to her.

"Then why haven't you taken him into Magia? Why haven't those dragons ripped him apart yet? You keep making excuses, don't you?"

How could she say that to me? Where had she been?

"This isn't you," she said. "The witch I know would have skinned him alive already. The witch I know showed her face the day you got your powers back. You were magnificent that day, Thea. I was in awe of your courage."

I hung my head.

"That right there," Delia said, pointing at me. "That is driving me crazy. The witch I know bowed her head to no one. Where the hell did *that* witch go? Now you've turned into this pathetic, self-loathing, whining witch. I don't even know you anymore."

"What do you want from me?" I shouted.

She got in my face. "I'm tired of waiting, Thea. I'm tired of living like this. I can't sit by and watch you turn into this sobbing witch I hardly know. I'm going to help you with something, but it better end all excuses."

"There's nothing you can do, Delia."

"Yes, there is. I know someone who knows the black witch, and I'm going to bring you to her."

Our conversation was put on hold when Cory pulled up with Donna. I was surprised to see Meaghan, Pam's daughter, with them. Joshua had the biggest grin on his face. He was completely in love with her. I smiled when he jumped out of the truck to open Meaghan's door. He even held out his hand to help her out of the truck. Meaghan also seemed smitten by Joshua. Her eyes lit up as she took his hand and stepped out of the truck. It made me wonder why Joshua thought she didn't like him. It was obvious to me that she did.

Donna hurried into the yard. "How is Helena?" she asked.

"She's a zombie," Delia said, never looking away from me.

"I'll see what I can do," Donna said as she headed into the building.

Meaghan still had hold of Joshua's hand when she reached us. I couldn't believe this was the same sick girl I had once healed. Her soft curls gently fell over her shoulders. Her eyes sparkled like two stars in the night. Joshua couldn't stop looking at her.

"Hello, Meaghan," I said. "You look well."

A beautiful smile lit up her face as she looked at me and said, "Thank you." Her eyes darted back up to him. "I've never felt better in my life, or happier."

Joshua was beaming with happiness. He squeezed her hand and pulled her a bit closer. Meaghan didn't seem to mind.

"Meaghan, come inside," Pam called from the door. A nasty look to Joshua followed.

Meaghan jumped back and looked at her mother. The smile faded from her face. She let go of Joshua's hand and ran to her mother's side. Pam gave Joshua a nasty look again before closing the door behind her.

What was that all about? I noticed that Joshua gave her the same nasty look back.

"Joshua," Delia said, "can you give Thea and me a minute?"

Joshua finally looked away from the door, nodded, and went into the house. I wanted to ask him what was going on, but I needed to finish my conversation with Delia.

Cory never got out of the truck. He said he was getting some tea leaves that Donna needed and headed out.

After he left, I looked at Delia and asked, "Why didn't you ever tell me you knew where she was? You knew I've been going crazy looking for her."

Delia flipped her hair and looked away. "I wanted to punish you."

"Punish me? You don't think I've been punished enough?"

"You made a blood promise, Thea. How stupid can you be?"

"I made a mistake. When are you going to let that go? Or would you rather get in line to torture me? Would that please you?"

She didn't answer. I could tell she was furious with me.

I'd had about enough of her attitude lately. "I guess you're perfect, huh, Delia? I guess you never make mistakes. It must be nice going through life like that."

She looked down. "I didn't mean it that way. I feel you keep making things worse. Making a blood promise was the last straw."

"And how many times do I have to ask for forgiveness? Do you want me to get down on my knees?"

She rolled her eyes. I would normally laugh when Delia did that, but right now it was annoying me. I knew my mood was getting dark. It was time for me to leave.

"You know what, Delia?" I said. "You keep punishing me. I'll find the black witch myself." I turned to walk out of the yard.

"I can show you how to find her, Thea."

"I told you, I don't need your help," I said over my shoulder.

I knew I was being stubborn, but Delia had really struck a nerve. I hated that she was right about me. I wasn't myself anymore. I remembered the day she was talking about, the day at the campground. Simon had captured me, and I still didn't remember who I was or that I had placed my son in the crystal. Delia was right—I was confident that day. That witch seemed like a distant memory to me. What had I done to myself? I never used to cry or think so little of myself. Nothing scared me; nothing stopped me. What had changed?

"Will you please slow down?" Delia said.

I hadn't heard her walking behind me. "Leave me alone, Delia."

"Something crazy is going through your head, isn't it?"

"Go away, witch."

She caught up to me and grabbed my arm. "What are you going to do, run to Simon?"

"Would that make you happy?" I pulled my arm away and kept walking.

"I'm just trying to make you realize how much you've changed," she said as she followed me. "Don't you remember who you used to be?"

I stopped and faced her. "You think I like who I am now?"

"Then snap out of it!" she yelled.

"I don't know how!" I shot back.

She took a step back. I knew my eyes were

getting darker. I could tell by the scared look on Delia's face that she thought I was going to hurt her.

I made a fist and tried to calm myself. "You have no idea what this promise is doing to me," I said, "but blaming me for my mistakes isn't helping. I'm trying everything I can to fix what I've done."

She seemed nervous but moved closer to me. "I'm not blaming you, Thea. I'm trying to help. Can't you see that? Everyone is only trying to help, but you keep pushing us away. We started this journey together, and we're going to end it together."

"I don't know how you can possibly help me, Delia."

She smiled. "Well, I do. Come on, we're going to go find that black witch."

"Where are you going?" Fish yelled from the door when he saw us walking away.

"Where do you think?" Delia snapped at him.

"I'm taking a walk with Thea." She rolled her eyes.

"I'm sorry, honeysuckle," Fish answered. "I'm an idiot, I know."

I wanted to laugh as Fish waved and went back inside.

"He's driving me crazy," Delia said as we began to walk. "I can't even go to the bathroom by myself. I'm getting tired of it."

"He's trying to protect you, Delia."

"Well, I don't need him to. He also needs to stop treating me like I'm made of glass or something. Out of nowhere, he wants to help me sit and get back up. It's driving me crazy."

I wanted to laugh again when Delia told me she had woken up to Fish standing over her that morning.

"He had this stupid grin on his face," she said. "He just stood there and stared at me. Why the hell was he so happy? I honestly wanted to slap him."

We both laughed. I knew exactly why Fish was so happy, but I didn't want to be the one to tell her.

"Halloween is over," two girls said in unison as they passed us. They began to laugh.

"Did you see the stupid clothes they were wearing?" one of them said.

"The fat one looks hideous," the other one added.

Delia spun around, but I put my hand up.

"I've got this one," I said to her.

I waved my hand and sent two spells flying at the girls. They gained forty pounds in an instant and ran off screaming as Delia and I laughed uncontrollably.

"Now *that's* the witch I know," Delia said.

I clutched my stomach, which hurt from laughing so hard. "You know we'll have to find them and erase their memories," I said.

"Who is going to believe them?"

We laughed some more, and it felt good. I finally had my friend back. We quickly put our little fight behind us and continued walking. After a few minutes, Delia seemed to be deep in thought. She kept glancing at me from the corner of her eye as we walked down Essex Street.

"Can I ask you something?" she finally said.

"What is it?"

"What does the blood promise feel like?"

"What?"

She stopped. "It's just that I've heard about it all my life. It's been the taboo subject no one ever talks about. I wanted to know if it's really that bad."

"It's bad, Delia," I said as we continued walking. "Sometimes the evil thoughts that go through my head are hard to control. As the days pass, I feel as if they're getting more and more evil."

"You seem pretty normal right now. You were even laughing."

"I usually am, after seeing James. But when I'm away from him, the darkness washes over me. It really scares me sometimes."

She stopped again. "Why don't you move back in with James? Stay there so you can stay strong. Just don't let Simon see you when you leave the house."

"I can't take that chance. Simon knows what the blood promise does to you. It kills the ability to love, to feel. If he saw me with James, he would know I found a way to stay strong."

"What's the big deal if he found out?"

"Don't you understand, Delia?" I said as we began walking again. "I made a blood promise, and with that promise I gave Simon some of my blood. If Simon ever suspected I had no plans to keep the promise, he would use that blood to call the demons from hell. I would be dead in seconds. I have a son to think about. I can't let that happen."

"And what happens if you keep the promise? Is it over then?"

"As far as the promise, yes. He can't use my blood against me anymore. I just don't know what happens to me after that. It's a question that keeps going through my head."

"And if you manage to break it? What happens then?"

I sighed. "I don't know. That's why I have to find the black witch."

"Then we'd better hurry."

Chapter 7
The Wooden Wicks

I noticed that Delia was headed to a shop I knew well. Melanie, the smiling witch, as I called her, had a shop in the middle of town where she sold T-shirts to tourists. Melanie was always happy, always smiling. Why were we going to see her?

"Is Melanie the black witch?" I asked.

"No, but she knows her . . . very well," Delia answered.

We walked into the shop before I could ask more questions. Melanie was behind the counter helping a customer. A wide smile spread across her face when she saw us. She had dark auburn hair that fell across her face a lot, and she talked loudly, with excitement in her voice. There wasn't any part of her that wasn't cheerful. She even had dimples to top off her smile.

"I'll be right with you ladies," she called out.

The customer turned to see who she was talking to. I instantly knew the woman was human.

When she looked into my eyes, she cringed and quickly averted her gaze. "I'll come back for the shirt later," the woman said.

"Don't be silly," Melanie answered. "I'll have it done in one second." Melanie put the shirt on a heating press. "It's going to look very cool."

The customer kept looking over her shoulder. I was scaring her.

I began checking out the little shop. Melanie had all the things tourists wanted. Anything that had the word *Salem* on it was in this shop. I noticed elaborate witch hats hanging off the walls and moved closer.

"I make those," Melanie said when she saw me admiring them.

I nodded and looked down at a table filled with candle jars. I picked up one that had a wooden wick.

"It crackles when you light it," Melanie explained.

"We're not here to buy, Melanie," Delia said, rolling her eyes.

As I set the jar down, I noticed more candles behind those on display. They were hidden away from the others, and I wondered why that was. They all looked like they had been lit before. I reached around the display and picked one up.

"Oh, those aren't for sale," Melanie said.

I ignored her and turned the jar in my hand.

"Is that a spell?" Delia asked, looking down at it.

"She puts spells in them?" I muttered, holding it up.

"I said those are not for sale," Melanie repeated behind us.

The little bell on the door dinged as the customer left. Melanie took the candle from my hand.

"These are made special for someone else," she said as she returned it to its place. "Please don't touch them."

"Then why do you have them out?" Delia asked.

"How may I help you?" Melanie asked, ignoring the question.

I stared at the candles. There was something off about them. Why would she put a spell into the wax, and what did the spell do?

"We need to find Irene," Delia said.

"Irene?" Melanie replied. "I'm afraid I don't know who you're talking about."

Delia narrowed her eyes. "Don't play stupid with me. I know she comes here."

"You must be mistaken. I have no idea what you're talking about."

Delia stepped up to her. "Lie to me again, witch. Watch what happens."

Melanie glanced at me. "She doesn't like to be bothered, Delia."

"That's really too bad," Delia said. "We need to speak with her."

The constant smile on Melanie's face was gone. She began to fidget and sweat. Where had the witch who said we were sisters gone to? She didn't seem to be in a helpful mood now.

"Do you know her or not?" I snapped.

"It's complicated," she answered.

I tried to remain calm. "It's a yes or no question."

"She'll be furious with me."

"Would you rather *I* be furious with you?" I asked, getting in her face.

She shook her head. "You don't understand . . . she's not the same person anymore. She's turned into something else, something that doesn't get along with others."

"I'll take my chances, witch," I said. "How do I find her?"

"Just tell us," Delia hissed at her.

Melanie looked into my eyes. "You're not going to find the answers you want, Thea. Soon you won't be you anymore, even if you break the promise. I've seen it happen firsthand."

Her words sent chills down my spine. I didn't like hearing that.

"Let us worry about that," Delia said.

Melanie kept looking into my eyes. After what seemed like forever, she finally agreed. "Meet me at Salem Willows at midnight. Come alone and unarmed. I can't promise she'll talk to you, but I'll try."

"We'll be there," Delia said.

"No, just Thea," Melanie said, looking back into my eyes.

Delia tried to argue, but I put my hand up. "I'll be there . . . alone."

"If I see anyone with you, I'll leave," Melanie warned.

"Don't worry, witch. I'll be alone."

We turned to leave, but Melanie grabbed my arm and said, "Wait. I must warn you, she may hurt you. Be prepared if she puts up a fight."

I smiled. "Does it look like I'm scared?"

She shook her head. "You don't understand. She may have broken the promise, but it changed her because of it. Her mood swings are hard to predict. She can get violent."

"Then we'll get along just fine," I said, yanking my arm away.

Delia argued with me all the way back to the house. "They say she's dangerous, Thea. You shouldn't go alone. You heard Melanie—she may hurt you."

I laughed. "Really, Delia? You're worried about *me*?"

"It's not funny. She's killed before."

"What a coincidence. So have I."

"Listen to me, witch," Delia said as we entered the yard. "She knows dark spells. They do horrible things. Why do you think she stays away from everyone? She can't control herself. Don't forget, she killed her own children."

I froze. "What?"

"You didn't know that?"

I looked away. Suddenly my father's words were making me nervous. He'd told me how the promise had made Simon kill what he loved the most. Was I going to turn into that monster? I thought of Simon again. He would kill James, his own son, in an instant, if he could. Was that the future I was going to give my son? Would he die at my hands? What about James? Would I be able to stop myself from hurting him?

I felt out of breath as I took hold of Delia's shoulders. "Tell me everything, Delia. What do you know about her?"

"Calm down, Thea. I know what you're thinking. You're not going to kill your son."

"Who was she? How does Melanie know her?"

Delia gave me a strange look. "Don't you remember? She's Melanie's sister."

I tried to think of the past. My memory of Melanie's sister Irene was vague. I hadn't known her well, but I remembered how beautiful she was. I'd always thought Irene had moved away or something. I had no idea she was the black witch. I could almost remember her face, picture her emerald green eyes. She had a beautiful smile, just like her sister. I remembered how friendly she was. Very sweet, very tender. What possible reason could she have for making a blood promise?

"Come on, Thea. Let's talk upstairs in your apartment."

We snuck in and hurried up the stairs and into my apartment before anyone could see us.

"What have you heard about her?" Delia asked, closing the door behind us.

I sat on the couch. "Just the legends everyone else knows. That she made a blood promise to someone and didn't keep it. They say she disappeared into the woods and hardly comes out. I never gave her much thought because I didn't believe half the stories."

Delia sat next to me. "I remember her. She was so beautiful. All the men chased her, even human men. She was such a nice person. I've always wondered what made her do that."

"Why didn't anyone else know she was the black witch—besides you, I mean?"

She looked thoughtful for a moment. "My house is near Melanie's shop. I used to see this old woman walking into it a lot. It took me a long time to realize it was Irene. Her shoes gave her away."

"Her shoes?"

Delia nodded. "She had this pair of purple shoes she always wore. She never took them off. I remember thinking how ugly they were. Then I noticed the old woman, and she was wearing those very same shoes. She always left Melanie's shop with a handful of witch hats. She looked my way one day, and her eyes sent chills down my spine. I'd heard about what the blood promise would do to them. It was then I realized she was the black witch. I never told anyone because they all thought Irene had gone mad for what she had done."

"Did she really kill her kids?"

Delia flipped her hair and sat back. "That's what they say. I never even knew she had kids. Someone said she married a human and kept her kids hidden from warlocks. They say she feared they would hurt them."

"How did she kill them?"

Delia gave me a nervous look. "Are you sure you want to know?"

"What do you think?"

"Thea, you're not going to hurt your son."

"Spit it out," I snapped.

She looked down. "They say she cut off their heads."

I froze. I couldn't make myself take a breath. All my worst fears filled my mind. What could have made her do that? Now I knew I had to find her. I had to know what had sent her over the edge.

Delia placed her hands over mine. "Thea, calm down. You're shaking," she said.

"My son," I whispered.

As Delia leaned into me, the scent hit me. She smelled like ink. My eyes traveled her body as she backed away.

"What are you looking at?" she asked.

"Did you get a tattoo?"

"What?"

"Did you get a tattoo? I can smell the ink."

Her eyes widened as she got to her feet. I realized it wasn't her with the tattoo, but perhaps Fish, who had been close to her.

"Um, I'm going to go check on Helena," she said and left.

I sat there staring at the door. What were my friends up to? Since when did Delia care enough to go check on Helena? I'd had enough of this. I wanted to know what the hell was going on. I quickly headed out the door.

I saw Pam almost dragging Meaghan out of Cory's apartment as I descended the stairs.

Pam looked angry as she pointed her finger in Joshua's face and ordered, "Stay away from my daughter!" She turned on her heels and headed out the front door, dragging Meaghan behind her.

Joshua slammed the door behind them. "Go to hell, witch!" he yelled.

"What's going on?" I asked.

He leaned against the door. "I wish I knew, Thea."

"What do you mean? What did I miss?"

I was blown away when Joshua told me what Pam had been doing to him. He couldn't understand why she sent him away every time he went looking for Meaghan. He explained how Pam would cross the street to avoid him if Meaghan was with her.

"I walked Meaghan home the other day," he said, "and Pam got furious when she saw us together. She said she didn't want me near her daughter. And today, when I asked Meaghan if she wanted to go for a walk, Pam got up and dragged her out of here."

"Did she tell you why?" I asked.

He shook his head. "I'm not good enough for her daughter. I'm sure that's what it is."

"That's not true, Joshua. Meaghan would be lucky to have someone like you."

"I love her, Thea. And I think she loves me, but she's scared of her mother."

Joshua was right. I saw the way Meaghan looked at him. The question was, what was Pam's problem? That was a question I planned on asking her face to face.

"Is Donna still here?" I asked.

"No. She put Helena in bed and left with James. They went looking for Sharron."

"Sharron?"

Joshua was obviously distracted with Meaghan when he kept looking toward the door. I gave him a kiss on the cheek and walked into the boys' apartment. I found Delia in Helena's room, whispering in a corner with Cory. Helena lay in bed, staring up at the ceiling.

~ 92 ~

She looked so lost.

"How is the patient?" I asked.

The moment Helena heard my voice, she jumped out of bed and ran toward me. She threw herself at my feet, wrapped her arms around my ankles, and began to cry. I wasn't sure what to do. I tried pulling my feet away, but she only held on tighter. I couldn't get over how distraught she was.

"Please, take me with you," she cried.

Cory crossed the room and tried to pull her off me, but she slapped his hands away and looked up at me.

"I won't see James anymore," she said as tears ran down her face. "I'll never look for him again, I swear. Just take me with you. Don't let Simon take me."

I wanted to kick her away, maybe even take her back to Simon myself.

"Helena," Cory said, trying to calm her, "if Simon walks in here, he'll have to get through me first. I assure you that you are safe here."

When Helena only clung to me tighter, Cory said, "Maybe you should go, Thea. It took me all morning to calm her down." He tried to pull Helena away again. "Come on, sweetie. I'll put you in bed again."

Helena ignored him and got a faraway look in her eyes. "No more needles," she said with a terrified look on her face. It was like she was talking to herself, reliving what she had gone through. "It wasn't me!" she yelled, slapping her hands to her head. "I didn't take them!"

"Helena," Cory said, gathering her in his arms.

~ 93 ~

"It's over, sweetie. You're safe now. We won't let anything happen to you."

"It wasn't me," she cried. She threw her arms around Cory and wept. "I didn't take them," she kept saying.

Cory chanted a spell and put her to sleep. I thought of erasing her memory, but the evil witch inside me wanted her to suffer. I'd felt pity for a split second when I rescued her, but now that pity was gone. I was glad to see her falling apart. My friends were foolish for being worried about her. I knew Helena would be back to her evil self when she got better. A witch like her could never change. And I, for one, had not forgotten all that she had done to me.

Cory picked her up and put her back in bed. He put a blanket over her and sat next to her. "Man, she's really bad," he said, shaking his head.

"No one forced this witch to help Simon," I snapped.

Cory looked shocked. "Thea, how can you say that? Look at her."

"Like I said, no one forced her to help Simon."

I forgot all about asking Delia about the ink and walked out the door. The minute Cory started worrying about Helena, it was my cue to leave. I had no time to join them in their sorrow. I had to think of what I was going to say to the black witch. My thoughts were consumed with her. Had the blood promise really caused her to kill her own kids? Now more than ever, I had to know what had sent her over the edge. I decided to go upstairs and clear my head and think of every question I would ask her.

As I was going up the stairs, Javier walked in the front door to the building. The smell of ink hit me at once.

I froze and slowly turned to face him. "Where did you just come from?" I asked.

He instantly became nervous. "I . . . I was just visiting Sharron," he said, tugging at his sleeve. He wouldn't look me in the eye. I looked at his arms but saw nothing. The ink smelled very fresh. Then I saw it—a small ink spot on his sleeve. I walked down the rest of the stairs as Javier looked away from me. "Have you been painting, too?" I asked, touching the ink.

"Um, yeah," Javier said with a fake smile.

"This paint doesn't dry very fast, does it?" I showed him my fingers.

He swallowed thickly as I wiped my fingers on my shirt again.

"What have you and Cory been painting?" I asked.

"Oh, um, Sharron asked us to paint her living room."

"All of you?"

"N-no, just me and Cory."

"That's strange. I wonder why Delia smells like paint?"

"Oh, she brought us something to eat. Maybe that's why." He was lying, that much was obvious. "Excuse me, Thea. I have to shower now."

Javier continued into the apartment while I hurried out the front door. It was time to find out what was going on. I was surprised to see Pam walking into the yard as I was leaving. I noticed Meaghan wasn't with her anymore.

"How is my cousin doing?" Pam asked as she walked up the stairs to the front porch.

"Where is Meaghan?" I asked.

"I took her home. She had chores to do." She was lying.

"It wouldn't be because of Joshua, would it?"

Her eyes shifted to the side. "N-no, not at all."

"Don't lie to me, witch. Joshua told me everything. What is your problem with him?"

Her chin jutted out stubbornly. "I think that's my business, Thea."

"Oh, I think you made it mine when you treated Joshua that way," I said, stepping up to her.

The color left her face as she looked into my eyes. Her auburn hair was almost turning white.

"What is your problem with him?" I asked.

"Why would I want them to be together? So Meaghan can get her heart broken?"

"What are you talking about, witch?"

"Everyone who comes into your life gets hurt or dies, Thea. I don't want my daughter to be a widow at such a young age. She deserves a better life than the one Joshua has been living next to you. I want her husband to have a future."

I was speechless. I had no words to defend myself. She was right.

"Look, Thea, he's a good boy, but he also worships you. I know he would follow you into hell if he had to. There isn't anything that boy wouldn't do for you. Even now, what they're doing with the tattoos, it's not what I want for my daughter."

My head shot up when she said that. "You know about the tattoos?"

~ 96 ~

"Yes, and I don't want my—"

I stormed out of the yard without waiting for her to finish. That was the last straw. I was getting to the bottom of this.

Chapter 8
Le Jardin de Parisienne

I took all the backstreets into town. I didn't want James to see me coming. I walked past the Hawthorne Hotel and the Witch Museum and crossed the snow-covered park. There in front of Sharron's house was James's car. I crept to the side of the house and peeked through a window. At first, all I saw was Sharron's country-style décor. The house was very neat and tidy. A tall glass vase filled with flowers sat on the dining room table.

I ducked down when Fish walked over to the table and pulled off his shirt.

"You think Helena will be okay in a few days?" he asked as he laid his shirt over one of the chairs.

My eyes followed him to the open living room.

I heard James's voice saying, "I'll go check on her after this."

I couldn't see James, but Sharron seemed to be sitting on a chair in front of him. *What is she doing?* She appeared to be leaning toward him, touching him.

"I'm getting a skunk this time," Fish said.

James laughed. "A skunk?"

"Yeah, I'll put a spell on it to spray Delia when she yells at me."

James laughed again.

I tried to see what Sharron was doing. She held a strange needle with what appeared to be thread wrapped around the tip. She dipped the tip of the needle into one bottle, then another, before leaning toward James again. "You'll have to get more ink soon," she said.

"I gave William three bottles today," James answered. "He's putting the spells on them."

"And you say the ink didn't make Thea weak?"

"No. She never complained once. We were together for a few hours and she never so much as yawned."

"That's good news," Sharron said. "I know William was worried about that."

Why would the ink make me weak? What was so special about the ink? I looked at the bottles. One was taller than the other. At first, I thought they were made of mercury glass, but I soon realized it was gold glass. They were very old-looking and chipped. The faded label on the taller bottle had a crown and the words *Le Jardin de Parisienne*. The shorter bottle was labeled *La Blanc Bordeaux Number 23*. The year on the bottle was 1829. I'd never seen bottles like these before. The glass was very strange looking. I had never seen any kind of glass that was made of gold. They looked hundreds of years old.

"Let me get a towel," Sharron said as she got to her feet.

When I was finally able to get a clear view of James, my jaw dropped. His shirt was off, and he was covered in tattoos. He now had full sleeves on his arms. He stood to stretch his arms, revealing a huge oak tree that covered most of his back. The tree was beautiful. Some of its branches draped down to the ground. Sharron had been working on what looked like an owl on his chest. The owl was white with black markings and bright yellow eyes. It stood on a snow-covered branch.

Sharron was quite the artist. I hadn't known that about her.

When she returned, James sat down again. "Here, I dripped some on your pants," she said, handing him the towel.

"This stuff gets everywhere," James said as he wiped the stain away.

"Make sure she doesn't see it," Sharron warned, and returned to the tattoo.

"She's already asking questions. I don't know how much longer I can keep this from her."

"You can't tell her, James. You know what she'll do."

"I don't plan on it. Not yet, anyway."

"If she wasn't so impulsive . . ." Sharron added.

As she worked on his tattoo, I wondered what was behind this. Why were they keeping it from me? What did the tattoos do for them? The moment that question passed through my mind, James looked my way. We made eye contact at once.

James gently pushed Sharron's hand away and rose to his feet. Sharron followed his eyes and gasped when she saw me. James made no attempt to hide his tattoos. He only looked into my eyes and said nothing.

I didn't need to hear the words he was thinking. I could see them in his eyes. He was asking if I trusted him, begging me to believe in him. I looked at his chest. I couldn't understand why he was doing this. One thing I did know was that I did trust him, and I wanted him to see that things really had changed.

Despite the million questions I wanted to ask, I let it go. I looked back into his eyes and nodded. James sat back down and asked Sharron to continue. Sharron looked nervously my way.

"It's okay," James said.

Fish turned to the window. "What are you looking at?" he asked. His eyes grew wide when he saw me. "Oh, shit," he said, quickly leaning back again.

James again asked Sharron to continue, and she finally picked up the needle. I thought of leaving, but I stayed put until Sharron finished the owl. I expected James to come out and talk to me, but when he lifted his arm and asked Sharron to give him another one over his rib area, I became worried.

"Are you sure?" Sharron asked him.

James glanced my way. "Just do it."

"I'm almost out of ink, dear. And I still have to do Fish."

"Then do it until you're out," James snapped at her.

Sharron sighed. "If people thought things over now and then, you wouldn't have to be doing this," she muttered.

"Please, Sharron . . . not now," James said.

Sharron gave me an angry look and continued her work. I instantly felt aggravated with her. I didn't like her judgmental glare. I was so tired of everyone being angry with me for what I had done. I knew it was my fault, but I didn't need them reminding me at every turn. I looked at James, wondering what he was putting on the line for me. I wasn't sure I wanted to know.

James finally looked my way again. "I love you," he mouthed to me.

I smiled. "I love you, too."

I stepped away from the window and started for home. I wouldn't question James when I saw him again. If he decided to tell me what he was up to, I would do my best to understand. That wasn't going to be easy; I was dying to know what the tattoos were for. Why was he getting so many?

I decided to wait for him at home. Maybe he would come over and tell me everything.

As I crossed the park, I saw the flash of a spell out of the corner of my eye. Two warlocks were chasing Vera. I broke into a run. As one warlock reached for her, I waved my hand, and he flew into a tree. Vera looked over her shoulder and spotted me.

"Run to me!" I shouted at her.

The moment the other warlock heard my voice, he turned and ran in the opposite direction. I reached the warlock I had thrown into a tree before he could get to his feet. I kicked him across the face and knocked him back down.

"Where do you think you're going?" I teased.

The warlock jumped to his feet. He towered over me. He was an older warlock, probably in his fifties, and had deep scars along his cheek. Once again, I couldn't believe how big these warlocks were getting. What the hell was Simon feeding them?

There was no fear in his dark eyes as he squared off with me and stood his ground. "Like it or not," he said, "that witch is coming with me."

Vera began chanting a spell that would prevent human eyes from seeing us.

I smiled at the warlock. "I'm afraid you'll have to get through me first."

An evil smile spread across his face. "That's not going to be a problem, witch."

"They were trying to take me to Simon!" Vera yelled.

"What does Simon want with her?" I asked the warlock.

"You're going to have to ask him yourself, witch. He's right behind you."

I spun around, but there was no one there but Vera.

Vera screamed, "Look out!"

It was the oldest trick in the book, and I had fallen for it. I felt a blast of pain explode throughout my back and ribs as the warlock hit me. His fists were so powerful. They took the breath right out of me.

Before I could recover, he punched me in the ribs again. I fell to the ground, gasping for air. Vera tried chanting a spell at him, but he spat out a spell, and she fell to the ground, shaking. I tried to get to my feet.

"Where do you think you're going?" the warlock said, kicking me in the ribs. I heard several of them break as I gasped. He was so strong. Why did his strikes feel so powerful? It was like he was hitting me with an iron bar.

I looked toward Sharron's house and prayed that James would hear the commotion and come running out. I didn't know how many more blows I could take. When the warlock began to walk toward Vera, I grabbed his leg.

"Vera, run!" I yelled. I felt his fist across my face, but not even that made me let go of him.

Vera was still shaky as she jumped to her feet.

"Run," I said again, before slipping on my father's ring.

I held on tight as the warlock spun into the vortex with me. I laughed at the look of shock on his face as the speckles of light surrounded us.

"What is this witchery?" he yelled.

I tried getting to my feet, but the pain knocked me back down.

The warlock kept trying to find a way out. He flapped his arms as if he were trying to fly. "Where are you taking me?" he yelled.

Finally, I felt the ground under me. The warlock said nothing as he looked around in amazement. His mouth was agape as he stared at the beautiful landscape around him. He'd forgotten all about me. He reached out and touched the glittering flowers.

"What in the world?" he said when the glitter from the flowers stuck to his fingers. He gasped when he looked up at the sun. "What kind of sun is that?" he murmured.

As he took in my father's world, I tried to heal myself. I waved my hand over my ribs and was shocked when my magic didn't work.

"Where the hell am I?" the warlock asked. His eyes darted from the lake and back to the sun. "It's Simon's home," he said with wonderment.

"No. This is *my* home," I hissed.

He turned to me with greed in his eyes. He kept looking at my father's ring. He slowly pulled out a dagger. "Give me that ring," he ordered.

"You're going to have to kill me, scum."

He smiled and raised the dagger. "So be it, witch."

Two gigantic talons grabbed him by the arms before he could strike.

"Attor!" I yelled as the dragon lifted the warlock into the air.

Attor flicked him away and blew fire at him. Nothing but dust came drifting back down when Attor was done. He flew back down and wrapped his talons around me. "I have to get you out of here," he said as he lifted me up.

Before I could tell him I was hurt, I was in the air. I screamed in pain as he flew over Magia, his talons like metal clasped around my waist. Every time he flapped his wings, he held me tighter. I tried to wiggle myself out of his grip.

"Attor, you're hurting me," I screamed. I was relieved when he descended to a clearing and laid me gently on the grass.

He spun around to check me. "What do you mean, I'm hurting you?" he asked.

I sighed when the pressure from his talons was gone. I grabbed my side again and tried to heal myself.

"What happened to you?" he asked.

"It's my ribs, they're broken. My magic isn't working for some reason."

He appeared confused. "It isn't working?"

"It's not working on me," I explained.

"Did you try?"

"Yes, Attor, I tried!" I snapped.

With a huff, he took the back of my shirt into his mouth and dragged me into the forest. Once he had me under a fig tree, he took to the sky again.

"Where are you going?" I called out.

He flew up and over the trees and was gone. I tried to heal myself again as I waited for him. I couldn't understand it. Why wasn't I healing? I waved my hand at a bush to make sure I still had magic. When the bush blew to pieces, I knew something wasn't right. I waved my hand at different things, sending leaves falling to the ground and a log flying into another tree. I commanded rocks and sticks into my hand. I tried everything, and it all worked. Why wasn't my magic working on me?

I waved my hand over my ribs. "Heal," I chanted. Nothing. I tried to stand up, but the pain wouldn't let me move. I heard a thump a few yards away. "Where did you go?" I called out. The sound of crunching leaves was getting closer. "Attor?" I searched my pockets for my father's wand and closed my eyes when I realized Delia had knocked it out of my hand back at Cory's apartment. I tried to drag myself behind the tree, but it was too late.

"I'm going to eat a pound of figs today," I heard a voice say. "I'm starving."

"Leave some for us," another said.

I heard laughter, and then I saw them. Three of Wendell's guards spotted me and quickly drew their weapons.

"She's alive!" one of them gasped. "It can't be. Wendell killed her."

Their red eyes widened as they fluffed their feathers. Leathery tails began whipping about in excitement. Their owl-like heads spun around, searching the area.

"She's alone," the biggest guard said.

They soon realized I was hurt and lowered their weapons. The biggest guard leaned down and spotted the ring on my finger. "Go tell Wendell she's still alive," he ordered the others.

One of the guards put his staff between his legs and took to the sky. When the big guard leaned over me again, I tried pulling off the ring. Pain filled my head, and the guard smiled at me. Their magic was torture. It was a buzzing sound that felt like a dagger being thrust into my head.

"Attor!" I shouted.

A net was thrown over me. Panic set in. The buzzing in my head got louder and made my body stiff. My head hit the ground. I could only gasp from the pain.

I couldn't let them take me to Wendell. He would kill me this time, no doubt. "A . . . ttor," I said as a single tear ran down my face.

I felt them trying to pull the ring from my finger. The big guard put his foot on my face for

~ 107 ~

leverage as he tried to yank the ring off. "Cut off her hand," the other guard suggested.

The big guard let go of my hand and stepped back. "We'll take her to Wendell. He'll be very happy to learn that the ring is still in Magia." He ordered his fellow guard to pick me up.

I wanted to scream as the guard gathered me in the net and threw me over his shoulder. But when he tried tying the net to his staff, something flashed across his chest and cut him in two. I fell to the ground with a *thud*. My eyes darted in every direction. There, with staff in hand, stood Martin, smiling at the remaining guard.

The big guard glared at him, but Martin laughed. "That doesn't work on me, Lofeus," Martin said. "It only works on her because she doesn't know how to control her mind. I'm afraid you will have to fight me."

I realized the guard was trying to cause Martin the same pain he was causing me. Martin didn't seem bothered by it. His smile only grew wider as the guard tried to cast his magic on him.

The guard named Lofeus finally gave up. "My battle is not with you, Martin," he said. "I just want the girl."

Martin spun his staff around. "Then I'm afraid we will fight to the death."

I heard a thump. It was Attor, with Morgan on his back. Attor held the guard that had flown off in his mouth. The guard was already dead. Attor spat him out and huffed, seeming very pleased with himself. Morgan smiled and patted Attor on the back, as if congratulating him.

Lofeus took a step back and raised his staff, but Martin was faster. He pointed his staff at the guard and released a ray of light like a bolt of lightning, which shattered Lofeus into a thousand pieces. I let out a sigh when the buzzing in my head finally went away.

Martin ran to me and pulled away the net. "Your Highness, what are you doing here? You shouldn't be here now." He tried helping me up.

"No!" I screamed.

Martin leaped back, confused.

Morgan jumped off Attor and ran to us. "Is she okay?" he asked.

I put my hand over my ribs. "I'm hurt. I think my ribs are broken."

"What happened?" Martin asked.

"It's a long story. Please, help me. My magic isn't working on me."

"Lie still. I'll take care of it," Martin said as he crouched over me.

Martin made a strange face when he saw the stain on my blouse. He lifted it up and waved his hand over my ribs. I could actually hear them putting themselves back together.

"Any news about my father?" Morgan asked.

"There's no time for that!" Martin yelled at him.

I felt bad for Morgan. Every time I came here, he asked about his father, and I never had an answer for him. I had no idea what had happened to him. All my father ever told me was that his father was still alive, but he never said more than that.

Wasting no time, Martin helped me to my feet and onto his staff. "You can't be seen here, Your

Highness. Things will get crazy again." He looked at Morgan. "Go with Attor and follow us back to the falls."

Morgan nodded and hurried back to Attor.

Martin jumped on the staff, and I grabbed onto his waist. "What's going on?" I asked.

"I'll explain in a moment."

Within seconds, we were in the air. The others followed closely behind us. I kept looking around for any sign of the guards or Wendell. It was then I realized how beautiful Magia looked. Nothing seemed out of the ordinary. The flowers bloomed more beautifully than before. I could see the waterfall from where we were, and it was breathtaking. The sparkles of light flowed from the water like before. Trees, draped in ivy, whistled in the wind. The ground was covered in a blanket of flowers.

"Has Wendell died?" I asked.

Martin laughed. "No, but he thinks you did. Those guards were only looking for food."

I thought back to that day, the day Wendell had tortured me. Of course, he thought I was dead. He never knew what had happened after he sent Porteus away with me. He probably didn't know Porteus was living in my world, either. That was no doubt the reason why things were so calm now. As far as Wendell knew, he had nothing to fear anymore.

Martin flew toward the lake. I heard the roar of the waterfall as we got closer. I didn't think I'd ever be back in this area again. This was the first place I had fallen in love with when I first came to Magia. I had run through these fields as a child with my father in tow, touching the flowers and getting my fingers covered in glitter. Why was it okay to come now? Things had seemed so bleak before, but now Magia looked more breathtaking than ever.

Martin landed near the waterfall. I looked up at the sun, its rays beaming down brighter than ever. The greenery was more alive than I'd ever seen it. Was it possible there were more flowers growing now? It was too beautiful to be real.

"Magia looks beautiful," I said.

Attor blew fire, and Martin grabbed my hand.

"In here," he said, pulling me behind him.

"Why are you hiding me?"

"Guards!" he yelled.

He was almost dragging me behind him. He pulled me behind a giant tree that had fallen on the forest floor. It gave us perfect cover. We stayed behind the tree as the guards flew over us.

"What about Attor and Morgan?" I asked.

Martin laughed. "They see us all the time, Your Highness. We've been banned from the village by the other wizards. I'm more worried about them seeing you."

I watched the guards disappear behind the mountain. They never gave Attor or Morgan a second glance. They didn't seem worried about them; I wondered why.

"Martin, what the hell is going on?" I asked, stepping away from the tree.

I couldn't get over how strong and vibrant Martin looked. His curly black hair glistened in the sun, and his eyes sparkled like my father's. I envied the look of confidence on his face, but the moment he looked into my eyes, that confidence was gone. His smile faded as a look of shock replaced it. Although I had told him what I had done, it didn't make it any easier to face him. I knew my eyes were darker than ever, and from the look on his face, that wasn't a good thing.

After a moment of silence, Martin finally spoke up. "I'm sorry I'm hiding you, but we can't let the guards see you. Wendell hasn't bothered us in weeks. It's better for everyone if he still believes you died that day."

"The guards don't bother you?" I asked.

"No. As long as we stay in this area, they leave us alone." He kept looking at my eyes. It was making me feel very uncomfortable.

"Please don't look at me like that," I said, glancing away.

He moved closer. "May I say a few words, Your Highness?"

I already knew what he was going to say. I nodded but didn't look at him.

"Do you know what makes a wizard strong?" he asked.

I shook my head.

"It's knowing who we are," he said. "We are born with the gift of confidence and loving ourselves. We know no other way to be. It's in our blood to accept the creature the gods meant us to be. Any doubt in that will make you as weak as a human."

I didn't say a word. I wanted him to stop talking. I think he figured that out.

"Wait here," he said. "I have to make sure there are no more guards around."

I nodded, and he handed me his staff.

"If you start getting weak, fly to Attor's cave. You'll be safe in there. I'll come back so you can explain what happened."

I nodded again, and he was off.

Why would I get weak? I wondered.

Chapter 9
The Tree Sap

I leaned against the tree as I watched Martin talking to Attor. After a moment, Martin jumped on Attor's back with Morgan, and they took to the sky.

As I stood there waiting, a strange odor wafted over me. I felt lightheaded. I wouldn't say I was weak, but I could have fallen asleep in an instant.

The odor hit me again, and I recognized it. I looked at the tree and saw some kind of syrup dripping out of it. I smelled it and gasped. "The ink."

I examined the tree more closely and realized that the two huge trunks were feet. This wasn't just any tree. It was one of the Onfroi, the half-man, half-tree people who lived here in Magia. The Onfroi fed on the leaves that took wizards' powers away. Just being near one of these Onfroi would make me feel weak. But if they touched me, they could drain the life right out of me. My magic couldn't hurt these giants.

The leaves they fed on served as a shield against it.

Was this Onfroi dead? I took Martin's staff and poked it. I jumped back when the tree moved.

The ground shook as the Onfroi sat up. Two eyes carved into the bark looked down at me. "Ah, Your Highness, it's you."

"Peter? I thought this was a dead tree."

The sound of trumpets filled the air when Peter laughed. "I was sleeping," he explained.

I looked at his peeling bark and the syrupy substance all over him. Peter followed my eyes.

"I'm shedding bark because I'm growing," he explained.

I was more focused on the syrup. I would have known that smell anywhere. It was the ink Sharron had been using on James. I reached out my hand to touch it.

"Don't touch my sap," he warned. "It will weaken your powers."

"Sap?"

Remembering the ink I had cleaned off my clothes, I looked down at the stain on my blouse, which was right over my ribs. So that's why my magic wasn't working on me. No wonder Martin had lifted my blouse up; that must have been what he was looking at. Then a thought occurred to me: How did James get his hands on the sap? I remembered Sharron telling him he had to get more of it. I looked at my fingers. *I gave William three bottles*, James had said.

I looked at Peter. "How many times has James been here?" I asked. When he didn't answer, I repeated, "How many times?"

After a moment, he said, "He comes every day, Your Highness."

I gasped. "How is that possible?"

"He has a ring," he said, looking down at my hand.

"A ring?"

"Yes, Your Highness."

What the hell was going on? How had James gotten a ring, and who gave it to him?

"My father," I muttered, realizing he was behind it. I tried to hide my shock from Peter. I needed him to tell me everything. "What does James do when he comes here?" I asked.

Peter knew there was no point in lying. "He's been trying to get near the secret river of life, Your Majesty. He and Martin have been trying to get the energy for Xander, but the wizards are keeping a watchful eye on it."

I moved closer to him. "James has been trying to get the energy?"

"Yes, Your Highness. But the wizards don't leave the river for one moment. The fairies had to give Martin and Morgan some of their magic to keep them strong because of it."

"Did James come today?"

"Yes, but only for the sap. The humans were not with him on this trip."

My heart sank. "Humans? James brings humans with him?"

"Yes, the ones like him."

"Cory," I said, looking away.

My friends were coming here. What was going on? Why all the tattoos? Even Delia smelled like the sap. What exactly did the ink do for them? I turned back to Peter. "I order you to tell me everything you know."

It took a lot of convincing before Peter finally mumbled the words, "I was only trying to help."

"Help? What do you mean?"

"Forgive me, Your Highness. It was I who told James about my sap and how they could use it. I only intended to protect them from your magic."

My heart was breaking. "Protect them from *my* magic?"

Peter avoided my eyes.

I looked at his sap. "I see."

He knew I would hurt my loved ones one day— and apparently, so did James. I thought about Irene, who had killed her own kids. It was obvious James knew where my mind was headed.

"They're scared of me," I said.

"Those tattoos they're getting with my sap won't stop your magic," Peter said, "but it will weaken it. Anywhere you strike, my sap—and Xander's spell—will heal the area. That's why they're getting covered with tattoos. It will be hard for you to kill them that way."

I closed my eyes. Just the thought of killing James sent a chill down my spine. I made a fist as the evil witch inside me took pleasure in those thoughts. In that moment, I knew I could no longer trust myself. I was no longer in control of my actions—even my loved ones knew that. I had to help them. I had to help them stop me. I would never forgive myself if I hurt any of them.

I began to pace as I tried to find a way to help. What spell could I teach them that would stop me dead in my tracks?

"The leaves!" I exclaimed. *Of course*. Those leaves were the best weapon I could give my friends and James to use against me. Hope rose inside me again. I had to meet with James and give him those leaves.

"I have to go," I said, dropping Martin's staff.

"You're not going to wait for Martin?" Peter asked.

"No. I have something I need to do." I pulled off my father's ring and disappeared.

It was dark by the time I got back. The park was quiet. Only Christmas lights from the surrounding houses lit the night. I looked toward Sharron's house and saw that James's car was gone. I slipped the ring into my pocket and started for home, hoping that James would be there waiting for me.

"Mistress, you're back," a voice said.

I spun around. Vera was sitting on a bench. "Vera, you're still here?"

She stood. "I was worried. You left so fast." She moved closer. "Did he hurt you?"

Vera looked frail and thin. She always had a worried look on her face. I was surprised she hadn't taken a potion to change what she looked like tonight, which she often did. The fear of Simon finding her had made her life a living hell. She was scared to death of him, and who could blame her? Simon had tortured her many times before. Yet here she was, loyal to the end.

"You shouldn't be alone right now," I said.

She looked down at her hands. "I can't go home. He'll find me."

She was talking about Simon, and she was right. I knew he wanted to question her about the leaves, but he was barking up the wrong tree. I had to watch over her. "Come on, Vera. You're coming home with me."

Her eyes filled with tears. "You don't have to do that."

"Yes, I do. Not another word. You're coming with me."

I began to walk away, but Vera didn't follow. "Is something wrong?" I asked.

She seemed scared. "Do you know why Simon sent those men for me?"

She deserved to know. "Yes," I said flatly.

"Why?"

"Simon thinks you may have something that belongs to him."

"What is it?"

I hesitated for a moment. "It's something I'm keeping safe," I answered.

A look of shock washed over her. "*You* have what he wants?"

"Yes, but not for long."

"What do you mean?"

"Never mind. Let's get you home," I said, spinning around.

She grabbed my arm. "No, please. I want to help."

The scared Vera seemed to have vanished now, but maybe that was a good thing. I did need help getting the leaves. I couldn't touch them, so Vera would come in handy after all.

"There is something you can do for me," I said.

"Anything."

"I have to get something to James. Will you help me bring it to him?"

Her eyes lit up. "What am I bringing?"

"I'll show you when we get there. Come on."

I waved my hand at a tree, and a branch flew into my hand. I put the branch between my legs, and Vera jumped on. She wrapped her arms around my waist as we took to the sky. It was a cold night, but the air felt good on my face. I could feel Vera shaking behind me from the cold.

"Where are we going?" she asked.

"I need to pick something up," I said over my shoulder.

As we flew deep into the woods, Vera grabbed me tighter. I could feel her heart racing against my back. I looked over my shoulder at her and saw a crooked smile on her face. I wasn't sure if she was scared or excited. I knew I was asking a lot from her, but she had offered, after all. There really wasn't anyone else around right now. Delia would be asking a million questions, and I wasn't in the mood for that.

"Why are you so happy?" I asked her.

Her smile vanished. She seemed nervous that I had caught her smiling. She became that frightened little bird again. "Forgive me, mistress."

I looked ahead of me again. "Stop calling me that," I said, flying faster.

I flew back to where the leaves were. The area was undisturbed. A boulder still sat over the water hole. There were no signs of anyone having searched the area. Things were as I had left them.

Vera seemed confused as she got off the branch. "Why are we here?"

I didn't have time to explain. It was getting late, and I had a date to keep. There was no way I would miss my opportunity to find the black witch tonight. I threw the branch aside and waved my hand toward the boulder. Vera's eyes followed the direction of my magic. Her jaw dropped when trees quickly shifted back to their original place and the landscape returned to how it had once been. The boulder protecting the water hole flew over us and landed a few yards away.

Eyes wide with disbelief, Vera leaned forward to see what was in the hole. We both stepped closer, and there they were—the leaves as green as ever, under the water. It was strange how the water was crystal clear. The leaves moved as if they were drifting in the wind and gave off a soft glow that lit up the hole. They seemed so harmless, but I knew otherwise.

Vera was my only hope of getting those leaves to James. I turned and grabbed her shoulders. "Vera, listen. I don't have time to explain things to you, but I need you to go in that water hole and get those leaves for me."

She looked into my eyes until it sank in what I was asking her to do. A look of concern washed over her. "You want *me* to get in there?"

"You'll be okay. I just need the leaves."

Her eyes darted to the hole. "I . . . I can't."

"I'm right here, Vera. I won't let anything happen to you." I gave her a gentle push toward the hole. "You can do it."

She swallowed thickly and made her way to the hole.

I had to step back when I felt myself getting weak. "Jump in," I said impatiently.

She looked over her shoulder. "What else is in there?" she asked in a shaky voice.

"It's only water," I snapped.

She looked back into the hole.

"Vera, I'm running out of time. Just grab the leaves."

She stood there staring down into the hole. Her back was to me, so I couldn't see her face. What was she doing? I thought I heard her mumbling something.

"Is something wrong?" I asked.

Without answering, she jumped into the hole. I tried to be patient as she began shivering. The water was very cold.

"I only need a few," I said.

She nodded and gathered some of the leaves in her hand. She kept shivering and began turning blue. Once done, she left the water hole, teeth chattering.

"Move away from the hole," I ordered.

She stepped aside, and I returned the boulder over the hole. The trees shifted and changed the landscape again. I stepped back as Vera tried moving closer and handing me the leaves.

"Don't come near me," I said.

"What do you want me to do with them?" she asked.

I couldn't fly her back into town. I couldn't get near those leaves. I was also running out of time. It was getting close to midnight, and I had to get to Salem Willows. A thought occurred to me: I could see

James right now. All I had to do was send the signal.

I waved my hand, and the sound of thunder filled the sky. I waited a moment and sent it again.

"What are you doing?" Vera asked.

"Sending a message," I said, and took out Delia's box.

I opened the box, grasped Vera's arm, and went into my memories. The moment we were there, I stepped away from her. She was drenched with the water from the hole, and it was making me weak.

"Stand over there," I said, pointing toward a tree.

Vera didn't move. She seemed to be in shock. She reached for a bush and gasped when she realized she was able to touch it. "Where are we?" she asked, looking around.

I stepped farther away from her. "We're in one of my memories," I answered.

She looked down at the box, seemingly amazed at what the box could do. It was like she was seeing it for the first time. "It's true," she murmured. She gasped when she saw the Thea and James that were in this memory. They were swimming in the lake, laughing and holding each other.

"Why do you look so surprised?" I asked. "You knew about Delia's box."

She looked at me. "I . . . I'm sorry. I've always heard about this, but never imagined it. I didn't know it was so real." She spun around when she heard the crunching of leaves behind us. Her eyes almost popped out of their sockets when she saw James emerge from the trees.

~ 123 ~

James stopped suddenly when he spotted her. Vera bowed her head as James approached me.

"What's going on?" he asked. His eyes darted back to Vera, but I grabbed his face and made him look at me.

"Do you still trust me?" I asked.

He seemed confused by the question. "You know I do, but why is Vera—?"

"Look at me." I turned his face to me again. "I know everything, James. Your visits to Magia, the sap—everything."

He looked surprised. "I can explain."

"You don't have to. I don't need you to."

He seemed shocked by my answer. "You're not angry with me? You're not wondering why or how I got there?"

I smiled. "No. But I could have spared you all these tattoos," I said, running my hand over his arm. "I could have given you something better than sap."

"What are you talking about?"

I looked at Vera. "Give him the leaves, Vera."

James turned to Vera. "What?"

Vera didn't move. She kept looking at James and back at me.

"Take them from her," I said. "Those leaves can help you more than any tattoo can. They can render my powers useless."

"Yes, I know!" James yelled. I wasn't sure why he was upset. "You've had them this whole time?"

I couldn't understand why he was getting so angry. "Well, yes."

"Why didn't you say anything? Do you know how long we've been searching? When did you find them?" He fired off so many questions.

I cut him off, saying, "It doesn't matter now."

"Why did you keep this from me, Thea?"

How could I tell him I had once thought about using those leaves to get rid of all of them? Greed had taken over my mind, and I wanted power. I planned on killing my father, killing James, killing everyone. But now those leaves could help them. "Just take them from her," I said, backing farther away. "You can stop me with them."

He seemed confused. "You think I'm trying to stop *you*?" When I didn't answer, he ran his hand through his hair, seeming frustrated. "I should be furious with you, witch."

"Listen, I know the monster I'm turning into. I don't blame you for wanting to stop me. I would be doing the same thing."

He was quiet for a moment, but then moved closer and took my face in his hands. "If this gives you peace of mind, I will take those leaves, but I want you to know one thing. I believe in you. Nothing you turn into will ever change that. Do you understand?"

I pulled away. "I have to go."

He pulled me back into his arms. "Do you understand?" he repeated.

I nodded.

"Don't ever forget I love you, Thea."

"I have to go," I said again. "I'll see you in three days."

"We don't have to wait three days, my love. I can see you when you need me."

"No. Three days is fine."

He nodded and looked at Vera. "I'll take those leaves now."

I stepped away as Vera, her hands shaking, gave him the leaves.

"Are you all right?" James asked her.

She nodded.

James looked down at the leaves. "Is this all of them?" he asked me.

"No, but that's all you'll need."

"Where are the rest of them?"

"I'll show you when I see you again."

His face reddened. "No. You'll show me now."

"We have to go," Vera said.

James shot a look at her. "What's the hurry?"

"She's right," I said. "We have to go now."

"No!" James said, taking my arm. "Now— you'll take me to the leaves now."

I pulled away from his grip. He had the leaves and was standing too close to me. I had no time to take him.

"I can't go now, but I'll meet you later," I said.

"What time and where?" He seemed so angry.

"Give me an hour," I said.

"And you'll take me to the leaves?"

"Yes." I had to get out of here. "I'll send the signal." I pulled out the box and grabbed Vera's arm.

"Hey," James called, "I love you."

I smiled at him. "I know."

Chapter 10
Finding the Black Witch

It was late by the time Vera and I returned to the park. We hurried back to my apartment, and I let her in.

"The blankets are in the closet," I said as I turned on the lights. "I'll be home later. You can sleep in my bed if you want." I gave Vera some dry clothes. I had to hurry. I still had to stop by Cory's and get my father's wand. I told Vera to make herself at home and headed toward the door. I didn't have a minute to spare.

"Wait," Vera called out.

"Later, Vera. I have to go." I knew she had a million questions, but I didn't have time to answer them.

"But it's so cold out, mistress. You'll freeze half to death."

"I'll be fine," I said, and slammed the door behind me. I hurried down the stairs and into Cory's apartment. Everyone was sleeping. I grabbed the wand and headed out into the night. My heart was racing as I flew to Salem Willows. I didn't have time to absorb all the information from today—James going into Magia, the sap, the tattoos. I had so much on my mind, but I had to concentrate on the black witch. She was the only thing that mattered right now. I had to look into her eyes and see the monster I was becoming. There was a question I needed to ask her: Why had she killed her kids? That question was tormenting me.

I flew faster as I thought of that. A blistering wind was blowing, and the night had become frigid. I regretted not grabbing a heavier coat. My teeth were already chattering. The chilling wind felt like speckles of glass hitting my face.

Braving the cold, I flew to Salem Willows and found it dark and quiet. I stopped at the front gate to the park. A sign on the massive green wrought-iron gate said *Salem Willows* in big gold letters. I waved my hand, and it slowly opened for me. I flew in and began to look around.

The willows whispered softly as the wind caressed their branches. A stage stood a good distance away, and closed vendor stands lined the edge of the park. I remembered summer concerts being held here. I wasn't used to seeing it so quiet. Campers usually flooded the park in the summer. Dead Horse Beach was a major tourist draw. They all loved hearing the legends of how people had buried their dead horses there in the nineteenth century. Even now, some tourist claimed to find a bone or two now and then. But those old horse bones had been moved years ago, leaving behind a white sandy beach.

The cold ocean air brushed against my face as I searched for the smiling witch, Melanie. I flew toward the back of the park and finally spotted her just as she was leaving. I flew in front of her, blocking her way, and jumped off my stick.

"I'm here," I said, tossing my ride to one side.

There was no smile on her face. "You're late," she hissed.

"Only by seconds."

"We agreed to midnight," she shot back. "I'm going home." She tried to walk past me.

I pushed her back and reached for my stick. I spun it around as it turned into the sword and held its glass blade to Melanie's neck. "I don't think so, witch. Unless you want to die today, you'd better take me to your sister."

Melanie's eyes were glued to the blade. She swallowed audibly and put her hands up. "F-fine, I'll take you to her."

When I grudgingly lowered the sword, she sighed in relief. "You have a bad temper, Thea."

"Where is your sister?" I demanded.

Melanie glanced at the sword and reached for a bag she had brought with her. I was confused when she began to pull out some candles. They were the same jars I had seen at her store.

"What are you doing?" I asked.

She set them on the ground. "I have to chant ten spells, all at once," she answered.

"How are you going to do that?"

She tossed the bag aside and began to light the candles. "You'll see, witch."

I noticed there were only nine jars, and each one had been lit before. She spread them apart and got to her feet.

"Don't disturb me while I'm chanting," she warned.

I nodded, and she raised her hands. She looked down at the jars and waited, but for what? All of a sudden, the wicks began to crackle, and the candle flames burned green. Soft whispering voices began to come out of them. It took me a moment to realize the candles were releasing spells.

Melanie chanted, "Change the moon and hide the stars, hear my spells within these jars. Leave the dark and show your face, meet us now within this space." And just like that, ten spells were chanted all at once.

When Melanie was done, the wind picked up, and some clouds moved in above our heads. The landscape around us began to change. The beautiful willows started to take on another form as their leaves began to fall. Their bark peeled, and their branches transformed into dried-out sticks. The trees now looked more like standing snags of centuries-old, lifeless trees, frozen in time.

I was shocked by how the park had changed. I felt like I was in a fortress of evil.

I heard the sound of a stream a few yards away. A cracking sound made me look down. The ground was turning brown and burnt-looking. As cracks revealed themselves, the smell of sulfur drifted into the air. I put my hand over my nose and looked at my surroundings. I gasped when I saw the sky turning a dark orange. The moon gave off a glow I had never seen before, as if the light were melting off it. I felt like I was in another world. The once-beautiful park was now a gloomy, dark place.

Sadness washed over me as this place dragged my spirit down. There was nothing but suffering here—no green leaves, no flowers or happiness. Only heartbreak and despair. I expected to feel scared, but instead it felt like home. I felt as if I belonged here somehow. I didn't have that heavy feeling I always felt. Instead, I felt free and uplifted. It was like someone had opened the cage I had been trapped in. For the first time in many months, my heart felt at peace. The evil witch inside me liked it here. This was her home, her palace.

This wasn't a good thing.

I found it funny to be standing here. This place was the stereotypical environment humans imagined for witches. All I needed was a pointy black witch hat.

"Irene," Melanie called out, but no one came. "Irene," she called again. No one appeared.

I glanced around and noticed where the sound of running water was coming from. I began to follow the stream.

"We have to wait here," Melanie warned, but I ignored her. I sensed the black witch nearby. Her black heart was calling out to me. I felt her pain, her anger. I understood her now, and she was suffering.

I broke into a run when I felt her heart beating. I heard the blood flowing through it, could almost hear every beat it took.

"Stop!" Melanie shouted, but I was gone. I was desperate to find her. I sensed her black soul making me run faster. I tried jumping over the stream but fell into the water. My sword went flying out of my hand.

"Where are you?" I shouted as I got to my feet. I felt the hair on the back of my neck stand. Then a cold chill made me freeze.

She was here, watching me. I slowly looked over my shoulder, and my heart leaped into my throat. Standing behind me, wearing a dark hooded cloak, was Irene, the black witch.

The light from the moon softly lit her face. I could see despair in her dark, glossy eyes. They were empty, soulless. I moved closer, but she held up her hand and stopped me dead in my tracks. I gasped when she lifted her hands and pulled back the hood. Only threads of what was once hair hung from her scalp. Her skin was old and wrinkled, with deep creases in her face. I didn't remember ever seeing her this bad. What had happened to her?

I was still frozen from shock when Melanie caught up to me. She saw her sister and apologized for my being here. "She insisted on talking to you," Melanie said.

Irene raised her hand. "Silence, my sister. I knew she was coming."

I felt breathless when her dark eyes found me. There was such a cold look about her. She was truly a wicked-looking witch.

"You're not going to find the answers you want, witch," Irene said in a raspy voice.

"Give me ten minutes, please," I answered.

Her eyes looked me over. "You have five."

I moved closer. "How did you break the blood promise?"

A smile spread across her face, revealing yellow teeth. She slowly shook her head. "Ask something else, witch."

I almost tripped as I stepped out of the water. "But that's what I came here to ask."

"Then you have wasted your time, haven't you?"

This witch was making me furious. I saw my sword lying in front of me. I slid my foot under it and kicked it up into my hand. "Answer my question," I said, pointing it at her.

She tilted her head. "Go ahead, witch—kill me. I've been ready to die for many years."

The sword shook in my hand as anger filled my heart. "You have to help me," I said through my teeth.

She laughed. "I don't *have* to do anything. You came to me, remember?"

I wanted to kill her. My mood was getting darker and darker. Didn't she know that I wasn't leaving this place until she told me what I needed to know? I pointed the sword at Melanie. "I'll kill your sister."

Irene smiled. "Do you really think I care?"

I put the blade to Melanie's neck. "Don't test me, witch," I said, glaring at her.

"Help me, sister," Melanie pleaded.

Melanie was shocked when Irene turned and began to walk away. I lowered the sword, desperate to stop her. "I'm with child!" I yelled.

She froze, looking straight ahead. I knew I had struck a nerve.

"You have to help me save my son," I continued. "I need to know how you broke the blood promise."

It felt like an eternity before she turned and faced me again. She looked at my stomach, confused as to why I wasn't showing.

"I'm hiding him," I said, stepping forward.

Shocked, she looked back into my eyes. I could feel the pain that washed over her. She was remembering what she had done—that much was clear.

I decided to use that to my advantage. I moved even closer to her. "I'm begging you, Irene. You have to help me save my son. I don't want to hurt him."

Melanie stepped forward. "Stop it, Thea. I know what you're trying to do."

"Silence!" Irene shouted at her. There was a hint of a smile on Irene's face as she looked back at me. "You've already doomed your child," she said. "There is nothing you can do to save him. He belongs to the darkness now."

My heart began to race with panic. I threw the sword on the ground and got inches from her face. I could see what the years of torture had done to her. Behind those evil eyes was incomprehensible pain. She knew nothing but suffering, nothing but regret.

"You listen to me, witch," I growled. "Something made you kill your kids, and I don't want to turn into that monster. You can help me, or you can live with regret for the rest of your life."

There was silence. I didn't know what to make of her as she stared into my eyes. For a moment, I thought she was going to walk away again, but then she whispered, "Drink the blood."

I almost fell over. "What?"

"The blood you gave when you made the promise—you must take it back and drink it."

Something inside me didn't like hearing that. I clenched my right hand into a fist as a wave of rage washed over me. I wanted to strike Irene across the face. I had never wanted anything so much in my life.

Irene smiled. "The darkness is already fighting you, isn't it? It doesn't like what I'm telling you."

I couldn't catch my breath. My eyes darted down to the sword. I thought of slashing her neck, then spinning around and killing Melanie.

Irene laughed. "You're too weak to break a blood promise. You're already giving into the darkness." She moved closer to me. "Have you started hearing the voices yet?" she asked in a teasing tone. "Have they told you to kill your loved ones?" She brushed her cold fingers along my face. "Have you started imagining them all dead?" Her rancid breath flowed into my mouth. I felt like I would vomit.

I tried turning away, but she dug her nails into my chin and made me look at her.

"Can you feel the black witch inside of you, wanting blood?" she asked. "Can you already taste it in your mouth?"

I didn't answer.

"It's only going to get worse, witch. I bet your child's blood sounds sweeter than any blood you can think of right now. I bet you're dreaming of the day you can give birth just so you can kill him."

Infuriated, I waved my hand and sent her flying ten feet in the air.

"Leave her alone!" Melanie screamed.

Irene hit the ground hard. I ran and pressed my foot on her neck. "I will never do what you've done!" I shouted.

Her cackling laughter filled the air. "Good luck trying to change the future," she said in a mocking voice.

I jumped on top of her and began to choke her. "I'll kill you," I said, banging her head on the ground. She did nothing to fight back. This witch wanted to die, and I was going to make it happen. I tightened my grip on her neck. "Die, witch. Die!"

"Get off her!" was the last thing I heard before I was struck over the head and darkness filled my vision. I fell over with the sound of Irene's laughter ringing in my ears.

Chapter 11
The Witch Hats

I heard a fire crackling as I opened my eyes. I was lying on an old sofa with a blanket over me and my clothes soaking wet. My head throbbed. I touched my head and found a big lump behind my temple. I wondered what Melanie had struck me with.

"Feeling pain is better than feeling nothing at all," a voice said.

I sat up and looked toward the fireplace, where Irene sat and gazed at the fire. She looked different. There were no wrinkles, no creases in her face. Although her eyes were still dark and glossy, she looked more like the old Irene I'd known.

"Where am I?" I asked.

We appeared to be in an old cottage filled with old, worn-out furniture. The place was dusty and covered in cobwebs. It smelled like a secondhand store.

"You're in my home," Irene said, never looking away from the fire.

I wondered why everything looked so old and worn. Even the staircase leading upstairs was broken and falling apart.

I was startled when Irene threw another log onto the fire. It was then I noticed the pointed black hat she wore. I'd seen her wearing these witch hats before whenever she was in town. I always thought she looked ridiculous in them. It was the same kind of witch hat all the vendors sold to tourists during the month of October. Everything about her screamed *witch*.

I sat there and watched her, wondering what was going through her head. I had to stay calm, so I could ask her my questions. I still had no answers, no hope. I was about to ask the first one when Irene reached up and pulled off her hat. She threw it into the fire and reached for another one.

That was odd. As she placed it on her head, I noticed all the hats sitting next to the fireplace. She had dozens of them. The fire crackled louder as the hat burned to ashes. The flames roared like an angry beast as Irene threw on another log. She lit a cigarette and glanced at me from the corner of her eye. "When is the child due?"

Why did she want to know that? I wasn't sure if I wanted to give her that information. She looked my way when I didn't answer. Her eyes darted down to my stomach, then back into the fire. "I see your eyes have already changed," she said, taking a puff from her cigarette.

I got to my feet, my heart racing. "What else is going to change?" I asked.

She got a faraway look in her eyes. "First your eyes. Then your heart will start to change. Soon the voices in your head will be the only thing you hear. They'll whisper spells you've never heard of, put ideas into your head you can never get out. You'll wake up one day and realize you've destroyed everything you loved." She took a puff from her cigarette again. "You can try and fight it, but it will only get worse."

"How are you fighting it?" I asked.

She smirked. "Who says I am?"

I swallowed thickly and moved closer to her. I had to ask the question I feared the answer to. I prepared myself for the worst. "Why did you kill your kids?"

She looked back into the fire and took another puff. Ribbons of smoke circled her head as I waited for an answer. She wouldn't move or look at me. Her eyes were glued to the fire. "Do you remember me from back in the sixteen hundreds?" she finally asked. "Before I made the blood promise?"

"Yes, I remember you. You were the most beautiful woman in town."

She laughed. "You thought I was beautiful? That's ridiculous."

How could she say that? Hadn't she seen the way men looked at her back then?

"You could have had anyone you wanted," I said.

"And yet, I only wanted one. He was a human, and I loved him like no other. I never understood what he saw in me. He was so handsome, I was so . . . plain.

No one knew of our relationship, no one knew we were meeting in the woods to be together." She paused as she pulled off her hat and threw it into the fire. She put on another one and continued, her eyes fixed on the fire. "His name was Richard. I fell in love with him from the moment I laid eyes on him, and to my surprise, he loved me back. It never bothered him that I was so beneath him, so little of a woman to stand by his side. Despite the differences in our lives, I gave him two beautiful baby boys. No one knew I had them. I had hidden my pregnancy just like you are. I feared warlocks would take my kids away and kill them for being half human." She stared into space. "One day when I was bathing my boys in the lake, a warlock found us. He was a warlock that had been chasing after me for years. He quickly realized my children were half human and threatened to kill them. I begged and pleaded with him not to. I even offered to never see Richard again."

She pulled the hat off with anger and threw it into the fire. As she reached for another one, I noticed that the creases of her face were back, but when she put the hat on, they disappeared.

Her eyes filled with tears as she looked into the fire again. "I offered him everything I had to save my kids, but he only wanted one thing, so I gave it to him. He knew witches couldn't bond with humans, so he bonded himself to me. He said he would spare my children if I killed my husband, the human who dared to love a witch. When he pulled out a knife, I knew what kind of promise he would be asking of me."

"You made a blood promise to kill your husband?"

She looked at me. "I had to save my kids. There was no other way."

"But they said you broke the blood promise."

"I did, when I drank the blood the warlock had taken from me. I watched Richard die of old age, happy with his new family. But it was too late to save my sons."

"What happened?"

She looked back into the fire, the pain clear on her face. "When I first made the blood promise, I felt the change in me right away. My mood got dark almost overnight. At first, my kids kept me strong. Being around them was enough to clear my head. Whenever I left them for the day, the black witch inside me would surface and change me. Then the voices started; I was consumed with them. The more I fought against the blood promise, the more I would change. I thought my love for Richard and the boys would be enough to bring me back, but I was wrong."

She wiped away tears and threw the cigarette into the fire. I knew what was coming next. "The boys were sleeping like angels one night," she continued. "I stood over them, watching them sleep. I don't know what came over me. They became something I had to destroy. They were the one thing in my life that I loved the most, and the black witch inside me didn't like that. I felt an ugly hatred in my heart. She wanted blood—*their* blood." She paused. "I tried to ignore what the voices where telling me to do. I stood over my boys, trying to bring myself back. When the voices got louder, I picked up an ax, looked down at them, and . . ."

She got to her feet and threw the hat into the fire. She screamed and began to turn things over. "Kill them all!" she shouted. She put her fist through a mirror on the wall, sending glass all over the floor. I ran and grabbed one of the hats near the fireplace, pushed her back, and put it on her head. It didn't take me long to figure out what Irene had done to the hats. She was using them to capture all her evil thoughts. Burning them was the only way she knew to get rid of them.

Irene dropped to her knees and sobbed uncontrollably. I tried wrapping my arms around her, but she pushed me away.

"Don't touch me!" she yelled. "I don't need your pity, witch." She looked at my stomach. "You should be more worried about what the black witch is going to make you do." She pointed at my stomach. "Have pity on him and destroy him now. Don't give yourself a chance to hold or love him. The black witch inside you will make you do it, anyway."

I took a step back and lay a hand protectively on my stomach. "Don't say that to me!"

A wicked smile spread across her face as she got to her feet. "Do you think breaking the promise will change you back into who you used to be?" She pointed at herself. "Look at me, witch. *This* is what you'll be for the rest of your life. Even if you drink the blood and break the promise, I'm what you'll turn into. It's the price the darkness makes you pay. You'll look old and tired. You'll never be what your friends and family need you to be again. The voices will never leave you. Evil will forever consume your life."

I turned my back to her. I couldn't listen anymore. I had come to her for hope, but all she had given me was a doomed future. I thought of Simon. He wasn't living like her. He didn't look as bad as she did, either. Simon looked young and handsome. Only his eyes showed signs that he had made a blood promise. Why wasn't the promise doing this to him? How was he able to live a life without the promise destroying who he was? And my father—he'd said I would find answers here. How could he send me to this place?

I heard the fire roar and knew Irene had thrown her hat into it. She was putting on another one when I faced her again.

"Our time is up, witch," she said. "You need to leave before I run out of hats. I'm done talking to you." She lit another cigarette and sat in front of the fire again.

As I stood there watching her, I realized something. She was just like me. It was like looking into a mirror. She even looked like me a little. She had the same body type, the same long, messy hair.

Sometimes it takes looking at ourselves to see what we're doing wrong. My father's words sounded like an alarm in my head. I felt numb as I thought of all the bad qualities Irene and I shared. Irene hated herself. She was insecure and self-loathing. Although she had once been a beautiful woman, she never considered herself good enough. I hated how much of myself I saw in her. I grabbed at my chest as I realized what I had been doing to myself all these years, thinking that I didn't deserve James, thinking of myself as fat and ugly, wondering how any man could ever love me.

I had even gone so far as to think Helena was better than me and convinced myself that she was a better match for James. How could I have been so stupid? All these years of fighting evil, and my worst enemy had always been me. I looked down at myself and touched the loose clothes I always hid behind. They had given me a sense of comfort I refused to let go of, but now I felt them almost burning me. I looked at my hands. What had I been so ashamed of? I had the hands of a warrior. They weren't manicured or soft like Helena's, but they were strong and marked with battle scars—scars I was proud of.

I looked at Irene again. She was such a pathetic excuse for a woman. She wouldn't know confidence if it hit her in the face. That thought rang out in my head. It was like hearing my father's voice telling me I had finally figured it out. This was what he had been trying to tell me. The blood promise was taking every weakness I had and making it worse. The less I thought of myself, the more I was feeding it.

Flashes of my past started going through my head. I remembered all the times I let other people's opinions change what I thought of myself. I put myself down, dared to think I didn't deserve the kind of happiness James was willing to give me. How could I have been so foolish? I felt myself slowly changing. My head began to clear. Something inside me was waking up, and it wasn't the evil witch. I was finding the wizard part of me, and it was making me strong. I could see all my mistakes now, all the pointless tears I'd cried. How many years had I spent doubting myself? How many times had I told myself I wasn't good enough?

My whole life was flashing before my eyes. I understood it all, understood how I was the one making myself weaker. There was no black witch inside me; it was just evil taking on the form I had given it. I thought of Simon again. He wasn't letting the voices control him, because he was confident. The darkness fed off our insecurities and fears; I realized that now. Simon wasn't the kind of man who feared anything, not even the darkness. In fact, he embraced it. There wasn't one thing he was insecure about, at least not that I knew. The blood promise couldn't control him; it had nothing to feed on.

"The weak-minded," I said as I realized what my father was talking about. At that moment, I knew what I had to do.

I looked at Irene again. I felt sorry for her. She had given up hope long ago. Although she was trying to fight the evil thoughts by wearing those hats, she was still weak. She was weak from the moment she allowed the voices to convince her to kill her kids. I would fight the devil himself before harming my son. There wasn't a force on this earth that could stop me from protecting him.

I closed my eyes as I finally accepted my mistakes. I looked deep within my heart and finally forgave myself. I couldn't change the past, but I sure as hell was going to change the future. I didn't need anyone to believe in me. I had to believe in myself. This was my battle, and I was going to win. The evil force inside me would not have its way. Irene had given in to the voices, but I was going to kick their ass.

"I said, get out," Irene hissed.

I opened my eyes. I saw the world in a whole new light. Irene was nothing but a soulless woman full of regret. She had given the darkness all the fuel it needed to change her. Even now, she was still feeding it, still thinking so little of herself. It was a mistake I didn't plan on making ever again. I had nothing more to say to her. I wanted to talk with the evil presence that lived inside of her. It was time to face all my fears, and that meant going into hell.

"You're a coward," I said.

Irene shot her glossy eyes my way. I stepped up to her, pulled off her hat, and threw it into the fire.

"What are you doing?" she asked when I reached for the rest of the hats and also threw them in. "Are you crazy, you stupid witch?" she yelled.

I spun around and slapped her across the face. I wanted to enrage her, bring the evil out so we could play. "You wretched, evil witch," I growled. "You deserve to live like this for killing your sons. I would have cut my own head off before touching my child."

Irene glared at me as her features began to change back into those of the ugly witch. The evil shone across her face. I knew I was standing before the evil presence that lived inside her. There was no fear in her eyes. She was cold and heartless.

"I'm not scared of you," I said, moving closer. "I'll fight you now, tomorrow, and forever. You'll never do to me what you've done to her."

Irene's eyes turned red. She laughed her cackling laugh. "You belong to me," she said in a deadly voice. "There's no turning back now, witch."

I smiled. "Haven't you heard? I'm already taken."

I struck her across the face again. A horrible sound escaped her lips as she wrapped her hands around my neck. A freezing, chilling wind made the fire go out, and the room turned pitch black as we fell to the ground.

My rage surfaced. I could feel evil trying to take me over. "No!" I shouted, fighting against it.

When Irene breathed into my mouth, a flood of insecurities came rushing back to me. "You can't control me anymore!" I yelled. I felt a force leaving my body. The floor under me opened up and swallowed me into it. I felt myself being transported into hell. The walls all around me were on fire. The sound of pleading souls echoed in my ears.

I jumped to my feet when I realized Irene was gone. I was back to where it all started, back to where I had first embraced evil. I grabbed at my chest when I noticed the rage that lived inside me was gone. I had done it; I had dragged the black witch out of me.

I looked around for her and knew she was here in this dark place. "Face me," I shouted.

The fire roared as the flames on the walls grew higher.

"You can never get rid of me," a voice said.

I spun around. It was her, the black witch, and she looked just like me. She was all the things I hated about myself, and all the things I had once wanted to be. Her hair was long and flowing, her face perfect and beautiful. She had the figure I'd always thought I wanted. She was tall, thin, and breathtaking. Her arms stretched out, calling me into them. "I'll take away the pain," she said in an angelic voice. "I'm part of you now, Thea. Come back to me. We belong together."

I began to approach her.

"Yes, that's right," she sang.

As I stepped up to her, she wrapped her cold arms around me.

"Your heart belongs to me," she whispered.

I pulled back and thrust my hand into her chest. I used every ounce of power I had to fight through the insecurities that lived inside her. I reach her heart and wrapped my fingers around it. I felt my connection to her break as I pulled it out and held it up to her. "I was going to say the same thing to you," I said triumphantly.

I waved my hand and set the heart on fire. At once, she turned to black smoke, and I was transported back into Irene's house. The room filled with light again. The fireplace made a loud puff as the fire started again.

"It can't be," Irene said.

I turned and faced her. Her eyes grew wider when she looked into my eyes.

"It's not possible," she said, shaking her head. "You never drank the blood."

I picked up a piece of the mirror Irene had broken earlier. It took me a moment before I nervously looked into it. I drew a breath when I saw that my eyes were back to normal. The old Thea was looking back at me. I had never been so happy to see her.

"It can't be," Irene said again.

I threw the piece of mirror on the floor and looked at her. "I hope one day you can find yourself, Irene. But I think Irene died the day she killed her kids. You're just the empty shell she left behind."

"I'm the shell you'll be one day," she answered.

I shook my head. "I'll never become like you, witch. I'm something you'll never be."

"What's so special about you?"

I smiled. "I'm not only a witch—I'm also half wizard."

Chapter 12
Travel Well, My Friend

I turned on my heels and walked out. The moment I was outside, I breathed in the fresh air. For the first time in many years, I felt proud of myself. I hadn't battled the black witch just now; I had battled myself. I had killed the shy, timid fat girl who was unhappy with herself. A beautiful, confident woman had walked out of this house. I felt reborn, alive. I wanted to jump for joy. Happiness flowed through me.

"Where is my sister?" Melanie asked.

I looked to my left. Melanie was sitting against the side of the house, waiting for me. I noticed she was holding the wand. I reached over and snatched it from her hands.

"What did you do to my sister?" she asked as she stood.

I looked at the house. "That's not your sister anymore. She died a long time ago."

"What do you mean? What happened?"

I looked into her desperate eyes. It was clear Melanie had only been trying to help her sister all these years. "Don't come back here anymore, Melanie. Let her go."

She hung her head. "I can't. She's my sister."

"Your sister died with those kids. There's nothing more for you here."

"But the hats—they were helping."

I ignored her and began making my way out of the cluttered yard. I didn't have the heart to tell her she was wrong. Maybe one day she would see the truth. There was no helping her sister if she couldn't help herself. Irene would forever feed the darkness the fuel it needed to keep her like that. Irene would have to forgive herself for killing her kids in order to find the light, and I knew that was never going to happen. She'd done the unthinkable. What mother could forgive herself for that? She was doomed to live in darkness.

I tried to find my way back. I had no idea how to get out of there. I heard Melanie following behind me as I found the stream again. "Light those candles," I said over my shoulder.

"Not until you tell me what happened."

I spun around and looked down at the bag she was holding. With a wave of my hand, I scattered the candles on the ground and made them burn. I pointed the wand at Melanie. "Chant that spell, witch," I demanded.

The trees came back to life as Melanie finished the spell. The moon once again shone in the night, and I could smell the ocean and feel its breeze on my face. I smiled when I heard the willows whistling in the wind. My beautiful Salem was back.

"Welcome home, Thea," I whispered. I felt the wind in my hair and smiled. I pulled away the rubber band I always wore to hide my knotted mass and let my hair down. I ran my fingers through it, thankful for every knot I felt.

This was a very special moment for me. I was happy—happy with everything about myself. Irene had made me take a long look at myself. I saw the pathetic, self-loathing woman I really was. I had been brave my whole life, but a coward when it came to loving myself. So what if I was larger than most girls? That didn't change who I was. I was Thea Hawthorne Wade, the witch who was going to end this nightmare.

Melanie's sobs kind of ruined my self-discovery moment. I knew there was nothing I could say to make her feel better. "I'm sorry, Melanie," was all I could think of. I left her behind and began running out of Salem Willows. I suddenly couldn't get out of there fast enough. I wanted to see James and tell him how sorry I was for acting so foolishly all these years. I couldn't wait to throw my arms around him. No longer would I think myself beneath him. In fact, he was lucky to have me. I was a new Thea, and from this moment on, I would never be apart from him again.

Without watching for human eyes, I jumped over trees and cars. I refused to use the wand. I wanted—needed—to feel the air on my face. My heart raced as I rushed home to send James the signal to meet me. My reasons for sending the signal had changed. Now, I only wanted to be alone with him. I thought of all the years we had spent apart because of my fears. I had been so stupid. I was a powerful witch who had allowed a mere half-human witch to make her hide. What had I been so scared of? Why had I allowed Simon to take so much away from me? None of that mattered anymore. I would put my mistakes behind me and look ahead to the future. No spell or promise would change me again.

All the lights to my building were on when I arrived home. I wondered what everyone was doing up. Cory had been sleeping when I retrieved my wand earlier. I made my way inside and found Delia and Fish sitting on the couch in Cory's apartment, each with a cup of coffee in hand. Cory stood across from them, looking annoyed.

"It's about time," Delia hissed. "Where have you been?"

"Were you waiting up for me?" I asked. I couldn't wait to tell them what had happened. I knew they would figure it out when they looked into my eyes.

Delia got to her feet. "No, but you left Vera alone in your apartment. She woke us all up talking about Simon and how he wanted to get her."

"She told us what happened at the park," Cory added.

"And she got *that* one all scared," Delia said, pointing to Helena's room.

"Try calming down two hysterical witches," Fish said.

I felt bad for leaving Vera now. I hadn't realized how scared she was. "Where is she?"

"James took her home," Cory answered. "Javier and Joshua went with him."

"He took her home? But I thought she was scared."

Cory shrugged. "James managed to calm her, so she asked him to take her home."

That was odd. Why would Vera want to go home, where she would be alone? It didn't make any sense. I knew James, and he would have insisted she wait here for me.

"She was being so annoying," Delia continued. "All she wanted to do was stay in the room with Helena. We had to almost drag her out of there when Helena started screaming."

"Helena was screaming?" I asked.

Fish nodded. "I think Vera got her all scared with her talk about Simon coming to get her. But don't worry, Thea." He put his arm around Delia. "Delia told Vera we would make Simon think he would die if he touched her. We told her how it worked for James."

My heart sank when he said that. I began to get an uneasy feeling.

"It was the only way to shut her up," Delia said, rolling her eyes.

"Vera calmed down after that," Fish said.

I said nothing as I slowly walked to the bedroom where Helena was. I opened the door and found Helena curled up in a corner with her arms around her legs. She was rocking back and forth, mumbling something I couldn't make out.

"Helena?" I said softly.

Her head shot up. Her eyes were still full of fear. She crawled to my feet and wrapped her arms around them. "Don't let him take me," she cried.

Years of hatred drifted away as I looked down at her. She was a broken woman. All her beauty couldn't pull her out of the hell she was living in.

Compelled to comfort her, I squatted down and wrapped my arms around her. "It's okay, sweetie. No one is going to take you, I promise."

When she began mumbling again, I gently put my fingers under her chin and made her look at me. Her lips were moving, but I couldn't make out what she was saying.

I leaned in, holding her face closer to me. "What is it, Helena?"

She slowly leaned forward. "Simon is here," she whispered in my ear.

I felt my heart stop. I jumped to my feet, spun around, and ran out into the living room. "Where did they go?" I asked the others.

Delia looked at me, annoyed, and sat back down. "I told you, James and the boys took her home. They should be back shortly."

I ran across the room and grabbed her shoulders. "What else did you say to her?" I said, shaking her. "Did you tell her about my father?"

"What did I say to who?" she asked.

"Vera!" I shouted.

"You're hurting her," Fish said, pushing me away.

"Thea, what's going on?" Cory asked.

"Have you lost your mind?" Delia said.

I pulled out the wand. "Stick!" I yelled.

Delia dropped the coffee. "What's going on?"

I put the stick between my legs. "If Vera comes back here," I said, "kill her."

In an instant, Cory jumped on with me.

Delia's face went pale as she realized what was going on. "Simon?" she asked.

"He made himself look like Vera," I answered.

Fish pulled out his hooks, pushed Delia behind him, and looked around.

"I'm so sorry," Delia said, putting her hands over her mouth.

Cory was already on his phone. "Ciro, get over here, and bring Jason and Justin with you."

I waved my hand at the door, and we were off. "Call James," I said over my shoulder.

"Got it," Cory said as he pulled out his phone again.

I flew like a bullet over Salem as Cory waited for James to answer. I closed my eyes when he said there was no answer. I flew faster, heading straight to Vera's house. My heart leaped to my throat when I didn't see James's car there. I had hoped I was wrong and I would find James here, but the truth was hitting me right in the face.

I waved my hand at the front door, sending it right off its hinges. The smell of death hit me as soon as I flew in. It didn't take us long to find Vera lying on the floor.

"Oh no," Cory whispered.

I jumped off my stick and knelt down beside her. I could tell she had fought for her life. There were still strands of someone's hair clutched in her hand.

"Oh, Vera," I said when I saw what Simon had done to her. My hands were shaking as I removed the needles from her feet. I waved my hand and removed the rope from around her neck.

Cory knelt down beside me and pulled out the knife from her chest.

"Look what he did to her," I said as tears ran down my cheek. "I wasn't here to help her."

"I'm going to kill that animal," Cory said through his teeth.

I held her hand to my cheek. "I'm so sorry, Vera. I should have been here."

Cory and I froze when we heard footsteps coming from upstairs. Cory tapped me on the shoulder and motioned to the kitchen table. Someone had been making themselves at home. There were dirty plates where someone had been eating.

"Warlocks," Cory whispered.

How dare they make themselves at home while Vera lay on the floor dead? I got to my feet and looked up the stairs. Cory held out my stick to me.

"No. Give me the needles," I said with my eyes fixed on the stairs.

I heard the warlocks turning things over as we slowly walked up the stairs. Cory followed closely behind me, weapons at the ready.

I saw their feet first as we ascended. There were four of them, all in Vera's room, laughing and joking with each other.

"I like how the spell is making me stronger," one of them said.

"Yeah, and I think it's making you stupid, too," another one answered.

I held my hand up to Cory as they laughed.

"That damn spell hurts, but it's worth it," one said.

"How much bigger do you think we can get?" one of them asked.

"I don't know, but I can't wait to face that witch and see the look of shock on her face when her spells do nothing to us," another answered.

So that's how these warlocks have gotten so big. Simon is casting changing spells on them.

I didn't know what kind of spell Simon was using, but not even that was going to save these warlocks. I walked up the rest of the stairs and entered the room. They all froze when they saw us.

"Who has a look of shock now?" I said.

They began spitting spells into their hands, but I waved my hand before any of them could throw them. They dropped the spells as their bodies were thrust into the air. The spells burned through the wood floor and exploded downstairs. I waved my hand again, making them float above our heads. With a hint of a smile, I sent their shoes and socks flying across the room.

"Let's see if *these* will hurt you," I said, holding up the needles.

The blond warlock smirked. "I'm sure not as much as it hurt your friend," he answered.

Before I could move, Cory stepped forward, grabbed a needle from my hand, and thrust it into the bottom of the warlock's foot. The warlock gasped but didn't cry out in pain.

"Tell me where my friends are!" Cory yelled.

Holding in his pain, the warlock shot back, "I would rather die."

"I can arrange that," I said. I held up the rest of the needles and waved my hand.

The needles floated all around the warlocks. I waved it again and turned the few into thousands. The warlocks' eyes widened. The needles made clanging noises as they grew bigger and sharper.

"Where are my friends?" Cory asked again.

There was fear in the warlocks' eyes as the needles floated around their feet. They looked around at each other.

"Death?" the blond one said.

When they nodded and closed their eyes, I knew they weren't going to tell us. Cory and I stepped out of the room and closed the door behind us. Cory kept his eyes on the door until he heard them screaming. It was the same sound of agony I had once made. Cory smiled as their cries of pain echoed through the house. After a moment, there was silence.

Cory finally looked away from the door. "That was too easy a death for them, Thea."

"It was justice, nothing more," I answered.

Back downstairs, we lay Vera on the sofa, and I began to clean her up. I didn't want Sharron seeing her like this. I waved my hand and made all the bruises fade away, then I touched her chest and sealed the hole. Cory grabbed a blanket and put it over her.

I held her hand to my cheek. "Travel well, my friend."

"The boys, Thea," Cory said. "We have to go find them."

I nodded and looked back at Vera. "I'll get him, Vera. He'll die screaming."

I kissed her hand, and we jumped back on my stick and flew out the door. The night had become even colder. Salem seemed different somehow. The town I loved so much was in danger, I could feel it. Something bad was headed our way, and there was nothing I could do to stop it.

"Where are we headed?" Cory asked.

"I think I know where they are," I said, taking to the sky.

Cory was back on his phone. I sighed in relief when I heard him say, "William, it's me." Cory put the phone on speaker as he explained what was going on.

"Where is Thea?" my father asked. "Did Simon take her, too?"

"She's right here, William. She can hear you."

"I want to hear her voice," he said.

I slowed down. "Father, I'm here."

There was silence.

"William, she's talking to you," Cory said.

"It's about time, Thea," my father finally said.

I understood what he meant. He could hear the change in my voice. I don't know how I managed to smile. "I'm sorry it took so long, Father."

"No time for that now," he said. "Think straight and do what you must. He won't kill James right now—not until he can kill him in front of you. Come see me as soon as you can."

"Yes, Father."

He hung up, and Cory quickly dialed another number. I soon realized he was talking to Sharron. He told her about Vera. I could hear Sharron's sobs, but Cory was all business.

"Get the other witches together and head to my apartment," Cory said. "Wait there until we get back." He closed his phone and put his hand on my shoulder. "Don't panic, Thea. We'll find them."

But he was wrong. There was no panic in me, only anger. I could think clearly, control the worry in my heart for James and the boys. I had to push all that aside and think like Simon right now. I knew exactly where he was headed. "Hang on, Cory."

The trees whipped by us as we flew through the forest. The water hole wasn't far from here. The first thing Simon would do was try to take the rest of the leaves. I was mad at myself for not putting a spell on the rock, so it couldn't be moved. I couldn't understand how Simon had gotten into the hole without his spell killing him like it had the other warlock. Then I remembered something. When I thought he was Vera, she had mumbled something before jumping into the water hole earlier.

"He was breaking his spell," I said, putting it together.

The thought of Simon outsmarting me made me fly faster. I should have known he would pull something like this when I couldn't smell him anymore. He had no doubt found a spell that could hide his rotten scent from me.

"Thea, I'm going to fall," Cory said as he dug his hands into my waist.

I hadn't realized how fast I was flying. I finally slowed down when we got near the water hole.

I knew it was too late when I saw that the boulder sitting over the hole was gone. I closed my eyes. Simon now had the leaves.

"Check the hole, Cory."

He jumped off and ran to the hole. I wasn't expecting the leaves to be there, but I still had to check. I bit my lip as Cory looked inside.

"Nothing," he said. As Cory walked back to me, he stopped suddenly and looked down.

"What is it?" I asked.

He picked up a piece of paper and began reading it. His eyes widened, and his hands shook. He broke into a run. "He's going after Fish and Delia!" he yelled.

Within seconds, we were in the air.

Chapter 13
Wall of Fire

Spells were flying through the air as we got close to my apartment. It seemed all hell had broken loose. The house was surrounded by warlocks. I gasped when I saw Ciro and the others trying to fight off about forty of them.

"Hurry!" Cory shouted. He jumped off before I could even land and hurried to help Fish fight off a warlock that was dragging Delia away.

I flew over them and began waving my hand, sending as many warlocks as I could into the air. I saw two warlocks I recognized, Netiri and Toby, helping my friends fight. Netiri was swinging his katana and sending heads flying into the air.

"Simon is half human," he kept yelling.

I waved my hand and sent all the warlocks into the street. I waved it again and put a wall of fire in front of my loved ones. The warlocks pushed back, looking up to the sky to where I was. I flew down and jumped off my stick to face them alone as the fire burned behind me. I spun my stick around, and it turned into a sword. My friends began screaming my name, begging me to let them help me.

I could hear the cries of panicked humans running out of their homes. Police sirens echoed everywhere. It was too late to cast a spell; human eyes had already seen us. The police were yelling for us to drop our weapons. I waved my hand and put a wall of fire in front of them, buying us a little time. I looked at the warlocks and took note of their smaller build. It was obvious Simon hadn't cast his spell on them yet. As much as I wanted to kill them, I had to give them one last chance.

"Hear me out!" I yelled. "I don't want to kill any of you. No one has to die today."

"No one but you," someone shot back.

"Just give me a moment of your time," I said. "If you still want to fight after what I have to say, I'll give you the battle you want."

I heard only soft voices as they talked among each other. This was my chance.

"You came here today fighting for a lie," I began. "Simon has been using you. He's kept a secret from you—a secret Jack tried to tell you about."

Silence fell when I said Jack's name. Many of them had known Jack, who had been one of Simon's top men.

"He tried to tell you that Simon was half human," I continued.

There were gasps.

"Simon lied when he told you I had taken his powers. He never had powers. He's a witch, just like my friends. The spells he knows he learned from a wizard. The new spells he's teaching you are spells he's getting from the darkness. Simon is marked with the blood promise, and he plans on killing all of you when he gets what he wants."

The warlocks looked at each other.

"He made you hate humans," I continued. "You hate my friends because human blood runs through their veins. Ask yourselves—did you hate them before Simon came here and turned you against them?"

More silence.

"I have dear friends who are warlocks. The difference between them and you is Simon. Their minds were never poisoned by him. They have nothing against humans or my friends. Simon needed you to hate them, so he could control you. He had to give you a purpose to fight. He knew putting hate into your hearts would blind you to the truth. He knew greed would motivate you."

When no one answered, I went on.

"Why hasn't Simon cast his changing spell on any of you? I'll tell you why: because he no longer needs you. He sent you here today to die."

I saw that my words were having an effect on them. I knew what they needed to hear next.

"I know we've never gotten along, but I humble myself now and ask for your forgiveness. I wish I could take back everything I've done. I'm not that person anymore. The witch you see now wants no more blood spilled. I just want us to live in harmony."

"You lie, witch!" a warlock yelled.

I scanned the crowd and saw a red-haired warlock step forward. There was so much rage in his eyes. "Simon warned us you would spit out lies!" he yelled. "We're taking back Salem tonight, and there's nothing you can do about it."

"Is that what Simon told you to do?" I asked. "That sounds like an easy way to get rid of you, don't you think? Look around you." I pointed at the police. "Do you think these humans are going to let you? If I remember correctly, bullets can kill us."

"What if she's telling the truth?" said a dark-haired warlock.

"Don't listen to this witch," the red-haired warlock growled.

"But she's right. I never had anything against these witches until Simon came along. It was he who convinced us that we should hate them."

I heard murmuring voices as the warlocks began talking to each other. An older, gray-haired warlock stepped forward.

"Don't tell me you're falling for this, Mark," the red-haired warlock said to him. "Can't you tell she's lying?"

The one named Mark looked at me. "I've been watching this witch for months. When she had no powers, she was still able to command things to do her will. I saw it firsthand. If Simon once had powers like her, why can't he do that?" He looked back at the red-haired warlock. "Why isn't he ever fighting these battles with us?"

"She's telling the truth!" Netiri yelled from behind the fire.

The one named Mark looked my way. "My battle with you is done, witch."

"What?" the red-haired one yelled.

Mark looked at him. "I am no one's puppet. If you fight, you fight without me."

I was shocked when he threw down his weapon and walked into the darkness. My heart began racing when a few more warlocks did the same.

"Cowards!" the red-haired warlock yelled. "You think this witch has changed?"

A few more warlocks walked into the darkness without saying a word.

The red-haired warlock faced me as the remaining twenty warlocks stood behind him. He held up his weapon. "You planning on fighting us alone?" he hissed.

"She's not alone," I heard Sharron say.

I looked up and smiled when I saw all the witches floating above me on their branches. I had never seen a more beautiful sky. I looked over my shoulder at the fire. Sharron was right; I wasn't alone. This was our battle—and tonight we would all fight together.

I waved my hand and extinguished the fire. As my friends filed in beside me, I looked at the warlocks. Greed and evil raged in their eyes. All they could think about was power. They were willing to die for the possibility of becoming wizards. They had heard Simon's lie for so long that they didn't want to believe the truth.

I looked at Netiri and Toby, knowing this would be difficult for them. "You don't have to fight," I said to them.

Netiri held up his katana. "I wasn't asking for your permission, witch."

I looked at Toby. He pulled his sword from its sheath and nodded.

"It's time to take back Salem, my brothers!" the red-haired warlock yelled.

They began spitting spells into their hands. The sounds of striking matches filled the air. I almost had to laugh when they threw the spells our way. I put my hand up and flicked my finger, sending the spells right back to them. The warlocks jumped out of the way as the spells exploded.

The red-haired warlock glared at me. "You make my skin crawl, witch!" he spat.

At once, Fish's hooks flew through the air and sank into the warlock's chest. Fish pulled them back, taking the warlock's skin with him. "Problem solved!" Fish yelled.

There was a roar of laughter as the warlocks ran toward us. I froze when I spotted a long-haired warlock holding James's whip. I ran straight toward him as my friends fought around me. I looked under his feet and waved my hand. The warlock screamed in agony as the ground began to swallow him. He threw the whip and clawed at the ground, trying to pull himself out.

I picked up the whip and looked down at him. "Where did you get this?" I asked.

"Go to hell, witch."

I swung the whip, cutting away one of his arms. "Answer me!" I shouted, "Where is the man who had this whip?"

When he didn't answer, I swung and cut away his other arm. "Shall we try for your head next?" I asked.

His eyes grew wide with fear. "Simon has them at Fort Rodman," he answered.

I spun around and waved my hand at the remaining warlocks, sending an explosion of dust into the air. I had no time to stay and fight. I had to find James.

When my friends realized all the warlocks around them were dead, they looked at me.

"Why didn't you do that from the beginning?" Fish yelled.

Sharron landed a few feet away. Her eyes were red from crying. Donna was next to land. Soon all the other witches were on the ground. I could see that Sharron had given them the news about Vera.

"Where is she?" Sharron asked. "Where did you leave her?"

I knew she was asking about Vera. "She's home," I said, hanging my head.

"No," Delia cried.

Sharron sighed. "Go get that son of a bitch, Thea. Make him suffer until he begs for death."

I looked up. "He'll beg, I swear it."

She nodded. "Think of how he made your mother beg, and then rip his heart out."

We both looked away when we heard more sirens.

"Oh no," Sharron said as the local news vans started pulling up. "You'd better hurry." She jumped back on her branch, and the other witches followed her into the sky.

~ 169 ~

I turned and tossed James's whip to Ciro. "I need you, amigo."

"Go do what you must, Thea," he said. "I'll stay here and watch over things."

Jason ran to my side. "We are not hurting these officers, Thea."

"I wouldn't dream of it."

We looked around and saw chaos all around us. Police cars were pulling up in every direction. Helicopters were flying overhead.

"Go," Ciro said. "We'll start cleaning things up here."

I nodded and yelled, "Stick!" at my sword.

"I'm coming with you," Cory said.

There was no stopping him. I agreed, and we took to the sky again.

The frigid air helped keep my mind clear as we flew through the clouds. Cory and I began to discuss our theory about what Simon was up to.

"Why would he take them there?" Cory asked.

"I don't know. What did the note say?"

Cory pulled it out of his pocket, unfolded it, and held it in front of me. I read:

> *Looking for something, my sweet?*
> *I'm afraid you're too late. Your*
> *little game is over, but mine has*
> *just begun. Let's see how long it*
> *takes you to figure out where I am.*
> *I'll give you a clue: follow the*
> *dead bodies of your friends. Shall*
> *we see how many of them you can*
> *save?*

I looked away. I didn't like the tone of the note. Simon was angry with me. I had made a fool out of him again. My fear for my husband and friends was rising to another level. All I could do was think of James. I kept hearing my father's words in my head: *He won't kill James yet, not until he can kill him in front of you.* How I hoped those words were true. That would mean James was still alive.

I tried to calm the panic that was rising up inside me. Simon had something up his sleeve. I could feel it.

"Stay calm, witch," I said, closing my eyes.

I felt Cory's arm on my shoulder. "You can't get weak on me, Thea. Don't give in to that evil witch inside you. We need you right now."

I opened my eyes, realizing Cory had no clue. I came to a sudden stop, looked over my shoulder, and stared into his eyes. "I thought if anyone would notice, it would be you, Cory."

He looked at me, confused. After a moment, his jaw dropped. "Thea, your eyes. They're not glossy anymore."

We almost fell from my stick when he pulled me into his arms. "You did it, Thea. You broke the promise." I couldn't believe he hadn't noticed my eyes before. We'd been together almost all night. How could he not see?

"I didn't break it," I said, pulling away. "I still have to keep the promise. It's a long story."

He smiled. "Tell it to me some other day, witch. Let's go get our friends."

"Music to my ears," I said.

I grasped my stick and began flying to Fort Rodman. It was in the town of New Bedford, about two hours away. I'd been to New Bedford many times on my way to Fall River when I worked at the bakery. New Bedford had once been the number one fishing town in the country, and a thriving whaling city in its heyday. Norm loved to stop there and admire the old fishing boats that were docked at the pier. I had always thought the town had a certain charm to it. I wondered why Simon had chosen to go there.

"Do you know where this fort is?" Cory asked.

"Yes. Hold on!" I yelled over my shoulder.

The ride was about to get bumpy. I was about to break a new flying record. It wouldn't take me long to get there. Cory kept holding me tighter and tighter the faster I flew. All I could think about was James and the boys. I had to prepare myself for the worst. I couldn't panic and do something stupid, something I knew Simon was counting on.

I slowed down when we reached the town of New Bedford. We passed all the fishing boats that were docked at the pier. The town was quiet. The moon was shining off the water. I came to a stop when the fort came into view. I drew a breath, reached for Cory's hand, and squeezed it.

"I'm ready," he said.

Chapter 14
Fort Rodman

    This fort had always captivated me. It sat on the ocean's edge, its stone walls towering over the park. It had been closed to the public for years, but humans had made holes in its brick walls to look inside. The place was an old Civil War military fort built in the nineteenth century. Piles of dirt had been placed around its roof to absorb cannon attacks. Now the roof was covered in greenery, making it look so mysterious. The gun bays where the cannons used to be were sealed up. An old, beautiful lighthouse stood on top of it.

    I flew to one of the holes in the wall and looked in. I was surprised to see torches burning inside. The vast open courtyard within the fort had lush grass and many corridors branching off from it. Someone had obviously been maintaining the yard. I noticed four nooses hanging off a platform to one side.

Cory also looked in and noticed the nooses. "Why four?" he asked.

"Maybe we should go find out."

The doors to the fort were immense. A cross beam had been lain across the wooden main doors, barricading them from the public. Cory tried to lift it away, but it was way too heavy.

"Get behind me," I said. I waved my hand and sent the door flying across the courtyard.

As my stick turned into a sword, we cautiously walked inside. I didn't like the silence that filled this place. Where were the warlocks? Why hadn't they come storming out yet?

"What the hell is that?" Cory asked.

I followed his eyes. I tilted my head in confusion when I saw an enormous flat-screen TV hanging off one of the walls. "I'm not sure—" I began to say, but gasped when I realized what that meant. "They're not here, Cory. It's a trap."

Simon's voice rang out: "I didn't think you would find me so fast."

Cory flicked his arms and exposed his weapons. I raised my sword and looked around. We were back to back as we waited for Simon to walk out. I kept looking down the corridors, waiting to see his evil face.

"Face me, you coward!" I yelled.

"Is my angel upset with me?" Simon said.

I kept trying to figure out where his voice was coming from. "Why don't you come find out?" I answered.

"You look pretty when you're angry," he teased.

Cory was looking in every direction. "Do you see him yet?" he asked.

"No, but keep your guard up."

"I see you brought a friend with you," Simon said. "Good thing I hung an extra noose."

"Did you save one for yourself?" Cory shot back.

Simon's laughter echoed throughout the courtyard. "So, tell me, my angel," he said, "how long did it take you to figure out Vera was me?"

I didn't answer.

"And here I was, only hoping to find out what you were up to. I never dreamed you would hand the leaves right to me, much less your husband."

"Where is he, Simon?" I yelled.

His mocking laugh pierced my ears. "In time, my sweet, in time. You know, I should be angry with you. You were the last person I thought would have the leaves. You're a very clever witch indeed, my little dove. I have to say, it was very interesting to see you and James still so in love. I knew something was making your eyes turn brown again. You never fooled me for one minute. But here's something you didn't think I'd find out about: it turns out I *can* touch James, and he *will* die."

"If you hurt him," I yelled, "I'll skin you alive."

"Now why would I hurt my own bastard son?" he said in a deviant voice.

"Let me see him!" I shouted.

"It would be my pleasure, dearest."

~ 175 ~

Cory and I spun around when the TV behind us came to life. My heart leaped to my throat when I saw James and the boys on their knees, with six enormous warlocks standing over them. I tried running toward the screen.

"I wouldn't move if I were you," Simon said. "You don't want to upset me now, do you?"

I froze and looked back at the screen. James and the boys appeared bloodied and beaten. Their hands were bound behind their backs. They looked like kids next to these warlocks. I noted the warlocks' dark, glossy eyes and realized they had made a blood promise to Simon. James looked like he was barely alive. One warlock had to keep holding him up by the collar of his shirt.

I examined the room they were in and tried to memorize every detail to see if I could figure out where Simon was keeping them. The room was poorly lit and had no windows or doors. The walls looked like they were made of dirt. I could tell Simon was keeping them underground. He wouldn't be stupid enough to keep them near this fort. I noticed how red the dirt on the walls was. I looked closer and saw that the side of James's face was covered in that same red mud. The clay-like mud was also all over the boys' clothes. I sorted through my thoughts, trying to remember where I had seen that mud before. Panic wanted to rise up inside me, but I couldn't fall apart right now.

I gasped when the warlock holding onto James hit him over the head for almost falling over. "James!" I screamed.

"I'm afraid he can't hear you," Simon said. "Don't you just love modern technology?"

Cory stood frozen next to me, his eyes glued to Joshua and Javier. One warlock grabbed Joshua's head and made him look up. Cory closed his eyes at the sight of Joshua's face. It was clear they had been taking turns beating them half to death.

"Simon," I said, "I'll give you anything you want, do anything you ask of me. Please, just let them go."

I tried desperately to find Simon as he laughed again. "I'm afraid the time for deals is over, my sweet. We do things my way. *I* am holding all the cards now."

My eyes searched every corridor. If I tried to use my magic to find him, the warlocks would surely kill my loved ones. "What do you want?" I asked.

"I was hoping you would ask that," Simon answered. Suddenly a blue shawl was thrown to the middle of the courtyard from a corridor above. "Put it on," he ordered.

I closed my eyes in frustration. I knew that the moment I put it on, Simon would have the upper hand.

"Do it," Simon called out. "Or would you rather we cut your husband's throat?"

My eyes darted up to the screen. There, holding onto life, were three of my greatest loves. I looked down at the shawl again. I knew I had to do it.

When I reached for it, Cory grabbed my arm. "Please don't, Thea."

I couldn't look him in the eye. "I have to, Cory. He'll kill them." Cory released me, and I picked up the shawl.

"Tell me what to do, Thea," Cory said in a low voice.

I finally looked into his desperate eyes. "Pray, my friend." I swallowed thickly and wrapped the shawl around myself. I instantly felt myself getting weak.

I heard footsteps coming from one of the corridors across from us. Cory quickly got in front of me with his weapons up.

Three massive warlocks came out first, spells spinning in their hands. A look of shock came over Cory's face when he saw how big they were.

"What the hell?" he murmured.

They didn't look real somehow. Their skin had a strange, shiny look to it. It was as if they were made of plastic. Simon's spell was having a strange effect on them. It was as if the spell was more than their bodies could handle.

Simon stood behind them, slowly applauding. An evil smile spread across his face. His glossy eyes were darker than ever. "What a good girl," he said in a sarcastic tone. As he walked toward us, he appeared triumphant. He had me where he wanted me. He looked so cheerful, it almost made me sick.

The warlocks stopped and let Simon through. They kept their eyes on Cory, ready to throw their spells if he moved.

Simon got a surprised look on his face when his eyes met mine. "Well now, look at you," he said, tilting his head. "You're stronger than I thought, my dear. Trying to fight the dark side, are you?"

I glanced away. He didn't know. He thought I was only trying to fight the promise.

Cory glared at him as he stood a few feet from us. "I'm going to kill you," Cory growled.

Simon's smile grew even wider. "Go ahead," he answered. "The instant you move, your friends will lose their heads."

Cory's eyes shifted to the screen.

"Wondering where they are?" Simon asked. "Say hello to them. They can see you." He pointed to several cameras installed around the courtyard.

I looked around and saw that he had cameras everywhere. His men were watching our every move.

Cory's eyes were on fire as he glared at Simon again. "If you kill them, you're going to taste my blade."

The three warlocks took a step forward, but Simon put his hand up. "At ease, my brothers. He's not going to let his friends die."

I fell to my knees as the shawl drained me of my energy. Cory tried helping me to my feet, but Simon took one giant step and kicked him away.

"Cory, don't," I said when he tried going after Simon. "Think of the boys."

Cory froze. He was fighting against himself. He looked at Simon and the warlocks with fury in his eyes.

"Please don't, Cory," I pleaded.

"Yes, Cory," Simon said in his most evil voice. "Think of the boys."

I was trying to force myself to breathe when Simon moved closer to me. He stood over me with a look of anger on his face.

"Look at me, witch," he growled.

When I looked up, Simon made a fist, took a deep breath, and struck me across the face. One warlock lunged forward and kicked Cory in the chest when he tried to help me. Cory made a horrible sound as the warlock knocked the wind out of him and sent him flying a few feet before he hit the ground.

Simon grabbed my hair. "That's for hiding the leaves from me, witch. And this," he said, striking me again, "is for lying to me about James."

Cory jumped to his feet.

"Cory, no," I managed to say.

A dark-haired warlock kicked him again. Cory flew twenty feet across the courtyard and crashed into the platform. It took him a moment to catch his breath. I knew he was about to go after the warlock.

"The boys!" I cried.

The warlocks laughed as Cory began pounding his fist on the ground in frustration. I was shocked to see him move. That blow should have shattered his chest.

Another warlock grabbed Cory's hair, dragged him back, and threw him next to me like he was a rag doll. I could see Cory almost convulsing from the anger that was consuming him.

Simon pushed me aside and looked down at him. "So this is Cory," he said, walking around him. "You have good taste, my dear. He's a very handsome man. Too bad he's going to lose his pretty face."

"What do you want, Simon?" I asked, trying to divert his attention away from Cory.

Simon looked at me. "Isn't it obvious, my angel? I want the same thing I've always wanted—your powers—and to be king, of course."

"Take them," I answered. "I've already promised to marry you."

Simon moved closer, bent down, and brushed the hair from my face. "I'm afraid that is no longer enough, my dear. You've given me more options now."

I looked into his eyes. "What else can you possibly take from me?"

He looked at James, then back at me. "I can think of something."

"I beg you," I cried, "please don't kill them."

Simon laughed. "I like it when you beg, witch."

"You bastard!" Cory shouted.

Cory flew back when a warlock kicked him across the face. They began taking turns kicking him as I screamed for them to stop. I could hear bones breaking as the warlocks kicked him over and over again. I tried to drag myself across his body, but the shawl had done its damage.

Simon reached down and grabbed my hair. "They're only having fun," he said, dragging me away from them. "Let's see what your precious Cory can do."

"Please stop them, Simon," I pleaded. I had to close my eyes as the warlocks beat Cory half to death.

Simon took hold of my face and made me look at them. "You caused this, witch. You *will* watch your friend die."

I pulled my chin from Simon's grip and glared up at him. "If he dies, you're next."

Simon struck me across the face again, sending my head pounding to the ground. He reached down and dragged me back to my knees. "I said, look at him," he hissed.

I looked at Cory, who was reaching his limit. Simon only laughed as Cory's rage escaped from his lips. He sounded like an angry lion roaring as he was hunted.

I put my head down and cried when Simon finally called his goons off. They backed away from Cory as he lay moaning. I couldn't look at him. My heart would break if I saw how badly he was hurt.

"You're all going to die," I said, shaking my head.

Simon squatted down. I felt his fingers under my chin. He had the biggest smile on his face when he made me look at him. "I was about to say that to you, my sweet."

I looked into his dark eyes. "You're going to die screaming, Simon."

His smile faded. He rose to his feet, but my eyes followed him.

"I'm going to pull your heart out so fast," I continued, "you'll still see it beating in my hand. But before that happens, I'm going to torture you until you beg me to kill you."

His eyes narrowed. "I don't think you're in any position to threaten me, witch."

"It's not a threat," I answered. "It's your future."

He looked at his warlocks. "Bring the ropes we soaked today. Tie this witch up." I had scared him.

One warlock gasped when he saw Cory moving. I had to admit, I was also shocked. I thought they had broken every bone in his body.

Simon didn't seem to notice what was going on. He was too busy keeping an eye on me. "I said, bring me the ropes!" he shouted.

"But Simon, he's still moving," the dark warlock said.

"I don't care! Bring me the ropes."

Simon seemed relieved when a warlock walked toward me with the ropes. I felt the life being drained out of me as they tied the ropes around my hands and feet. I could hardly bring myself to take a breath. I felt as if my chest was caving in as I struggled for air. I kept telling myself to stay focused. I could hear the warlocks beating Cory every time he tried to come and help me.

"Now, where were we?" Simon said as he squatted back down.

I wanted to close my eyes and sleep. My body wanted nothing more than to give up. I kept looking toward Cory; I couldn't understand how he was still moving. Only his face showed signs of the beating he was taking. "Please, leave him alone," I cried.

Simon finally called them off. "I don't understand your love for these disgusting humans," he said. "You are above them, my dear. Don't you know that?"

I stared into his eyes. "There is only one human I'm above, and that's you."

Simon glanced over at his men and smiled when he realized they hadn't heard me. He leaned into me. "I wouldn't talk about such things, my angel. Your friends may lose their tongues."

"What are you afraid of, Simon? That I've already told all your other men?"

His eyes grew wider. He grabbed a handful of my hair. "I didn't realize you were so informed about my past," he whispered in my ear. "But if you say one more word about that, I'm going to burn your friends alive." He pushed me away. "It's a good thing I changed my plan, isn't it?"

I looked into his eyes, wondering what he meant.

He smiled. "I am always one step ahead of you, witch. I haven't gotten this far by taking chances. I leave no stone unturned."

"There's one stone you forgot about, Simon."

"Really? And what stone is that?"

"You'll know when it hits you right over the head."

Simon started laughing. "I think I have all the power I need right up there," he said, pointing up at James. "But don't worry, my angel," he added in a soft voice. "I'm not going to kill you or your friend." He turned to Cory. "I'm not finished with you yet. You see," he said, stroking my face, "there's something I want you to bring me. Something that will solve all my problems."

I could hardly keep my eyes open as he put his face inches from mine. "I've been driving myself crazy wondering how to get around this, but I finally have the answer." He leaned in even more and whispered, "I want you to bring me Wendell's head."

I felt my head spinning when I heard his words.

He slowly backed away and smiled. "I can't go into Magia knowing he's waiting for me, can I? You see, my angel, I know you've been going there. I have no doubt you've been setting a trap for me and my men. I've been trying to figure out who's been helping you, but as it turns out, you've made things easier for me. I don't have to storm Magia with the leaves anymore—I've got you. I always said you could fight an army alone. I guess we will see if that's true." He rose to his feet. "I'm afraid I've been keeping secrets as well. I don't know if you're aware of this, but I haven't kept a little promise I made. Although it's true I planned on keeping it, being king sounds so much better. That, my dear, I owe to you. You handed me what Wendell never could. I never imagined I would realize my dream of taking it all away from him." He looked up at the screen and then at me. "And I want you to know something. I wouldn't plan any tricks, if I were you. I am well prepared for anything you throw my way. Besides, I don't think you want to anger me any further. You see, I've got a few tricks of my own." He winked at me playfully, sending chills down my spine.

I drew a breath. I didn't like the cheerful smile on his face. My heart began racing when he walked over to the screen and clasped his hands behind his back.

"I'll show you one of my tricks now," he said over his shoulder. He looked at one of the cameras and nodded.

My eyes darted up to the screen as one of the warlocks standing behind Javier stepped forward. James struggled to free himself when the warlock stood over Javier and grabbed his hair. Joshua fought his restraints like an enraged animal.

"No!" I screamed.

Simon nodded again, and without hesitation, the warlock pulled out a knife and thrust it through Javier's heart.

A heartbreaking sound of anguish escaped Cory's lips as he jumped to his feet. Shocked, the warlocks began throwing their spells at him, but they did nothing to stop Cory. He ran toward Simon as warlock spells bounced off his back. I noticed every time a spell hit him, his tattoos glowed and healed the area in an instant. Cory continued running toward Simon like a madman.

I had to search deep inside myself to stop him. If he touched Simon, the rest of my loved ones would die. I closed my eyes and imagined Cory falling, hoping my mind would be enough to stop him. When I opened my eyes, he was on the ground. I kept my eyes on him, forcing my mind to drag him back.

Cory kept clawing at the ground, trying to fight my magic. "I'm going to kill you!" he yelled at Simon.

Joshua sobbed with pain as the warlock kicked Javier's body in front of him. James stopped fighting and began shouting something at the warlocks. I couldn't hear what he was saying, but the warlocks only laughed at him. It was strange how calm I was. Although my heart was filled with anguish and pain, my mind was clear. I had to concentrate on keeping my friends and husband alive.

I managed to drag Cory back again. The pain on his face was breaking my heart into a million pieces. I tried to crawl to him. "Cory," I cried.

When Cory reached for me, a warlock threw a spell, hitting Cory in the arm. Cory glared at him when the spell bounced right off him. A confused look washed over the warlock's face. He threw another one, and it, too, bounced right off him.

The warlock reached down and tore open Cory's shirt. His jaw dropped when he saw that Cory was covered in tattoos. "He's wearing a spell?" the warlock said, amazed.

It was then I realized why they were getting the tattoos. They weren't trying to protect themselves from me; they were trying to protect themselves from the warlocks. My father knew Simon was teaching them wizard spells, and this was the only way he knew to help them. I looked up at the screen again, wondering why James had gotten so many.

"As you can see," Simon said, "that spell didn't stop a knife."

I closed my eyes again when Cory tried getting to his feet. "Down," I whispered.

I heard Simon's laughter as Cory hit the ground again. "If he gets up again, just kill him," Simon ordered.

I looked at Cory. "Please," I begged him as our eyes finally met. "He'll kill them."

Cory slammed his blades into the grass and began pounding his head on the ground. His veins were bulging from the anger that was consuming him. He let out a loud roar as he fought to keep himself down. I breathed a sigh of relief when he finally lay his head on the ground and began to sob.

I looked at the screen again. Joshua was inconsolable. James leaned his head over Javier's body and sobbed. I closed my eyes as I fought against the rage I was feeling. I wanted to tear Simon into a million pieces. His death would not be quick. I would pull him apart, limb from limb, as he screamed from the pain. But I had to stay calm. I still didn't know where he was keeping James and Joshua.

"And now for the final show of the day," Simon said, walking back to us. He stood over me, his dark eyes beaming with happiness. "There's a spell I need you to cast, my sweet. We can't be together until you break all ties now, can we?"

I already knew what spell Simon was talking about. He wanted me to cast the divorce spell. It was the only way I could marry him.

"I'm waiting," Simon said in a jubilant voice.

I looked at the ground. "You'll have to remove the shawl," I said.

"Do you think I'm a fool?" he answered. "I've been watching you. You can chant that spell just fine." He looked up at one of the cameras. "Maybe I'll cut a head off this time."

"Cast it!" Cory shouted at me.

I looked down and began chanting the spell. "I break the bond that sealed our life, I crush the years I was your wife. I turn my back and cast my spell, I send our love right into hell."

Streams of energy began leaving my body and funneling into the middle of the courtyard high above my head. The sound of shattering glass filled the air as the streams of energy disappeared.

I looked at the screen. James was shaking his head. He'd heard the same sound I had.

"Well done," Simon cheered, and added with a mocking voice, "I hope you don't look this sad on our honeymoon." He squatted down in front of me. "You have two days to kill Wendell and bring me his head. If you are not back here in two days, I'll kill them both. And I promise you this—their deaths will not be

~ 188 ~

quick. I will torture them until there is nothing but bones left. And if you don't have the ring and the crystal with you, I will set them on fire. And remember, no tricks." He got to his feet again. "I'll be waiting, my pet." He signaled his men to follow and disappeared into one of the corridors.

The screen suddenly went black. Silence filled the courtyard again.

I hung my head and began sobbing.

Cory pulled the shawl off me and flung it across the courtyard. His body was covered with burn marks where the spells had hit him. He cut away the ropes from my hands and feet. "I'm going to kill that son of a bitch," he said as he flung the ropes across the courtyard.

All I could do was look at the ground. There were no words I could say to comfort him. His heart was broken. There was nothing I could do to change that.

I looked up when he slapped his hands to his head. "Javier," he said, breaking down.

I reached over and tried to gather him in my arms. I was shocked when he slapped my hands away. He grabbed my shoulders with force and shook me. "Now you listen to me, witch," he said through his teeth. "I'm going with you into Magia. I'm going to make sure you bring back that head. If you try and leave me behind, I will never forgive you."

"I wasn't going to stop you."

He pushed me away and jumped to his feet. He looked up at the screen, wiped away his tears, and kicked the sword to me. "Let's get the hell out of here."

Chapter 15
Speckles of Light

The ride home seemed so long as we flew back to Salem. I kept thinking of Javier. My heart was aching. I kept picturing his face, seeing him smile as he talked about his latest conquest.

Cory and I talked about how we would break the news to Delia and Fish.

"Let me tell them," Cory said in a shaky voice. He was blaming himself, and probably me, too. There was no magic in the world that could have changed things. Simon had played his cards right. He'd put me in a position where I couldn't do anything to save Javier.

The anguish was killing me. I kept imagining what those animals could be doing to James and Joshua. Simon had no intention of letting them live. He couldn't wait to take it all away from me. Cory was probably thinking the same thing.

He lay his head on my back and wrapped his arms around my waist. "We have to save them, Thea. Please tell me you can do this."

I looked straight ahead when he said that. The only thing I could think of was talking to my father. I didn't want to tell Cory I had no idea what I was going to do. I had never fought a wizard before. What if I lost? "I can do it," I lied.

He let out a big sigh. "We'll have to go look for Javier's body when this is over. I'm not leaving him like that," he said, breaking down.

I looked for a spot to land and threw my arms around Cory the moment we were on the ground. We cried in each other's arms. I knew Cory's pain was tearing him apart. He'd been with the boys for so long, he was like a father to them.

"I failed him, Thea," he moaned.

I held him tighter. "No, you didn't. Don't you ever say that again."

"He was going to get a tattoo on his chest tomorrow," he said, shaking his head.

"That would have only stopped a spell," I said. "It wouldn't have saved him from that dagger."

"I let him die," he cried. "I let him die!"

"There was nothing we could have done."

"It's my fault. I'm the one who told them to go with James when he left to take Vera home. I shouldn't have done that." He pulled away from me and hit a nearby tree. "I want Simon dead!" he shouted.

That was something I could promise. "He'll die, Cory. I give you my word."

He looked at me. "I want to be the one who kills him. I want to do the same thing to him that he did to Javier."

"I can't promise you that."

He stepped up to me. There was so much anger in his eyes. "You can, and you will, witch. This is your fault. You owe it to me. Sammy and Javier would still be alive if it weren't for you. You brought us into this nightmare. You don't get to live happily ever after without them."

My eyes spilled over as his words cut through my heart. "Maybe we should leave now," I said, turning away.

I kept my back to him as I tried to hide my tears. I knew it was only his pain making him talk that way. He knew I would have traded places with Javier in an instant. There was only one person to blame here, and that was Simon. I wiped my tears away as I heard Cory sigh.

"I'm sorry, Thea. I shouldn't have said that. I didn't mean it, I swear."

I turned and faced him. "We'd better get going now."

Frustrated, he moved closer and put his arms around me. "I'm so stupid sometimes."

I wrapped my arms around his waist. "It's okay, old friend. No harm done."

He sighed. "How is this going to end, Thea? Tell me it will end with us saving our friends."

I looked up into his green eyes. I had to tell him the truth. "I don't know, Cory. I don't even think I'll make it back from Magia alive."

"You mean you don't think *we'll* make it back alive, right?"

I didn't answer. How could I expect him to die with me?

"Together, old friend," he said. "If we die, we die together."

I looked down at his arm and ran my fingers along his tattoos. There wasn't a scratch on him. The burn marks were already gone. I looked back into his eyes. "Together, old friend."

He backed away. "Come on, let's go kick some wizard ass."

I tried to keep myself together as we flew home. I felt myself about to come unhinged. There was panic in my heart for James. I couldn't imagine my life without him. If he died, I wanted to die with him. Would I ever get a chance to kiss him one last time? The thought scared me.

Simon was going to suffer for this. If I did anything before I died, it would be to torture him before I killed him.

Salem was quiet and peaceful as we flew over the town. There wasn't a single human outside as we passed the streets below. Things seemed so calm. There were no sirens, no humans running around and screaming. It was as if the town was sleeping.

I saw Jason standing guard in the yard as we approached my apartment. Delia was sitting on the porch with Fish. The two warlocks, Netiri and Toby, were also there.

"What are the witches doing?" Cory asked.

I looked around and saw them flying over Salem, chanting and casting spells. "Erasing human memories," I answered.

Delia ran across the yard when we landed. She stopped dead in her tracks when she saw the anguished look on Cory's face. "Cory?" she said nervously.

The others soon filed in behind her. "Where are the guys?" Fish asked.

Cory hung his head. I did the same as Fish looked at me.

"No," Delia said, stepping back.

"Look at me, Cory," Fish said. "Tell me they're okay."

Cory wouldn't look up.

Delia shook her head. "Please, no."

"Where are they?" Fish yelled. "Are they all dead?"

"Just Javier," Cory said, never looking up.

Delia burst into a sob as Fish gathered her in his arms. "It's my fault," she kept saying.

"It's no one's fault," Cory said. "I don't want everyone blaming themselves for what happened. And it won't help matters if we start blaming each other."

I could see the rage in Fish's eyes. He looked at Cory as Delia cried in his arms.

"Simon?" Fish asked.

Cory nodded.

Fish made a fist. His face turned red as tears streamed down over his cheeks. "Where is he?" he asked.

"No," Delia said, holding him tighter. "I can't take this anymore."

Fish pushed her away, his eyes fixed on Cory. "I don't know about you, Cory, but I'm going after him."

"What are you doing?" Delia screamed.

"I'll come with you," Ciro said.

"So will I," Jason added.

Cory stepped forward. "You think this isn't killing me?" he yelled, his face wet with tears. "They killed him right in front of me. I had to watch him die on a monitor and do nothing. It was a trap. Simon had them somewhere else. He'll kill Joshua and James if we do anything stupid."

There was silence. All that could be heard were Delia's sobs.

Fish pulled her into his embrace again and closed his eyes. "It's okay, baby. It's going to be okay."

Cory ran his hand through his hair. "Listen, I want you all to pack your bags. Leave Salem, and don't come back until we call for you. I'm not going to lose anyone else."

"What?" Fish said in disbelief. "You want us to run and hide?"

"No," Cory answered. "I want you to stay alive."

Fish pulled away from Delia and walked up to Cory. "Since when did you start thinking of me as a coward?"

"It's not like that, Fish," Cory replied. "Simon still has Joshua and James. I won't have him capturing you and giving him more power over us. My only concern is keeping you and Delia safe and away from him. He'll use anyone in order to hurt Thea. I'm not giving Simon any more ammo."

"He's not going to let them live, Cory," Fish said. "You know that."

~ 195 ~

There was silence again as Cory tried to find the words to explain what we had to do. "We have a chance to save them," he said. "Thea and I have to go somewhere. If we don't come back in two days, I want you to promise me you will get the hell out of here."

Fish studied Cory's eyes as he spoke. He looked at me, but I looked away from him. I didn't want him to know there was a possibility we wouldn't be coming back. But Fish wasn't fooled for one second.

"I'm coming with you," he said. "He was my friend, too."

"Fish, no," Delia cried.

Delia's tears did nothing to change Fish's mind. "I'm sorry, Delia, but I won't be able to live with myself if I stay behind," he said.

She looked down, knowing he was right. "Let me come with you," she pleaded.

Fish gathered her in his arms. "Listen, I need you to stay here, okay? You're carrying something very precious to me. I don't want anything to happen to either one of you."

Delia stared up into his eyes, shocked by his words. She looked down at her stomach and back into his eyes.

Fish smiled. "Besides, who's going to tell my kid what a badass their father was?"

Delia was speechless.

Fish ran his fingers along her face. "I love you, Delia. You'll never know the amount of happiness you've given me."

Delia threw her arms around him. "Please don't go."

"I'll come back to you, baby. I give you my word."

I looked at Cory. No words were needed to know that we both agreed Fish would not be coming with us. He would forgive us one day.

"Fish," I said, laying my hand on his back, "why don't we bring Delia with us and leave her with my father? She'll be safe there."

He nodded and picked Delia up in his arms. "I'll go pack some of her things," he said and headed into the house with her. Cory and I watched him carry her in.

"So we're agreed?" Cory asked.

I knew he was talking about leaving Fish behind. "Yes."

"Good. I'll go get Helena, so we can bring her to your father's home as well."

I turned to the others as Cory walked inside. Netiri and Toby had expressions of shock on their faces.

"Did you say your father?" Netiri asked.

"Yes."

They looked at each other.

"I thought he was dead," Toby said.

I smiled. "You thought wrong."

"I don't understand," Netiri said.

"You're not supposed to," I said, turning on my heels.

I ran up to my apartment to change clothes. When I came back down, I found Cory in Helena's room, carefully wrapping her in a blanket. She looked tired, her hair disheveled.

~ 197 ~

"I'm going to take you somewhere safe, okay?" Cory said soothingly to her.

Helena said nothing in reply and only looked at him as he bent down and reached for her shoes.

"Do your feet still hurt?" he asked.

She shook her head.

He gently slipped on her shoes and rose to his feet. Helena's eyes followed him as he put on his coat. When he picked Helena up, she closed her eyes, sighed, and lay her head against his chest.

Ciro was standing behind me when I moved out of Cory's way.

"I'll be waiting in the living room," Cory said.

I leaned my head against the wall and closed my eyes. What was I going to do? I kept thinking of James and Joshua. I couldn't fail them.

Ciro put his hand on my shoulder. "I don't know where you're going," he said, "but I want you to know I'll watch over your friends."

I turned and threw my arms around him.

"We'll find him, you'll see," Ciro said.

I held him tighter. I didn't want to tell him that I needed someone to hold me right now. The chances of me killing a wizard were close to zero, but I couldn't bring myself to say those words out loud.

Helena was like a zombie as Cory put her into his truck. "Why don't you sit with her?" he suggested to me.

I nodded and got into the back seat with her. Delia was still crying when she and Fish jumped in the front seat with Cory. Jason hopped into Ciro's car with the others, and they followed behind us as we drove to the mansion.

"What about the witches and Salem?" Fish asked.

Cory and I looked at each other in the rearview mirror.

"They'll be safe, Fish," Cory answered, "for two days, anyway."

"Why? What happens in two days?" Fish asked.

Cory glanced at me in the mirror again. I knew what we were both thinking. There was no telling what Simon had planned if we failed. I looked down at Helena. Her eyes were empty. Despite the horrified look on her face, she still looked beautiful. Her golden hair fell across her face, making her look like an angel. I wondered if she would be a different person once she came out of her torment.

"How is she?" Cory asked.

It was then I noticed his concern for her. He kept checking on her in the rearview mirror. He'd also been staying in her room ever since I brought her to his apartment. Could it be he was falling for her? I found it hard to believe that someone like Helena could steal his heart away. Cory didn't have patience for arrogant, conceited women like her.

"Is she awake?" he asked.

Maybe I was wrong. "She's just staring into space," I answered.

I looked out the window as we approached the mansion. The entire house was dark, with the exception of a single candle burning in my father's room. I leaned forward when I noticed that the gates to the mansion were open. Something was odd. I didn't like the feeling I was getting. Then I gasped when I saw the front doors to the house hanging off the hinges.

Before Cory could stop, I jumped out of the truck and stormed into the foyer. My feet immediately sank into something on the floor, and I fell down. It was too dark to see what it was, but it felt like a pile of dirt. I staggered to my feet and waved my hand at the lights.

I gasped when I saw what I had fallen into. The floor was knee-high in dust. It was everywhere, piles and piles of it, scattered all over the house.

"Your Highness?" I heard Porteus say.

I looked toward the stairs. Porteus stood with an enormous sword in his hand. He wasn't in human form anymore. His owl-like face gazed down at me as his leathery tail whipped around. Now I understood why he had all the lights off; he didn't need light to see in the dark. I looked down at the dust again.

"Warlocks," he said flatly.

I gasped. "My father?"

"He's fine," Porteus assured me.

The house looked like a war zone. There wasn't an inch that wasn't covered in warlock dust—except behind Porteus, that is. The dust ended at his feet. Everything behind him was clean and dust free. He had guarded my father with his life. Not a single warlock had gotten past him.

"How many?" I asked, amazed.

He ruffled his feathers. "A hundred or so," he said proudly. "They don't fight very well, Your Majesty. They seem to rely on their spells to do all the work."

"Why did they come here?"

"They were searching for the leaves, Your Majesty."

Cory and Fish ran in, weapons at the ready.

"What the hell?" Fish said. "Did someone dump a truckload of dust in here?"

"Where is my father?" I asked Porteus.

He looked upstairs. "He's in his room with the boy."

"Steven," I said and ran up the stairs.

A soft ringing sound was coming from behind my father's door. I put my ear to the door and heard voices.

"What happened next?" Steven asked.

"All the dragons and wizards became friends," my father answered.

"Tell me another story," Steven begged.

I knocked on the door and walked in.

A wide-eyed Steven jumped to his feet. "Sister!" he yelled, running into my arms.

All noise outside the room was gone. There was only the soft, pleasant ringing coming from the candle. I smiled at my father, knowing what he had done. He didn't want Steven to hear the commotion downstairs as Porteus slaughtered the warlocks.

My father rose to his feet. I noticed the door to his secret room was open. It was a room he used to remind himself where he had come from. He'd always told me how human air would weaken a wizard's memory, turning them human if they forgot where they came from. I'd wondered if that was the reason he never went outside. That was still a big mystery to me.

Speckles of light streamed out from the room, the same speckles that carried me into Magia. At least, that's what they looked like.

"I missed you," Steven said, squeezing me.

I squatted down. "I missed you, too, sweetie. And you know who else is here? Auntie Delia and Fish are downstairs."

"Really? Can I go down and see them?"

"Steven," my father said, "why don't you go wait for them in your room. I'm sure they'll be up shortly."

Steven nodded and ran out of the room.

I rose to my feet and met my father's gaze. He studied my eyes, and a look of sadness followed. No words were needed for him to see what had happened.

"He was a good boy," my father said, shaking his head.

"I don't understand," I said. "I saw his future. I saw him married with kids."

He took a deep breath. "The future can change, Thea. I've always told you that. Nothing is certain. You must accept what is."

I wanted to run into my father's arms, to cry and tell him that I had no idea what to do. I was ashamed for him to know that fear was growing in my heart. I wasn't scared about what I had to do; I was scared for James and my friends. I didn't want to fail them—I couldn't fail them. I swallowed my fear.

"He still has James," I said. "I have no idea where Simon is keeping him. I fear he's already killed them." I couldn't believe I had just said those words.

"Yes, I know," my father said. "I've been trying to locate them, but my mind is too weak."

"Is Simon going to kill them?" I asked, not really wanting to know the answer.

My father didn't look me in the eye. My heart sank. He didn't know the answer to that question. I could see it in his eyes—he really didn't know. It was clear now that I would have no choice. I would have to face Wendell.

"I'm going into Magia, Father, and you can't stop me."

He looked at me. "I wasn't going to. I don't think you have a choice now."

"So, you know what Simon wants?"

He nodded. "I think you should bring it to him at once."

Huh? He made it sound so easy, as if I could just stroll into Magia and ask Wendell for his head.

"Father, I'm not sure if you understand—"

"I understand perfectly," he cut in.

I stared at him, confused. Why wasn't he worried? He seemed perfectly at ease. "I don't think you do. I have no idea how I'm going to kill Wendell."

"Who said you were going to kill him?" He put his hands behind his back.

Now I was really confused. "Father, Simon wants his head."

"Yes, and you should bring it to him."

I shook my head. "I'm sorry, but I don't understand."

"Perhaps you will understand this: Wendell is not going to die. His punishment is for me to give, not you. This started because of him, and I will be the one who ends it."

"Then how am I supposed to bring what Simon wants?"

"I'm more worried about finding James and the boy, Thea. What Simon wants is easy."

"What? How can you say that? I've never fought a wizard before."

"I believe Simon asked for a head, not a dead body, correct?"

My face twisted with confusion. What was he up to? I was still trying to make sense of what he was saying when more speckles of light started coming out of his secret room. They floated around his head, almost whispering in his ear.

My father leaned in, as if he were listening to them, and nodded. "Yes, I will ask her at once."

Who was he talking to?

"Thea, can you please grab that blanket and wrap it around yourself?" He pointed to the bed.

"What? Why?" I asked, more confused than ever.

"They can feel you," he explained. "You're hurting them."

"Them?"

He motioned to the bed. "The blanket, please. Put it on." As I wrapped the blanket around myself, he said, "Yes, this is her."

"Who are you talking to?" I asked.

He motioned toward the secret room. I warily walked over. My jaw dropped when I saw the leaves I had given James in the room. I quickly realized they were the source of the speckles. They weren't underwater like Simon had had them. Here, my father had them hanging from a small plant. They clung to it as if trying to root themselves into it.

"Don't get too close," he warned. "They don't like it when you hurt them."

"You can talk to them?"

He stood next to me and looked into the room. "Yes. I discovered that when James brought them home earlier. I don't have enough energy to hurt them. I was actually able to hear them because of that. It was quite an amazing discovery."

I looked at the leaves again. "What are they saying?"

"They want to go home, of course. They don't like it here, so I promised them you would take them back to Magia. We won't be destroying them as we planned."

"What?" I said, snapping my head up. "They'll kill me."

He looked at me from the corner of his eye. "Would we be standing here if that were true?"

I looked at the leaves again. I noticed that every time they shook, they sent speckles of light into the air straight at my father. He would lean in, smile, and nod his head to them.

"What did they just tell you?" I asked, amazed.

"They want me to show you how to stop hurting them, so you can take them home."

Chapter 16
The Wand

My father blew out the candle as I looked into his secret room. I wondered how I could possibly take the leaves back to Magia. Just being near them would make me feel weak. How was I supposed to take them without them killing me?

"They're not going to kill you," my father said. "In fact, they are going to help you."

"How do you know that?" I asked.

He walked over to his desk and pulled out a box. I had seen this box before. He kept leaves in it, the same gold leaves the boys had once taken. My father had given them those leaves the first time we had gone into Magia. He said the dragons wouldn't hurt them if they ate these leaves. I remembered how their skin had taken on a soft, pearl-like look after they ate them.

"Do you remember these?" he asked as he held one of them up.

"Yes. They made the boys smell funny, so the dragons wouldn't hurt them."

He looked at the leaf. "Yes, but today I found out what they can do to you."

"Do to me?"

He held it out. "Eat it. I will show you."

I took the leaf from him and slowly put it in my mouth. It had a very sweet taste as I chewed it. I swallowed and waited for its effect. At first, I didn't feel any different, and my skin wasn't changing. Then I felt a soft tingling all over my skin. I looked at my arm and couldn't see any changes in it, but I could feel a certain numbness all over my body.

My father reached over and pulled the blanket away from me. "Walk into the room," he ordered.

I wasn't expecting him to say that. What if this didn't work? Who was going to pull me out?

"We're running out of time, Thea. You need to leave soon, and they want to go home."

I drew a steadying breath and walked in.

My father's room was so magical. I could hear the roar of a waterfall that wasn't there. I could feel the warmth of a sun that was nowhere in sight. I looked at the leaves, expecting them to attack, but that didn't happen. They didn't seem bothered by my presence. They shook and sent speckles of light into the air. I gasped when the speckles surrounded my head and spoke to me.

"I can hear them!" I said with excitement.

Their voices sounded like soft whispers in my

ear. They all spoke at once, but I could understand them perfectly. They wanted nothing more than to go home. My father was right—they didn't like it here. They were sick of being underwater.

I took a step back when the leaves came off the plant and hung in the air.

"They're not going to hurt you," my father said from the door. He nodded at the leaves, and they began to cover my arms and hands.

I smiled at my father when they had no effect on me.

"See if your magic is working," he suggested.

I glanced around the room and saw a glass of water my father had been drinking. I held my hand out, and the glass flew right into it. I gasped when I realized what that meant: Simon couldn't use the leaves on me anymore.

"And so it begins," my father said. He had the biggest smile on his face. He nodded at the leaves again, and they flew back onto the plant. "Now to get them home," he said, turning around.

I walked out of the secret room, wondering what my father's plan was. He opened his spell book and began searching the pages. What kind of spell was he looking for?

"Father, what about James?" I asked. "We have to find him before Simon kills them."

He turned another page. "Believe me when I say he won't kill him without you there. He wants you to see it."

Cory and Fish walked in before I could ask another question.

"I put Helena in one of the rooms," Cory said to my father. "Delia is with Steven. The others are cleaning up the mess downstairs."

My father nodded and closed the spell book. "I am very sorry for your loss, gentlemen. Javier was a good boy. He will be missed."

"Thank you," Cory answered.

My father's eyes drifted over to Fish. He looked down at Fish's hooks and realized Fish wanted to come with us. "How is young Delia doing?" my father asked.

"She's not doing so well," Fish answered.

"She's going to need you, young man. Your little girl is also going to need her father."

Fish's eyes lit up. "Delia is having a girl?"

My father smiled. "Yes, and she's going to look just like her mother."

I could almost hear Fish's heart racing. I understood what my father was doing. He was trying to give Fish a reason to stay behind, taking that burden off our hands.

"Why don't you stay behind," my father suggested.

"I'm not a coward," Fish said. "I have to go with them. I owe it to Javier."

My father walked up to him and put one hand on Fish's shoulder. "Dying will not prove you're a man—but being a father will. Go be with your wife, son. You have a family to think of now. Imagine their life without you to watch over them. You can't bring your friend back, but you can give your daughter a future."

Fish looked thoughtful for a moment, probably picturing the future Delia could possibly have without him.

When my father pulled out a small dagger, I knew what he was about to do. He made a small cut on his arm, then reached for Fish and did the same.

"What are you doing?" Fish said, trying to pull away.

My father put their arms together and closed his eyes. Fish had a distant look on his face as my father showed him pieces of his future. We all kept our eyes on Fish as he gasped and looked at my father.

"You see?" my father said, pulling his arm away. "You must stay here. Your family is going to need you."

Fish was amazed.

"Tell no one what I've shown you," my father said.

Fish nodded. "Thank you, William." He hurried out of the room, no doubt going back to Delia.

Cory thanked my father as soon as Fish was gone. "What did you show him?" he asked.

My father ignored him and looked at me. "My wand," he said, holding out his hand. "I would like it back now."

"What? But I need it."

"Then I suggest you use yours," he answered.

I shook my head. "I don't have one."

"I beg to differ. You've always had one." He held out his hand again. "My wand, please."

I took out his wand and placed it in his hand. "What am I going to use now?" I asked.

He placed the wand on his desk and motioned to the wall behind me. "I kept it safe for you."

I turned, but only saw my old stick leaning against the wall. I had forgotten all about it. I'd thought I no longer had a need for it since I had my father's wand. Why would my father be giving me that? "That's just my stick," I said. "Your wand turns into whatever I tell it to, into whatever I need."

"No, Thea. My wand turns into whatever *I've* told it to. It works with my mind, not yours." He motioned to my stick again. "It's time you start commanding your own wand. I believe there is something you need at the moment."

I looked at my stick again. I remembered the few times I had used it as a weapon. I always thought it was my spells that were controlling it. I never imagined it had been a wand this whole time. I walked over and took it in my hands. "Hello, old friend," I said as I held it up. My hand slid right into the grooves my fingers had left behind. I was amazed when it turned into a sword. It looked nothing like my father's glass sword. This one looked like it had been cut right off a tree. I wrapped my fingers around its branch-like handle. I felt connected to it at once. The leaf-shaped blade made a faint chiming sound as I held it up.

"What was it that Simon asked for?" my father said.

I gasped when I understood what he was talking about. I looked at the sword again. My heart raced as I thought of what Simon had asked for. I heard Cory gasp as the sword turned into Wendell's head.

"Only a confident wizard can truly command their wand," my father said. "You've never been ready until now."

I looked at his desk to where his wand lay. Why hadn't his wand turned into what I needed?

"I can't ask it for something that has been directed to you," my father explained. "I've always had a need to protect you, and the wand did just that. But this is something you need, not me."

I looked at Wendell's head. It truly looked like I had cut it off his body.

"Let's go get our friends," Cory said, "before Simon kills them."

"First you must go—" My father suddenly stopped talking. His eyes were glued to Cory's hands. Every time Cory moved them, his eyes followed.

"Father, what is it?"

He stepped forward and reached for one of Cory's hands.

"Is something wrong?" Cory asked as my father examined it.

I was surprised when he let go of Cory's hand and left the room. I put down Wendell's fake head, and we followed him out. He was walking down the hall, straight to Helena's room.

"Father, what is it?" I asked again.

Without answering, he stormed into her room. When we walked in, Helena was curled up in a corner with her hands wrapped around her ankles, rocking back and forth. My heart went out to her. This witch was suffering, and possibly losing her mind.

My father walked over to her. She stared at his feet but didn't look up. He reached out his hand. "I think the bed would be more comfortable," he said to her.

Helena stared at his hand. Huge tears ran down her cheeks as she looked back down. "I don't deserve your kindness," she cried.

"Forgiveness is good for the soul, young lady. Especially when you can forgive yourself." He stretched out his hand again. "You are among friends. I will not harm you."

Helena looked at his hand. After a moment, she finally took it. I noticed my father's eyes widen when their hands met. The moment she was standing, he put both his hands on her head. The look on his face told me he was seeing something.

"What is it?" I asked, moving closer.

He spun his head to look down at something on the floor. "What are you looking at?" Then I froze. There, lying on the floor, were Helena's shoes, with red mud on the soles. It was the same mud I had seen on James's face.

Cory followed our eyes and gasped when he saw the shoes. He looked down at his hands. "I put her shoes on. Why didn't I see it?"

"What . . . the mud?" Helena said. "That mud is—"

My father put his hand over her mouth. "No."

He pulled his hands away from Helena and nodded at me. I saw it in his eyes: he knew where James was. As soon as I realized that, he nodded again.

"You can't tell me, can you?" I said.

"It will change, and he'll move them," he answered.

I finally understood. It was like hearing the truth for the first time. My father had told me before, but it never really sank in. We weren't meant to know our future. Our lives in the human world were not written in stone. Destiny made those choices for us. Here, if those words were spoken, destiny would change them, assuring we had no idea what was to come. My father had told Fish he was having a girl because destiny had already chosen what Delia would have. He had given nothing away, only shared what he knew.

My father smiled as I finally made sense of my life. He had known how this was going to end the whole time, and he was trying to make sure the future wouldn't change. He knew I had to make mistakes along the way to get me to where I was right now. He let me suffer, let me cry, all to know the person I really was inside. Destiny had plans for me, and my father knew I would have to find myself first. I had to live through every human emotion to get strong. In the end, I would be the wizard I needed to be, both for Magia and for my son.

"Wisdom does not come cheap," my father said.

I looked into his eyes. "I understand now."

I heard his voice in my head. I hadn't heard it since my memory was erased. My father had always blocked his thoughts from me, but now they flowed freely. I saw the vision he had shown Fish, with my son in it. I locked eyes with my father. He nodded and closed his eyes. I took in all the information he was giving me.

His mind came back to the present. I saw James and Joshua in a dark room. My father was careful not to give away the exact spot. They were being tortured by warlocks.

"No!" I said as the images raced through my head.

Simon was nowhere in sight as the warlocks beat James and Joshua half to death. Then I saw it—I saw who would be saving the man I loved. I gasped as my heart pounded. I was surprised to see that Fish would have a hand in this after all. I knew where I would be standing the very moment James and Joshua were being rescued. I understood what I had to do. Before saving James, there was something I needed to do in Magia.

I opened my eyes and looked at my father. "I'm ready."

He smiled. "Yes, I believe you are."

Chapter 17
Swarm

I stuffed several gold leaves into my pocket before leaving for Magia. My father had warned me not to forget to eat one every hour or so. He gave me instructions to find Levora, the queen of the fairies, and said she would show me what I needed to see. I already knew what he needed me to bring back to him.

"Anything you want me to tell her?" I asked.

My father looked thoughtful before saying, "Please tell her not to blame herself."

That was an odd thing to say. What was she blaming herself about?

"Go. I'll be waiting," my father said.

I shrank my stick down to the size of a wand and placed it in my pocket. Cory didn't ask a single question as we spiraled into my father's world. I knew Joshua was on his mind. We were both sick with worry, that much was clear.

"Did you see where they were?" Cory asked.

I didn't answer.

"I know your father showed you, Thea."

"Not exactly," I answered. "He can't show me the exact spot."

"Is he going to tell you?"

"He can't, Cory. You heard him—things will change, and Simon will move them."

He shook his head. "I hate all these stupid rules."

I was as frustrated as he was, but my father was right. What if Simon did move them? How would we find them then? At least my father knew how to get to them. "I'm not going to let them die, Cory."

He huffed. "What makes you think they're not already dead?"

I shot a look at him, instantly angry. "You think I like this?" I yelled, pushing him. "I'm going crazy with anguish. If I knew exactly where they were, I would be there already. Don't you ever say they're already dead."

Frustrated, Cory hung his head. "I'm sorry, Thea."

"We're going to find them, Cory. Please don't lose hope."

He put his arm around me. "I won't, kid. I promise."

Speckles of light began floating around our heads. I had forgotten Cory was holding the leaves my father had in his secret room.

"What are they saying?" Cory asked, pulling away from me.

"I think they're thanking me for taking them home."

"I can't believe they can talk."

"They can do much more than that," I answered.

Cory stared at me.

"What?" I asked innocently.

He shook his head. "You're starting to sound like your father."

I smiled. "I'll take that as a compliment."

"So what are we going to Magia for?" he asked.

"My father needs a ring so he can go home."

He sighed. "Finally."

He looked down at the leaves again as they continued to shake and release speckles of light all around us. They got more excited the closer we got to Magia. Cory got spooked when they flew out of his hand and began floating in the air.

"What the hell are they doing?" he asked.

I reached out and touched one. "They're getting ready to fly home."

The moment our feet touched the ground, the leaves took off flying. They made squeaking noises of happiness as they disappeared over the falls. Although it was a good distance away, I could hear the rustling sound the other leaves made as they saw their friends returning.

The sound of the leaves seemed to wake Magia up. Flowers began to open and release their sparkles into the air. The waterfall roared even louder as Cory and I turned to face it. The grass under our feet seemed to grow greener and longer. Ivy hanging off the trees whistled in the wind.

"What's happening?" Cory asked, looking around.

I wasn't sure myself. It was as if Magia was welcoming the leaves home. One of their own had been gone for so long. It made me wonder how Magia would react when my father returned.

As fast as Magia reacted to the leaves being here, it stopped just as fast. Things suddenly got quiet.

"That was weird," Cory muttered.

I had a bad feeling. "Yeah, I don't like the sound of this."

"What do you mean?"

I looked toward the waterfall. The roar was gone. "Something isn't right."

"Take the ring off. Let's get out of here," Cory said.

"No. We have to find Levora."

"You mean the fairy lady?"

"Yes, she's going to take us to get a ring for my father."

"Where?"

I looked up at the sky. "I don't know, but I'm sure she'll show us."

There was something odd about the clouds. Something was blowing them away.

"I thought the ring wasn't working on your father," Cory said.

I pulled out my wand. "That's why he needs another one."

I spotted Attor flying high over our heads alongside two other dragons. They were flying very fast. It took me a moment to realize they were fleeing from something. When I saw two wizards flying behind them, I grabbed Cory by the arm and we ran into the trees and hid behind some brush. Above, the wizards were waving their hands at the dragons and sending a net over Attor. Attor came crashing down when his wings got tangled in the net. He hit the ground hard just a few yards away from us. The earth shook as the other two dragons fell next to him while trying to flap their wings. The more they fought, the more tangled they got.

I pulled Cory back when he tried to run and help them. I pointed at five guards that landed and threw more nets over the dragons.

"Three!" one of them yelled. "Wendell will be more than pleased with us."

The two wizards landed soon after and joined them. They wore beautiful velvet robes adorned with multicolored gems. One wizard had beautiful blond hair and deep blue eyes. His skin was milky white and flawless. The other was gray-haired with honey-brown eyes. Although he was an older wizard, he looked perfect in every way—strong, tall, and very handsome. He moved with such grace as he neared Attor.

We watched as both wizards calmly walked around the dragons and smiled.

"I believe we have caught this one before," the blond one said, pointing at Attor.

The older wizard looked down at Attor and waved his hand. Attor huffed and blew fire as shackles appeared on his legs.

"We have to help them," Cory said.

I held him back. "No, not yet."

Attor screeched as the wizards waved their hands and put an iron clamp around his mouth. You could see their spells making sparks around the iron and sealing Attor's mouth shut. The guards pulled out iron bars and began nailing the nets to the ground. Attor had stopped fighting. The other dragons seemed to lose hope when they saw Attor give up.

"You know what to do," the older wizard said to the guards. "I will inform Wendell that we have found the black dragon and killed him."

The guards bowed their heads as the wizards mounted their staffs. The moment the wizards took to the sky, the guards pulled out their swords.

One guard pulled out a stone and began sharpening his blade. "You ever have dragon meat before?" he asked the others.

They all laughed.

I stepped out from behind the bushes with Cory right behind me. Attor met my eyes. I put my finger over my lips. He glanced at the guards and slowly nodded. Cory already had his weapons out.

"Kill the black one first," one guard said. "We'll take some of his meat to Wendell, so he can feast on it tonight."

"Does Wendell like owl meat?" I asked.

They spun their owl heads around, eyes wide in shock.

"It can't be," one of them gasped.

The one who had been sharpening his blade spun around and glared at me. Cory fell to his knees when the guard began causing him pain. He dropped like a log as their magic paralyzed him on the ground. All five guards were soon glaring at me and tried casting their magic. I could actually see the waves of pain they were sending my way.

~ 221 ~

I blocked the magic from my mind and smiled. "I'm afraid that doesn't work on me anymore, my lords."

Their red eyes filled with fury as they raised their swords. I waved my hand and sent pain shooting into their heads. All five fell to their knees, grabbing and shaking their heads.

"How do *you* like that?" I said.

I looked at Attor and waved my hand again, sending the nets and bars flying into the trees. I removed the clamp from around his mouth and waved my hand at his shackles, and Attor jumped to his feet. The three dragons stood over the guards, huffing and puffing as they walked around them. Attor took one deep breath, glared at the guards, and blew a wave of fire all over them. The other dragons followed suit, leaving nothing but ashes when they were done. Attor spread his wings and sent a roar of fire into the air. He looked down at the ashes on the ground, huffed, and blew fire at them again.

I helped Cory to his feet. He didn't look very well. I knew the pain he had just gone through. It was like being stabbed over and over in the head. It was the kind of pain that made you wish for death rather than suffer through it.

"What the hell was that?" he asked, grabbing his head. "Did I get shot in the head?"

I laughed. "Yes, with pain spells."

"Remind me to never piss off Porteus," he said.

I laughed again.

"Thank you," I heard from behind me.

I turned. It was Attor. The other two dragons were behind him. Attor looked into my eyes for what seemed like forever. Finally, he bowed his head and leaned down. "Welcome home, my queen."

The other dragons also bowed. "Your Majesty," they said in unison.

Attor raised his head, saying, "I owe you my life."

"You owe me nothing, friend. You have saved me more than once."

"Friend," Attor said, bowing his head again.

"Why did the wizards attack you?" I asked.

Attor huffed when I mentioned the wizards. He looked at the other dragons and motioned for them to leave. "Find the others," he told them. "Tell them the wizards are on the hunt."

The dragons nodded and took to the sky.

"What's going on?" I asked.

"They found out about the guards we killed the other day," Attor answered. "The one Martin killed was Lofeus, one of Wendell's top guards. The wizards are not happy about that. They've declared Martin fair game and have been hunting him down."

"Where is he?" I asked.

"He and Morgan are with the Onfroi, just beyond the mountain."

"Take me to them."

Within moments, Cory and I were on Attor's back, flying through the air. Attor stayed low to the ground and mostly flew through the trees.

"I can't believe I'm flying on a dragon's back," Cory said excitedly. "No one is ever going to believe this."

"Who would you tell?" I yelled over my shoulder.

We both laughed as Attor made his way through the forest. When he began to fly over a mountain, my heart leaped to my throat. Six wizards were flying in our direction, searching for Martin, no doubt. They looked as surprised as we did when they spotted us. Attor tried flying in another direction, only to find two more wizards flying toward us.

"Make a circle around them!" one wizard yelled. We were being herded like cattle.

As the wizards began throwing spells in every direction, Attor shifted directions suddenly, and I had to grab Cory when he almost fell. Nets flew through the air. I had to keep waving my hand to make them miss us. When one spell hit Attor on the wing, I knew we were going to fall.

"Fly down!" I shouted.

It took everything I had to protect Cory from the wizard spells. Attor was trying his best not to let us fall. I saw another spell heading our way and waved my hand, but I missed the spell completely. Attor let out an ear-piercing screech when the spell hit his other wing.

I reached for Cory as we began crashing down. Then a wizard spell hit him in the face, and his hand slipped away from mine. He grunted and fell away.

"Cory!" I screamed.

I tried to jump off after him, but Attor wrapped his bloody wing around me and held me tight. We hit the ground hard, with Attor taking the brunt of the impact.

"Cory!" I kept screaming.

I heard thumps as the wizards landed all around us. I tried jumping to my feet but couldn't get my leg out from under Attor. Attor only huffed in pain as the wizards got closer.

My eyes darted in every direction, searching for my friend. I finally spotted him, and he wasn't moving.

"Please, no," I said, trying to pull myself out. I pushed Attor as hard as I could and finally got my leg out from under him. I jumped to my feet and began running to Cory.

The wizards gasped when they realized who I was. "You!" one wizard said. He waved his hand and sent his magic my way.

I spun around and saw his spell flying straight toward me. I waved my hand, and the spell exploded before it could reach me.

All the wizards raised their hands, ready to send more spells flying my way. I readied myself, placing my feet firmly on the ground. There wasn't a force on this earth that could keep me from returning to James. I knew this: I would die fighting to get back to him. Perhaps Cory would get his wish, and we would indeed die together.

I was preparing myself for battle when the wizards looked up. A strange sound, like a swarm of bees, began blaring behind me. The sound grew louder and louder. Whatever it was, it was getting closer. There was a look of horror on the wizards' faces as they slowly lowered their hands. They began backing away with terror in their eyes.

I finally had to look behind me to see what they were looking at. I gasped when I saw what appeared to be a tidal wave of leaves hovering over me. They released a heart-rending cry of agony as the wizards' energy began to hurt them. The leaves froze for several seconds before descending on the wizards. They sounded like a huge flock of birds flapping their wings as they covered the wizards and drained them of their lives. One wizard tried mounting his staff, but the leaves knocked him off and covered his body.

I closed my eyes and looked away as the wizards' old, wrinkled bodies fell to the ground. Then there was silence. I heard a soft whispering in my ear but couldn't bring myself to open my eyes.

"It's over," the soft voice said.

I opened my eyes. Speckles of light were floating all around me. I reluctantly looked at the carnage on the ground, but the leaves had left behind nothing but bones.

"Are you well?" a childlike voice asked.

I was speechless. Millions of leaves were waiting on my answer.

"Yes," I finally said. I was surprised when the leaves began making that horrible sound again. They flew high above my head and prepared to strike.

It took me a moment to realize who they were getting ready to attack. I hadn't heard Martin and Morgan land a few yards away. They were with the two dragons Attor had sent away. Martin was standing with his mouth open, his eyes fixed on the leaves. Morgan wouldn't move; he only stared at the leaves with an expression of shock on his face.

I looked up at the leaves. "Fly away, quickly," I commanded. "They're my friends." I heard Martin gasp when the leaves did as I asked them to. I spun around and ran to Cory, who still wasn't moving.

As I neared him, my feet refused to get any closer. I froze at the sight of his bloodied body. I couldn't bring myself to face the truth. I knew if Cory was gone, I would lose my mind. I forced myself to approach him and dropped to my knees. I turned him over and slapped my hand over my mouth. His ear was hanging on by a thread of skin. Half his face was gone, ripped away by a spell.

"Cory!" I cried. My hands shook as I tried to feel a heartbeat. "Please don't be dead." I gasped when I felt the faint pulse of his heart. It was very slow, but he was still alive. "Stay with me, my friend." I closed my eyes and chanted, "Heal."

"Use the petals," one of the dragons called to me. "The petals from the flowers—place them on his face. They'll work much faster."

I quickly did as he said and began pulling petals from the flowers. I scattered them over Cory's face and waited. After a moment, he began to move. My heart rejoiced as he moaned. It was music to my ears. New skin was already forming on his face.

Tears trickled down my cheeks as he opened his eyes. I flicked some of the petals away from his face, which was covered with the glitter from the flowers. I wrapped my arms around him. "Cory," I said, squeezing him.

"Are we dead?" he asked.

I laughed and pulled away. "If we are, I died with you."

It suddenly occurred to him that he was lying on the ground. "What happened?"

"You got hit by a spell and fell off Attor."

"The wizards," he said, remembering what had happened.

"Don't worry—they're dead."

"Dead?" he asked, confused. I nodded. He looked at Martin and Morgan. "And what happened to them?"

I looked over my shoulder. They were both frozen, staring in the direction of the leaves. "Oh, the leaves just left," I answered.

"I'm not even going to ask," Cory said.

I helped him to his feet and began checking him. "Are you okay now?"

"Yes, but I don't think they are," Cory said, motioning to Martin and Morgan.

It was true—they were in shock. They kept looking down at the bones the leaves had left behind. Morgan wouldn't look away from the direction the leaves had gone.

Cory gently elbowed me, "Thea, look at his eyes." Morgan's eyes were changing color from brown to green, then to sky blue.

Cory and I looked at each other.

"Netiri," I whispered.

"Yeah, and he kind of looks like him, too," Cory said.

Why hadn't I noticed that before? Morgan really did look like Netiri. They could be brothers.

Martin finally unfroze from the shock and looked at me. "How did you do that? How did you get the leaves to go like that?"

"She can talk to them," Cory answered.

"She can what?" Martin exclaimed.

~ 228 ~

Chapter 18
The Tree of Kings

As we finally left the area, I brought Martin up to speed about the leaves. He couldn't believe they could actually communicate with us. I told him about the gold leaves my father had given me and explained what they did. When I told him about James and what Simon was doing, I could see he was as worried about it as I was.

"Don't worry, Thea. You'll get to them in time," he said.

"You're damn right we will," Cory cut in.

We began to fly to a safe part of Magia—well, as safe as possible, anyway. I told Martin I needed to speak with Levora and explained what my father needed. Martin knew at once where to take me. As we flew to find Levora, I kept looking over my shoulder at Morgan, who was flying behind us with Cory.

"Why do Morgan's eyes change like that?" I asked Martin.

"Ahh, he got that from his father," Martin answered. "It's something some wizards are born with. It serves no purpose that I know of."

I looked over my shoulder again. Could it be that Netiri's father was the same man? My father had told me once that Morgan's father was alive, that he'd stayed in the human world for so long that he turned human, but he said nothing more than that.

"Why did Morgan's father leave Magia?" I asked.

"His name was Aldore, and he went looking for Xander."

"He what?" I asked, surprised.

"Yes, he left when Xander didn't come back," Martin explained. "He said he had a bad feeling and went in search of your father. No one knows what happened to him or why he never came back."

"He just disappeared?"

"Yes, that's why Morgan keeps asking you for him. He expected you to say that his father was with Xander. Has Xander told you anything about him?"

"No, he hasn't," I lied. I couldn't bring myself to tell him that my father hardly brought him up. I didn't even know that Morgan's father was named Aldore. "Maybe he never found my father," I suggested.

"I think you're right," Martin said. "If he had found Xander, he would have killed Simon the moment he found out what Simon was doing."

"Do you think Aldore was helping Wendell?"

~ 230 ~

Martin laughed. "Wendell and Aldore are enemies," he said. "They've never liked each other."

"Why do you say that?"

"Aldore was Xander's best friend. Wendell hated him for that. He thought your father favored Aldore when it came to rank. Wendell thought he should hold top rank, not Aldore."

We began to fly faster, over a part of Magia I'd never seen before. Here there was nothing but big oak trees. They looked hundreds of years old. They were massive in size and breathtaking to look at. Some of their branches were so thick and heavy that they lay on the ground, almost like arms welcoming someone to climb them.

I jumped off Martin's staff and looked up at the towering oak we had landed under. It had what seemed like a hundred branches stretching out as wide as a house.

"Wow," I said.

"Magnificent, aren't they?" Martin said.

I gasped when I recognized a nearby oak. It was like the one James had on his back. Had he been here before? This tree was larger than any of the others. There were hundreds of orbs floating all around it, sparkling like stars in the night. The oak looked magical and alive, each of its branches twisted and curved like a ribbon. I'd never seen anything so beautiful in my life. If a tree could be a king, this one would be it.

I looked closer at the orbs and realized they were fairies. Was this tree their home?

The others landed behind me as I gazed at the tree. I paid no attention as Martin continued our conversation. I was too amazed by the beautiful tree in front of me. I felt it calling out to me somehow and pulling me toward it. I felt connected to it at once. I wanted to touch it, feel its bark in my hand.

Martin finally realized I was paying no attention to him. "Oh, that's the Tree of Kings," he said when he saw me staring at the tree.

"The what?"

Before Martin could answer, someone walked out from the inside of the tree. It was her—Levora.

"It's the fairy lady," Cory said.

She looked more breathtaking than ever. Her hair was greener than I'd ever seen it, and her eyes were pink like sapphires. Her peacock-like wings spread across her back like a fan painted with vivid colors. I drew a quick breath when she smiled at me.

"I've been waiting for you," she said in an almost musical voice.

I was captivated by her beauty as she walked toward me. The others dropped to one knee and bowed their heads. Cory followed suit.

"Your Majesty," they said.

I began to bow my head when she stopped me.

"Let me look into your eyes," she said, putting her fingers under my chin.

I lifted my head. She raised her brows when my eyes met hers. As the others got to their feet, she pulled away her hand and kept her eyes on me, a look of relief on her face.

"Well done," she finally said. She looked down at my hand and held hers out to me. "If you would, please."

I looked at her pearl-like skin and placed my hand in hers. She got a faraway look in her eyes as she wrapped her fingers around it. She swallowed thickly and closed her eyes, then suddenly held my hand tighter. I could swear she mumbled the name "Xander."

A single tear fell from her eye. I could feel the pulse of her heart through her hand. She spread her wings and sighed. It was then I noticed something odd about them. All the feathers in her wings were shaped like leaves. There were purple, blue, orange, and gold ones. There were also empty spots where there used to be feathers, as if she had plucked them out.

"It was you," I said. "You gave my father those gold leaves."

She opened her pink sapphire eyes. I stared into them, trying to look into her soul.

"I've been eating your feathers?" I asked, shocked.

She laughed.

"Eww," Cory said.

"Are you ready to meet the Tree of Kings?" Levora asked. "I believe Xander is in need of a ring."

I didn't overlook the fact that she had changed the subject. I also didn't miss her whispering my father's name. "You want me to *meet* a tree?" I asked, confused.

She looked toward the giant oak. "This is our tree of life. Only this tree can give you what you came here to find."

"We're here to see a tree?" Cory asked.

Levora smiled at him. "This is not just any tree. Its roots stretch for miles and draw water from the secret river of life. The roots fill the river with its magic and make the water give life and energy. It's what keeps Magia alive and wizards strong. This tree can feel your heart and knows your intentions. It can sense where you are at every moment of the day. This is why it chooses our king."

"A tree chooses your king?" I asked.

"Our true king," she added.

I looked at the massive oak. "That tree chose my father?"

Levora nodded. "Yes. It has chosen all our past and even our future kings."

"It's not a very smart tree if it chose Wendell, is it?" I snapped. "Wasn't he next in line for the throne?"

Martin tried to cut in, but Levora held her hand up. "We don't question whom the tree chooses," she said. "And we don't go against its wishes. There is always a reason the tree chooses the way it does."

"And how does it choose?" I asked.

"Five kings are chosen every thousand years or so. The tree grows five names in its bark, naming the future kings of Magia. Your father was number four."

"And Wendell was the fifth name?" I asked.

"Yes, but he never proved himself to Magia or the tree," Levora said. "He believed his fate as future king was sealed because the tree had shown his name on its bark. But when he never showed his worth, his name began to fade from the tree. You're still able to read it, but it's not as vibrant as before. That means the tree of life is uncertain."

"What happened to the first three kings?" Cory asked.

Levora, Martin, and Morgan all looked at each other, a bit of shame on their faces. It didn't take me long to figure out what they couldn't bring themselves to say.

"Wendell killed them, didn't he?" I asked.

"We didn't realize that until a few months ago," Levora said, looking down.

Cory shook his head. "You mean Wendell has been picking off your kings and you had no idea? How can that be? Thea figured that out in a matter of seconds."

"You don't understand," Martin said. "We didn't know it was him. We thought the dragons had killed those kings. That's why we enslaved them."

Attor huffed behind him.

Martin spun around. "I'm sorry, Attor. We didn't know."

Attor moved closer, his eyes locked on Martin. "We tried to warn you about a traitor amongst you," he said. "No one would listen to us. Only Xander believed what we had to say. That's why he freed us. He knew someone else was behind it, he just didn't know who." Attor turned to me. "When your father and I became friends, Wendell convinced the others that Xander had helped us kill those kings."

"How could you believe that?" I asked Martin. "I thought my father was your friend."

Martin seemed frustrated. "He was . . . is, but when he left Magia and his name disappeared from the tree, we thought Xander was dead and Wendell was telling the truth. We had no reason to doubt him at the time.

"My father's name disappeared from the tree?" I was shocked.

"Yes," Levora said. "We thought it would grow your name next, since you are Xander's heir. But a few weeks ago, it began growing a new name."

"A new name?" I asked. "Whose?"

There was silence. Martin looked away from me. I glanced at the dragons, and they, too, were looking away.

My gaze shot toward the tree. I got an uneasy feeling. Though I feared the answer, I asked Levora again, "Whose name is it growing?"

When she didn't answer, I felt my heart leap to my throat. Cory tried reaching for my hand.

"No," I said, slapping it away. I didn't want his comfort. I didn't deserve it. I had to face this alone. I had made one mistake after another; it was time I face the music. I looked toward the giant oak, swallowed thickly, and made my way toward it.

I already knew the name I was going to find, but I had to see it nonetheless. I knew it wouldn't change what I had to do. This was my mistake, and I was going to deal with it. *Get on with it, witch.*

The closer I got to the tree, the bigger it seemed. As I approached the entrance Levora had walked out of, I heard a dripping sound. I stopped just outside the entrance as my eyes searched the bark for the name I knew would be there.

"It's inside," Levora said from behind me.

I took a deep breath and walked in.

My heart seemed to come alive the moment I stepped inside. I was in awe of the beauty as I looked around. The tree was hollow, and what appeared to be beads of water were coming out of its walls. The strange water almost had a gel-like appearance that shimmered like diamonds as more and more beads emerged from the walls. I gasped when I looked up and saw how far up inside the tree the beads went. Hundreds of fairies were flying about, gathering the beads of water and flying out of the tree. I realized they were the ones taking the magic to all the plant life in Magia.

My eyes began searching the walls for the names. There, carved in beautiful writing, were two names. There were blank spots where the first three names had once been.

"This is the first time the tree has grown only one name," Levora said from behind me. My eyes darted down to the fourth name; I could still see Wendell's name clearly. I looked under his and wasn't surprised to see the name *Simon Wade* carved into the bark.

Levora seemed to be waiting on my reaction.

"Looks like your tree picked a dead king," I said.

Levora looked confused. "He's not dead."

I smiled grimly. "Yet." I touched the spot where my father's name had once been and noticed something odd. His name didn't look like it had faded away at all, but rather as if it had been carved away. The blade of a knife had left deep gouges in the wood. "Someone carved my father's name out," I said.

"That's not possible," Levora replied. "Only Xander himself could have done that. Otherwise, anyone would be able to carve their name into the tree."

I ran my fingers along the bark again. I could almost make my finger follow the outline of his name. It made me wonder: Had my father truly carved his own name out? And if it was true that this tree could feel your heart, why didn't it know my father would never betray this land? Why would it doubt him now? And why would it think he was dead if it knew where he was at every moment of the day?

I thought of the day I saw my father; the day James had taken him into my memory. I had tried bringing him home using the ring, but it hadn't worked. My father's words rang in my head: *"The ring can't sense you here, Thea. It doesn't know where you are."*

I gasped.

"Thea, was it—?" Cory asked.

I spun around, my jaw hanging open. "I know why my father can't go outside."

I thought of the many times he had stepped away from the door or any open window. He was right: the answer had been there the whole time. It wasn't that he couldn't go outside—it was that he didn't want to. He knew the ring would sense him the moment human air hit him.

"Prisoner to a spell," I murmured.

That was it. My father had a spell on the house, so the ring couldn't sense him. He knew the moment he went outside, the tree would find him and put his name back on its bark, sending wizards in search of him. It was like a puzzle coming together in my head.

My father knew Wendell would devise a way to escape from Magia and find him. Without his powers, my father would be helpless. Being dead was the only way my father had found to keep Wendell away from the human world. He needed time to fix what Simon had done. He needed me to be strong, needed me to be the wizard he knew I could be. I had to find myself.

This revelation was like a breath of fresh air. Hope rose inside me for James and my friends. Now I knew why my father needed a ring. He was about to go outside. I spun around and faced Levora. She wore a smile from ear to ear.

"How do I get that ring?" I asked.

I followed her eyes to the beads of water on the walls of the tree. She touched them and removed one of the strands. The strand fell on her palm like a strand of pearls. She held it gently to her mouth and blew. The beads quickly came together to form a ring. She closed her hand and put it over mine. "Tell Xander we'll be waiting for him," she said as she placed the ring in my palm.

The ring looked like the one I had on. I had always thought my father's ring was made of glass; I never imagined it was made of water. The same jewels floated inside it that were in my father's ring.

"Come on, Thea," Cory said. "Let's go get our friends."

I nodded and put the ring in my pocket. I looked at the names again. Simon's name was getting clearer and clearer, while Wendell's faded away even more. "Time to erase two names," I said.

When we walked out of the tree, I asked Attor to take me back to his cave. It wasn't really his cave I wanted to see, but rather the forest where the leaves lived. A plan was coming together in my head, and I was going to need them. Martin and Morgan stayed behind when I told them where I was going. I gave them each a gold leaf and told them to save it for when I came back.

"We'll be ready," Martin assured me.

I turned to Levora. Her stunning face was so beautiful.

"Thank you for helping my father when no one else would," I said. I didn't bother giving her my father's message. I had a feeling she already knew.

She smiled. "Please give him my love."

"How about you give it to him yourself when I bring him home?" I suggested.

The thought of seeing him again clearly made her happy. Her secret was out. She loved him. There was no mistaking her feelings for him. "He's waiting," she said.

Cory and I jumped on Attor and took to the sky. We both kept our eyes out for wizards.

"Aren't you worried they'll see us?" he asked.

"No," I answered. There was no fear in me anymore. If the wizards did see us, they would die.

When Attor landed near his cave, I asked Cory to wait inside. Attor left to rejoin the others when I told him Cory and I would be leaving shortly. After he left, I pulled out a leaf, ate it, and walked into the forest. There was a little favor I needed from the leaves.

Chapter 19
The Humble Witch

I walked out of the forest, feeling thankful the leaves had agreed to help me. I made my way back to Attor's cave and found Cory kneeling in a corner.

What is he doing? He had his back to me and his head down. "Why are you kneeling?" I asked.

"Isn't it customary to kneel before a king?" a voice said.

I pulled out my wand. My heart sank when Wendell walked out from behind the enormous oak that stood in the center of the cave. He looked more evil than I remembered. His beard had grown longer, his eyes darker. Wendell was a tall man, with a pointy nose and beady eyes. He had the classic look of a villain. If he had appeared in a movie, the audience would immediately guess he was the bad guy.

Wendell's eyes were glued to me as he pointed his wand at Cory's head. "Well, look who's alive and well," he said in a teasing tone.

I had my wand pointed between his eyes. "No thanks to you," I answered.

He laughed. "Come now, did you not enjoy our time together?"

"Of course, I did. That's why I came back for more."

His eyes traveled over my body. "You may not be so lucky this time, witch."

"That's funny. I was going to say the same thing to you."

He poked his wand into Cory's cheek. "I can promise you this: you will not leave this cave alive."

I smiled. "Worried the others will find out you killed all those kings?"

His eyes widened. A smile slowly spread across his face. "You've been talking to Simon, haven't you? How is my little puppet?"

This was a surprise. I didn't realize Simon knew Wendell's secret. "Actually, he's waiting for your head," I answered.

He laughed again. "And I suppose you're the one who is to bring it to him?"

"That's the plan."

"Perhaps we can come to some kind of agreement."

I shook my head. "I didn't come here to make any deals, Wendell."

"That's a shame, witch. I could have made good use of you."

~ 242 ~

There were burn marks on Cory's shirt from where Wendell had thrown spells at him.

"Cory, are you okay?" I asked.

"Oh, he can't hear you," Wendell said in a deviant voice. "I'm afraid my spell has him rather frozen."

I took two steps forward.

"I wouldn't do anything foolish if I were you," Wendell said as he touched his wand to Cory's head. "You wouldn't want me to get jittery, would you?"

"Did you and Simon take speech lessons together?" I asked sarcastically.

Wendell's laughter echoed throughout the cave. It reminded me of Simon. I made a fist and stepped closer.

"Move again, and I'll kill your little human friend," Wendell warned.

I froze and looked at Cory. All I could see was his back. He was helpless under Wendell's spell.

"I must confess," Wendell said, "I thought it would be Martin walking into this cave. I never expected to see you again. How on earth did you survive?"

"Let him go, and I'll tell you all about it."

I got worried when he kept digging his wand to Cory's head.

He chuckled. "I think I'll keep him, if you don't mind. He could prove to be quite useful. It's amazing what people will say when they're being tortured." He pressed his wand into Cory's temple. "I have a feeling your friend has an amazing story to tell m—" He suddenly stopped talking and stared at me. I wasn't quite sure what he was looking at. "Well, well, well," he finally said. "Simon is smarter than I ever imagined."

Confusion washed over me. What was he talking about?

"Painful, that blood promise, don't you agree?" he asked.

I almost gasped when he said that. I had forgotten about the scar on my neck. I had tried so many times to use a spell to remove it, but there was no erasing what I had done.

"What did you promise him?" Wendell asked.

When I didn't answer, he looked down at my father's ring, and then at Cory. I could almost see what he was thinking as his eyes lit up. He knew if I took off the ring, Cory would come with me. I had a bad feeling Wendell wanted to go for a ride.

I wasn't surprised when he grabbed a handful of Cory's hair and wrapped his fingers around it. "Take off the ring," he said, glaring at me. "I think Simon is waiting for us."

"That's not going to happen, Wendell."

He seemed to be debating what to do. I moved closer, my wand pointed steadily at his head.

"Looks like one of us is dying today," Wendell said.

"Yeah, and that someone looks like you," I answered.

Before I could move, Cory suddenly pushed Wendell into the wall. Surprised, I pulled off my father's ring before Wendell could wave his hand at us. Cory was pulled into the vortex with me. He slammed against me, and we fell to the ground.

I heard Wendell's faint, angry voice yelling, "No!" as I pushed Cory off me.

"I thought you were frozen," I said.

He didn't answer. There was a strange look about him. He put his hands up to his face. It was then I noticed his face was like a stone.

"Can you talk?" I asked.

He pointed at his face. I touched it; it felt like solid ice. I touched his arms and chest and found that the rest of him felt normal. Again, I was thankful for the tattoos he had gotten.

"Wendell's spell hit you on the head, didn't it?"

He waved his arms around. I felt horrible for laughing, but I couldn't help it. Cory squeezed my leg when I wouldn't stop.

"Okay, I'm sorry," I said, composing myself. I pulled out some of the petals I still had and forced them into Cory's mouth. I knew they would be faster than trying to break Wendell's spell. "Can you chew?" I asked, then broke into laughter again. I was still laughing when Cory's face finally began to unfreeze itself.

"I hate wizards," he said in a funny voice.

"They really seem to love you," I joked.

"Today is not my day, Thea."

I heard my father jump to his feet when we reached his room.

"What happened?" he asked.

"Wendell threw a spell at him," I answered.

"Wendell?" he gasped as he rushed to Cory's side. "Are you all right, son?"

"I'm fine," Cory said, shaking his head. "I can feel my face again."

"Do you need to sit for a moment?"

"I'm fine now," Cory repeated.

My father turned and looked into my eyes. After a moment, he politely asked Cory to leave the room.

"I'll go check on Helena," Cory said.

My father closed the door behind him and looked into my eyes again. "I would have preferred that no wizards were killed," he said.

"And I would have preferred they didn't try to kill me."

He sighed. "I see they are still under Wendell's control."

I walked across the room. "They're traitors, Father. All they seem to crave is power."

"No, Thea. They've done nothing but try to protect Magia. Remember, they think I am the traitor, but they will soon see the light. They will have to answer to me for their actions. I will not tolerate arrogance any further. I will not forget how they reacted when I told them I was going to marry a witch."

"What makes you think they'll listen? They believe everything Wendell says. They think themselves above all others. I can see where Simon got that from."

He gave me a sideways glance. "They'll have no choice but to listen. I will soon set them straight."

I knew he was upset with the wizards. They had allowed Wendell to make fools of them.

"He made a fool out of me as well, Thea. I can't blame them for not seeing what I also missed."

"Did you know Wendell killed those kings?" I asked.

"Yes, I realized that when he tried to kill me."

"Wendell knows, Father. He knows I made a blood promise to Simon."

He did not seem to like hearing that. "This may complicate things," he said, looking away.

"What do you mean?"

"That means he'll be prepared now."

"That doesn't matter anymore." I pulled out the ring and showed it to him. "Are you ready to get some fresh air?"

Before he could take it from me, the room began to spin. It felt like someone had pulled the ground right out from under me. I was slammed hard against the wall.

"Put away the ring!" my father shouted.

I tried to hand it to him.

"Put it away," he repeated.

I had no idea what was going on. The weight of the ring felt like I was holding a million bricks. It seemed glued to me somehow. My father tried to help me, but every time he got near me, I was slammed across the room and into another wall.

"Close your hand around it," he ordered.

The moment my father took a step forward, I flew across the room and slammed into the door. I hit face-first, with my feet dangling in the air.

"Close it, Thea!"

"I . . . I can't," I managed to say.

The ring wanted no part of him. It was as if it wanted to get as far away from him as possible. I tried to close my hand, but the weight I felt kept my fingers opened. I panicked when I began to slam into the door, over and over again.

"What's going on in there?" Fish yelled.

I heard some of my bones breaking as the ring slammed me harder against the door. Was this door made of iron?

Light suddenly filled the room. I heard a door open and close. I knew my father had gone into his secret room. I fell to the floor, closed my hand, and tried to catch my breath.

The door hit my feet as Fish kicked it open. "Thea, are you okay?"

I squeezed the ring in my hand before darkness filled my head.

I felt someone wiping my face with a damp towel as I opened my eyes. Beautiful golden locks slowly came into view. Soft, milky white fingers stroked the hair away from my face. I was shocked when I realized the one attending to me was Helena.

She pulled away the towel when she saw that I was awake. "Oh, sorry," she said nervously. "You were sweating a little. I thought the damp towel would help you."

I looked around to see that I was in her room. I wanted to jump out of bed and find out what the hell had happened, but the truth was, I still wasn't feeling very good. It felt like someone had hit me over the head with a bat.

"You broke some bones, but I used a spell," Helena said.

I looked down at my hand and saw that the ring was gone.

"Cory has it," Helena said.

"Cory?"

"Yes. He was the only one that seemed able to take it from your hand."

I tried to sit up. "Where is he?" A bolt of pain shot through my head, causing me to lie back down. I put my hand over my head, realizing I had a rather large bump.

"You want me to cast a headache spell?" Helena asked.

I shook my head no. "What time is it?"

"About two in the morning. No one has been able to sleep."

It was then I realized that she had finally showered and was back to her beautiful, striking self. She was wearing one of Delia's black dresses. I had to admit, black was definitely her color.

As she fidgeted with the towel, I wondered what I should say to her. I thought of asking how she was feeling. "How long have I been out?" I asked instead.

"Just a couple of hours. Your father left to get you some food."

I suddenly realized I couldn't remember the last time I had put something in my stomach. Come to think of it, I couldn't remember the last time I had slept, either. My stomach growled the moment Helena mentioned food.

"How do you stay so sane?" she asked.

I looked at her. "What are you talking about?"

She looked down at the towel. "How do you endure that kind of pain and not lose your mind? How do you find the strength to keep going after him?" I knew she was talking about Simon.

~ 249 ~

"What doesn't kill you makes you stronger," I answered.

She huffed. "Didn't make *me* stronger."

"I wouldn't say that. You seem different already."

She forced a smile. "You were calling his name," she said.

"James?"

She nodded and looked down at her hands. "I know he never loved me. As much as I tried to make him forget you, I always knew his heart belonged to you. I was a fool to think he could ever leave you for me."

"You don't have to do this, Helena."

"Yes, I do," she said as tears swelled in her eyes. "I know I don't deserve your forgiveness, but I want to say how sorry I am for everything I've done to you. I'm ashamed of all the harm I've caused. You could have left me there that day, needles and all." She shook her head. "I deserved nothing less."

I tried to sit up again. "Helena, you don't have—"

"No, please," she cut in, "let me finish."

I nodded and sat back again. She wiped away tears and continued. "Despite all the things I put you through, you saved me, anyway. I know the old me would have left you there to rot. But you took pity on me. You saved the witch who did nothing but try to rid the earth of you. I truly hated you, and I am so ashamed of that now. I'm grateful that you didn't hold that against me. You saved me in spite of the person I was. But I hope one day I can win your trust and forgiveness. Nothing would make me happier than if you could one day consider me a friend."

I saw the sincerity in her eyes. She was speaking from the heart. At last, Helena had become a humble witch.

I reached for her hand. "We both made mistakes," I said. "Life has taught us both a lesson. We were both arrogant and headstrong, thinking we needed nothing from others. Truth is, I would be nothing without those who surround me. Even you served a purpose in my life, Helena. I always envied your beauty, thought it would make me a better person. But in the end, I realized the most beautiful part of me had always been inside me. I would have never seen that if not for you. I have nothing to forgive. And I'm sure as the days go by, you and I will become good friends."

She let out a sigh and threw her arms around me. My bitterness for this witch had all but vanished. I knew deep in my heart that I could learn to love her one day.

Someone knocked on the door, and Helena pulled away and rose to her feet. Moments later, my father walked in with a tray of food. I didn't like the look on his face. He was worried about something. Helena quickly crossed the room and took the tray from him. His face was somber as he watched her place the tray of food on my lap. I wanted to push the tray away and jump to my feet. What was wrong with him?

"Helena, I left some tea downstairs," he said. "Can you please go and bring it up for me?"

"Yes, of course," she said, heading for the door.

The moment Helena closed the door, I looked at my father. "What is it, Father?"

He walked the length of the room and sat on the bed. "I don't know how to say this . . ."

"You're scaring me."

"It's the ring," he said.

"What about it?"

"I was afraid this would happen."

"What are you talking about?"

"The ring—it doesn't know who I am," he explained. "I'm too weak for it to realize I am the person it was meant for. Without energy, it doesn't see me as a wizard."

"What does this mean?" I had never seen my father so worried before. "Father, tell me."

He sighed. "My intention was to get the ring and go immediately into Magia. I planned to return after I got some energy and rescue James and Joshua. I never planned on allowing you to see Simon again. It was I who would bring him Wendell's head."

I stared at him. "Now what do we do?"

He sighed once more. "I think our only option is for you to go into Magia and bring me the energy first. I know it will be difficult with the wizard watching over the river so much."

"But there's no time for that, Father. What about James and Joshua?"

At that moment, Helena walked back in. Porteus was behind her, which surprised me. Helena had been frightened of Porteus when she first saw him, but now she didn't seem scared or bothered by his appearance. In fact, she was smiling from ear to ear as she put the tea on a table. She looked at Porteus with loving eyes and asked, "Would you like some tea, Cory?"

"No, thank you," Porteus answered.

I was instantly confused. I looked at Porteus again as his leathery tail whipped about. His red eyes looked even scarier than before. I couldn't understand why Helena thought he was Cory.

Helena gave him the biggest smile before excusing herself.

The moment she walked out, I jumped out of bed. "What the hell is going on?" I asked.

My father rose to his feet. "He was scaring her. I thought it best that she see one of us whenever she looks upon him."

I looked at Porteus. "You can do that?"

"It takes a lot of concentration on my part, but yes, I can do that."

"Why don't you just take the potion my father made for you?" I asked.

"It never worked on me, Your Highness," Porteus replied. "I've had to trick minds since I've been here."

"Is that what you did when you went to see Simon?" I asked.

"Yes, he only saw what I wanted him to see. I made you see Xander because that's who you needed to see, but Simon only saw an old man."

"And why didn't I see you as Cory just now?"

"That's because I wasn't concentrating on you, Your Majesty."

An idea began brewing in my head. "Show me," I said.

Porteus looked at my father for an approving nod.

"Show her," my father said.

My heart began racing when Porteus made me see him as Fish. He switched to Sharron, and then Delia. "Who would you prefer to see, Your Highness?" When he made me think I was seeing James, I almost felt my heart stop. "Is this better?"

I was speechless. I couldn't look away from him. I moved closer and touched his face. "James," I whispered.

"Porteus, what are you doing?" my father asked.

In a blink of an eye, Porteus was back to himself. "I'm sorry, Your Majesty. I didn't mean to upset her."

"Do that again," I said.

"Thea, I don't—"

"Do that again!" I yelled, cutting my father off.

Porteus looked at him. When my father gave him an approving nod, he made me see James again.

"How many people can you make see James?" I asked.

"As many as I want, Your Highness."

"Even if they're not there?"

Porteus got a confused look on his face. "I don't understand."

I was beginning to get excited. "How far does your magic go?" I asked.

"I'm not sure, Your Highness."

"Thea, this may not—"

I spun around and cut my father off again. "I have to try!" I yelled.

He didn't answer.

I moved closer. "Father, you said yourself you needed the energy first. I'll never get back in time to save James. This is the only way. You have to show me where he is."

"Thea, you know I can't speak the words. I can't even think them."

"You don't have to," I replied. I took his dagger from his waist and cut into my wrist. "Please, father," I said, holding it out.

My father looked thoughtful for a moment. "You know this may change things, don't you?"

"I don't have a choice."

After several moments, he finally took his dagger back and cut into his wrist. When he put our wrists together, I drew a breath. I saw a long, dark tunnel deep underground, with an entrance that began right behind the Witch Museum. There were three men guarding the entrance. As my father showed me the way to James, I saw how many tunnels met up with this one. I was careful to follow every step he showed me. Some of his vision was blurry, but I was able to make out the way. I finally saw James and Joshua. I knew exactly where they were now.

I pulled my arm away, wiped off the blood, and headed for the door.

"Thea," my father called.

I opened the door and looked back at him. He seemed so stressed. Could it be he knew something bad was going to happen?

"I'll come back to you, Father." I grabbed my coat and headed for the stairs. I could hear Porteus walking behind me. Fish was coming out of the kitchen when we reached the bottom.

"Where are you going?" Fish asked.

I tightened the grip on my coat.

"I'm taking a walk," I answered.

"At two in the morning?" He looked at Porteus and then back at me. "Is Godzilla coming with you?"

I didn't smile. "Yes," I said flatly.

He studied my eyes. He looked down at the cut on my wrist and raised his eyebrows. He looked into my eyes again. Fish could always see right through me. I didn't have to speak a word. He knew; I could tell. He reached for his hooks and began to strap them on.

"What are you doing?" I asked.

He opened the closet and reached for his coat. "What does it look like? I'm coming with you."

"Stay here, Fish," I ordered.

"Not a chance, witch," he said as he threw on his coat.

Delia came out of the kitchen holding some hot tea. She noticed Fish had his coat on and immediately got upset. "Where do you think you're going?" she asked.

"I'm just going for a walk with Thea," he answered.

"At two in the morning?"

"We'll be right back," he promised.

Delia glanced down at my arm as I tried to hide the cut I had made on myself. Her eyes drifted to Porteus, then back to me. She sighed and placed her tea on the foyer table. "Good. I'll come with you," she said. "Let me grab my coat."

"Why don't you wait here?" Fish suggested.

Delia opened the closet door. "Why don't you wait with me?" she shot back.

"We're just going for a walk," Fish snapped at her.

Delia glared at him. "And I'm in the mood to walk right now," she hissed.

"You're staying here!" I yelled.

Delia's eyes moved over to me. She glanced at my arm again as she yanked the coat from the hanger. "I'm afraid you have no say-so in this, witch." She put her coat on and pointed at Fish. "If he goes, I go. You may like doing things alone, but I follow him, no matter what." She walked past us and out the door. "You coming?" she said over her shoulder.

I looked at Fish, hoping he would stop her.

He shrugged his shoulders. "Sorry, Thea."

I shook my head, and we all headed out into the night.

Chapter 20
Tunnel of Daggers

I was surprised to see how the night had warmed up. The chilling wind was gone. Salem was peaceful and quiet. Not one soul was out and about. It almost felt like Salem was bracing itself for what was to come. Truth was, so was I. My father said things might change a little because he had shown me where James was. I just didn't know how much.

I was grateful it was so late. Sharron lived nearby, and I didn't want her to see us. I didn't need yet another person to look after. It was bad enough Delia had tagged along; I didn't need another witch here right now. I knew Delia would have refused to stay behind. Even Fish would have found a way to catch up to me. I thought of sending them both away, but I knew deep down that Fish was meant to be here.

As we made our way down the street, Delia kept looking behind her at Porteus. "So why is he here?" she asked, pointing with her thumb. "Since when do owls like taking walks?"

"Where are we walking to, anyway?" Fish asked.

"The Witch Museum," I answered.

"That's a short walk," Delia said.

I stopped and faced her. "Then go home, Delia. I really don't need you here right now."

She stared at me for a long moment, eyes narrowed. "I knew you were up to something, witch." She pulled off her belt and tossed it above her head. "To my blade I command, come flying back into my hand." When she caught it, she smiled at me. "Lead the way, witch."

"I'm not going to babysit any of you," I said.

"Just go home, Delia. Please," Fish begged.

Delia gave him a dirty look. "Together, remember?"

"I have to go with Thea," he said.

"So do I," Delia shot back. "If you don't let me come with you, I'll never be able to forgive myself for what I've done. Don't you understand that?"

Fish looked at her with caring eyes. "It wasn't your fault, Dells. None of us knew it was Simon."

"Tell that to my heart," she said, looking away. "I don't think it understands that."

Fish and I exchanged glances. I understood her need to be here. I knew I would be doing the same thing. I gave up on trying to send her away and pulled out my wand. "Keep your eyes open, both of you," I

~ 259 ~

said.

As we neared the Hawthorne Hotel, Porteus told us to stay out of sight. "I will approach them alone," he said. "Try to find a place to stay out of sight."

I reached for his leathery arm. "Be careful with them. They're very strong."

He laughed. "You haven't seen these warlocks fight, have you? I don't know what kind of spell they're using to get so big, but it's done nothing but weaken their spells and slow them down."

"Are you sure?" I asked.

"I'll be perfectly fine, Your Highness."

"What did he call you?" Delia asked.

Porteus crossed the street toward the museum while we followed in the shadows. I kept Porteus in my sights as we hid behind a maple tree near the park. I was grateful it was such a dark night. It would be easy to hide from the warlocks.

Fish pointed to a house next to the museum. "Let's hide in that yard. We can get a better look from there."

I nodded, and we carefully made our way across the street and into the yard. Fish scooted in beside me.

"What the hell is that?" he said when he looked across the street.

"Oh my God," Delia gasped.

It was one of the warlocks. He had long brown hair and was enormous. Two other warlocks filed in behind him as they approached Porteus. Again, I was shocked by the appearance of their skin. It was being stretched to its limit, causing it to appear shiny and plastic looking. Even their heads looked odd. They had bald spots from where the hair had been pulled apart from their heads growing so fast. It made me wonder what part of the spell Simon was getting wrong. It was a mistake he made often. They were even mixing the anti-aging potion wrong. They always turned to dust when they died.

"They're real-life Frankenstein monsters," Fish said.

They were only about twenty feet away from us. "Be quiet, Fish," I hissed.

"I thought you were supposed to be at the fort," the long-haired warlock said to Porteus. It was clear Porteus was making them see another warlock.

"I came for the half humans," Porteus answered. "Simon said to move them."

Delia shifted closer to me. "Why isn't he attacking Porteus?" she asked.

"It's a long story," I said.

"What the hell has Simon been feeding his dogs?" Fish asked. "They look like one big blister."

I motioned for him to be quiet as Porteus spoke to the warlock.

"Move them?" the warlock was saying. "Why wasn't I told about this?"

Porteus stepped closer to them. "If Simon wanted you to know his every move, you'd be with him, wouldn't you?"

As Porteus spoke to the warlocks, my eyes searched for the entrance to the tunnel. It was too dark to get a good look from here.

"Is that a camera?" Fish asked.

My heart sank. "What?"

"I think it is," Delia said. "I've never seen a camera there before."

I followed their eyes. The moment I spotted the camera on a huge statue across from the museum, I knew I had to stop Porteus. Simon would surely see us and give the command to kill James and Joshua. The odds of Simon being asleep right now were high, but I knew I couldn't take any chances.

Before I could move, I saw Cory climbing the statue and doing something to the camera. Jason and Ciro were with him. Ciro spat a spell into his hand and climbed up to Cory. I wasn't sure what they were doing as Ciro held the spell up to the lens.

"Why didn't Simon call me himself?" the warlock asked Porteus.

"Do you want me to call him so you can ask him yourself?" Porteus answered.

Cory climbed down from the statue and exposed his weapons. It was then I noticed his arm was bleeding a little. I knew at once that my father had shown him what I was doing.

"I'll call him myself," the warlock said, pulling out his phone.

Porteus picked the warlock up by the neck, and we ran from the yard. The other two warlocks drew their weapons, but Porteus sent them to the ground, grasping their heads as they screamed in pain. Dust drifted into the air when Cory and Ciro swooped in and finished the two warlocks off.

I ran and searched frantically for the entrance to the tunnel.

"Where is it?" Cory said. "We don't have much time before that spell on the camera is going to wear off." I couldn't see the entrance my father had shown me. "It moved," I said, touching the walls of the museum. I thought of going back to the house I had used when I found Helena. I knew there was a tunnel there, but I also knew it would take us hours to find where it led. Simon wasn't dumb enough to keep them where I had found Helena.

"We have to find it!" Cory yelled.

He and Ciro kept searching the area but found nothing. We checked every brick and stone in the wall, but I couldn't find the entrance. I was about to wave my hand when Ciro stopped me.

"Do you think Simon wouldn't be prepared for your magic?" he said. "I'm sure he put a spell here to warn him if you found this place. We can't take that chance."

I looked at Porteus, who was still holding up the long-haired warlock. "Make him tell you," I ordered.

Porteus nodded. A look of terror came over the warlock's face when Porteus showed him his true form. He began to shake as Porteus took hold of his tail and put it into the warlock's ear. The man gasped from the pain. I knew that pain, because Porteus had once done that to me. I was surprised when Porteus snapped the warlock's neck and tossed him aside.

"What about the entrance?" I yelled as the warlock turned to dust.

Porteus walked over to a maple tree and tapped it three times. I felt a wave of relief wash over me when it revealed the entrance to the tunnel.

Porteus was the first to enter. I stepped in behind him, and the others followed. I could smell the mildew as we crept inside. The tunnel was huge. It almost looked like it had been a railroad tunnel at one time, but there were no tracks in sight.

"You could fit a car in here," Jason whispered.

I put my finger over my lips, motioning him to stay quiet.

"What is that horrible smell?" Delia said, putting her hand over her nose.

The walls were covered in mold and red mud. The smell was almost unbearable. As we made our way deeper into the tunnel, the mud and mold gave way to brick walls.

"Looks like someone has been building down here for years," Cory whispered.

"What is that buzzing sound?" Fish said in a low voice.

I heard the faint sound of matches being lit. I knew that could only mean one thing. "Warlocks," I said, raising the wand.

"Get behind me, Your Highness," Porteus said as he moved to take position in front of me.

"Remember, we can't kill them," I reminded him. "We need to leave two of them alive."

"For what?" Cory asked.

"You'll see," I said, moving forward.

We talked in low whispers as we made our way down the tunnel. Old layered bricks covered the walls. Some of the bricks were falling off. I could still hear that faint sound of warlock spells but couldn't see any warlocks. The tunnel began to curve.

"Wait here," I said, trying to get a better look. I inched my way forward and peeked around the curve in the tunnel. The moment I tried walking around it, something shot out from the wall and pierced my shoulder. I was slammed against the wall, only to get a dagger thrust through my leg. I fell to the ground, trying not to shout out in pain.

"Don't move," Ciro said, pointing at the walls.

It was then I noticed the spells along the walls. They were embedded in the bricks. That was the sound I was hearing. It wasn't warlocks—it was their spells. They had booby-trapped the tunnel.

Cory got on his stomach and tried reaching for me. "Grab my hand," he said.

The minute I moved my hand, I set off another spell, which sent a dagger straight into my arm.

"Dammit," Cory said and dragged himself back.

Jason pulled off his belt and swung it to me.

"Hold on to it," he said. "I'll pull you back."

I looked at his belt, fearing I would set off another spell. I considered using my magic, but Ciro was right—Simon would be prepared for that. I thought better of it and didn't reach for the belt. I leaned my head against the wall, closed my eyes, and pulled out the daggers from my arm and leg. I tried pulling the one from my shoulder, but it was too painful.

"We have to get her out of there," Delia said.

"No. Stay back," I answered. "I'm fine."

I looked at the walls, trying to figure out what to do. How were we possibly going to get past all these spells without setting them off? I looked down the tunnel and noticed that the spells were only along the sides of the walls, and only where there were bricks. The bricks ended a few yards away. But how would we get from here to there? An image of Sammy came to me. I pictured him climbing the walls. *Of course— that would work.*

I looked at the others. "Sammy's shoe spells," I whispered.

Cory looked back at me, confused for a moment, but I pointed down the tunnel to where the bricks ended. He instantly knew what I meant. He began whispering a spell to the others. As they all began chanting spells on their hands and feet, I tried to pull the dagger from my shoulder again. I put my hand over my mouth and gave a yank. I finally got it out and tossed it aside. I feared healing myself and decided to wait until we were out of the tunnel.

"Is this going to work?" Delia asked.

Fish put his hand up to the wall. When his hand stuck to it like glue, he smiled. "I think so," he said.

One by one, they began climbing the walls.

"Spiderman, Spiderman, does whatever a spider can."

"Fish!" Cory said in a low whisper.

"Sorry, I couldn't resist," Fish answered.

When Porteus was over my head, he checked the walls around me for more spells. "I think we're clear," he said, lowering his hand to me. He pulled me up as if I were a feather. "Hold on to me, Your Highness."

"Why does he keep calling you that?" Fish asked.

"Keep moving, Fish," Cory snapped at him.

We crawled a few yards before the sound of spells faded.

"I think we cleared the spells," Ciro said. He jumped off and waved his hand over the walls. "All clear," he said, looking up at us.

"Thea, you're bleeding everywhere," Delia said when we came off the wall.

I tore off a piece of my shirt and wrapped it around my leg.

"We have to hurry before you bleed to death," Cory said. He ripped a piece from his shirt and wrapped it on my arm.

"I'll be fine," I answered.

A distant scream made our heads spin around.

"That was Joshua," Fish said.

He tried to break into a run, but Cory grabbed him and held him back.

"We have to be careful, Fish," Cory said. "We're only going to get one shot at this."

When I heard the sound of James's agonizing screams, I felt my heart stop. They were doing something horrible to him. I tried with all my might to stop myself, but it was too late. By the time Ciro and Jason tried reaching for me, I was gone.

Not even the pain from my leg could stop me from running. James's cries sent a surge of anger through me. What were they doing to him? I kept telling myself not to kill the warlocks, but I feared my anger would win the battle. Every time I heard his cries of pain, I ran faster. I knew I had to stop myself. If I killed the warlocks, the plan would never work. I heard the others running behind me and prayed they would catch me and hold me back.

James's cries became louder. My heart felt like it would leap out of my chest. Finally, when I felt a sharp blast of pain through my head, I allowed the pain to stop me. I knew at once it was Porteus causing me that pain. I fell to my knees, grasping at my head.

Cory caught up to me and dragged me a few feet back. He held onto me as the buzzing in my head stopped. "They're right around the corner," he whispered into my ear.

"Everyone stay calm," Jason whispered.

I pulled away from Cory and peeked around the corner. There it was, the dark room I had seen in my father's vision. It was nothing less than a torture chamber. I was reminded of Wendell's dark dungeon. Joshua and James were strapped to a large wooden table in the middle of the room. The floor was covered in their blood. They had been tortured.

Eight enormous warlocks filled the room. They seemed to be enjoying themselves as my loved ones begged for mercy. Javier's body was still in the room, the dagger still thrust into his heart. They had tossed him in a corner as if he were trash.

Cory pointed out the camera so I wouldn't storm in. "Not yet," he whispered.

A black-skinned warlock spat out a spell at James, and I covered my ears as James shook and cried out in pain. The spell began to burn and tear apart his skin. The warlocks watched in amazement when James's tattoos began glowing and healing the injury.

"See, the tattoos are some kind of spell," an older warlock said.

"Throw one on the owl that's on his chest," the black warlock said.

A warlock leaned over and spat onto James's chest. He instantly began to shake and convulse as the spell made a deep hole in his chest. A moment later the hole began sealing itself shut.

"That's amazing," one of them said.

I understood now why James had gotten so many tattoos. My father must have known he would be going through this.

The black-skinned warlock spat out another spell, this time hitting Joshua in the stomach. They laughed as Joshua cried out for them to stop.

"I've never seen anything like it," the black warlock said.

"Throw another one," said a young-looking warlock. "I don't get tired of seeing this."

"Do something," Delia cried from behind us.

I looked at Porteus. "It's time."

He nodded and walked into the room. The other warlocks didn't seem surprised to see him. I knew Porteus was making himself look like one of them.

Ciro began making his way to the camera. "Wait for my signal," he said.

I nodded as Porteus spoke to the warlocks.

"They're being moved," he said.

"And take away the fun?" the black-skinned warlock answered.

"I'm killing him first," Fish whispered.

"We have to leave two of them alive," I hissed at him.

The other warlocks resumed spitting spells at James and Joshua as the black-skinned warlock spoke to Porteus.

"Simon never said anything to me about moving them," he said.

In an instant, Ciro whistled, signaling that he had put a spell on the camera.

Fish's hooks flew through the air and sank into the black warlock's chest. "Die, you son of a bitch,"

Fish said, pulling his skin away.

The room filled with dust as we stormed the room.

"Leave two alive," I shouted. I wanted to wave my hand and send them all into hell, but I knew I couldn't take that kind of chance. Warlock spells began flying all around the room. Several hit Jason and sent him crashing into the wall. He shook on the ground from the pain but was soon on his feet as his tattoos began to heal the area.

The warlocks had unbelievable strength. One of them grabbed Ciro by the neck and almost snapped him in two. But Ciro was faster. He used his machete to cut the man's hands clean off, releasing himself from his grip. Ciro swung it again and cut off the warlock's head. Meanwhile, Fish pulled Delia out of the way when one warlock tried going after her, but Delia pushed away from him and plunged her spear through the warlock's head. I was having a hard time helping them fight. My leg and shoulder wouldn't let me move much.

I noticed how slow the warlocks were moving. Porteus was right—their large size did nothing to increase their speed. If anything, it made it worse. Their minds didn't seem capable of keeping up with the chaos. They spat spells wildly as the others ducked out of the way. I almost waved my hand when Jason got hit with another spell. He jumped to his feet and shot off his guns, sending dust drifting into the air. Another warlock sent a spell at Cory and knocked him to the ground, but Ciro was right behind him, slicing the warlock in two with his machete.

I spotted the warlock who had killed Javier. "There!" I shouted at Cory.

All at once, Porteus forced the warlocks to their knees and grabbed their heads. He whipped his tail and sent the warlock who had killed Javier to Cory's feet.

Cory's eyes were on fire as he held up his blades. "I'm going to savor this moment," he said, almost salivating.

Porteus already had the two warlocks we would need by the neck. He held them high against the wall as he let them see what he really looked like. I almost had to laugh as a look of terror washed over them.

The remaining warlock tried running from the room, but Jason shot off his gun, sending a death spell right at him. Everyone turned to Cory, who still had the warlock on his knees.

Cory stood over him, his face red with rage. "Fish," he said, never looking away from the warlock, "let me borrow your hooks." He unstrapped his weapons, dropped them to the ground, and held out his arms. Fish quickly strapped his hooks onto Cory.

The warlock tried spitting a spell at him, but Cory kicked him in the face and sent the spell across the room. The warlock jumped to his feet and tried to run, but Cory sent the hooks straight into his back. I had to look away as Cory pulled the hooks back as slowly as he could. The warlock screamed in pain, and I couldn't blame him. Cory was taking his time skinning him alive.

When I finally heard the warlock turn to dust, I limped my way over to James, who was still convulsing from the pain. "James," I said, grabbing his face.

He looked at me. "W . . . hat t . . . ook you s . . . so l . . . long?" he mumbled.

"I'm so sorry, my love," I said, kissing his face. "I'm here."

"A . . . bout t . . . time."

I couldn't get over how bad he looked. His eyes were swollen shut; his face was black and blue. I shook my head and looked at Joshua. He was barely alive. Both of them looked like they were on death's door. I glanced over my shoulder at my friends. Jason had burn marks all over him. Ciro had also been hit with a spell. He was trying to be brave, but I knew he was in pain.

"J . . . Joshua, I . . . is he still a . . . alive?" James asked.

"He's hanging in there," Cory said as he ran to the table and began to cut away the ropes. He called for Fish to come help him with Joshua, but Fish didn't answer. "Fish, get over here!" Cory yelled.

Again, Fish didn't answer.

I looked over my shoulder and spotted him and Delia crouched over Javier's body.

Delia dropped to her knees, shaking her head. "Look what they did to you," she cried.

Fish reached over and pulled the dagger from Javier's chest. "We're taking you home, buddy," Fish said as tears streamed down his face.

Ciro helped me cut the ropes away from James's legs. I gasped when I noticed the needles impaled in the soles of his feet. Joshua's feet had needles in them, too. Both men were covered in burn marks from spells hitting their bodies. The areas with tattoos had healed, but that didn't mean they didn't

~ 272 ~

feel the pain.

I spun around and stared at the two warlocks Porteus was still holding.

"Don't do it, Thea," Cory said. "Remember, you said you needed them."

I ignored him and limped over to the warlocks. "I want you to know," I said through my teeth, "that today your life will end. You will learn that you've been helping a half-human witch all along. You will die knowing that your life meant nothing to Simon. These last few moments of your life will be spent realizing you were only his puppets."

"What are you talking about, witch?" one of them said.

I smiled. "You'll see."

"We have to get them out of here!" Cory yelled.

I leaned over and whispered instructions into Porteus's ear.

He nodded and said, "Yes, Your Majesty."

I called Ciro and Jason over. As much as I hated to ask, I knew I needed their help. It was the one thing I hadn't thought about: Who would stay here with these men? My father had been right to send them looking for me.

"I need you both to stay here tonight," I said. "Just until the sun comes out. Simon needs to think his men are still alive. I want you both to tie these men down on that table James and Joshua were on. Porteus will fill you in on what's going on. If more warlocks come in here, let Porteus take care of them."

"As you wish, Thea," Ciro answered.

I spun around when I heard James gasping. Cory was pulling the needles out of his feet.

~ 273 ~

"I don't think they can walk," Cory said.

Porteus dropped the warlocks like bags of rocks. They both clamped their hands to cover their heads as Porteus came to help Cory. "My head!" one warlock screamed.

"Hurts, doesn't it?" I said.

Porteus threw James over one shoulder and Joshua over the other. Cory and Fish wrapped up Javier's body and picked him up. As we made our way out of the dark room, I thought it best if we took a different tunnel.

"Wait here," I said. I limped into another tunnel and began searching for an easier way for us to leave. It took me several long moments to find the tunnel I had used when I rescued Helena. The exit to the tunnel was near my apartment.

I returned to the others and told Porteus to rejoin Jason and Ciro. I don't even know how I managed to drag James out of there. He was so weak. Joshua didn't look any better. Cory was having a hard time keeping him up. I knew every step they took was filled with pain because of their feet.

"We're almost there, my love," I said, holding James up.

"Joshua," he said in a labored voice.

"I've got him," Cory answered.

When we finally reached the exit to the tunnel, James collapsed on the living room floor. Joshua broke down when he realized they were really out of there. I wanted to wave my hand and heal them, but I knew I had to wait.

Cory put Joshua next to James and ran to the window. "I don't see a soul out there," he said.

I helped James onto the sofa. "Go get the truck, Cory. We'll drive them home from here."

"I'll get Delia's wagon. It's right down the street."

He was out the door in an instant. I helped Fish put Javier's body near the door.

Delia wouldn't stop crying.

Fish gathered her in his arms. "Everything is going to be okay, baby," he murmured.

Cory pulled up moments later. We hurried and got everyone into the wagon. I finally breathed a sigh of relief when we pulled away from the curb. We had done it. I couldn't believe we had actually done it. I knew the hardest part was still ahead of us, but that was nothing compared to having James back in my arms.

Delia broke into a sob and leaned her head on Fish's shoulder. "We did it," she cried. "We did it."

Fish wrapped his arm around her. "I think we all feel the same way, baby."

Chapter 21
Stupid Blind Witch

I stood by the window of my father's room, looking out into the darkness. My father was tending to James and Joshua. He'd been giving them a healing tea since we brought them home. Some of the spells had really done their damage, and Joshua and James were healing slowly.

I couldn't bring myself to stay in the room with James. It was breaking my heart to see him like that. I had to walk out of the room when my father said he'd found more needles in their legs. Rage was coursing through me. I had to calm myself down.

I felt numb as I waited to leave. The sun would be coming up in a few hours, and I knew Simon would be waiting. I had gone through my plan in my head a million times. There was no looking back now. The good news was that Simon had no power over me anymore. I had taken back the only weapon he had to use against me. My James was safe.

Fish and Delia couldn't understand why I wouldn't just go kill Simon.

"We have James and Joshua back now," Fish said, looking confused. "What's stopping you?"

I had never answered his question. Instead I had sneaked into my father's room and was now waiting for him to return. It wasn't that I didn't want to answer the question; I just didn't know how. The events of tonight had affected me more than I bargained for. There was a heavy feeling in my heart. I feared I would lose someone else today. My friends all planned on going with me to kill Simon, but they didn't know was that I had no intention of letting them go. I knew Simon was not a stupid man. He would be ready for whatever I had planned. No, this was going to be between me and him. If anyone had to die today, it would be me.

There was also the small detail of the promise I had made. I still didn't know what would happen to me when I broke it. I had chased the black witch inside me away, but what was waiting for me after that? Was I going to be dragged into hell? One thing I did know— my loved ones would be nowhere in sight when that moment came. I thought of that horrible scene in the dark room, with James and Joshua strapped to the table. Visions of their bloodied bodies kept flashing through my head. I just couldn't shake it. It was an image burned into my mind.

"James is asking for you," I heard my father say.

I turned and faced him. He was standing by the door. "How is he, Father?"

He looked somber. "He'll be better in a few hours."

"And Joshua?" I asked hopefully.

He sighed. "His body will heal, but his mind will take some time."

I looked down, knowing I couldn't put them through this again.

"This wasn't your fault," my father said.

I returned to the window and stared out again. I heard my father's footsteps as he approached me.

"Look at me, Thea."

I turned and stared into his eyes.

"You look so much like your mother," he said, touching my face. "Every time I look at you, I'm reminded of how much I miss her." He wrapped his arms around me and drew me closer. "If I hadn't had you, I would have lost my mind without her. You gave me hope. You gave me a reason to live. Everything I've done in my life has been to protect you."

"I know," I answered.

He put his fingers under my chin and made me look at him. "Then why would you think I would let you die now?"

"What about them, Father?" Tears filled my eyes. "Would you let my friends die?"

"I would have saved that boy if it were possible, Thea."

"Who's next?" I asked bitterly. "Who will destiny take from me now?"

"Is that what worries you?"

When I didn't answer, he pulled away and reached into his pocket. I was surprised when he pulled out the green crystal, the same crystal I had put my son into once. He held it out to me. "I believe this belongs to you," he said.

"Yes, of course—Simon wanted me to bring it," I said, taking it.

"That's not why I'm giving it to you, Thea."

I looked at him, confused.

"I always knew you would need it," he said.

Was he expecting me to put my son back in it?

"I know you'll figure it out," he added softly.

I shook my head. "I don't understand, Father."

He looked toward the door. "Your husband is waiting."

I didn't have time for his puzzles. I put the crystal into my pocket and headed for the door.

"Thea," my father called.

I paused. "Yes, Father?"

"I know you'll make the right choices."

I nodded and hurried down the hall to James's room, but stopped when I heard him and Fish talking.

"We'll burn his body in the morning," Fish said.

"I tried to save him," James said. "I swear, I did all I could." I knew he was talking about Javier.

"It wasn't your fault, James," Fish answered.

There was silence. "How is Delia doing?" James asked.

"I think she's sleeping," Fish answered. "I'm about to jump into bed with her."

"And Joshua? How is he holding up?"

"He's in the next room, sound asleep," Fish said.

"Go get some rest, kid. You look really tired."

"Yeah, it's been a long night. You should get

some rest, too, James."

"I do feel like I could sleep for a year," James answered. "I'm just waiting for Thea."

"Big day tomorrow," Fish said. "I can't even imagine how life is going to be without Simon lurking around the corner."

James sighed.

"Are you feeling bad because he's your father?" Fish asked.

"No. I've never seen him as my father. His life means nothing to me. I only wish I would have known how much suffering he would cause one day. I would have killed him a long time ago."

"Don't think about that. Tomorrow he'll be a distant memory."

"I'm sorry, Fish, but I can hardly keep my eyes open."

"Get some rest. I'll see you in a few hours."

I snuck into one of the rooms as Fish walked out. I decided to let James get some rest. I knew I would only keep him up. When he was sleeping, I would go in there and kiss him goodbye.

"Is that you, Thea?" a voice behind me said.

I spun around. It was Joshua. I hadn't realized he was sleeping in this room. I noticed there was a pot of tea on the nightstand—my father's potion, no doubt. Joshua looked so much better than the last time I'd seen him.

"Did I wake you, sweetie?" I asked, stepping away from the door.

He shook his head. "I wasn't sleeping."

I crossed the room. "You should get some rest," I said as I sat by his side.

"I can't," he answered. "I keep hearing James screaming in my head."

I ran my fingers through his red hair. "You want me to cast a sleeping spell on you?"

He looked away. "Will it make the images go away?"

I took his hand and squeezed it. "I'm so sorry this happened to you, Joshua."

When he looked back at me, his eyes were wet with tears. "They killed him, Thea. They killed Javier right in front of me. I had to see his body lying on the floor the whole time we were there. They tossed him aside like he didn't matter." He turned away as tears streamed down his face.

I didn't know what to say. He was in so much pain.

"Where did they put him?" he asked, still looking away from me.

I sighed. "He's in the guest house. They're going to burn him in the morning."

Fresh tears rolled down his face. "I want to go see him."

"Stay in bed, Joshua," James said behind me.

I hadn't heard him enter the room. As he crossed the room, I noticed he was still having trouble walking.

James sat on the other side of the bed. "How you doing, kid?" he asked Joshua.

Joshua wiped away his tears. "I've seen better days."

James reached for his hand. "I told you we would make it out of there, didn't I?"

Joshua sat up and threw his arms around James. The two squeezed each other as James gave Joshua a hard pat on the back. "I love you, kid," James said.

"I love you, too, man," Joshua cried. A special bond had formed between them. They had lived through hell together.

"Now get some rest," James said, pulling away. "I'll be right next door if you need me, okay?"

Joshua nodded. James glanced at me and gave me a subtle nod. I knew exactly what he wanted me to do. I waved my hand and sent Joshua into a deep sleep.

James sat there watching Joshua sleep. "I don't know how you haven't gone insane, Thea," he finally said. "I nearly lost my mind down in that tunnel."

I shrugged. "I had to stay sane, so I could come back to you."

He looked at me. "You really are a wizard. No normal person could endure what you have and retain their sanity. I'll never get over how strong you really are."

I smiled. "The only thing that would drive me mad is losing you."

He stood up and walked around the bed toward me. "I missed you, forest girl," he said as he touched my face.

I choked on a laugh and threw my arms around him. I finally allowed myself to break free of my tears. "I thought I'd lost you," I said, squeezing him.

James sighed. "You have no idea how happy I was to see you."

I squeezed him harder. "I would have died with you. I would have gone mad."

"But you found me, my love. You found me."

"I was so scared," I cried.

He looked into my eyes and wiped away my tears. "You, scared? I find that hard to believe."

"I love you, James. I love you."

"And I will forever love you," he said and kissed me.

I helped James back to our room and put him in bed. He fell asleep the moment his head hit the pillow. The others had also gone to sleep. The house was dead quiet. I sat next to James, touching every curve of his beautiful face. Yet the image of him strapped to that table wouldn't leave me. It was only cementing my decision to leave without him. I knew he would be furious with me, but I couldn't let him get hurt again. He had suffered so much because of me. My own stupidity had led me to make all the wrong choices.

I thought of the boys. I had taken so much away from them. Javier and Sammy were dead because of my choices. I wasn't sure if I was prepared to keep allowing them to risk so much.

Fish's words began going through my head. *We have James and Joshua back now. What's stopping you?* What was stopping me? I could kill Simon right now. No one had to get hurt. All I had to do was get the blood I had given him. The black witch herself had said all I had to do was drink it. I could end this tonight and send Simon into hell.

I looked down at James again. I knew in my heart I couldn't let him get hurt again. I leaned down and gave him a kiss on the lips. "You will always be my greatest love," I whispered. I gently pulled away from him and headed downstairs. I threw on a coat and grabbed my stick and a bag.

"So, you're leaving?" my father asked as I entered the kitchen. He was sitting at the table with a cup of tea in front of him. He wouldn't look at me. He kept his eyes on the back door to the kitchen.

"Why? Are you going to stop me?" I asked.

He looked down at his tea. "I really hate when that happens," he said.

"When what happens?"

He sighed and began running his finger along the rim of the teacup. "When you know what's going to happen, but you can't say a word because it will change how it ends."

"I wouldn't know, Father. I never know what's going to happen."

"And maybe that's for the best. But I must say, this is the one time I wish I could tell you." He sighed again and put something on the table. He pushed it forward and looked at me. "I think you may need this. At least, I'm hoping you will."

I realized it was the capsule he needed me to fill with energy. "So, you're not going to try and stop me?" I asked, looking back at him.

He glanced toward the door again. "This is the one thing I hoped wouldn't change, the one thing I hoped you would do. I only wish that you didn't have to suffer so much to get there."

So, I was right. He knew James and my friends would be killed if they came with me. "I love you, Father. I wouldn't be so strong if it were not for you."

He nodded but didn't meet my eyes. "Go. Destiny awaits."

I grabbed the capsule and headed out the door. I soon found myself in the guest house with Javier. They had put his body on one of the beds. He looked so peaceful. I could have sworn he was only taking a nap.

I sat next to him and touched his face. I could already smell the foul odor of death. "I'm so sorry, Javier," I whispered. This wasn't the way I had wanted things to end for him. I wanted to see him married and with kids. If I were able to turn back the years, I would have never entered his life. I reached for his hand and held it to my face. "I love you, sweetie."

"I don't think he can hear you," I heard from behind me.

I spun around. It was Delia. "I didn't know you were here," I said, getting to my feet.

She was sitting in a corner, holding a cup of tea. She put it down and crossed the room. "You are so predictable, witch. You're leaving without them, aren't you?"

I didn't answer.

"Stupid, blind witch. Are you going to get yourself killed? Is that your plan?"

"Stay out of this, Delia."

I was shocked when Delia slapped me hard across the face. I didn't flinch.

"How dare you cheat them out of helping you end this?" she growled. "You owe it to them, witch. They deserve to feed on the spoils just like you. Nothing is going to make them feel better about the last four hundred years than helping you kill that son of a bitch." She put her face inches from mine. "You've killed warlocks to ease your anger, but what about them? When do they get to ease their anger?"

I looked away from her.

"Do you think dying alone will set them free?" she asked.

I didn't answer.

"Go ahead!" she yelled, pointing at Javier. "Tell him he died for nothing."

I tried to walk away.

"It's not going to be that easy, witch." She spun me around.

Angry, I grabbed her arm and practically dragged her over to Javier. I put my hand on the back of her neck and made her look at him. "Look at him," I said, pushing her face down. "You want that to be Fish? How about Cory? You want to see Cory like this?"

"Let go of me!" she yelled.

"Look at him!" I ordered, pushing her face down again. "You want me to take Fish, so he can end up like this? Would that make you happy?"

"Shut up!" she screamed, pulling away from me.

I stepped up to her. "Come on, Delia. Tell me how wrong I am for leaving without them. Slap me again and tell me what a stupid, blind witch I am."

She looked at Javier.

"What's wrong?" I asked. "Don't you want to burn Fish's body with Javier's in the morning? Maybe Joshua will die, too, and we'll be able to burn them all together."

"Shut up!" she said, pressing her hands over her ears.

"Isn't this what you wanted?" I said. "How dare I leave without them, remember?"

She didn't answer.

"Maybe you're right, Delia. Maybe they should come with me. I shouldn't be thinking of saving them; I should be thinking of letting them die. I really am a stupid, blind witch. What was I thinking? I'll go wake them up now, so they can come with me." I turned to leave.

"No," Delia said, grabbing my arm. "Please don't take them." She let go of my arm when she realized those words had come out of her mouth. She looked at Javier again and then bowed her head. She'd realized I was right for leaving them alone.

"Tell them not to hate me, Delia," I said quietly. "Tell them I did it out of love."

She threw her arms around me. "Please be careful."

"Don't worry about me. I've got this."

"I love you, witch," she cried.

"Now who's the crybaby?" I teased.

I said my goodbyes to Delia and headed out into the cold air. I flew over Salem, wishing I had kissed James one last time. I knew he would be angry with me. After all, I had promised him we would do this together. But something inside me knew I had to do it alone, and from the looks of it, so did my father. His words kept going through my head. He'd said this was the one thing he'd hoped I would do. Was it because he knew James would die?

I shook my head as that thought entered my mind. No one was going to die today. I had already come to terms with my own demise. If this was to be the end, I was ready for what destiny had prepared for me.

Chapter 22
One by One

I stopped near the ocean, about a mile from the fort. I thought it best if I commanded my wand to turn into Wendell's head under the cover of darkness. The sun would be coming up soon, and I didn't want human eyes to see me. I also didn't want to get too close to the fort, in case Simon was watching for me. It was still early, but I knew he would be ready for anything. I only prayed that my little plan with Porteus was going to work. If I was right about Simon, he had no intention of letting my loved ones live. Rescuing James and Joshua was the only way they were ever going to get out of there alive. Now when Simon looked at that TV, he would think James and Joshua were still there.

I decided to walk toward the dock and wait for the sun to come up. I would sit in one of those old fishing boats and think about what I was going to do. Would I just grab Simon and take him into Magia? Better yet, would I be required to keep my promise the moment we arrived? This only reminded me of how important it was that I take back the blood I had given to Simon. Once I drank it, I would end Simon's life. At last, my father could return and take back his place as king. My friends would be free and able to live happy lives. It was the only thing that mattered to me anymore.

I jumped onto the fishing boat and let the ocean air hit my face. This fishing boat looked like it had been out of commission for many years. Floorboards were missing, and the mast was cracked. The galley was sealed up with wooden boards. I sat on the deck atop the old hatch, looking toward the fort. Here, I would wait for dawn, so I could make my way to Simon.

I began to fantasize about how I would kill him. I considered cutting off his head, but I knew that would be too easy a death for him. No, Simon had to suffer for all that he'd done. I would pull him apart slowly and enjoy every moment. I could already see myself laughing as he screamed in pain. I gasped when I thought of that. I remembered the day I had put my sword up to Simon's neck.

It was the same day he had captured Fish and thought it was Cory. I had felt every slash I had given him. It was then I realized the pain I would have to go through in order to kill him. I swallowed thickly and tried to prepare myself for that pain. I let the thought of James give me the strength I needed to endure it.

I pulled out a gold leaf and ate it. I knew Simon would be using that shawl to weaken me.

I sat for about two hours before the night gave way to dawn. It was time to leave now. I ate another leaf, sat up, and pulled out my wand. Before I could command it to turn into Wendell's head, I saw something odd. Warlocks were standing near the shore, looking up at the sky. I could see only six of them. Then I spotted more, about forty, all staring up at the sky.

I ducked out of sight and began searching the sky, but it was empty. There wasn't a cloud in sight. I couldn't understand it. What were they looking for? I looked toward the warlocks again. They were clearly trying to stay out of sight. They all carried their weapons at the ready.

It finally occurred to me what that meant. These men were looking for me. They were expecting me to fly across the sky on my way to Simon. I shook my head as I realized Simon was trying to trap me. I didn't even know why I was surprised. This was so like him. Of course, he would be distrustful right now. He didn't want anything to go wrong. Well, things were about to go very wrong for him.

Suddenly a thought occurred to me. I knew James would come looking for me sooner or later. Even my father wouldn't be able to stop him. I couldn't let him walk into this trap. These men were no doubt looking for any kind of help I was bringing with me. If they took one look at James, they would certainly tell Simon that James was no longer his prisoner. I had to get rid of them. I decided I would let them follow me to the fort. But first, I had to let them see me.

I looked at my wand, and it turned into Wendell's head. I threw it in the bag I had brought with me, jumped off the boat, and began walking toward the warlocks. I knew once they spotted me, they would warn Simon I was on my way. I made it a point to walk near the shore and make some noise. I coughed and sneezed, and finally they saw me. I pretended not to notice them when I heard them gasp.

"There she goes," one of them said.

I was almost tempted to taunt them as I passed by a group of them. I could easily see them in the bushes. They weren't very smart. They were so big, I could spot them a mile away. They followed behind me as I made my way to the park where the fort sat. I passed the *Closed* sign and made my way across the grass. I could almost hear the warlocks' hearts beating as I neared the fort. I glanced over my shoulder to see that all of them had followed me here. When I reached the two massive wooden doors to the fort, I stopped and waited.

After a few minutes had passed, I finally yelled, "Are you going to let me in, or should I break the door again?" The doors slowly opened. I heard the warlocks come out of hiding and step in behind me. "You didn't hide very well," I said as I walked in.

"She saw us," I heard one say.

The moment I stepped through the door, the TV came to life. I swallowed hard and looked up. I still didn't know if my plan was going to work, or if Porteus's magic would go this far. I gasped when I saw James and Joshua on their knees, with two warlocks standing over them. I wanted to jump for joy. The two warlocks were Ciro and Jason. James and Joshua were the two warlocks we had kept alive. I knew that all Simon and his men could see was James and Joshua. It had worked. Porteus's magic was tricking their minds.

Ciro and Jason were playing the part well. Their faces looked absolutely evil as they smiled into the camera. The two warlocks were caged and trying to break free. They kept looking into the camera and shaking their heads, trying to warn the others. Ciro and Jason were holding daggers up to the warlocks' necks. They looked like they were waiting on a command from Simon. Laughter erupted around me when Ciro hit one of them over the head.

"Filthy humans," one called out.

I wanted to smile. They had no idea those men were their friends.

I couldn't see Porteus anywhere. Maybe he was concentrating on sending his magic this way.

Relieved, I began looking around the courtyard and spotted the three giant warlocks that were always by Simon's side. They stood near one of the corridors, arms crossed in front of them. They looked even bigger than before. I knew they were the warlocks I would have to kill first. One of them gave a signal, and a shawl was thrown to the middle of the courtyard. Warlocks began pouring from every corridor, all of them armed to the teeth. The courtyard was soon filled with them. There must have been at least a hundred.

Simon's army had shrunk. I had expected to see three times as many today.

"Put it on," Simon's voice rang out as the warlocks who'd been following me entered the courtyard.

I looked around for him. "First, let my friends go," I answered. I knew Simon would be expecting me to say that.

"Put it on!" he shouted.

A few warlocks took a step forward. I watched them out of the corner of my eye. I wanted to laugh. Did they really think they were scaring me? I looked away from them and threw the bag with Wendell's head on the grass. I reached for the shawl and slipped it over my shoulders.

"What a good witch," Simon said.

I pretended to look weak and dropped to my knees. I heard Simon's footsteps coming from one of the corridors and finally spotted him. His face was lit up with joy. He was almost skipping his way to me. The three warlocks hurried ahead of him and cleared a path for him to walk through.

Simon was all dressed in black. I noticed how dark his eyes were. Could it be that they were darker than the last time I'd seen him? My heart began racing when I spotted a vial hanging from his neck. He wore it like a medal. I knew at once that it was my blood.

Simon glanced at the bag on the grass and smiled. He looked around to see who was with me. "What's this?" he asked. "You came alone?"

I didn't answer.

"What am I supposed to do with all these nooses now?" he asked.

"Why don't you use them on your men?" I answered.

Simon laughed. His men took another step toward me.

"Now, now, brothers," he said, "She's only teasing. Aren't you, my little dove?"

"I don't tease," I answered.

Simon began laughing again. He squatted down in front of me and rested his elbows on his knees. "What's in the bag, witch? Did you actually pull it off?"

I looked into his dark eyes. "What do *you* think?"

His eyes lit up as he stared at the bag. A smile spread across his face. "And what kind of spell did you put on the bag?" he asked.

I pretended to be confused. "What do you mean?"

"What's going to happen to me when I open it?" he asked. He was truly expecting anything from me.

"Why don't you open it and find out?"

He looked at the bag like he was expecting it to bite him. I have to be honest, it never occurred to me to put a spell on the bag. That was actually a good idea.

Always the untrusting witch, Simon rose to his feet and called over one of his goons. I knew he was too much of a coward to open it himself. "Bring her the bag," Simon ordered.

The warlock nodded and dragged the bag over to me.

Simon took a few steps back. "Open it, witch."

I slowly reached for the bag, pretending to get weaker by the minute. I grabbed the bottom of it and shook out the head. Simon's eyes widened in shock when he saw that I had actually brought him Wendell's head. His jaw dropped as it rolled to his feet.

"Impossible," Simon murmured.

"Now let them go," I demanded.

He stood frozen and would not answer. When he leaned down to looked at the head more closely, my heart sank. But the amazement in his eyes told me he truly believed this was Wendell's head. I almost thought he was giving me a look of respect when his eyes looked at me again. "You never stop surprising me, witch. Never a dull moment when it comes to you."

"We had a deal, Simon. Let them go."

He glanced up at the cameras. "Oh, that. Yes, I'm afraid there's been a change in plans."

"Let them go, please," I begged.

His glossy eyes looked more evil than ever as he moved closer to me. "You broke our deal, witch. Not me."

"What are you talking about? I brought you Wendell's head."

"Really? Where is Cory? I don't recall telling you to leave him behind."

"Maybe he had things to do," I answered.

Simon punched me across the face, and I flew back. His men erupted into laughter. As he grabbed a handful of my hair, the vial swung back and forth right in front of me. I wanted to reach for it, but knew it wasn't the right time. He yanked on my hair and put my face inches from his. "Have no doubt, witch. Your precious Cory will die. He will take his last breath in a pool of his own blood."

"That's funny," I said. "I was going to say the same thing to you. That always seems to happen, doesn't it?"

His face twisted with anger, and he punched me again. I wasn't sure how many more blows to the face I could take before he knocked me out. "Where is the crystal?" he yelled.

"First, let them go," I answered.

I didn't like the evil smile spreading across his face. I had always known Simon intended to kill my loved ones. I already knew what he was going to do next.

He stepped away from me and looked up at the screen. "Give me the crystal, or they die."

I played the part to the end. With shaky hands, I reached into my pocket and pulled out the crystal.

Simon's wide eyes matched the happiness on his face when he saw it. He looked at it as if he were looking at an angel. "Give it to me," he said, holding out his hand.

When I placed it in the palm of his hand, he drew a breath. "So long I've waited," he said as he held it up.

"Now let them go, Simon."

He kept his eyes on the crystal. "I don't think so, my angel. Not now that we are so close to happiness. I'll let them go when you give me your powers."

"I'm not giving you anything until you let them go."

Smirking, he looked at me from the corner of his eye and put the crystal into his pocket. "I don't like distractions," he said, "and it seems that my bastard son is distracting my little angel. We'll just have to fix that now, won't we?" When he looked up at the screen, the two warlocks, who were Ciro and Jason, were holding the real warlocks, who were now squirming and kicking. Simon nodded, giving my friends the signal to kill the prisoners.

It was over in a moment. Ciro slit the throat of the warlock that looked like Joshua, while Jason cut the head off the one that looked like James.

Simon looked at me, expecting to hear my screams. When I only smiled, his head shot back at the screen.

"You're right," I said. "They really were distracting me."

Simon gasped when he saw his warlocks turned to dust. Porteus's magic faded, and Simon was able to see Jason and Ciro. Jason slowly raised his hand, smiled, and flipped Simon his middle finger. I pulled away the shawl and rose to my feet. As I held out my hand, the head transformed into my sword and flew into my grasp.

The fear in Simon's shocked eyes almost made me laugh. He seemed to be moving in slow motion as he turned and began to run. "Kill her!" he ordered his men.

I waved my hand and sent Simon soaring high above our heads. I left him floating there while I dealt with his goons, spinning my sword as his men surrounded me. I held it up and smiled at them. "Shall we play, my lords?"

The sound of matches being lit filled the courtyard as they began spitting spells into their hands. I heard the sound of weapons being drawn from their sheaths. I'd never seen so many swords before. This was going to be fun.

"You want to die one at a time, or all at once?" I asked.

"I said, kill her!" Simon shouted from above.

The three giant warlocks began running at me. I slammed my sword into the ground, waved my hand, and made the sword wrap itself around their ankles. "Enjoy your trip to hell," I said. I pulled back the sword, and the men were pulled into the ground. I left no mark where they had once stood as the sword snapped back into my hand.

I looked at the others and smiled. I could feel the wizard part of me filling me with confidence. There was no fear, no doubt. These men were not only going to die, they were going to suffer. Some of them were already running away, but I only cared about the ones who dared to stay.

When another group came at me, I waved my hand and sent about forty of them floating into the air. I threw my sword up and made it spin like a helicopter blade. The sword spun in front of them as I waved my hand again and made the men slowly drift toward the sword. I heard gasps of fear from the others when my sword began cutting away heads. They stumbled backward as heads landed all over the courtyard.

I held out my hand for my sword. As dust drifted through the air, I looked up at Simon, smiled, and began walking in his direction.

"Stop her!" Simon shouted.

This was it. Nothing was going to stop me, not even the rest of the warlocks.

I kept my eyes on Simon as the warlocks attacked. I waved my hand and sent four warlocks to the nooses Simon had intended for my friends. With another wave, their necks broke. I shook my sword once, and it turned into my whip sword. When a group of warlocks came at me, I swung the sword and wrapped it around their waists. I smiled at Simon as I pulled back hard, cutting the men in two.

One by one, they fell. I didn't bother chasing after the ones who were getting away. My prize was right in front of me. Simon was about to die a horrible death. I would feel no pity for him. I would give him the same sympathy he had shown when he thought he was killing James. I knew the pain I was about to go through, but I didn't care. No amount of pain could stop me now. I was going to end this. I was going to send Simon back to the hell from where he had come.

When only dust surrounded me, I looked up at Simon. He began floating down to where I was. He looked like a true coward, shaking as if he had seen the devil himself. I let him fall the rest of the way. He began dragging himself away from me, but I waved my hand and made him face me.

"No, please don't hurt me," he said as I got closer.

"Hurt you?" I answered. "No, Simon, I'm going to kill you." I leaned in closer. "I'm going to tear your face away and make you look at it."

"P-please, I'll do whatever you want."

"Yes, beg some more, scum. I like it when you beg."

"I'll forgive you your promise. I'll leave and never return."

What a coward he was. This was his true nature. And I knew he was lying about forgiving the promise. There was no forgiving that. Besides, I didn't need him to forgive the promise. My way out was hanging from his neck.

Simon pulled away as I reached for the vial. "What are you doing?" he said, leaning back.

I wrapped my fingers around the vial. "Taking my life back," I said, and yanked it off his neck.

"That won't break the promise," he said.

"Says you." I pulled off the cap and emptied its contents into my mouth. I closed my eyes as the blood slid down my throat. Suddenly my throat began to burn, as if I had swallowed hot lava. I dropped the sword and put both my hands around my neck.

Simon erupted into laughter, which echoed all over the courtyard. He got to his feet, clapping his hands. I dropped to my knees in pain. What was happening to me? I tried reaching for my sword.

"You won't be needing that," he said, kicking it away.

I drew back my arm and grabbed my neck again. It felt as if a fire was roaring in my throat. I wasn't even sure if I was breathing.

"Come out, my dear," Simon called out to someone. "Let us celebrate the happy occasion."

I almost screamed when I heard that unmistakable cackling laugh. Then I saw her. It was the black witch, Irene. She came out of one of the corridors with a smile from ear to ear. She didn't look old like the last time I had seen her. In fact, she looked beautiful. She wore one of her witch hats and a long, flowing black dress.

I was shocked when Simon greeted her with a kiss on the cheek. "My lord," she said.

"You see," Simon said to her. "She did the one thing I hoped she would."

"No!" I screamed. I thought of the day I had gone searching for Irene. I was now catching what I had missed before. She had known I was coming. I remembered the words she had spoken to her sister, Melanie.

"She insisted on talking to you," Melanie had said.

"Silence, my sister. I knew she was coming," Irene had answered.

I fell over, clutching at my neck. I could hear a strange buzzing in my head. Flashes of my life began passing through my mind. They were all of happy times. With every memory that crossed my mind, something grabbed it and tore it apart. "No," I gasped, realizing that I was being robbed of every happy event I had experienced in my life.

"Oh, did I lie and say to drink the blood?" Irene said. "I meant to say *not* to drink it. It kills your soul, witch."

"No!" I screamed again. All I heard was their echoing laughter as my mind sank into darkness.

Chapter 23
Simon's Secret

I could only feel the cool grass on my cheek as I lay at Simon's feet. I was trying with all my might to fight the darkness that was traveling through my heart. Every happy thought I tried to hang on to was shattered and pushed out of my head, leaving behind only memories filled with sorrow and pain. Those days were clear in my mind. I tried not to think of James. I was too scared that he, too, would be pushed out from my thoughts.

"I'm going to kill you," I said as I tried to stand.

Simon laughed and put his foot on my back, pushing me back down. He squatted down next to me and pulled out a dagger, which he twirled around his fingers. "In a minute, I'm going to tell you what this dagger is for," he began. "But first, I want to thank you. You taught me a great lesson today. I learned that your mind is more clever than I was expecting. I can only imagine what you have waiting for me in Magia." He looked at the dagger. "It's a good thing I plan on changing how things turn out."

He looked at the dagger. "I suppose I should also thank you for today," he continued. "I wasn't sure how to get rid of all those pesky warlocks. I had to keep promising them more and more in order for them to help me. My spell was taking too long to kill them. All they kept doing was getting bigger and bigger. They actually thought I was helping them grow stronger. They had no idea they would be blowing up soon." He smiled and ran the tip of the dagger along my face. "But I knew if I had them all come here, you would take care of them for me. They were starting to get suspicious of me. It was time for them to go. They are almost as useless as humans. Those warlocks will believe anything if you offer them power." He leaned in closer. "Did you know I was killing some of those idiots and telling them it was the half humans? Why do you think they hate them so much? I've been doing that for hundreds of years. I'm the one who fed them that story about the bloodline. They were only too eager to believe me."

"You're an animal," I hissed.

He threw his head back and laughed. Irene laughed with him.

He looked up at her and then back at me. "You are quite predictable, my angel. I knew you would go looking for this witch. That's why I tracked her down. I told her how you were going to live happily ever after if she helped you. Apparently, she didn't like hearing that. You know, she's been telling me some very interesting things. Of course, I won't be making the same mistake she did. She broke her promise, and I plan on keeping mine."

Irene smiled her devilish smile.

"She's the one who suggested lying to you," Simon said. "I thought it was brilliant. You see, I knew that drinking the blood would render you helpless at my feet. I learned that when I told Wendell I could never kill your mother. He made sure I would never be able to say no. He knew the power behind that spell. Once you dance with the devil, there's no way out. But there's one catch: you have to drink the blood of your own free will. Soon, you will deny me nothing. Why do you think I wanted you to kill Wendell? I am a slave to no man."

I closed my eyes, realizing my own stupidity. I had fallen right into Simon's trap. I should have known he would go looking for Irene. He had even told me himself that he knew I was trying to find her. It was the reason why Simon didn't want me catching his scent; he didn't want me to smell him on Irene.

As I writhed in pain, Simon continued, "Of course I had no idea you were going to trick me like that today," he said. "I was ready for anything, but not that. I was rather hoping to see my bastard son die today. What did you do with him, anyway?" he asked. "Is he going to storm the fort with reinforcements?"

I didn't answer. I could think of nothing else but the pain in my throat that was now moving to my chest.

"I hope he does," Simon said. "It will be interesting to see the two of you fight. You know how I love to see your powers at work." He reached into his pocket. "Speaking of powers," he said, pulling out the crystal, "I knew Wendell would never keep his word to use this on me. He's probably very angry with me. I was supposed to kill you, you know." He looked at the crystal again. "Wendell had already killed all those kings. He only needed your father out of the way. I almost said no. Your father was my friend, after all. But then I found out Xander had not only taken the only woman I ever wanted, but now he was having a family with her. That's when I agreed to help Wendell kill you both. He made me make that blood promise to assure him that the job would be done. He armed me with the leaves and that black spell to cast on your father and sent me on my way. But I had other plans," he said, turning the crystal in his hands. "How could I trust a man who would kill his own king? No, I had to plan and find another way."

He laughed and shook his head. "I was such a fool. After killing your father, I thought it would be easy to control you. Plan after plan had failed. I tried using James, but he ended up falling in love with you. Then you went into hiding. I thought I had you when you resurfaced again. I thought my spell would make you love me, but you somehow found a way to fight it. I was starting to lose hope. Until you walked into my house that night." He gazed down at me. "Never in a million years did I expect you would make a blood promise to me. Everything fell into place then. I knew I had you. You made things quite easy for me after that." Simon slammed the dagger into the ground, reached into his coat, and pulled out the leaves. "The only thing left is to kill Wendell. Too bad that wasn't really his head. Now I'll have to keep my promise to him before I kill him. I don't want to end up like this witch," he said, looking up at Irene.

I closed my eyes as Simon laughed. I could feel my heart getting darker and darker. It was becoming almost impossible to think a happy thought. The burning in my throat was slowly fading, leaving behind a dead feeling in my heart. This wasn't like the night I had made the blood promise. This was different. Something inside me was dying. It was the happy part, the part that felt any kind of love. I began to shake as a cold chill spread across my body. My hands felt like I had plunged them into ice water. An ugly anger began rising up inside me.

Simon noticed I was shaking. He smiled and put his face inches from mine. "Don't worry," he whispered into my ear. "It's almost over. You'll be whispering the words 'I do' without hesitation. After that, your heart will stop beating. You will only feel the cold touch of death. It will wrap its fingers around your heart and make it feel alive again. You will be free, my dearest. Any pain that lived inside you will fade away. Nothing else will ever hurt you. Not even those disgusting humans." He got a faraway look in his eyes. "Humans are such trash. I've never come across a more disgusting species. I dream of the day I can rid the world of them. It will be the first thing I do when I get powers." He looked down at me. "I don't know why you've spent so many years protecting them. They'll only break your heart."

Years of despair were evident on his face. He shared the same look of suffering with Irene. She was a tortured soul because of what she'd done, but now I understood that Simon was tortured because of what had been done to him. I was starting to understand his pain, his reason for hating humans so much. Simon had always hated that part of himself. It was the reason he wanted to change. I was finally putting it all together. Simon's father had robbed him of his innocence as a child. It was like my father had said: Simon's father had done the unspeakable to him. No wonder he hated humans. He thought they were all the same.

Irene tapped Simon on the shoulder. "We had a deal," she said. "I don't have time to listen to your speeches. I want what was promised to me."

Simon looked up at her. "And I will keep my end of the bargain, dear lady. There are just two more things we need from this witch." He looked down at me, his eyes on fire as I lay at his feet. He reached for the crystal and put it in my shaky hands. "Give me your powers, witch."

I tried to fight the need to please him. Simon's wish was like a command I couldn't refuse. I felt evil rising up inside me, tasted its bitterness in my mouth. A battle between good and evil was underway in my head, and good was losing.

Tears streamed down my face as I tried to remind myself who I was. I couldn't find the strength to wave my hand and save myself. The darkness was too strong. It was time to pay for what I'd done.

My eyes grew wide as I found myself opening the crystal. What was I doing? I put a hand over my mouth to try to silence myself as I chanted the spell needed to give Simon my powers.

"Don't fight it," he said, moving my hand away.

I cried as the crystal began to glow. Streams of energy flowed from my body and into the crystal. A crackling laugh escaped my lips. The darkness had won. My life was doomed. I had just killed any hope of saving my friends.

Simon beamed as he took the crystal from my hand and held it up. "At last," he said.

"What about our deal?" Irene hissed.

"Patience, witch. Just one more thing." Simon smiled, leaned down, and put his lips to my ear again.

"Do you take me as your husband and bond yourself to me?" he whispered.

The word "yes" came freely from my mouth. It was as if my lips couldn't wait to spit it out.

"And I take you," Simon answered.

The ugly feeling in my heart drifted away. The rage inside me subsided. I began to feel like myself again. The deed was done. My promise to Simon was fulfilled. I expected to see ribbons of light bonding us together, but that didn't happen. There was no magic sealing our marriage together like it had with Fish and Delia. I knew the reason, but I was hoping Simon wouldn't notice. He closed his eyes and took in a deep breath.

"Me, a married man," he said, shaking his head. Evil flashed across his face as his eyes moved to the dagger. What was he going to do with it? My eyes followed his hand as he pulled the dagger out of the ground and stood over me, a grin from ear to ear. "Looks like I don't need you anymore, witch. I heard the spell I needed to open the crystal. I don't even need you to get into Magia. It turns out my ticket has been inside you all along. Hasn't it, my dear?" He looked at Irene.

Irene stared at my stomach. "Yes, she's still pregnant. She's hiding him from you with a spell. She told me herself."

I felt my heart stop. I suddenly realized what Simon had promised her. She wanted my baby. I started to panic as I looked at the dagger in Simon's hand. This was my worst nightmare. It was my vision coming to life. Simon was about to cut my son out of me.

I willed myself to wave my hand at him, but I had no powers left to fight back. I choked on words that wouldn't come out of my mouth. I felt paralyzed by what was happening to my mind and body. I wanted to warn Irene that Simon was going to kill my son. There would be no baby for her to take.

"He wants his heart," I managed to say.

I tried to stand, but Simon pushed me back down. He rolled me on my back and lifted my blouse.

"Please," I begged. I dug my fingers into the ground as I tried to shake the heaving feeling that was holding me down. I had to save my son. I couldn't let Simon take him.

Simon pulled at my skirt and lifted it over my head. I saw a shiny object fall from the skirt's pocket and onto my chest. It was my father's ring.

With every ounce of energy I had, I broke through what was keeping me down. I quickly wrapped my legs around Simon and slipped my finger through the ring.

We were instantly sucked in and began spiraling into my father's world. I heard Irene yell Simon's name as he was pulled into the vortex with me.

"You fool," Simon said, thrusting the dagger into my leg. He pushed me away and held up the crystal. He began chanting the spell he'd heard me cast. Fear washed across his face when the crystal did nothing. He shook it and commanded, "Open."

I dragged myself away from him and smiled. "Only I can open it, you bastard."

Simon began to panic. He knew we were almost there. He growled as he reached down and grabbed a handful of my hair. "Open it, witch. Open it now!"

I reached for the dagger still in my leg and pulled it out. "Go to hell," I said and thrust the dagger into Simon's stomach. I screamed as the pain shot through me. It took the breath right out of me. Simon fell to his knees as we arrived in Magia.

Chapter 24
The Secret River of Life

We were in Attor's cave, the last place I had used the ring. I struggled to my feet and began limping my way out. I heard Simon grunting behind me as he pulled the dagger from his stomach.

"I'm going to kill you!" he yelled.

Outside the cave, I headed for the trees. I had to get myself into the forest. I knew the leaves would help me. They were my only saving grace against the wizards, who would be here any minute. Without my powers, I would be defenseless against them.

I could hear Simon following me as I reached the forest and began calling out to the leaves for help. Simon was having a hard time catching up to me. I knew he was hurt badly. I went deeper into the forest as he struggled to keep up. Why were the leaves not helping me? They had promised. Yet they lay still on the trees and didn't move. I called to them again, but nothing.

Then it occurred to me that I had no powers. They couldn't sense me anymore. My heart sank.

I looked across the woods and saw a beam of light a short distance away. It was the secret river of life. If I could only get to the river and fill the capsule my father had given me, maybe I could use it to get my powers back. I moved faster, ignoring the pain shooting through my leg. I could already hear the force of the river. My heart began racing with excitement.

Every time Simon shouted for me to stop, my body wanted to halt and turn to face him. I had to fight through the power that was within me. This was my last chance. Evil would not have its way with me. I was stronger than it. My father was right: only I had power over my heart. I had to remember who I was and keep running.

I tripped on fallen branches but jumped right back up. I had no idea how far Simon was behind me, and I didn't care. I was going to make it out of here.

Finally, I saw the end. The river was right in front of me. Tears of happiness spilled over as I made a final leap toward the water.

"Now!" I heard someone yell.

I felt the most horrible pain I could remember as I was hit with a spell and launched twenty feet into the air. Another spell hit me, sending me crashing to the ground. I heard bones break from the impact. I could do nothing but scream from the pain.

I heard thumping on the ground from wizards landing all around me. They looked magnificent. It was a sea of beautiful robes and long beards. Some wizards came from across the river as they all left their posts. The sky was soon filled with hundreds of them. They hovered over me as Wendell emerged from the crowd, wearing a beautiful jeweled crown that seemed too big for his head. His beady eyes almost danced with happiness as he looked down at me. An evil smile spread across his face.

"I knew you would be back," he said. "Did you bring Simon with you?"

My eyes searched the trees for him. He hadn't followed me out.

"Answer me," Wendell said, waving his hand.

I choked on sobs as his spell caused pain to vibrate all over my body. It felt like I had put my finger into a wall socket. I tried dragging myself away, but Wendell waved his hand again. I could only gasp as my hair began to pull itself from my scalp. In seconds, my head was bald, covered only in blood. My hair scattered all around me as Wendell began to laugh. I was convulsing from the pain when the rest of the wizards began to land near the edge.

"Kill the traitor's daughter and be done with it," a long-haired wizard said.

"She dies slowly," Wendell said, eyeing me. "I know this witch did not come alone."

I searched the skies for any sign of my friends. I prayed that Attor and the other dragons would get here soon. I knew I was about to die. Wendell's spells were powerful. There was no way my body could take another hit. My only hope was to at least get the energy back to my father, even if he had to take it from my dead hands.

"Where is he?" Wendell asked again. "Tell me, or I will skin you alive!"

Before he could wave his hand at me again, two guards emerged from the trees, dragging Simon behind them. Wendell lowered his arm as Simon tried to pull away from the guards. There were murmurs amongst the wizards. "Wendell was right," one of them said.

Wendell seemed pleased that his warnings had come true.

The guards threw Simon at Wendell's feet. "He was performing a healing spell on himself, sire," a guard said.

"A healing spell?" Wendell asked. He saw the blood on Simon's shirt. "Don't tell me this witch hurt you." He laughed. He leaned down with a huge smile on his face. "It will take more than a healing spell to save you from what I'm about to do to you, Simon."

Simon kept his head down and didn't answer.

Wendell looked at the guards. "Go check the area and see if he brought anyone else with him. Kill anything that doesn't belong here." As the guards took to the sky, Wendell's eyes scanned the wizards. "Who doubts me now?" he asked. "Did I not say this witch would bring him here? I told you he would use the leaves against us. He was in the forest, wasn't he?"

The wizards kept staring at Simon.

Wendell looked down at Simon, who was cowering at his feet. "Asking for my head, were you? I assure you that the only head being cut away will be yours, Simon."

I was surprised when Simon looked at me from the corner of his eye and gave me an evil grin. I looked down at his hand as he slowly reached into his pocket. Wendell was too busy gloating to notice what Simon was doing. "Don't hurt me, my lord," Simon said. "I

~ 314 ~

am your servant. I will be your slave if you wish it so."

As Wendell laughed, I kept my eyes on Simon's hand. What was he reaching for? I froze when I saw him pulling out his dog whistle. I knew what was about to happen. That dog whistle was about to cause the nearby leaves pain.

I pretended to moan and tried to inch my way closer to the river before Simon could blow on it. I was trying to get as close as I could when a hook came flying out of the water and landed right in front of me. I looked over my shoulder at the wizards, but no one had noticed. I frantically searched the river's edge. My heart rejoiced when I saw four pair of eyes slowly popping out of the water. James and the boys were swimming toward me. James pointed to the hook. It took me a moment to realize what he wanted me to do.

I pulled out the capsule my father had given me and inserted it into Fish's hook. Fish gave a tug, and it was quickly dragged underwater.

"Take him to the village," Wendell ordered. "Put him in my dungeon and guard him. Looks like I'll be having some fun tonight."

"What about this witch?" a wizard asked.

Wendell smiled. "She's about to die."

"No," Simon said, looking up at him. "*You* are."

The forest behind us came to life when Simon blew into the whistle. At first, the wizards had no idea what was going on. Then that horrible sound filled the air. Wizards began mounting their staffs and flying away. Wendell's eyes grew wide as the leaves began coming off the trees. He tried reaching for his staff, but Simon held onto his leg.

"You die today!" Simon yelled.

Wendell lost his balance and fell to the ground, but he held out his hand as his staff flew into it. Wendell was in the air in seconds. Simon jumped to his feet and blew the whistle harder.

Suddenly, a hand emerged from the water. It was James. He tried to stay out of Simon's view as he reached for me. "Take my hand," he said.

I clawed my way to him. "James," I said, reaching out. I couldn't reach him.

James thrust himself forward and grasped my hand, but Simon grabbed my feet and dragged me back, pulling me out of James's reach. I heard James shouting, "No!" as he spiraled away. The boys were pulled into the vortex with him. "What?" I said to myself. I looked down at my finger as Simon dragged me away. The ring was gone. It was then I noticed that my hand was full of my own hair. I had threaded it through my fingers when I was crawling to James.

I remembered when Attor had done the same thing when he needed Cory to take Delia back home. He had wrapped some of my own hair on the ring so it would think it was still on me.

Simon began dragging me into the safety of the forest. He knew the wizards would not follow us there. "We have unfinished business, witch," he said.

"Attor," I screamed.

Simon dragged me deep into the forest before he finally stopped and pulled out the crystal. "Open this now," he said, holding it up to my face.

"Go to hell, Simon."

His face turned red with fury. He dropped the crystal and wrapped both hands around my neck. "You're coming with me!" he said, choking me.

I had no strength to fight him off. I could only gasp for air as he squeezed the life out of me. I tried slapping at his hands, but it only made him squeeze harder.

The horrible sound around us began to fade. Leaves soon started flying back into the trees. My hand dropped to the ground as darkness filled my head.

"Die, witch," Simon said, squeezing harder.

I felt something cold under my hand. It was the crystal. I wrapped my fingers around it and closed my eyes. If Simon wanted my powers, he was about to get them in the worst place possible. I began chanting the spell in my head to open the crystal. Simon looked down when he noticed the crystal glowing under my hand. He pulled his hands from my neck and lifted my arm.

"I give my powers to you," I said in a shaky voice.

A vibrating wave pulsated through the forest. The trees shook as streams of energy began coming out of the crystal.

Simon's face lit up as he realized what I had done. He rose to his feet and spread his arms. "At last," he said, closing his eyes. Ribbons of light began flowing through him. He drew a deep breath as his body began healing itself. He looked stronger in seconds.

The glow from the crystal faded. Simon opened his eyes and looked at his hands. "Magnificent," he whispered. He threw his head back and laughed. The forest echoed with the sound of his happiness. "Come get me now, Wendell," he shouted. He began waving his hand at branches and rocks and laughed harder when they shattered into hundreds of pieces. His eyes moved over to me. He sighed and smiled the most wicked smile I had ever seen. "And now for the final piece of the puzzle," he said, moving closer to me. "I'm afraid you must die so I can be free, my dearest." He looked at my battered body and shook his head. "I promise to kill you quickly. I owe you that, at least. I will not scalp you like Wendell has. You deserve a much better death than that. I can admit this now: I think you are the strongest witch I have ever encountered. I have always admired your bravery. It almost seems like a waste to have to kill you. But I'm afraid there's no getting out of my promise. I will regret killing you more than I regretted killing your father." He raised his hand, preparing to wave it.

"I think there's something you should know before I die," I said.

He paused with his hand up. "Humor me, witch."

"Remember that stone I told you about? The one you left unturned?"

His eyes narrowed.

"It's coming," I said. "And it's going to hit you right over the head."

He quickly looked up. He began to laugh when all he saw were the trees.

Then that horrible sound of agony began shaking the trees. Simon froze. His jaw dropped as he looked around at the leaves. I knew it was finally hitting him as to where he was. Leaves began tearing themselves away from the branches. Simon spun in every direction trying to find a way out. Thousands of leaves hovered above him.

I covered my ears as that horrible sound got louder and louder.

"No," Simon said, backing away.

Just as the leaves were about to descend on Simon, they froze in midair and did nothing. Out of nowhere, guards began flying into the forest from every direction. I could hear Wendell shouting, "Find them!" from a good distance away. Simon began waving his hand at the guards.

I kept my eyes on the leaves. What was wrong with them? Why were they not attacking Simon? Then, as fast as it had started, that horrible sound stopped. The leaves flew back into the trees and simply blew in the wind. Both Simon and I looked around. I couldn't understand it. Why were they not attacking him? Even the guards halted and took notice.

The earth began to shake. It felt like an earthquake was spreading across the land. Guards began falling from their staffs. Clouds moved in and cast a shadow over the land. Simon looked shocked when the roots of the trees tore themselves out of the ground and began to simply walk away. In a matter of seconds, we all stood in an open field with nothing around us. Even the wizards who were outside where the forest had once stood were frozen with shock.

A dark cloud was moving closer and closer. It hovered over the river as the wizards tried to figure out what it was. There was fear in everyone's eyes when something shot out of the cloud and dove into the river. Then the cloud cleared, and James and my friends appeared, riding the dragons. James sat atop Attor, his eyes desperately searching for me. I began to cry.

The guards gasped when they saw Porteus on one of the dragons. They seemed shocked to see that he was still alive.

Attor blew fire into the air. A roar emanated from the river. The wizards drew back when a wave began rising from the water.

"Father," I cried.

The land began coming alive. I'd never heard such a sound like the one Magia was making now. All eyes were on the wall of water. Wendell ordered the wizards to protect him. They all flew in front of him and held their places. There were gasps as the water began falling back into the river and they saw who had been inside of it.

My father sat upon his glass staff, looking down at them. He looked so radiant and strong. There wasn't one gray hair on his head. His green eyes sparkled like I'd never seen them before. Decades had been erased from his face. A beautiful green robe was draped around him.

I looked at Simon. There are no words to describe the fear that was in his eyes. He was shaking and almost falling to his knees. I couldn't help but watch Wendell. I wanted to see him squirm like Simon was.

Wendell stared past the wizards at my father. His lips trembled with fear as he realized who was right in front of him. "Impossible," he said. His face shook with anger as he looked at my father with rage in his eyes. "Kill him!" he commanded.

At first, the wizards didn't know what to do. They only looked at each other as Wendell ordered them to attack.

"You fools!" Wendell shouted. "He came here to kill us!" Wendell waved his hand, sending a spell right at my father. My father made no effort to block it. He held out his hand and caught the spell in his palm. Then he smiled, wrapped his fingers around it, and crushed it with a sound like shattering glass.

In seconds, spells began flying through the air as the wizards attacked. The dragons broke formation and blew fire at the wizards. The sky lit up with spells as a war broke out between my father and the wizards. I wasn't sure why he didn't just kill them. He only kept blocking their spells as he glared at Wendell.

Wendell pulled out a horn and blew into it. The sound was so loud that it made my ears vibrate. Within seconds, hundreds of guards came out of nowhere. They flew next to Wendell and drew their weapons. Wendell's courage seemed to be restored when the guards awaited his command.

"Kill the traitor," he ordered. Swarms of guards flew at my father.

Then the ground under me began to vibrate. Something was shaking the earth. I turned and saw the Onfroi making their way to the battle with Peter in the lead. He began blocking spells as he stood in front of my father. The other Onfroi were slapping the guards and sending them to the ground.

James finally spotted me and tapped Attor on the head. "There," he said, pointing in my direction.

Simon frantically began searching the ground. He spotted a staff one of the guards had dropped and reached for it.

"James!" I shouted as Simon grabbed me and threw me over it.

Simon turned and began to fly away from the battle. I tried to kick myself off the staff, but Simon waved his hand and glued me to him.

"If I die, so shall you," he said, wrapping his arm around my neck.

Simon had to change direction when the earth lifted and made a wall in front of us. He made a hard left, only to find Cory and Fish waiting on two dragons. Simon flew straight up, but James was fast on our heels. We flew into the midst of the battle as Simon tried to fly over my father. My father spotted us and waved his hand, sending a stream of energy that wrapped itself around Simon's staff. It looked like a rope coming from my father's hand as he held on to it.

"Kill her!" Wendell shouted at Simon.

My father began pulling the rope-like energy toward him. The Onfroi started blocking any spell that was being sent at me. Wendell ordered the wizards to send fire spells at the Onfroi and light them on fire.

"Burn them down!" Wendell shouted.

The guards began casting nets over the dragons and sending them crashing to the ground. I saw Fish and Joshua hit the ground hard. My father ignored the chaos and pulled the rope faster.

"I'll kill her," Simon said, holding the dagger to my throat.

My father stopped but didn't let go.

"Release us so we can fly away," Simon said. His shaky hands held the dagger closer to my neck.

"You know I will never do that," my father answered.

I felt the blade cut into my skin.

"William!" James shouted. "He's hurting her."

We were surrounded by wizards as the Onfroi tried to hold them all back. My father wouldn't break away from his grip on the rope. Joshua jumped back on Katu and took to the sky. He drew his arrow and pointed it straight at Simon's head. Fish flew next to him, ready with his hooks. Cory was closing in behind us.

"Stay back," my father warned them. "She is his only way out of here. He's not going to kill her."

Simon laughed. "You don't know me very well, Xander. Did you forget I killed your wife?"

My father's eyes narrowed.

"She would have been happy with me," Simon continued, "but you poisoned her against me and took her from me."

"She never belonged to you, Simon," my father replied. "You never loved her enough to say no to Wendell's plan. It was your greed that betrayed you, not me."

"Wendell promised me powers if I killed you, but what did you ever do for me?" Simon shot back. "I was never anything but a half human to you. At least Wendell tried to give me what you never offered."

Some of the wizards stopped sending spells when they heard what Simon was saying.

"But I have all I need right here," Simon continued, poking the dagger at my neck. "We are married now, and there's nothing you can do to change that. She has promised to make me king. You have no choice but to surrender your ring to me. She is your heir."

~ 323 ~

My father held up his hand to show Simon the ring on his finger. "You're right, Simon. She has indeed made her choice. And I will surrender the ring willingly."

There were murmurs among the wizards. "Xander, what are you doing?" one of them said.

My father looked at the ring. "I give this ring of my own free will. May the next king rule with courage and honor. May the river bless him with powers and wisdom. And may the tree of life forever hold his name."

Simon held out his hand as the ring came off my father's finger. His face twisted with anger when the ring flew straight into James's hand. You could have heard a pin drop as everyone looked at James.

My saving grace had worked. No one had known what James and I had come here to do. We had married in Magia the day after I made my promise to Simon. It had been my insurance policy in case I was forced to keep my word to him. The promise had been made in the human world, and I had kept my end of the bargain. I had never promised Simon I would marry him here.

Simon shook as anger traveled through him. He knew it was over. He seemed resigned to his fate now. He put his mouth next to my ear. "Say goodbye to your king," he whispered.

I drew a breath and looked at James. I knew Simon was about to kill me.

"I love you," I said as Simon slid the blade across my neck.

Chapter 25
The Tree of Life

I choked on my blood as Simon pushed me off the staff. James leapt off Attor and dove through the sky, shouting, "No!" I felt I was falling in slow motion as I plunged toward the river, looking into James's desperate eyes. I took one last breath and reached out for him before I hit the water hard and began sinking to the bottom. I could see James's shadow above me as he, too, hit the water and swam toward me.

It was like one of the stories in his books. The hero had risked it all to save the woman he loved. But I sensed that this story would not have a happy ending.

I closed my eyes as I drifted downward. At last, I would be put out of my misery. My pain and suffering would be no more. I could finally rest and be with my mother. I had no strength to keep fighting. There was nothing left inside me that wanted to live— yet I was brokenhearted that I was taking my son with me. He was the reason I had endured so much. I'd only wanted a happy life for him. I would have gone to the ends of the earth to hand him the world. But now, together, we would watch over his father. I would tell him of the love we had shared.

I let go of hope as I sank to the bottom, where I would die. There was no pain here. I felt only sorrow because I was leaving my husband behind. I let my mind drift to happier days, wanting my last thoughts to be of my James. I thought of the first day I had laid eyes on him. It was the first time I had felt my heart race. He never knew this, but my heart belonged to him from that very moment. I felt my life had a purpose when I was with him. His arms always felt like home. I belonged there; I was safe. He would never know how much I'd believed in him. I wouldn't live to tell him that he was the reason I stayed so strong.

As I waited to die, I felt something wrapping itself around me. It pulled me closer and enveloped me in its arms. I was too frightened to open my eyes. Was death here already?

After a few moments, my body began to get warmer. A strange sensation traveled through me. I twitched as something started shooting through my body. It was like a blast of electricity going through my bones. The feeling of weakness turned into strength. I felt as if I could crush a stone between my fingers. Then my hair brushed across my face, wafted by the river's current. How was that possible? Wendell had pulled all my hair out.

The pain from my injuries began to fade. My body shook as my bones began to put themselves back together. The cut on my neck was sealing itself shut. Even the pain from where Simon had stabbed me had vanished. My mind became clearer and clearer. All my human weaknesses were crushed and destroyed in seconds. The feeling of confidence came flooding through me. Something was changing me, making me stronger. Spells that had been cast on me broke away. I felt lighter as that feeling of dreadfulness ran away from me.

I dared to open my eyes. The first thing I saw was James. He had his arms wrapped tightly around me, his eyes closed. He looked peaceful as the current moved his head back and forth. Why wouldn't he look at me? It took me a moment to realize that he hadn't jumped into the river to save me; he had jumped in to die with me. He thought Simon had killed me. He had no way of knowing the river was healing me. I grabbed his shoulders and shook him. A thin stream of blood came drifting out of his nose.

I felt pain like no spell could give me. It shot through my heart like a dagger.

He was dead. My James was gone.

Slowly, a staff came drifting down in front of me. I looked at the staff and back at James. I would fight one last time for him. His death would not be in vain.

I grabbed his face and gave him one last kiss. I felt as if the anguish would tear my heart into a million pieces. I gently pushed him away and let the current take him. He belonged to Magia now. I knew I would be joining him very soon, and we would at last be together for all time.

I stood for a moment and watched James disappear with the current. My heart ached as I felt my soul being torn apart. I would have joined him now if not for my son. I knew I had to do the right thing and give birth to him here in Magia. My father would take care of him. My place was with my James.

I grabbed the staff and looked up. It was time for Wendell to pay.

I came flying out of the river as the battle raged on. Explosions rang out from every direction. Some of the Onfroi were scattered in pieces on the forest floor. The dragons had guards in their mouths and were chewing them up. Meanwhile, my father was doing his best to protect my friends. Hundreds of wizards were throwing spells at him. I searched the skies for Simon, but he was nowhere to be found. I flew high into the sky so that Wendell would see me. As I expected, all the wizards froze.

Spells flew toward me. I felt a surge of energy as I waved them away. This was like no other feeling I'd ever had. I could actually feel my powers inside me. I knew I was strong. The word *doubt* wouldn't register in my head. It felt almost impossible to understand what that word meant now. I could see things clearly like never before. I knew exactly where Simon was. He was hiding like a coward nearby. I sensed his heart beating and could almost hear every breath he took. I would deal with him later. Right now, it was time for all the wizards to pay.

But as I raised my hand to wave it, a feeling of compassion washed over me. I was shocked when the need for blood and vengeance vanished in an instant. Something inside me knew better than that. The clarity the river had given me was making me think straight. I looked at my father as he held off the wizards. I finally understood why he hadn't killed them yet. Although he could destroy them in an instant, he didn't want to hurt them.

My father was wiser than I had imagined. His need for justice was greater than the need to kill. It was no wonder Magia had chosen him to be its king. It was clear to me now: having powers didn't mean having to kill—it meant using your mind to find a solution. My father had always lived his life that way. He killed only when needed, and not a moment sooner. He respected life and the lessons it could teach us.

I understood now. Today would not be the epic battle I had thought it would be. The battle was over. I had already lost what mattered the most. James was gone. Nothing I did now was going to change that. The time for peace had come.

When my father saw me, he waved his hand and sent a sea of wizards crashing to the ground. Bars of energy shot up from the earth and enclosed them inside of it. Wendell tried escaping, but he slammed into the bars and was thrust back. Dragons landed all around them, huffing and puffing as they circled them. The Onfroi soon joined them and began making a wall all around them.

"Help us, Xander!" the wizards yelled.

"He doesn't care about you," Wendell shot at them. "He only came to kill us."

My father gave me the signal to fly down. The guards seemed too frightened to fight now that the wizards were helpless. They dropped their weapons the moment my father's feet hit the ground.

"Your Majesty," they said, bowing their heads.

I heard Attor and Katu landing behind us. Cory and the boys quickly jumped off.

"You fools!" Wendell shouted at the guards. "Do not bow your heads to him. He is a traitor."

My father's eyes pierced through him. He was angry, I could see that. When he moved closer, Wendell took a step back.

"I have waited years to look into your eyes, Wendell," my father said. "You have betrayed Magia and all who live here. Because of you, I lost my wife and almost my daughter. But today, these wizards will learn the truth. They will be held accountable for their part in helping you destroy my kingdom. But you— you will suffer the most."

Wendell's beady eyes squinted with anger. "You have no proof of anything, Xander. These wizards know you only want to kill me like you killed all those kings. I have done nothing but try to save them from you. You are the one who chose a witch over them."

My father made a fist. "Magia chose my bride, you animal. She was to be your queen and rule next to me. But you used Simon to make sure that would never happen."

Wendell smiled. "You are a good liar, Xander. Everyone knows you left the witch Simon here to kill me. I'm the one who figured out your plan and cast Simon from this land. Because of you, Simon knew he could use the leaves against us."

My father turned to me and nodded. I knew exactly what he wanted me to do. I put one finger up to my head and pulled out a single memory. It was of the day Wendell had tortured me. I was in his dungeon, strapped to a wooden table, as he pushed needles into my feet. I looked at Wendell, smiled, and flicked the memory into the sky. It looked like fireworks as the image of me in Wendell's dungeon appeared. The truth was about to play out like a movie for all to see. Then Wendell's voice from the memory rang out through the land . . .

Wendell was reaching for a box on the floor. "Did you know there is a part of the body that feels pain more intensely than any other?" He opened the box. "Simon knows of it. I'm the one who told him." He pulled out three long needles. "I told Simon about a lot of things. I even taught him a spell to render your father useless." He walked back to me. "You see, wizards can be killed in your world. Our defenses grow weak in the human air— something your father has learned the hard way." He placed the needles by my feet. "I should have been king. I was next in line for the throne. But Xander decided to have a daughter, an heir. My chance at becoming king floated away. And that's where Simon comes in. Your father was a fool to bring that witch here. He was even more foolish when he began leaving Simon behind in Magia. He never suspected the evil thoughts going through that boy's head." He held up one of the needles and inspected it. "But I did. I began to mold Simon, shape him in my image. While your father was busy falling in love, I was busy turning Simon against him."

All eyes were on Wendell as he put his hands up. "I can explain," he said, backing away.

"Explain what?" one wizard asked. "That you made fools out of all of us?"

"That was you up there," another wizard said, pointing to the sky.

My father waved his hand and removed the bars of energy from around them.

"That memory is false," Wendell said, backing away again. He backed away until he backed into one of the guards.

The guard put his tail into Wendell's ear. Wendell froze and gasped from the pain. When the guard looked at my father, I knew he had seen the truth.

"That memory is *not* false," the guard said, throwing Wendell to the ground.

The wizards pointed their wands at Wendell's head.

"Traitor!" one of them yelled.

Wendell put his hands over his head to protect himself. They were about to kill him when my father put his hand up to stop them.

Wendell began shaking like a coward on the ground. "Mercy, my king," he said, getting on his knees.

I couldn't get over how radiant my father looked as he moved closer to Wendell. Confidence oozed from his face.

The wizards dropped to one knee and hung their heads in shame. "We beg forgiveness, Your Majesty," they said.

My father looked around at them all. "It is me who should be forgiven," he said. "I should have seen what greed was doing to my kingdom. I never saw what having so much power was doing to all of you. Even I had become arrogant at times. But being trapped in the human world has taught me a great lesson." He looked down at Wendell. "If you take away what Magia has given you, you must be prepared to live with the powerless soul that stays behind. It's a lesson you will all learn." He looked up at the wizards again.

They kept their heads down, clearly ashamed.

"Power has turned your hearts into stone," my father continued. "You see only what you choose to see, and not what Magia is trying to teach you." He gestured to the dragons. "We are not above these creatures. In fact, we are beneath them. But today, your lesson begins. You will have to earn back the trust of this land. Magia will decide when you are worthy of its magic." He moved closer to Wendell as the other wizards rose to their feet. "But you, Wendell—you have betrayed Magia like no other. There is no room for someone like you here. There is only one place fitting to send you."

Wendell crawled to my father's feet. "I beg mercy, Your Highness. Please allow me to live."

My father smiled. "You will indeed live, Wendell. But you will live as a human. You will not be taking the gift of magic that Magia has given you. You will live your days trying to remember who you are. It is the same fate you wished upon me at one time."

When my father turned to face the river, I saw a smile creep across Wendell's face. He tried waving his hand.

"William!" Cory shouted.

My father closed his eyes, and Wendell was thrust into the secret river of life. The wizards tried to run when my father waved his hand, and he also sent them crashing into it. He kept them under the water for several moments before letting them come up for air.

"What the river gives, may it also take away," he said, waving his hand again.

There was an explosion of light from the river. The sun came alive and began sucking the beams of light into its rays.

My father looked away as the wizards begged and shouted for him to forgive them. He closed his eyes as the river took away their powers. I knew it was breaking his heart to have to do that.

When the beams of light disappeared, my father looked up to the sky and waved his hand. A cloud began spinning and forming a vortex. He looked into the river and held out his hand. Wendell came flying out and floated in the air.

"You'll pay for this," Wendell shouted.

My father smiled. "I look forward to seeing you again, Wendell. I give you my word: the next time you see me, you will die." He waved his hand and sent Wendell spinning into the vortex.

"No!" Wendell shouted as the vortex pulled him in.

The wizards gasped as Wendell's feet were the last to get pulled in. My father waved his hand again, and the vortex disappeared. A sense of calm spread across the river. The sun shone brighter than ever. Speckles of light began circling my father's head.

"Xander, where did you send him?" Attor asked.

My father kept his eyes to the sky. "Where he needed to be," he answered.

"Why not kill him?" Attor asked.

My father sighed. "Because today is not the day Magia wishes it so."

Wizards began walking out of the water. My father turned to face them. Their eyes no longer sparkled. They looked tired and weak.

One by one, they dropped to their knees. "Forgiveness," they said as they hung their heads.

"It is Magia that must forgive you," my father said. "Even if it takes a thousand years, you will all learn what it means to be humble. You will work hard until you have proven your worth. Only then will Magia restore your powers."

I was surprised when the guards began to laugh. They were celebrating as if they had won a battle. I understood their happiness. They had been under Wendell's control for so long and had lived almost likes slaves under him.

"Long live the king!" they chanted.

The dragons spread their wings and blew fire into the air. My father smiled as Porteus rejoined his men. They greeted him with open arms. I heard the trees returning to their places behind us. The wizards began walking out of the water and disappearing into the forest.

When my father turned to look at me, I choked on sobs and threw myself into his arms. We almost fell over when the boys threw their arms around us.

"I can't believe it's over," Cory said, squeezing me.

Joshua pulled back and looked around. "Hey, where's James?"

I didn't answer as I cried in my father's arms.

"Thea, where is James?" Fish asked.

Cory pulled on my arm. "Thea, where is he?"

I couldn't look at him. I turned my head as tears streamed down my face.

Fish looked toward the river and back at me. "Did he come out?"

I threw myself into my father's arms again. I wanted to die. I couldn't stand hearing them ask for him.

"Please say he's okay, Thea," Fish said.

I only cried harder. Joshua hung his head and began to sob.

"What the hell?" Fish shouted.

Cory was like a statue as he stared at the river. "I thought he made it out," he whispered.

My pain was tearing me apart. That feeling of vengeance began rising up inside me. I could feel it pulsing through my veins. I pulled away from my father and held out a hand. A roar of anger escaped my lips as I commanded Simon out of hiding. Simon came flying out of the forest and was slammed into my waiting hand. I squeezed my fingers around his neck and held his face to mine. He waved his hand at me, but his eyes filled with fear when I blinked my eyes and sent his spell into the river. The spell was put out as if it were a lit match.

Simon looked back into my eyes. I wasn't surprised when I saw a wicked smile shine across his face. "I regret nothing, witch," he rasped.

I put my other hand over his heart. Simon closed his eyes and readied himself to die. I was about to pull out his heart when Cory and the boys took a step forward. They all looked at Simon with rage in their eyes. They couldn't wait for me to kill him. They were almost salivating as they waited to see what I would do to him. I looked at my father. He didn't have the same look in his eyes; there was no anticipation, no need to kill Simon himself. He nodded at me. I looked at the boys again. Something inside me knew they needed this more than I did.

I held Simon up and turned him to face the boys. The boys looked at Simon and then at me. Slowly, smiles broke across their faces when they realized what I was about to do. Cory flicked his arms and exposed his weapons. Joshua threw his bow and arrow on the ground and pulled his sword from its sheath. Fish almost drooled as he held up his hooks. With one last nod from my father, I threw Simon at their feet. Before he could even put his hand up to wave it, Fish sank his hooks into Simon's chest and skinned him alive. Simon's cries of pain did nothing to soften their hearts. Cory leaned down, smiled at Simon, and slowly cut out his heart. Joshua shouted like an animal as he swung his sword and chopped Simon's body up into hundreds of pieces. Cory had to pull him away when Joshua wouldn't stop swinging.

"Die!" Joshua kept yelling.

There was no dust drifting into the air. Here, Simon's blood flowed freely onto the ground. The boys backed away and began to celebrate. It was like years of pain had drifted away from them.

It was over. Simon was finally dead.

My father walked over to Simon's mangled body and stood over him. "That was for my Emma," he whispered. "May you rot in hell, Simon." A smile spread across my father's face.

Yet I didn't feel the happiness I should have. Sorrow was taking it all away from me. I hung my head and began to cry. "James," I said, clutching at my heart.

I felt my father's fingers under my chin. He gently tilted my face up and made me look at him. "What did I promise you long ago, Thea?"

I gazed into his sparkling green eyes as tears streamed down my face. I tried to remember the promise he'd once made. He smiled as I read his thoughts. "I told you I would keep my promise," he said.

As it sunk in, I began choking on sobs. I dropped to my knees and put my hands over my face.

"What's going on?" Cory asked.

My father motioned to Attor. "You know where to take her," he said.

Attor nodded and wrapped his talons around me. I couldn't control my emotions as Attor flew over the forest. I felt as if my heart would leap out of my chest. My vision was blurred from the many tears I had cried.

I cried harder when Attor landed near the Tree of Kings and released me from his grip. With no strength to stand, I fell to the ground as my father and the boys landed behind us. Loud, choking sobs took me over when I looked at the tree. I put my trembling hands over my mouth.

A bright light was flowing from inside the tree.
Then Martin and Morgan came into view, both
carrying beautiful gold swords with jeweled hilts. It
almost seemed like they were guarding the tree.
Levora emerged, looking radiant. She smiled at my
father and stepped aside with Martin and Morgan.

They dropped to one knee and said in unison,
"Your Majesty."

The boys' mouths dropped open as someone
began walking out from the tree. I staggered to my feet
but fell back down. Fish ran and helped me up. At
first, I saw nothing but light, but then it faded,
revealing who was there.

Fish gasped. "It's James!"

A joyful smile broke across James' face. He
wore a delicate crown with precious jewels embedded
all around it. He still wore the clothes he'd had on
earlier, rather than a robe like my father's. His honey-
brown eyes sparkled as he looked at me. The blue had
all but faded away.

I pulled away from Fish and broke into a run.
Years of anguish were floating away. My heart was
overcome with happiness. I could hardly make out
James' face through the tears. His smile grew even
wider as I leapt into his arms.

"James!" I cried.

He enveloped me in his arms and pulled me up.
"Thea."

I tried to stop crying, but my happiness was too
great. My father had kept his promise. He hadn't let
James die. I couldn't believe this was happening. I
kept touching James' face to make sure he was real.

"Don't cry, my love," he said, wiping away my tears. "Nothing will ever keep us apart again." He took my face in his hands and smiled. "It's a new life for us, a new beginning." He winked and pulled me to his lips. They were as sweet as ever.

I felt like my heart would explode from happiness. I heard the others cheer as his kiss brought my heart back to life. There were no words to describe the joy I was feeling. Nothing could compare to this moment. I was finally home. I was safe now.

James kissed my face over and over again. "I thought you were dead," he kept saying.

I couldn't find the words to tell him that I had thought the same of him. I only pulled him closer and cried in his arms. "I love you," I said, closing my eyes.

James pulled away from me when my father laid his hand on his shoulder.

"I believe there are others who wish to greet you," my father said, motioning to the boys.

James looked at the boys and smiled. "Will you guys get off your knees?" he said, pulling away from me.

Fish jumped to his feet. "Everyone else was doing it."

James threw his head back and laughed. My father put his arm around me as James walked over to the group. Cory was the first to extend his hand. James slapped it away and gave Cory a hug.

"Thank you, old friend," James said. "I will never be able to repay you for all you've done."

"You can start by not scaring us like that again," Cory said.

James smiled. "Deal."

"We don't have to drop to one knee and bow every time we see you, do we?" Fish asked.

Laughing, James shook his head. "Only Delia," he said as he wrapped his arms around Fish.

"Gee, thanks," Fish answered.

"I love you, kid," James said, squeezing him.

"Yeah, I love you, too."

Suddenly, Joshua picked both of them up and spun them around. "I love you guys."

"Put us down, ginger!" Fish yelled.

I looked up at my father as the boys rejoiced with James. "How did you pull it off?" I asked.

He glanced at me from the corner of his eye. "You already know that answer, Thea."

"I do?"

"The river gives life; it doesn't take it. You couldn't drown in that river even if you wanted to." He looked at James. "You can, however, be reborn. He truly does belong to Magia now."

"Thank you, Father," I said, wrapping my arms around him. "I will never be a able to repay you."

"Xander?" I heard from behind us.

My father's face lit up as he turned and looked into Levora's eyes.

"Welcome home," she said in that musical voice of hers. "Magia has missed you."

"Thank you, old friend," my father answered. "I have missed it as well."

She smiled her golden smile. "I must confess, Xander, I lost hope when I realized your name had vanished from the tree. You never warned me you would do that. I honestly thought you were dead."

My father chuckled. "I'm afraid that was the point. Please forgive me if I caused you any sorrow. I only intended to keep Wendell here . . . in Magia."

"And why the name?" Levora asked. "Why ask the tree to grow Simon's name?"

"You asked the tree to grow Simon's name?" I said.

He nodded. "It was the only way it would give James a ring. He was Simon's heir, after all."

"But how did you know I would—"

He raised his hand to cut me off. "I am more connected to you than you think, Thea."

James grabbed my hand. "May I have a moment with my wife?" he asked.

My father nodded and handed him his staff. James placed it between his legs and reached for me. Within moments, we were flying through the air.

"I could get used to this," James said as we flew over Magia.

I leaned my head on his chest as he flew us to my favorite waterfall. The flowers came alive when our feet hit the ground.

James threw the staff to one side and pulled me into his arms. "Thank you," he said, pulling me closer. "Thank you for believing in me enough to give me this gift."

I trailed my fingers along his face. His liquid brown eyes were sparkling. "You will make a good king," I said.

"That's not the gift I was talking about."

"What do you mean?" I asked, confused.

The most beautiful smile spread across his face. "I meant the gift of your love. I've never felt worthy until now. And not because you made me king, but because of the wonderful things that went through your head when you were in the river."

"You heard my thoughts?" I asked.

He pulled me closer. "I feel I have a purpose when I'm with you, too. And your arms have always felt like home to me."

My eyes filled with tears as he pulled me to his lips. Everything around us disappeared as we lost ourselves in the moment. For the first time in hundreds of years, my life finally felt complete. We had gone through so much pain to get to this moment, and it was as sweet as I'd thought it would be. I let his love wash over me as I felt the ecstasy of his touch. We became one as flowers opened up all around us.

It was the perfect moment, the happy ending in one of his books. The girl had gotten her hero. But he hadn't saved her—they had saved each other.

Chapter 26
Saying Goodbye

We watched the falls roar as James held me in his arms. He kept running his fingers through my hair. The river had all but restored it to how it was before I met him.

"You don't have to go back to wearing it messy," he said. "I don't need any signs to show me that you love me."

I looked up at him. "Delia will be happy to hear that," I answered. I gently touched his eyelids. "I like your eyes brown," I said. "They make you look distinguished."

He laughed. "You realized you're the only one who ever saw them blue, right?"

We laughed. James held me tighter, and I put my face to his chest and breathed him in. He smelled different now. The scent I had marked him with was gone. Now he smelled musky, with traces of oak. It was the most wonderful scent I had ever inhaled.

"You see, my love," James said, kissing my head, "you were perfect all along."

"What do you mean?" I asked, looking up at him again.

"The river only changed your hair. The rest of you is as beautiful as before."

I knew what he meant, but I didn't want to change that part of me anymore. I was never going to be thin or tall. My hands were never going to look like Helena's. My figure would always be full and curvy. I was exactly the person God meant me to be and I was beautiful. "Thank goodness," I answered.

We jumped to our feet when we saw my father and the boys flying toward us. Martin was with them. James frantically gathered our clothes, which were scattered about. We couldn't dress ourselves quickly enough.

Fish was already shaking his head when they landed. "Will you two get a room already?" he teased.

James stood in front of me as I finished dressing. "Um, we were just talking," he lied.

"Hey, James," Fish said, "you have grass in your hair."

My father's shoulders bounced up and down with laughter as he looked away.

"Shut up, Fish," Cory said, slapping him over the head.

"What?" Fish answered. "I wasn't even going to bring up the fact that James has his shirt on backwards."

James quickly pulled his shirt around as he laughed. "I'm going to miss you, kid."

The smile vanished from Fish's face. "What do you mean, you're going to miss me?"

"They're staying here, Fish," Cory said.

"What?" Joshua chimed in. "I thought we were going back together."

"We are," my father informed him, "but we won't be staying long."

I looked down as Fish glanced our way. That was the one thing I hadn't thought about. How could we *not* stay here? James was king now; it was obvious we would have to stay.

"Will we ever see you again?" Fish asked.

"We're not saying goodbye yet," James answered.

"Come on," Cory said, grabbing Fish by the arm. "We have to get out of here."

"Martin will be in charge until we get back," my father said. "So, don't be too long."

Martin flew away as my father gathered the boys. Then he took off his ring, and they were gone.

I felt heaviness in my heart as they spun into the vortex. How could I say goodbye to them? They had been such a big part of my life for years. I'd never given living without them much thought. I thought we would be in each other's' lives forever.

I tried to imagine my life without Delia. It broke my heart just thinking about it. How could I ever say goodbye to her?

"We'll think of something," James said, pulling me to him. "Maybe we can go visit them."

~ 346 ~

I didn't answer. I knew that wouldn't be possible. My father would never allow it.

"Hey," James said, lifting my chin. "I thought I was king." He smiled and held me closer. He pulled off his ring, and we were gone.

We were in my father's room. I pulled away from James, feeling a great sadness inside me. I wanted to cry when I stepped out into the hallway. I hadn't expected to miss this place so much.

James grabbed my hand, and we started downstairs.

Delia was at the bottom, her arms wrapped tightly around Fish. "So, it's true? He's really dead?" she kept saying.

"Ding dong, baby," Fish answered. "The wicked witch is really dead. Oh, and Thea is a princess, and James, a king."

"What?" Delia asked confused.

Cory and Joshua stood next to them. Delia looked up when she heard us. I ran the rest of the way down the stairs and threw my arms around her. Cory and the boys soon joined us. I held them like never before. I wanted to tell them how much I loved them, how much they meant to me. There wasn't a thing in the world I wouldn't do for them. If I could have waved my hand and erased what they had lost, I would have done it in an instant. I wasn't sure if I could live without them.

"I love you all," I cried.

"You're leaving, aren't you?" Delia asked, pulling away. "I can tell you're going to leave."

Before I could answer, my father came walking out of the kitchen, holding Steven's hand.

~ 347 ~

"Sister!" Steven yelled. Delia and the boys stepped away as Steven ran into my arms. I lifted him up and squeezed him. I knew it was time to erase the life I had given him. I began crying as I held him tight.

James laid his hand on my shoulder. "You have to," he said.

I nodded and set Steven on his feet. I squatted down and took his hand. "I want you to know that I love you very much," I began. "No matter what happens, you will always be my little brother. I hope one day you can forgive me. I never meant to hurt you. I only wanted a better life for you."

Steven looked at me with confusion. "What are you talking about?"

I closed my eyes. I couldn't bring myself to do it.

"It's time, Thea," my father said.

With my eyes closed, I tapped Steven on the head and gave him back all the memories I had taken out.

He seemed lost for several moments. Then it began to sink in. He suddenly looked at me with anger and took a step back. "You killed my father," he said.

I tried reaching for him.

"No!" he said, slapping my hand away. "I was there. I came back when you sent me away. I saw what you did to my father. You killed him, witch!"

I had no idea Steven had seen that. I tried reaching for him again.

"I hate you!" he shouted. He ran to Delia and threw his arms around her. "Please get me away from here."

James pulled him away from Delia. "Steven, this is your home. The love we felt for you was real. Thea never meant to hurt you. She only wanted to protect you."

"I hate her!" he yelled and started running up the stairs.

"Leave him," my father said when I tried going after him.

"It was the right thing to do, Thea," James said.

I couldn't deal with all the pain that was filling my heart. I looked at Delia and the boys before running up the stairs. ~~~

Days passed, and I refused to go back to Magia. There were no words my father could say to convince me. I knocked on Steven's door many times, but he never wanted to speak to me. Delia and Fish were the only ones he would talk to. He ignored my father and even James.

I spent every moment I could with Delia and the boys. There were moments when it felt like old times as we walked the streets of Salem. I must have sat in my apartment for hours on my second night home. I thought of the old Thea who had found so much happiness there. I opened my closet and looked at my old, loose clothes. I couldn't believe how much of myself I used to hide. In a strange way, I knew I was going to miss that Thea a little.

I looked around my apartment and knew this would make someone a good home one day. I hoped Cory would find the perfect tenant. My final walk down the stairs of my building was heartbreaking. I left my apartment knowing I would never come back.

There were days when I went to the lake with Delia and the boys. We usually just sat there for hours and stared out into the water. James was patient with me. He knew how hard it was for me to let them go.

My heart ached when I stopped at the bakery one day. I smiled as I watched Norm through the window, making his bread. I imagined myself working next to him. I could almost hear him yelling at me for reading my books. I was going to miss this little bakery. Although Norm was a bit of a grouch sometimes, I had loved every minute I spent there.

I walked through Delia's alley and stopped. I could almost picture her all dolled up for Halloween as she set up her stand. I imagined the tourists around her and could almost hear them walking about.

This had been my home for so long. Salem had been my palace, my second love. I didn't want to leave this town. My heart belonged here. How could I tell James that I didn't want to leave?

"It's really over?" I heard a voice say. I opened my eyes. It was Melanie, the smiling witch. News had traveled fast.

I turned to face her, trying not to hold what her sister had done against her. "Yes," I said, "it's over."

"No wonder all the warlocks left," she said, looking toward the street.

"Were there many of them?" I asked.

She ignored my question. "She won't come out anymore, you know. I've been there twice, and she won't see me. I think she's gone."

I knew she was talking about the black witch, Irene. "Stop going there, Melanie. She's only using you. That's not your sister anymore."

~ 350 ~

She nodded. "I know. I was only hanging onto hope."

"Where do you think she went?" I asked.

"I'm not sure, but she'll show her face again. She always does."

We said goodbye, and she was off.

I walked through the streets of Salem, visiting all my favorite spots. I looked into the window of Lori Bruno's store, Magika, which was always busy. Kim and Donna were visiting her. They saw me looking through the window and waved hello. Kim studied my eyes and stopped waving. She finally smiled and mouthed, "Goodbye, witch."

I nodded and stepped away from the window. I made my way over to the pirate ship and sat near the water for what seemed like hours. I gazed at the ship and smiled, remembering the day Delia and I were trying to distract the warlocks. I could almost see us walking down the pier with our swimsuits on. It felt silly now to realize how insecure I was then. If I could only go back and tell myself that the one who had to love me was me. There was no greater love than the love you could give yourself.

I soon left the ship and began walking toward the park. I took a seat on a bench, closed my eyes, and breathed in the cool air.

"Everyone has been looking for you," I heard Cory say.

"Tell them you didn't find me," I said, looking away from him.

"Mind if I join you?" he asked.

I scooted over, and he sat next to me. I lay my head on his shoulder, and he held my hand.

"You okay?" he asked.

"I don't know."

"What's going on in that head of yours?" he asked, nudging me.

"It's a mess in there right now, Cory."

"Care to share?"

I squeezed his hand. "I don't want to leave. I don't know why James won't just stay here."

"Um, because he's king now, Thea. How is he supposed to rule from here?"

I let go of his hand and looked away. "I don't want him to be king if it means leaving Salem."

"Leaving Salem . . . or leaving us?" He took my hand again. "We're going to be fine, Thea. Life will go on for us the way it always has. Your place is with James now. It's time for all of us to get on with life."

I looked into his eyes. "I'm being selfish, aren't I?"

"Not really. I understand why you're having such a hard time. You think we're going to be lonely without you. But it's not going to be that bad. Delia and Fish are having a family. Joshua and Meaghan seem to be doing great. Helena and me, well, I think I love her. I may even ask her to marry me."

My head spun in his direction. "Why, Cory Urban, who would have thought?"

He laughed. "Right? Me and Helena? I still can't believe it," he said, shaking his head. "But I love her, Thea. I see the changes in her, and I like them. She was completely heartbroken, just like me. I think we can both help each other out. It's worth giving it a shot, anyway."

"I'm so sorry, Cory. I never meant to hurt you."

He put his arm around me. "I'm okay now. Besides, I could never give you what James has. That guy really loves you. He's going to make a good king."

I lay my head on his shoulder again. "You're wrong about something," I said.

"Wrong about what?"

"I don't think you would be lonely without me. I'm pretty sure that I'm the one who would be lonely without you."

"You're talking like you're never going to see us again, Thea. According to your father and James, we're allowed to come visit."

I looked at him. "Really?"

"Yeah, I heard them talking about that this morning. Your father didn't expect you to have such a hard time with this."

"Are you sure?" I asked, sitting up.

"Yes. Your father even said he was going to give us a ring."

I threw my arms around him.

"You're going to break my neck, Thea."

I pulled away and grabbed his face. "You will never know what your friendship has meant to me, Cory. You're part of my heart, part of my soul. I could never live without you."

He smiled. "You'll always be my girl, Thea. I will never stop loving you."

I threw caution into the wind and pulled him to my lips. It wasn't my intention to kiss him, but my heart wanted nothing else. Years of being next to him couldn't be erased. Although I had never loved him

~ 353 ~

like James, he had been a great love to me. I knew that if I hadn't met James, Cory would have been the man I married. As our lips came together, I knew this would be the last kiss we would share. I would never get this close to him again. I ran my fingers through his hair. Cory squeezed me and held me tighter. He kissed me slowly until I thought I would go mad. He finally pulled away from me and smiled.

"I love you," I whispered.

"Yeah, let's keep that between us, okay?"

I laughed and got to my feet. "Come on," I said, holding out my hand. "Come with me to say goodbye to Sharron."

"She's at the house," he said, taking my hand. "I think she's having a hard time saying goodbye to your father."

We began walking home.

"I always knew she loved him," I said.

"Yeah, it was kind of obvious."

"Why do you say that?" I asked.

"Who do you think taught him how to cook?"

Ciro and Jason were walking out of the mansion when we arrived. Justin popped out right behind them. I noticed they were carrying their bags.

"Are you leaving?" I asked.

Ciro set his bag down. "It's time to spread the word about Simon," he said. "What happened here should never happen again. Warlocks have to know they were being lied to."

I looked at Jason.

"I'm going with him," he said.

"Me, too," Justin added.

I started to reach for them to say goodbye.

"No," Ciro said, pulling away. "This is not goodbye. We'll see each other again, *amiga*."

"*Que dois te bendiga, amigo*," I said.

"*Y a ti tambien*, Thea."

"What did you say to him?" Cory asked as they walked away.

"I said, 'May God bless you.'"

The smell of food hit me the moment we walked into the mansion. We went to the kitchen and found James with papers scattered all over the table. As usual, my father stood in front of the stove. Sharron stood next to him, a somber look in her eyes.

"Are you hungry?" my father asked. He held out a plate of scrambled eggs.

I snatched it from his hand. "I'm starving."

I sat next to James and gave him a kiss. "What's all this for?" I asked, looking at the table.

He seemed surprised by my happy mood.

"I was just working on some legal papers," he said, eyeing me. He looked at me for several long moments before exchanging glances with Cory. I knew he could sense what had happened between us.

After a moment, James began fiddling with the papers again. "I don't know what you said to her, Cory, but thank you. I assume that was the final goodbye?" James glanced at me.

"The very final," I answered.

Cory smiled nervously. "So, what's all this for?" he asked, pointing at the papers on the table.

"Oh, I'm leaving my house and all my possessions to you all. There's a good amount of money in the bank, too. I don't think I'll be needing it anymore."

~ 355 ~

"Are you serious?" Cory asked.

Delia walked into the kitchen and didn't say a word. She walked right out the back door and headed into the garden. I pushed my food aside and followed her out. She didn't look at me when I took a seat next to her on the bench. I reached for her hand.

"You okay?" I asked.

She sighed. "You know what I was thinking about today? I thought about when we were kids. We got into so much trouble in those woods." She looked at me. "We had so many adventures then, didn't we?"

"I would say we had quite the time."

"I'm going to miss those days, Thea. I will always remember that little witch who saved the day."

"More like got us into trouble," I said.

She laughed. "Yeah, I guess you did."

I moved closer. "I'm going to miss you, witch. No one ever stood up to me the way you did. Even as kids, you always told me how it was. I will always love you for that."

She began to cry. "Someone had to put you in your place." She threw her arms around me. "Don't forget about me, witch."

"You're my heart, Delia. How can I forget about you? You will always be my sister."

"Why is everyone so sad?" my father asked.

I still wasn't used to him being outside. "We were saying goodbye," I said.

"Goodbye? As far as I know, you two will be seeing each other all the time."

Delia wiped her tears. "What? You mean that?"

"The matter has been settled, young Delia. Not another tear."

Delia got up and threw her arms around my father. "Thank you, William."

"I have only one request," he said, pulling away.

"Anything," she answered.

My father looked toward the mansion. "That you look after Sharron."

"Yes, of course," Delia said, giving him another hug.

My father looked at me. "I think it's time that we go, Thea. There's someone who wants to meet his brother." He motioned to the back door to the kitchen as Netiri came through it. His katana was strapped to his back, and he held a small bag of belongings in his hand. "It's time for his destiny to begin," my father said.

I looked at Delia and then back at my father. I felt ready now. It was time to let go. "I'm ready, Father."

Sixteen Years Later

Chapter 27
You Can't Have Him

I sat near my favorite waterfall, book in hand. It was one of the many things I had brought with me when we left Salem. I would sit here alone for hours and read all day. I still loved escaping into my books, but now my books were about Salem. Delia brought me all the new releases when she came to visit. While Fish and the boys went off with James, Delia and I sat and talked for hours. I wanted to hear every single detail about what was going on back home. It made me feel like I was still back in my precious Salem.

Delia told me about Vera, her daughter, and how she seemed to be almost glued to Steven's side. "I think she loves him," Delia said.

Steven was still living with them in the mansion. He hadn't forgiven me yet. I sent him notes often with Delia, but she told me how he only tore them up.

"I don't like Vera falling in love at her age," Delia said. "Steven is much older than her. She should have fallen in love with Ethan."

I knew it was Delia's dream that my son, Ethan, take Vera for a wife someday. But it seemed that Vera had already made her choice. James tried to take Ethan around to other women in the village, but my son only had eyes for Vera. He was completely in love with her. It broke my heart to see him get so excited when Delia brought Vera with her. There was nothing Ethan wouldn't do for her. But I knew Vera saw him only as a friend. They had been around each other since childhood. They had spent many years here in Magia running around and playing with the dragons.

Joshua and Meaghan had married. It was one of the few times we had gone back to Salem—that anyone knew about, anyway. They still had no kids, but Joshua seemed happier than ever. There were no signs of the horror he had lived through. He and Meaghan were living in my old apartment. That made me very happy.

Cory had waited two years before finally proposing to Helena. They decided to marry here, in Magia. My father had performed the ceremony. Martin was the best man, and many of the wizards attended the wedding, which was simple but beautiful. It surprised me to see that Helena had picked a very modest dress with no train, no veil, and just a few flowers in her hair. She seemed to be a whole new person now. Cory had changed her in more ways than one.

I was surprised when Delia told me that Helena was working at the bakery. She and Cory had bought it from Norm when he retired. Cory was sad to learn that Helena couldn't have children, a result of what Simon had done to her. But that didn't seem to tarnish their happiness. Surprisingly, Helena seemed to be flourishing in the bakery. Delia told me how Helena loved working there. We were both shocked to hear that.

Cory came here often with Fish. James had given them a ring so they could travel here, and they spent many hours flying around Magia. I knew it made James happy when they were here.

Netiri had adapted to Magia well. Morgan had expected him to tell him all about his father, but come to find out, Netiri hadn't seen his father in years. Netiri spent most of his days with my father. I had this gut feeling that my father was preparing him for something—I just didn't know what.

I often asked Delia about the witches back home. There was a new council, and the boys were part of it. They all kept a watchful eye on the city of Salem. Warlocks were welcome, but only if they kept the peace. The battle between them and half humans was over, but I knew they still couldn't be trusted. There were many who thought Simon would come back. They didn't want to believe he was actually dead. It was the reason James and I snuck away sometimes. No one knew this, but we would go into Salem and check on our friends. We often found ourselves at my favorite lake, where we sat for hours and talked. I knew James missed Salem as much as I did.

I always hated when we had to leave, but I knew our place was here. The river had given me back my powers, but now I needed it to keep me strong. I realized that when we left for Joshua's wedding. I felt very weak after only three weeks of being there. My father explained that I had given the powers I was born with to Simon, and now I needed the river the same way he and all the other wizards did, including James.

Magia was back to its splendor. Wizards and dragons alike were now friends. Some of the wizards had earned back their powers. They spent many years proving to my father and James that they had changed. They had learned the secret of the leaves and had nothing to fear now. They had gained respect for what could possibly destroy them and used caution when entering that forest. The walls to the village had long been demolished. There was no sign of the prison Wendell had once made.

People were free to roam now. Villagers built homes all over the land. My father had expected us to stay in the castle with him, but James insisted we build a house near the falls. He stood aside and gave my father back his kingdom. He said he would take his place as king when my father was no longer with us. Yet my father still looked to James to make decisions, and he demanded that everyone still view James as king.

Magia had welcomed my father back with open arms. There was a big celebration when he returned. Creatures came from hundreds of miles away to welcome him back. He put rules in place with the wizards to make sure that someone like Wendell would never be able to hurt Magia again. He made Martin and Morgan royal guards and put certain things into law. If any wizard cast a black spell, he would immediately be stripped of his powers and banished from Magia.

The land was quiet again. Dragons became protectors to the king and were well respected and honored. Attor held the highest place possible. He sat next to my father and gave counsel. As for James and me, our life had never been happier. We never talked about Simon again. It was as if it had never happened. I lived for the moments I could spend alone with James. The need to hold him in my arms never grew old.

My son, Ethan, spent most of his time with his father. He loved hearing James tell him stories about the human world. Ethan had never been there before, and it was the one place he wanted to go. The stories about humans fascinated him. He couldn't wait to see his first car. "Humans don't fly?" he asked as a child. He couldn't comprehend how humans got around. Ethan had begged us many times to take him to Salem, but James knew his real reason for wanting to go.

"She'll break his heart," James said to me one day.

James and I had talked about taking him there, but the thought of the dangers kept us away. I wasn't sure what it was that I feared, but something in my heart told me my son was in danger. I always had Wendell in the back of my head. My father had never told us where he had sent him. His only words were, 'He is where he needs to be,' which drove me crazy.

~ 363 ~

"Mother," I heard from a distance.

I peeled my eyes away from my book and smiled as my son came running down the hill. He looked so much like his father. Although he was only sixteen, he was already as tall as James. He had the same liquid brown eyes and dark hair, and he was just as handsome. My son had grown into quite the young man. Years of being around wizards had done him well. He was polite and well-mannered. His heart was tender and kind. James was proud of how brave his son was.

"He got that from you," he often told me.

Ethan loved to playfully torture the dragons. He pretended to slay them all the time. "Blow fire at me again," he would tell Attor.

James would cheer him on as Ethan flew through the fire without getting burned.

Now I got to my feet as my son approached me. He looked very happy about something.

"Mother, they're here," he called.

I knew at once that it was Delia and her daughter, Vera. "Did Uncle Fish come with them?" I asked.

"Yes, he's with Father. They're not far behind." My son's eyes were lit up as he waited for Delia and Vera to catch up. "She's near the falls!" Ethan yelled to them.

"Of course, she is," I heard Delia say.

I smiled as they came into view. Delia looked as beautiful as ever. She was obviously still taking the anti-aging potion. In fact, they all were. "I don't have a river to keep me young," she'd said to me one day. Vera wore a beautiful yellow sundress, and her long dark hair was draped over her shoulders. Her eyes were an emerald green like her father's, but she was the spitting image of Delia. Ethan couldn't take his eyes off her.

"Don't you have normal clothes?" Vera asked as she passed him.

Ethan looked down at his robe. "What's wrong with my clothes?"

"You're wearing a dress," Vera said over her shoulder. She had obviously inherited Fish's sense of humor.

"I've already told you," Delia said to her, "that's what they wear here."

"Why? What do humans wear?" Ethan asked as he followed behind them.

"Not a dress," Vera answered.

"Stop it," Delia hissed at her.

Vera didn't seem happy about being here today. I looked at Delia with questioning eyes.

"She wanted to go with Steven to a party," Delia explained.

"I see." I looked at Vera. "Aren't you a little young to go to parties?"

Vera rolled her eyes. "I'm sixteen, almost seventeen. Besides, it's Steven's birthday, and I wanted to celebrate with him."

"You, young lady," Delia said, "are far too young to be celebrating."

I looked at my son. I could tell he was bothered when Vera mentioned Steven's name. All Vera did was talk about him sometimes. Ethan knew about her feelings toward Steven.

"Where are you taking Vera today?" I asked him.

He looked at her. "Wherever she pleases."

"Can he take me home?" Vera shot back.

"Vera!" Delia snapped.

It was like seeing a young Delia all over again. Vera was like her in so many ways. She shared her mother's same spunky attitude and was never afraid to speak her mind.

"Sorry," Delia said, giving me a kiss on the cheek. "She's been a handful lately."

"She takes after her mother," I answered.

"Then I'm doomed," Delia said.

Ethan kept looking at Vera as she flipped her hair. It broke my heart to see him yearn for her like that. "Vera," Ethan said, holding up his staff, "would you like to take a spin around Magia?"

Vera looked at him. "Are your eyes getting bluer?" she asked.

Delia and I exchanged glances.

"Vera," Delia said, "why don't you go with him? Thea and I need to talk."

"Okay, but can we stop to visit my godfather? He said he had a surprise for me."

"My father would love that," I said.

Ethan hovered the staff in front of him. "I'll take you there now," he said, holding out his hand to her. I could almost hear his heart race as Vera took her place in front of him. I caught him leaning into her and smelling her hair.

"Please be careful," Delia said.

"She's in good hands," Ethan assured her.

We watched them fly off into the clouds.

"He's a good boy," Delia said. "He's polite and untainted with human habits. I wish my daughter could see his worth."

"It wasn't meant to be, Delia. He'll find his true love one day."

"I'm not losing hope. I'll leave her here if I have to. They belong together."

"You can't force love, my friend. No amount of time can make you love someone."

Delia looked at me. "That's not true. Look at me and Fish."

We sat, and she began to tell me about Steven.

"He's changing, Thea. I don't like the person he's becoming. He started hanging around the new warlocks in town. He won't listen to Fish anymore. Even Cory tried talking to him, but he won't listen to anyone."

"He's a grown man, Delia. Let him make his own choices. If that's the kind of life he wants to lead, let him go."

"Oh, I want to let him go, all right. I don't even want him around Vera anymore. I don't like the way he looks at her, as if he owns her."

"That doesn't sound like him."

She sighed. "He's not the same little boy anymore. The Steven who used to call you 'sister' is gone. The grown-up Steven is bitter and angry. I don't know him anymore."

"What does Fish say about this?"

She sighed again. "He thinks it's time to kick him out, that there's no reason Steven can't venture out on his own. Like you said, he's a grown man. But I think he's grown used to all the money James left him.

It's taught him nothing but selfishness."

I didn't like hearing that. I had hoped that Steven would grow into the kind soul he was as a child. That little boy was so tender and full of love.

"He used to call me auntie before," Delia continued. "Now he just says 'Delia.' Fish is getting pretty tired of him and his attitude."

"Be patient with him, Delia. He's been through a lot."

"He's been through nothing," she hissed. "So you erased the horrible life he used to have. Big deal. He needs to get over that already. He never went through the hell we did."

James and Fish interrupted us.

"Hello, ladies," James said. "Having your usual conversation?"

"Salem hasn't changed, Thea," Fish said.

I smiled and got to my feet. "Hello, sweetie," I said, giving him a kiss.

"Do I get a kiss?" James said, pulling me away from Fish.

I was about to kiss him when something flashed through my head. My body stiffened, and I dug my fingers into James's shoulders.

"What's wrong?" he asked.

I couldn't answer him. I drew a breath as something made my body freeze.

"Thea, what is it?" James said, shaking me.

Flashes of my son's life began going through my head. I was having a vision. My mind drifted off into a dream-like state. I couldn't feel the ground under me. Even James's voice sounded like it was miles away. I tried to tell James what was going on, but my mind was getting pulled farther and farther away.

"Thea, answer me!" James shouted.

I soon felt James flying through the air with me. I heard the panic in his voice as he called my name. Something had hold of me, something that wouldn't let go. The images in my head got clearer. I felt as if I were being pulled into them.

James's voice began to fade. The last thing I heard him say was, "What's wrong with her, Xander?"

Although I couldn't hear him, I was able to feel my father's hands touching me. I drifted off, knowing he was there. I faced the future that destiny was showing me: I saw my son being tortured. He was tied to a tree, deep in the woods of Salem. A man with dark eyes stood over him with a dagger in his hand while a woman cried next to them. I couldn't see her face, but she was begging the man to let my son go.

I felt my father's touch as the vision continued.

"I'm with you," he whispered into my ear.

I was taken away again, but this time I could see faces. I cleared my head and tried to engrave every detail on my mind. I thought of nothing else as the moments turned into hours. Soon the hours turned into days. My body was drenched in sweat as the vision continued. I felt my father holding my hand the whole time.

Gradually I began to hear James's voice again. "How long will this last?" he asked my father.

"As long as it needs to," my father answered.

I felt James's kiss on my lips. "I'm here, my love," he said.

I wanted to open my eyes, but destiny had one last image to show me.

At first, I only saw my son's body on the ground. And then a woman's lips hovered next to my son's ear. I heard her whisper, "You're coming with me into hell." And then that unmistakable cackling laugh made my eyes shoot open.

I jumped to my feet and waved my hand wildly as everyone ducked away from my spells. "You can't have him!" I shouted.

James tackled me from behind and held my arms down. "It's over!" he yelled.

"You can't have him," I screamed.

Epilogue

I didn't talk to anyone for days. I sat atop the mountain, thinking of my son. I was angry at my father for stopping me from going into Salem. It was the first thing I had tried to do.

"You can't change things," my father kept telling me.

James still didn't know what I had seen, but he understood how important it was that I not tell him. My heart knew he had figured it out. Every time I looked at my son or held him, I started sobbing.

It killed me to know that my son would soon leave me. Destiny had already chosen where he would go. The mother in me wanted to protect him, but the wizard in me knew I had to stay here. I was not strong enough to watch him suffer. I knew I would kill the moment he was hurt. I was trying to find ways to help him, but how could I do that from here?

"You have to let him go," James said from behind me.

I didn't turn. "I can't," I answered.

"He will leave, anyway, my love." He sat next to me and took my hand. "I don't know what you saw, but I know our son is a strong man. We have taught him well. We must believe he will make all the right choices."

I looked into his eyes. "What if he doesn't? What then?"

He smiled and brushed the hair from my face. "I know a witch who made all the wrong choices. But she was strong. She lived through hell and came out the other end smiling. I have faith that our son will do the same thing."

"I have to go with him, James."

"You can't, my love. You don't have it in you to leave things alone."

"I do," a voice said.

I spun around. It was my father. I was shocked to see him wearing human clothes. I jumped to my feet. My hands began shaking when I looked into his eyes.

He smiled. "I told you we're connected more than you think, Thea."

I couldn't breathe. He knew; he knew the vision I'd had of my son. I felt a wave of relief wash over me when I realized my father would be going with him. I ran into his arms. "Please take care of him, Father."

He pulled back and looked into my eyes. "I give you my word—I will not let him die."

My anguish vanished in an instant. I looked at him, knowing his words were true. "You always knew you would go back, didn't you?" I asked.

"I knew from the moment you were born."

I wrapped my arms around him. "Thank you, Father."

~~~

James put his arm around me as I watched my son gather his belongings. My father was already outside waiting for him. Ethan couldn't believe our change of heart. He didn't care why we were okay with him leaving now; he was just happy to go.

"I promise I'll come see you every chance I get," he said as he threw another robe into a bag. "I'm sure Grandfather will come with me."

I looked at James, knowing that wasn't true. My father didn't trust me enough to stay away. He planned on blocking the way out of Magia. Only he knew the spell to get back in. But I knew my father would have to return now and then. He needed the river to keep him strong. I smiled when I thought of that. Maybe I would sneak out, just to check on my son.

"I don't think you'll need those robes," James said to him. He held up a bag. "Here, I packed some of my human clothes for you. I'm sure Cory will buy you some more."

Ethan dropped his bag and took the one being offered. "You have human clothes?" he said.

"Don't use your magic around humans," I warned. "They don't know about that."

My son's eyes were lit up with happiness. "I promise, Mother."

"Your grandfather is waiting," James said.

I pulled away from James and held out my hand. "Come, I'll walk with you."

I was surprised to see Netiri standing next to my father when we walked outside. I had already had my suspicions that my father was getting him ready for something.

"You're going with him?" James asked Netiri.

Netiri's eyes began to change color. "We're going to find my father," he answered.

My father smiled and looked at Ethan. "Are you ready, son?"

"Yes, Grandfather. I'm ready."

I turned to my son and put my arms around him. "Promise me something," I said.

"Anything, Mother," he said as he stepped back.

I looked at James and nodded. He pulled out a wand and handed it to him. "Promise you will think of us when you use this," I said. "Think of all the love we have for you."

He put the wand into his robe and hugged me again. "I'm going to miss you, Mother."

I held back my tears. "You have no idea how much I'm going to miss you."

Ethan pulled away and looked at his father. James hugged him and gave him a hard pat on the back. "Remember everything I taught you, son. Your mother and I will be waiting. I love you."

Ethan stood next to my father as James put his arm around me. "Take care of him, William," James said. "I'll watch over Magia until your return."

My father nodded and looked at me. "I'll keep my word, Thea."

I smiled. "I know, Father." I had to close my eyes as my father pulled off his ring. When I opened them again, they were gone. I took a deep breath. "Come back to me, Ethan."

I felt James's fingers on my cheek. I looked up at him.

"You're not going to have this long face the whole time he's gone, are you?" James asked.

When I didn't answer, James reached for his staff and took to the sky with me. "Where are you taking me?" I asked.

"To show you something," he said, flying faster.

We flew to a part of Magia I had never been to before. I kept asking James where we were going, but he only asked me to close my eyes. I felt him fly a bit slower. "Okay, you can open your eyes," he said as we stopped.

My eyes fluttered open, and I looked down. My jaw dropped, and I gasped.

"Do you recognize it?" he asked.

I saw trees filled with the colors of autumn. Yellows and reds surrounded a beautiful lake. A small wooden sign hanging off a tree read, *Welcome to Salem.*

"It's my lake!" I cried. It looked just like the one back in Salem. Even our tree was there.

James smiled as my heart came alive with happiness. "I've been working on this for months," he said.

"This is where you've been coming?" I asked, gazing at it.

"Cory and Fish have been coming with me. I wanted to get it just right."

He landed near the edge of the lake, and I jumped off the staff. "Oh, James, it's beautiful," I said, taking it all in.

He threw the staff to one side and stood next to me. "Fish said that tree was over there," he said, pointing, "but Cory assured me it was here."

He pointed to a tree. I didn't look in the direction he was pointing. I only kept my eyes on him.

I thought of all the horrible things we'd been through. James had never once lost hope. Even when things didn't go right, he believed in me to the end. I thought of my son. James believed in him the same way. In that very moment, I knew I had to believe in him, too.

"He's coming back to us," I said.

James turned and looked at me with those honey-brown eyes. "Of course he is." He pulled me into his arms. "I don't doubt it for a moment, my love."

I smiled. "I don't either, and you know why?" I touched his face. "Because he's just like his father."

I closed my eyes as James pulled me to his lips. I lost myself in his arms, knowing things would work out. It was time to let go of worry. I knew my father would keep his word. There was no doubt left inside me: James and I would see my son again. Our love would keep us strong. We would find strength in each other's arms. There would be nothing to tear us apart again. We would live our happily ever after.

"I love you," I said, holding him tighter.

"My wife, my life, my love," James said, enveloping me in his arms.

Chapter One: The Vortex

I felt I would fall into space as we traveled into the human world. I waited in anticipation to feel the ground under my feet. I was in a vortex of travel with my grandfather and a friend. It was the door to my realm, the world I'd only heard of my whole life. My grandfather's ring served as the key that opened the door to the human world. The moment he pulled it off his finger, we were pulled into this vortex.

Speckles of light surrounded and carried us as if we were feathers. I could feel only the wind blowing all around us. I was far too excited to pay attention to anything else.

We moved through the vortex with ease. I truly felt I would fall at any moment. Although my grandfather, William, had been in this vortex many times, this was my first time going with him. I had waited my whole life to leave Magia, the magical land I came from. The human world had only been a story told through the eyes of my parents. My mother, a wizard, and my father, a witch, were born in the human world. They lived there for most of their young life. My mother never told me why they left the human world, but I knew it broke her heart when she left all her friends behind.

She grew up with the people I knew as my uncles and aunt. Although we were not blood related, my mother always told me they were family nonetheless. She had been friends with them since childhood. My mother said she would not be alive if not for them. She often said they were closer than family. Even now, they came to visit us frequently. My grandfather gave them a ring so they could travel into our world. Their visits were the only time I saw my mother truly happy.

I thought of the worried look my mother gave me right before we left Magia. I was her only son, and for a moment, I thought she would never let me find my own way. I was speechless when she finally agreed that I should see the human world. Her decision came suddenly one day. I didn't question her, only gathered my belongings before she could change her mind. Her reasons didn't matter to me—I was finally free.

I felt suffocated for years. I was always under the watchful eyes of the royal guards and my parents. Even my grandfather, the Wizard King of Magia, wouldn't let me spread my wings. I would be turning seventeen soon, and I wanted nothing to do with being a prince. They could keep their royal titles and thrones. I didn't want any part of that.

Magia was filled with rules and prophecies. I was taught as a boy, that certain things would happen. "There is no changing the future," my grandfather always said. And part of that future is that I be king one day. But there was one thing he didn't know; I didn't want to be king. A life of commanding others was not the life I wanted to live. It was bad enough just being a wizard; I didn't need the pressure of being a king as well.

I looked at my grandfather as we travelled through the vortex. His green eyes had not met mine once. I couldn't help but wonder why he left his kingdom to come with me. His decision to leave was as sudden as my mother's to let me go. I had a strange feeling he only wanted to protect me. But why would I need protecting? I had no enemies, that I knew of.

No one in the human world even knew who I was. I spent the last sixteen years sheltered from them, the humans. It was a decision my parents made when they left the human world. Although they lived for years in a town named Salem, they had never taken me there once. I never understood that, and my parents never explained why. All they ever said was that I belonged in Magia. Went on about how it was my home. I always knew they were only trying to get the idea of leaving out of my head.

I was born and raised amongst wizards and dragons. Magic has always been the only life I knew. I knew nothing of human possessions or the thing called *money* that was needed to live. Coming into the human world was a way to escape my obligations of being a prince.

My mother spoke of Salem frequently. She called Salem her first love. I wanted to see the strange sun that gave light there. My father once said it was the other side of our sun. He said his world was unlike our realm. There would be no magical garden or Tree of Life. "*Humans can't fly,*" he explained one day. "*No staff in the world can give them that power.*" He never knew this, but his stories only fueled my need to leave the kingdom.

The human life he spoke of seemed simple and uncomplicated. I was tired of being praised for what I had not yet done. I wanted to earn my way, not have it handed to me. Just because I had been born into royalty, didn't mean I expected things to come easy. I welcomed the challenge.

I wanted nothing else but to prove to myself and to others that I was much more than just a prince. The human world seemed like the perfect place to start. There, I would be just like the others, just another boy. I would use no magic or spells. I would put away the wand my mother gave me and blend into the masses. I had many reasons for wanting to come into the human world, but right now, I can think of just one.

"Vera will be happy to see you, Ethan," my grandfather said.

I hadn't noticed he was finally looking at me. He was smiling. Did he know I was thinking of her? It couldn't be. No one knew I loved Vera, or that she was my real reason for wanting to leave Magia.

Vera was a half-human witch that lived in the human world, a world she seemed to be quite happy in. My title or magic never impressed her. We'd been around each other since we were kids. Her mother, Delia, had been bringing her into my world ever since I could remember. As Vera grew, I began to look forward to those visits more and more. I found myself feeling empty when she wasn't around.

For Vera, coming into my world had become a nuisance. I knew she only did it to accompany her mother. I could see she had no desire to be in the magical world I lived in. The human world was the only place she spoke of. She'd been coming to Magia for so long that she no longer found my world enchanting.

She thought it strange that we lived without the modern technologies of her world. *"What do you do besides fly around all day?"* she would ask. *"What about watching movies or listening to music?"* I never knew what to answer. I had no idea what those things were.

Her visits to my world had become almost torture. I was finding it harder to hide how I felt. Her brotherly love for me didn't help matters. She thought nothing of sitting close to me and holding my hand. *"Let's sit on that rock,"* she would say, pulling me toward the waterfall.

I couldn't remember half the things she said sometimes. I was always too busy trying to stop myself from pulling her into my arms. *"Ethan, don't sit so close,"* she would say scooting away from me.

My usual answer would be, *"Then don't pick such a small rock."*

Her long, dark hair smelled like a beautiful garden. Lavender was my favorite scent. I often got lost in her emerald-green eyes. She was short tempered like her mother, but I always loved that about her. She looked even more beautiful when she was angry, I thought.

"I wonder what Steven is doing," she would say. She certainly had a way of ruining a good moment.

That would only make me back away. He was a constant reminder that her heart was already taken. It didn't help that Steven lived in the same house where she lived. He was a just a boy when her parents took him in. Vera talked of nothing else. Steven this and Steven that. I often got very annoyed with her because of that. Here she was, in the most magical place ever, and all she wanted to do was talk about Steven.

"Ethan, did you hear me?"

I broke away from my thoughts of her. My grandfather was looking right at me.

"Does she know we're coming?" I asked in a calm voice. I didn't want to give away how excited I was to see her.

My grandfather smiled. "You'll have to change out of that wizard robe when we arrive," he said, looking down at what I was wearing. "I'm sure your father's clothes will fit you just fine."

Netiri, a friend that was traveling with us, began to laugh. "What's so funny?" I asked.

He pointed to my robe. "You're going to stand out like a sore thumb in that thing."

I looked down at my robe, taking note of the new ruby and sapphire my mother had added. I didn't like the draped robes my grandfather wore. Mine were more fitted and slimming. It was black velvet with gold threaded edges along the front. The jewels I earned were sewn along the collar. Apparently, this wasn't what humans wore. Even Vera had teased me about what she called, *my dress* when she came to visit. I never understood why she teased me so much.

In our world, robes were a sign of courage and wisdom. The more you learned, the more stones were sewn onto your robe. I was proud to display so many. I had earned every single stone with hard work. My robe was like a badge of honor to me. I felt no shame wearing it. Although my father, James, had given me some of his human clothes, I had no desire to wear them. It was the one thing about being a wizard I didn't want to change.

"Hey," Netiri said, nudging me with his elbow. "I'm just kidding, kid. But you'll have to wear human clothes if you're planning on fitting in."

"Who are you calling kid?" I asked. "We're almost the same age."

"No," Netiri said, shaking his head. "You're *actually* sixteen. I just look sixteen because of the aging potion I drink. No one would know I am really two hundred years old."

"Perhaps I should call you Old Man," I answered.

We laughed as Netiri nudged me again.

Netiri had been in my life since my birth. He was the only true friend I had. He left the human world many years ago with my parents. I didn't know much about his back story, but I knew he and my mother were once enemies. I heard that Netiri had spent his whole life not knowing he was half-wizard. He'd always assumed he was just a warlock. It was my grandfather, William, who informed him of who he really was.

I was surprised when my Uncle Cory said warlocks and witches didn't get along back in the day. He explained how Netiri once hated my mother. I asked my mother about that one day, but she only answered, "That's a story for another day,

Son."

I always thought it strange how Netiri's eyes would change color. Whenever he was in a foul mood or excited, his eyes would go from green to blue in the blink of an eye. His brother, Morgan, passed away before I was born. I wasn't sure how or why, I only knew Netiri had taken it very hard. He never even knew he had a brother until my grandfather brought him into my world. I wondered why Netiri was going back now.

As I thought of Netiri's past, the smell of food slowly began to fill the air. I knew what that meant; we were almost there. My mother always said she could smell Magia before she got there. I assumed it worked the same way coming back.

I knew we were traveling to my parents' old house. The mansion, as my mother called it, was a house my father left for Vera's parents when he and my mother left the human world. Although my father meant it as a gift, my uncle and aunt refused to take it. Even though they were living there now, it was always said that my parents would return one day. I didn't know how true that was.

I felt my heart would leap out of my chest when the speckles of light began to fade. I swallowed thickly, bracing myself for what I was about to see. The smell of food became more intense. The air under me was now a floor. We were here, *I* was finally here.

The wind died down and I began to make out four walls. I instantly knew we were in my grandfather's room. I'd heard so many stories through the years, I could almost picture the rest of the house. This room looked just as I had imagined. Two huge windows covered one wall. There was a large table with papers scattered over it. It almost seemed like my grandfather had never left. Had he been coming here this whole time?

There was a bed in one corner with a chair next to it. I quickly noticed a pair of slippers had been placed right in front of it. I glanced at my grandfather; it was obvious he was avoiding my questioning eyes. Why didn't he want to tell me he had been coming here? What was the big deal? There was no law that said he couldn't leave our world. He was the king. He could leave whenever he wanted.

I looked around the room again. Jars filled with something I couldn't make out, lined the shelves. Dried leaves hung all around the room. The smell of lavender filled the air. It was a pleasant smell that reminded me of Vera.

I spun around when I heard birds chirping just outside the room. My grandfather stood to one side, motioning me to look out the window. I moved closer, my heart racing as I stretched out my hand. I pushed aside the curtain— and drew breath.

This world was not what I was expecting. The light from the sun was strange. It had no rays beaming down like in Magia. Surprisingly, it hurt my eyes to look at the sun here. My eyes moved down to see what the humans called cars. They were parked below. My father was right, humans couldn't fly.

"*They drive cars*," I remembered him saying. He had shown me images of them when I was younger. He even told me how he had owned a few at one time. "*I gave them all to your uncles and aunt*," he explained. "*I have no need for them here in Magia.*"

My mouth was agape as I took in every detail of this world. I almost put my head through the glass when I saw some humans walking by. A tall, wrought iron gate wouldn't let me get a clear view of them. Greenery grew on the fence that surrounded the whole mansion. I tried to look past it. I wanted to see what kind of clothes the humans were wearing. What color were their robes? Did they wear the same kind of shoes?

A door opened before I could get a better look. A small, older woman came walking in. I instantly knew she was a half-human witch. I could see her eyes light up behind her glasses. I couldn't help but notice her smile grew wider as she neared my grandfather.

"Xander, you're here," she said, greeting him. Xander was my grandfather's middle name.

"Hello, Sharron," my grandfather answered. "I didn't expect to see you here today."

They spoke as if they had seen each other the day before. She didn't seem surprised he was here.

"We've all been waiting," she said, looking my way.

"Ah, yes," my grandfather said, motioning toward me. "This is Ethan, my grandson."

The curly haired woman seemed alarmed or shocked for some reason. She slowly moved closer as I stepped away from the window. I was a little surprised when she reached out and touched my face.

"Oh my," she whispered. "You are the spitting image of your father, James. If I didn't know any better, I would have confused you for him. You have his dark hair, his brown eyes, and you're just about as tall as him, too."

"You know my father?" I asked.

"Yes, dear," she said, pulling her arm back. "And I also know your mother, Thea. How is she?"

"Mother is fine," I answered. "She said to send everyone her love."

The woman named Sharron looked at my grandfather. "He's so handsome, Xander. Delia was not exaggerating his good looks."

"He's a good boy," my grandfather said, putting his arm on my shoulder. "He's grown into quite the young man."

"I feel as if I'm looking right at James," Sharron said, seeming amazed.

"I think he has Thea's eyes," my grandfather added.

Sharron raised one eyebrow. "Does he have her temper, too?"

What did she mean by that? My mother didn't have a bad temper. I never knew her to lose her composure once. She was a sweet, gentle woman.

As they laughed, I couldn't help but look toward the window. I wanted nothing else but to go outside. I wanted to see the town that had captured my mother's heart. Would I love this place as much as she did? I was really counting on that. Through the years, as she told me her stories, I felt I loved Salem as much as she did.

Sharron greeted Netiri before he headed out of the room. "I'll come back later, Ethan," he said over his shoulder. He was out the door before I could respond.

What was his hurry? I was hoping he would show me around town. He talked about Salem as much as my mother.

I glanced at Sharron, she wasn't taking her eyes off me. I think my grandfather sensed that I was uncomfortable about it.

"Where are the others?" he asked her.

"They've gone food shopping," she said, looking down at what I was wearing. "They should be home shortly."

She looked back at my grandfather. "Should I get him some clothes? I know James left all of his behind."

Why does everyone want me out of this robe?

"I am wearing clothes," I pointed out.

Sharron seemed surprised by my answer. "Sorry, dear. I only meant to say it might be best if you dressed in human clothes."

"Why?"

My grandfather cleared his throat. "I think I should show Ethan the house."

"Yes, of course," Sharron said, giving my robe another glance. "I'll be downstairs if you need me."

My grandfather shook his head when she left the room. "You don't have to change out of that robe, if you don't want..."

The sound of someone shouting made us both turn our heads, cutting our conversation short.

"What on earth?" my grandfather said, heading for the door.

We both stepped into the hallway to find a man pointing his finger in Sharron's face. He must be in his late twenties. He towered over her.

"You need to stay out of this," he was telling her. "She's not your daughter or your concern."

Sharron pointed her chin up. "She will always be my concern," she shot back. "You're a twenty-seven-year-old man, and she's just a child. You have no business chasing after her. You should be ashamed of yourself."

"I've already told you, witch. I've started taking the aging potion. I can wait until she comes of age. But until then, you will keep your nose out of our business."

"Why don't you make me," Sharron spat.

The man narrowed his eyes, moving inches from her face. I readied myself. It looked like he was getting ready to strike her.

"You don't want to cross me, witch," he hissed.

"You took the words right out of my mouth," I said, stepping forward.

The man did a double take when he looked my way. He instantly got a confused look on his face when he looked at my robe. I saw fear shine across his face when he saw my grandfather standing next to me. He clearly knew who my grandfather was.

He slowly backed away from Sharron. "I...I didn't know you were here," he said nervously.

"And now you do," my grandfather answered.

"He was just leaving," Sharron said, crossing her arms.

The man eyed me, a subtle streak of evil in his droopy, brown eyes. He was dark skinned with messy black hair. He wore the same kind of clothes my uncles, Fish and Cory, wore. *Jeans*, as they called them, seemed to be the thing to wear in this world. There was such an angry look about him. I got the sense that he was angry at the world.

He seemed to be very at ease here. Did he live here? Then it hit me, this man was Steven. The same man Vera was in love with. I had no idea he was that much older than her. Vera had never mentioned that to me.

It was obvious he already figured out who I was. The angry look on his face made that clear. I knew this man hated my mother, although I didn't know why. It was obvious he hated me too.

He gave my grandfather another glance before turning for the stairs.

"Wait," I called out. He froze and looked my way. "Apologize to her," I demanded.

It wasn't because Vera loved him that I wanted him to apologize to Sharron. He had been very rude to her just now. In my world, we had manners. If I even raised my voice an increment, I was made to apologize.

Sharron became visibly nervous.

"It's not necessary," she quickly said.

I ignored her, taking another step forward.

"I said…apologize to her."

Steven made a fist, his face shaking from anger. I thought I saw him reach for something near his belt, then stopped and glanced at my grandfather again. He slowly pulled his hand away from his waist. "I'm sorry," he spat and quickly headed down the stairs.

Sharron looked at me, shaking her head in disapproval. "You didn't have to do that, dear."

"But he was rude to you, madam," I answered.

"Madam?" she laughed. "Please, just call me Sharron." She looked at my grandfather. "He's got his mother's temper alright."

I heard a door slam shut. I knew it was Steven leaving the house. I thought of Vera, why did she love such an angry man?

"Come, I'll show you around the house," my grandfather said, leading me toward the stairs.

Chapter Two: The Mansion

As we descended the stairs, I recalled all the stories my mother told me about this house. Everything looked just as I imagined it. There was a foyer that was large enough to be its own room. A large sitting area was just to the left of it. A beautiful fireplace welcomed you as you entered the main floor. Priceless works of art hung on almost every wall. I was no expert on homes, but I could tell this was a very nice one.

As I looked around, I saw sections I could only guess were pathways leading to other rooms. My mother once said this house even had a ballroom. In fact, she told me my Uncle Fish and Aunt Delia were married there.

My grandfather led us through a door near the foyer. "The kitchen is through here," he said, with a big smile.

I could see this room was his favorite. I looked around the enormous kitchen. Pots and pans hung over a huge counter. It looked nothing like the kitchens in Magia. We usually just made a fire to prepare our meals. A simple wooden table served as our place to share our evening dinner.

The table in this room looked like a dozen people could share it. It was elegant and had fancy chairs. I was surprised when my grandfather said there was another room called a *formal dining room* that they used from time to time. The room we were in now was apparently where they had breakfast. Why did they need two rooms for that? How odd, I thought.

My parents didn't seem like the types to own possessions like these. I was surprised this used to be their home. Back in Magia, my father built my mother a modest home. It was small but served its purpose. Our lives were spent living outside, exploring what Magia had to offer. Money or possessions had no value in my world. Magic gave us everything we ever needed. Although my grandfather lived in a castle, he rarely stayed there. Most of the time, he would stay with us. He said he had become accustomed to living in a small space. This mansion was anything but small.

I had been to the castle to see my grandfather many times. Its glass looking walls towered over the land of Magia. Precious jewels were embedded in every space available. It was very rare to see my grandfather sitting on his throne. He always said the castle was too big and empty for him. Now, I understood why. The castle wasn't cluttered with furniture like this place. He obviously had become accustomed to the clutter.

A glass door at the end of the kitchen caught my attention. I could see a beautiful garden was just on the other side. "My mother's garden," I whispered.

I moved towards the door, my heart racing.

"Go on," my grandfather said, "step outside."

I felt the strange sun the moment I walked out. Here, the sun made me feel too warm for the robe I was wearing. It was so bright, almost hurting my eyes. It was nothing like the subtle sun in Magia. I could fly around all day and not feel the heat from our sun. Here, it felt like a blanket was being wrapped around me. I wasn't sure if I liked it. I touched the back of my hand, noting how the sun was warming my skin.

I made my way across the massive yard, and to my mother's garden. It was not what I was expecting. Although it was beautiful, the flowers didn't sparkle like the ones in Magia. Where I came from, flowers gave out speckles of light that drifted into the air. They carried healing powers to everything that lived in Magia. I remember playing with them as a child, laughing when the speckles stuck to my fingers.

I scanned the garden, noticing another house at the far end of the yard. It wasn't as big as the main house, but it was just as beautiful.

"That's the guest house," my grandfather said from behind me. "I think Steven is living there now."

I looked down at the strange grass that grew here, noticing dirt patches where the grass didn't grow. In Magia, the grass looked like a lush, green carpet covering every mountain in the land.

I closed my eyes, allowing the sounds of the city, just outside the gate, to flow through my ears. They were sounds I hadn't heard before. I smiled when I heard a car horn for the first time. It was just as my father described it. I opened my eyes when I heard it again.

"Delia is home," Sharron called from the kitchen door.

We walked back into the kitchen to find my Aunt Delia holding several bags. I always thought Vera was the spitting image of her mother. My Aunt Delia also had long, dark hair. There was always an angry look about her. It didn't help that she was rather moody sometimes.

She quickly put the bags on the counter and ran to my side. "You're early," she said, wrapping her arms around me. "I wasn't expecting you until tonight."

"Are they really here?" I heard my Uncle Fish say.

He came storming into the kitchen with far more bags than my aunt was holding. He couldn't put them down fast enough. I couldn't help but notice he had a few bruises on his face. Had he been in a fight?

"Come here, kid," my uncle said, pulling me away from my aunt.

"Hello, Uncle," I said, embracing him.

"I've already told you, just call me Fish," he said, pulling away.

I was happy to see him. I loved my uncle. He always made me laugh. He didn't look any older than me, something I knew to be not true. He and my Aunt Delia took an aging potion to stay young. At least that's what my mother told me.

Vera had her father's green eyes. She didn't inherit his dirty blond hair; rather, her mother's dark hair. My mother always said that my uncle had the face of a fifteen-year-old boy. He was always in a good mood, always very funny. My father loved being around him, laughing the whole time they were together.

"Joshua and Meaghan will be sorry they missed you," my Aunt Delia said. "They left on vacation two days ago."

She pulled me into her arms again. I could feel her love flowing through me. These people had been in my life for many years. My mother loved them more than life itself. They were her best friends and she considered them family. She spoke of them often, always making it a point that I knew how much she loved them.

"How is your mother?" my aunt asked.

"She sends her love," I answered.

"So, what do you think?" my Uncle Fish asked. "Like it here?"

I smiled. "I haven't seen much yet."

I noticed my Aunt Delia's eyes moving down to my robe. "Did you bring clothes?" she asked.

"James left a ton of clothes," my uncle said to her. "I'm sure he'll fit into them. September has been very warm this year," he said to me. "I bet you're melting in that thing."

"Who's September?" I asked, confused.

They laughed, although I didn't know why.

"We should give him a moment, so he can change out of his robe," my aunt suggested.

"If you don't mind," I said, "I'd rather keep what I'm wearing."

My aunt looked at my grandfather. "Is that wise? He'll stick out like a sore thumb."

My grandfather smiled. "He'll change out of it when he's ready."

Again, I took notice how no one seemed surprised to see my grandfather. My aunt and uncle hadn't even said hello to him yet. It was as if they had spoken moments ago.

I caught my grandfather and uncle exchanging glances. I think my grandfather noticed the bruises on his face.

"Is everything okay?" my grandfather asked him.

My uncle nodded. "We'll talk later."

"Are you hungry?" my aunt asked.

I smiled politely. "If you don't mind, I would rather see the town first."

Everyone looked at my robe again. Why did they keep doing that?

"May I ask something?" I said, trying to get them to stop staring at my robe.

"Shoot," my uncle answered.

"Why is everyone's thumb sore?"

The room erupted into laughter.

"Why don't I show you to your room?" my grandfather said, composing himself. "You can put your things away before we see the town."

"Come on, kid," my uncle said, showing me the way. "You can stay in your parent's old room."

My grandfather followed as we ascended the stairs. "We removed all the flowers," my uncle was saying.

"Flowers?" I asked confused.

My uncle nodded. "I didn't think you'd like the way your father left it. He put a spell on some flowers to make them live forever. He did it for your mother, she loved flowers. He had them everywhere."

"I love flowers," I informed him.

My uncle stopped half way up the stairs. "Kid, no," he said, shaking his head. "Guys don't say things like that. No flowers, okay?"

Confused, I nodded, and we continued our way up. I looked at my grandfather, wondering why it was a bad thing that I love flowers. He only smiled.

We walked down the same hallway we had been in earlier. We stopped at my grandfather's room, so I could collect my things.

"Your room is at the end of the hall," my uncle said, leading the way. "Vera's room is right next to yours. So, no sneaking around," he joked.

My head shot up when he said that.

"Is she home?" I quickly asked.

"She's at the bakery with Cory and Helena," my uncle answered. "Delia thought perhaps making her get a part time job would keep her out of trouble."

I came to a stop. "She's in trouble?"

He laughed. "No, but she will be if she doesn't keep that job. She has too much free time on her hands. Keeping her busy will do her some good."

My uncle looked at my grandfather. "I don't know what's got into her lately. I don't think I like the influence Steven is having on her."

My grandfather nodded knowingly.

We continued walking. I had to stop myself from asking more questions about Vera. What kind of trouble was she getting into?

"How many rooms does this house have?" I asked looking around.

"Eight bedrooms," my uncle answered. "Ten, if you count the ones upstairs, but we never use them."

He stopped at a set of double doors, pulling a set of keys from his pocket. "Plenty of room for you in here," he said as he unlocked the doors.

When he swung them open, I saw a beautiful sitting room. Two large chairs sat in front of a huge fireplace. Hundreds of books lined the walls.

"Where is the bed?" I asked.

My uncle walked over to another set of doors which were made of glass. "We made a few changes," he said, as he swung them open.

A huge bed sat near another set of doors that seemed to lead outside.

"That's the terrace," my uncle explained.

I quickly noticed the room was cluttered with furniture. Why would anyone need anything else besides a bed?

My uncle walked over to yet another set of doors and opened them. "This is the closet. There are plenty of clothes for you to change into. I bet you and your father wear the same size."

I walked over and looked in. I'd never seen so many human clothes before. I noticed there wasn't a robe in sight. Strange shoes lined the bottom of the closet. I remembered my father calling some of them sneakers.

"We'll give you a minute to change out of that thing," my uncle said, looking at my robe.

I looked at my grandfather again. He smiled and put one finger over his lips, motioning me to stay quiet. As soon as my uncle was gone, my grandfather closed the door.

"Grandfather, I don't want to change out of my robe."

He crossed his arms behind his back. "So, don't. No one is forcing you."

I looked around the room again, wondering how many more doors there were.

"Do you not like your room?" he asked.

I looked at the bed, several people could easily sleep in it. I wanted to say no, but the thought of being right next to Vera was making it very hard to turn this room down.

"It's fine, Grandfather."

He stepped closer to me. "There are more important things I need to speak with you about." He put his hand on my shoulder. "I'm going to ask you to do things that may not make any sense, but I want you to obey my wishes and do them anyway. Do you understand?"

"Yes, Grandfather," I said, putting my things down.

"For starters, I don't want you calling me grandfather in this world. Refer to me as simply, William. I also don't want you referring to Delia and Fish as your aunt and uncle, even in your thoughts. Simply, Delia and Fish. Do you understand?"

"But, why?"

"For reasons I cannot tell you, I don't want strangers knowing who you are…yet. And when you see Cory, you will do the same. Understood?"

"Yes grandfa…I mean, William."

~ 404 ~

"And most importantly, do not use your magic in the presence of humans. No matter the situation, refrain from using it. Is that clear?"

"Crystal clear."

My grandfather smiled. "I wish your mother would have followed my instructions as easily."

He motioned toward the door. "Come, it's time we see the town."

"May I ask you something?" I said, as we made our way into the sitting room.

"Of course."

I faced him. "Why did my parents finally agree to let me come here?"

He looked thoughtful for a moment. "Because it was time," he finally answered.

"You're not going to tell me, are you?"

He only smiled.

"Will you tell me soon?"

"Very soon," he answered. "I give you my word. There will be no secrets between us."

I looked around the room again. I couldn't imagine my mother living here. She seemed to love the small home we lived in now.

"Why do you like it here so much?" I asked.

My grandfather sighed, looking around the room. "I was a prisoner to this house once. I suppose I'm attached to the memories I left behind. I became fond of this place, though not because it's a mansion. I would feel the same if it were a shack."

"A prisoner?" I asked confused.

"It's a long story, Ethan. I'll tell you about it another day."

We made our way downstairs and back into the kitchen. "I'm taking Ethan into town," my grandfather said. "We won't be gone long."

Sharron was putting away the food my aunt had purchased. She made a funny face when she realized I was still wearing my robe.

"Did the clothes not fit, dear?" she asked.

"Want to try some of mine on?" my uncle offered.

I didn't answer and only looked out the window. Steven was coming out of the guest house, and he was not alone. Three other men were with him. They had the same kind of angry look Steven possessed. They all looked to be the same age. They began making their way toward the house. One had blond hair and was rather short. The other two were tall with dark hair.

My Aunt Delia spotted them. "Oh, I hate when he brings warlocks here, especially the new ones in town. They've been acting very odd, causing all sorts of trouble. Everything was so quiet until they got here."

Again, my grandfather and uncle exchanged glances.

"I'll take care of it," my uncle assured her.

Steven stomped his way in but froze when he saw me. We stared at each other for several long moments. His hatred toward me was obvious. I had to admit, I was starting to feel the same towards him.

"I won't be home for dinner," Steven said, storming past me.

The three men looked me up and down before following him across the kitchen and out the door.

"I need to speak with you, Steven," my uncle said, following behind them.

My grandfather looked at Delia. "When?" he asked.

"Few weeks ago," she answered.

He nodded. "We'll be on our way now. I'll be back to help you prepare dinner." He turned to me.

"Come Ethan, I'll show you the town."

Chapter Three: Salem

We stepped outside to find my uncle arguing with Steven. The men that were with him were not far away. They waited near the gate as Steven's conversation with my uncle began to get heated.

"I'm not having this conversation with you again," my uncle was saying. "I don't want you bringing the likes of them into my house."

Steven glared at him. "This isn't your house, remember? You're as much a guest as I am."

My Uncle Fish stepped up to him. "And, as of this moment, your reservation has been cancelled."

Steven laughed. "What? You're kicking me out now?"

"Would you rather I just kick your ass?" my uncle shot back.

I saw Steven reach for something around his

belt, but my uncle was faster. He flicked his arms, revealing two hook-like weapons from his sleeves.

"Go ahead," he said, getting in Steven's face. "Let's see how tough you are. Pull that thing out, I dare you."

Steven's eyes darted down to the hooks. He made a fist, slowly moving it away from his belt. I stepped forward when the other men moved closer. They also seemed to be reaching for something.

"Fish," I said awkwardly. "Is everything okay?"

"I don't know," he answered. "Is it?" he said, glaring at Steven.

"Why don't you go back inside, pretty boy?" one of the men said to me. "You might get your pretty dress all dirty."

Steven's eyes grew wide when he saw my grandfather. He looked back at my uncle. "I'll be back for my things later," he hissed.

"I'll have your things waiting by the door," my uncle said getting closer to him. "And if you come near my daughter again, I'll skin you alive."

Steven gave my grandfather one last glance before turning on his heels. My uncle stood there until Steven and his friends disappeared down the street. He flicked his arms again, causing the hooks disappeared into his sleeves.

I'd never seen my uncle so angry. My mother was right; despite being a half-human witch, he was very brave. I wondered about the strange weapons he had up his sleeves. I knew my uncle couldn't wave his hand like me. My mother told me that half-human witches need spells to use their magic. Is that why he carried a weapon?

I watched Steven and his friends walk away. I thought the bad blood between warlocks and witches was a thing of the past. My uncle didn't seem to like them very much. I couldn't help but wonder why. Were all warlocks bad? Did they all have bad tempers like Steven and his friends? That couldn't be. I knew my parents had plenty of friends that were warlocks.

"You did the right thing, Fish," my grandfather said, eyeing the men.

Fish turned and faced us. "I never wanted this for him, William. He gave me no choice. His new friends are nothing but trouble. I have to look out for my daughter."

"No need to explain," my grandfather answered. "His new friends seem to have changed him."

Fish looked down the street. "Tell me who your friends are, and I'll tell you who you are."

My grandfather followed Fish's gaze down the street. "Indeed."

I was suddenly aware that I was outside. My heart began racing all over again. I looked beyond the gate, eager to explore this world.

"Hey, are you really going into town wearing that thing?" my uncle asked.

"Yes," I said, gazing all around me.

The mansion was much bigger than I

thought. I saw the name *Wade* on another building next to the house. "That's the garage," my grandfather explained.

He motioned towards the gate. We walked across the massive driveway, making our way out the gate, and onto the street. My uncle quickly filed in behind us, staring at my robe the whole time.

"It even moves like a dress," he said, under his breath.

Trees lined the street the mansion sat on. I walked in amazement at what my eyes were taking in. There were no wizards flying above us, no dragons for me to mount. It was a world paved in stone. The ground was covered in it. Why did humans need to walk on stone?

There were subtle yellows and reds on some of the trees. I remembered my mother telling me about the changing of the leaves. It was her favorite time of year. She called it autumn. I knew that soon, the trees would transform and become radiant with colors. At least, that's what my mother said. That didn't happen in Magia, so I was looking forward to it.

"What do you think?" my uncle asked, as we made our way down the street.

I forced a smile. "It's lovely."

He stopped. "Kid, no," he said, shaking his head at me. "Guys don't say that. No lovely, okay?"

Confused, I nodded, and we continued

walking. Again, I glanced at my grandfather, wondering why it was a bad thing that I say lovely. And again, he only smiled.

My eyes almost came out of their sockets when I saw two humans walking our way. I got a little confused when they gave me a strange look. They stared at my robe as they past us.

"Is it October already?" one of them said to the other.

What did they mean by that?

A large vehicle full of humans caught my attention. "Oh look, it's a warlock," one of them said. They began holding up small boxes. I couldn't help but wonder; why did they think I was a warlock?

My uncle began laughing. "See, you should have changed out of that robe."

Confused, I looked at him.

"That was a tour bus," he explained. "They were taking pictures of you because they think you're in costume."

I looked at the thing called a *bus* again. The humans were still holding up their boxes as the *bus* drove away.

"Ethan, they're just taking pictures of you," my uncle assured me.

Why would they take pictures of me?

"Come on," my uncle said, putting his arm on my shoulder. "Essex Street is just a few blocks from here. The bakery is just off it. We'll stop by and see Cory."

I was taken aback when we reached the street named Essex. I quickly stopped. There were hundreds of humans walking around. Some were even dressed as witches. I saw one human dressed as, what I could only say was, a monster. He had what appeared to be fake blood running down his face. That was odd. Why did this human feel the need to put fake blood on his face like that?

My uncle laughed as we continued walking. The street was lined with shops. Stands with what my uncle called t-shirts were everywhere. Most of them had the word *Salem* imprinted on them. There were witch hats, brooms, and trinkets of all sorts.

I looked at the human that was dressed as a monster. The fake blood on his face looked very real. Was he trying to scare people? I stopped again as he got closer to us.

"Hey," the bloodied man said. "That's a cool costume," he said, pointing at my robe.

Bewildered, I watched as he smiled and walked past us.

"Ethan," my grandfather said. He waited until I tore my eyes away from the human.

"How did you know that man was human?" he asked.

"What do you mean, grandfa...I mean, William?"

He looked at the humans around us. "Them, how do you know they're human?" he asked again.

I wasn't sure how to answer his question.

"I'm not sure," I answered. "Something inside of me just knows."

"And, can you spot the real witches?" he asked.

I looked around the busy street. I saw a witch standing behind her stand. She seemed to be selling trinkets. "She's a witch," I said, pointing. "And her, she's also a witch," I said, pointing to a woman walking into a building. "But him," I said, pointing to a man sitting at a table. "He's not half-human or a witch. He's a warlock."

My grandfather shook his head and mumbled, "Thea. I should have known."

"Did you really expect her to stay out of this?" my uncle said to him.

My grandfather ignored him. "And the men Steven was with today, did you know they were warlocks?" he asked me.

"Yes."

"I see."

"Even I know Thea wouldn't send him without tools, William," my uncle said.

"What are you both talking about?" I asked.

My grandfather only smiled. "Come, Cory is waiting."

We continued walking through the crowded streets. I felt all eyes were on me. One man stopped and asked where I had purchased my robe. When I said Magia, the man asked where that store was. "I have to get me one of those," he said, admiring my robe.

My grandfather was quick to say I shouldn't tell people about my world or say the word, Magia. "Try to pass off as human," he suggested.

"Good luck with that," my uncle laughed.

"Ethan," my grandfather said, nudging me. "I told you, not even in your thoughts. Think, Fish. Simply, Fish."

"Yes, William," I answered.

I was starting to realize that humans had no idea wizards and witches were real. I found it amazing they had no idea we walked among them. It would appear witches went to great lengths to keep it that way.

The smell of bread hit me the moment we walked into the bakery my Uncle Cory owned. I smiled as I pictured my mother working here. She'd shown me images of this place my whole life. She loved this bakery. When Norm, the original owner, retired, my uncle purchased it. My mother said she had lived some of her happiest moments working in this small, little place. She explained that this was where she had reunited with my father.

The bakery was small with two huge glass counters, both filled with pastries. A few small tables were scattered around. Boxes and bread lined the walls. Two wall-sized windows gave perfect views of the tourist walking by.

"Cory, he's here," I heard his wife say.

My uncle's wife, Helena, was a striking woman. She was tall, thin, and very beautiful. She had golden locks that shimmered in the sun. I could never understand how my mother had once hated her. She seemed to be a very pleasant person.

I was shocked to learn that she and my mother had once been enemies. My mother had said Helena was once a very bad person. Of course, my mother loved her now.

Helena walked from around a counter and gave me a hug. "He'll be so happy to see you."

"Where is he?" I heard my Uncle Cory call out.

He came out from the back of the bakery, a smile spread across his face. I was a little shocked that he too, had bruises on his face. I wasn't surprised to see him and my grandfather exchanging glances.

I had never ignored the special relationship my mother shared with Cory. She talked of him often, calling him a beautiful Polish man.

"*Even that nose can't take away from his beauty,*" she once said.

His visits into my world were something my mother looked forward to. She always referred to him as her brother. Truth was, even I couldn't ignore how handsome he was.

"Come here, kid," Cory said, pulling me into his arms.

"Hello, Uncle."

"Please, just call me Cory. How is your mother?" he asked, pulling away from me.

"She sends her love."

"And your father? How is he?"

"Father is well."

Again, I noticed my grandfather's presence surprised no one.

"How do you like Salem?" he asked, looking down at my robe.

Before I could answer, Vera came walking out of the back room, holding a tray of pastries.

Our eyes met. I slowly smiled. She looked different somehow.

"Hello, Vera," I said softly.

"I see you're still wearing a dress," she said, placing the tray on the counter.

I could smell her lavender scent from here. She looked more beautiful than the last time I'd seen her, and that was just a few days ago. Her dark hair fell across her face like an angel. Her green eyes spoke to me and called me to her.

"Don't be rude," Fish hissed at her.

She rolled her eyes. "Hello, Ethan," she said, strolling to the back room again.

"I'm walking you home," Fish called to her.

She was back within seconds. "Why? I know where I live."

"Oh good," he answered. "Then maybe you can show me."

She rolled her eyes again. "I really wish you wouldn't do that. People always think you're my boyfriend or something. I hate having to explain why my father looks like he's seventeen. I really wish you and mother would stop taking that aging potion."

"Then, maybe Ethan can walk you home?" Fish suggested.

Vera slowly looked at my robe. "No, I'll walk home with you," she said, heading to the back again.

I stepped forward. "I was hoping you could show me around, Vera."

She gave my robe a sour look. "Are you serious? In that thing? All you need are heels and maybe some lipstick."

She flipped her hair and strode off to the back. I heard her mumble, "What a loser," as she disappeared.

This wasn't the reaction I expected from her. I thought she would at least be a little happy to see me. I hoped she'd want to show me around, like I had done with her on her visits to my world. Here, she seemed a little rude, spoiled even. I wasn't sure I liked this side of her. I always found her temper charming, but the rude part of her, well, it wasn't very pretty.

She was only gone a few moments when she returned, holding up one of those boxes like the humans had on the bus.

"You threw him out?" she shouted at Fish.

He smiled. "What? Did the baby call and tell you?"

"Where is he supposed to go?" she asked.

"Tell him to sleep in the woods. Maybe he'll

~ 418 ~

learn some manners there."

"I hate you!" Vera shouted.

Fish stepped up to her. "Did I ever tell you about my belt collection? I have several of them. I have leather ones, suede, even alligator skin. Want to see them?"

Vera burst into tears, stomping her way past him and out of the bakery.

Fish sighed. "Time to go be a dad," he said, chasing after her.

"He threw Steven out?" Cory asked my grandfather.

"Yes, and I think it was time," he answered.

Cory looked thoughtful for a moment.

"I was really hoping that kid would straighten his life out. Those warlocks he's been hanging out with are bad news. Maybe I'll go look for him and try to talk some sense into him."

"I believe the time for talking is over, Cory. There is only one way he's going to change his life."

They both glanced at me. Why did they keep doing that? It was starting to get a little annoying.

I had been quiet this whole time. This world had me a bit unsettled. I thought of the one place my mother said she had always found peace.

"Grandfa…I mean, William. Do you mind if I go explore the town on my own?"

"I'll show you around, kid," Cory said. "Just give me a few minutes. You might get yourself lost."

I smiled politely.

"If you don't mind, I'd rather go on my own. I'd like to see the places my mother told me about. I think I can find my way back."

Cory and my grandfather looked at each other.

"Don't be long," William said. "I'll be back at the mansion, waiting."

"Thank you, grandfa…William."

I walked out, disappearing into the crowd. I ignored all the strange glances and odd comments about my robe and finally made my way into the woods. Once clear of human eyes, I pulled out the wand my mother had given me. When I waved my hand, the wand quickly turned into a long, wooden staff. It was old and rustic looking. It had once belonged to my mother. It still had indentations from where her fingers once had been.

I slowly put it between my legs. The wind suddenly picked up beneath me, made me hover, then took me away.

It felt good to feel the wind in my face again. Flying always gave me the feeling of freedom I so desperately wanted.

My original plan had been to never use the wand. It was my intention to live without my magic. But this world had me on edge. I wasn't finding the feeling of freedom I thought I would. Surprisingly, I was missing Magia and my parents.

Vera's reaction to me didn't help matters. I expected to find the sweet girl I had fallen in love with. Her eyes showed no sign of happiness when she saw me just now. In fact, she could care less that I was here. Something was different about her, I could feel it. She had never been this rude.

I flew through the trees, using them as cover, and found my way to my mother's lake. So many times, she had shown me images of this place. I knew exactly how to get here. I would have been able to find it with my eyes closed.

The lake was just as she had shown me. I landed and tossed the staff to the ground. Trees surrounded the murky lake. It was nothing like the crystal-clear lake in Magia. There were no flowers or draping ivy. I found no waterfall or dancing fairies. I began to question my mother's reasons for loving this place so much.

I stood at the edge, trying to understand her love for this world. It wasn't the world I had expected. Everything seemed so dull and lifeless, I thought. Even the leaves that blew in the wind seemed lifeless. What had my mother fallen in love with? Were her eyes blind to the dullness of this world? Magia was full of life and color. You could hear the leaves whistling in the wind a mile away. Here, the forest was silent and dull.

I looked down at the ground, happy to see it wasn't covered in stone. I removed my shoes, sighing as I felt the grass under my feet. It was only making me think of Magia more and more. Had I made a mistake by coming here? I didn't feel very welcomed in this world. Things were off to a bad start.

"Well, look who's here," I heard from behind me. "It's pretty boy, and he's still wearing his pretty dress."

I looked over my shoulder. It was the three warlocks that had been with Steven.

I turned and faced them.

"What's the matter, pretty boy?" one of them asked. "Did you get lost?"

"Look at his stupid shoes," the blond one said, pointing to where my shoes lay. "Are they bedazzled?"

They laughed.

"His dress is bedazzled too. These half-human witches sure do dress odd."

I couldn't understand it. Why did these men think I was a witch? Better yet, why did they hate me?

"These stones are badges of honor," I informed them.

"Did the girl scouts give them to you?" a dark haired one asked.

They laughed again.

"No, my mother did," I answered.

They laughed even harder.

"Did you hear that?" the blond one said. "His mommy gave them to him."

I couldn't understand why they were laughing at me. "Don't laugh at my mother," I demanded.

"Why? Are you gonna cry, pretty boy? Or,

are you gonna run and tell your mommy?"

I didn't like the way the word *mommy* flowed from their mouths. I had a feeling they meant it as an insult.

I stepped forward. "If you call her *mommy* one more time, you will find out why I earned these badges."

They stopped laughing. The blond warlock slowly put his hand near his mouth. When he spat into his palm, a spell came out, spinning and making a strange sound. It would seem these warlocks couldn't just wave their hands like me. The other two quickly followed suit, spitting spells into both of their hands.

"Are you preparing to fight me?" I asked.

The blond one slowly smiled. "No, we're preparing to tear you apart, pretty boy."

I had no idea why they wanted to fight, but if it was a fight they wanted, I was prepared to give it to them.

I stood there, looking deep into their eyes. I could feel hate coursing through their veins. It wasn't just hate for me, they hated everything. I grew more curious about these warlocks by the minute. Did they not have the capability to love? Why had my mother been at war with them? It was a question I would pose to my grandfather when I got back.

"Thinking about running, pretty boy?" the blond one asked.

I want to thank all the fans of The Witch Series. I've often said there would be no Witch Series without you. Thank you for supporting and believing in me. I promise to always keep you on the edge of your seat in my next ventures. Stay with me!

L.S. Gagnon

Made in United States
North Haven, CT
03 January 2022

14117148R00241